a HEX for HUNGER

THE RUNE TITHE ♦ BOOK TWO

ALISTAIR REEVES

All rights reserved. No part of this publication may be reproduced, stored in a retrieval system, or transmitted in any form or by any means electronic, mechanical, photocopying, recording, or otherwise without prior written permission from Podium Publishing.

This is a work of fiction. Names, characters, places, and incidents are either products of the author's imagination or used fictitiously. Any resemblance to actual events, locales, or persons, living, dead, or undead, is entirely coincidental.

Copyright © 2025 by Alistair Reeves

Cover design by Alistair Reeves

ISBN: 978-1-0394-7592-2

Published in 2025 by Podium Publishing
www.podiumentertainment.com

To every trans person reading this,
I hope your heart never goes hungry

CONTENT WARNING

I want to preface this with a warning that *A Hex for Hunger* is much darker than its predecessor, *A Spell for Heartsickness*. Horror, violence, and themes of abuse are dominant elements, so please take care, as this story's themes may be unsuitable for some readers.

Content warnings include: animal death/murder, graphic violence, body horror, abuse (physical, emotional, psychological), taboo relationships, gender dysphoria, self-harm, slurs, sexually explicit scenes, transphobia, entomophobia.

a HEX for HUNGER

CHAPTER 1

Resurrection hurt worse than dying.

Ambrose recalled the eerie peace of his soul rent from his body. Pain followed by sweet sleep. Now, the marrow refilled his hollow bones until they were fit to splinter. Tendons laced him back together like an ill-fitting corset. The muscle and meat for which he'd been long feared hung heavy on his newly assembled skeleton.

When, finally, his skull's sockets swelled with eyes and he blinked them open, he anticipated the face before him with a dread swoop in his half-knitted belly. Better than the way he remembered dying, Ambrose remembered the witch king—his cherubic smile, the rich thunder of his voice, the soft caress of his magic. These recollections were far gentler than the flood of guilt that followed.

Ambrose's last act had been a failed attempt to protect the man he'd sworn himself to.

The man before him, though, was not the witch king. He was a necromancer, dusted in grave dirt and the flickering green sparks of the resurrection spell. His raven hair had gone prematurely silver. He wore no armor, only alien clothes. Neither the rough-spun of peasantry nor the fine satin of nobility, but something in between. His mouth held the vaguest memory of a smile.

At his feet lay the slain body of his familiar. A white hound, its chest ruptured to tithe the heart inside and power the spell putting Ambrose together piece by piece.

It painted a bloody picture. A witch who readily killed his familiar wasn't likely to have benign intentions in bringing Ambrose back from the dead.

The spell finished. The green light abated. Ambrose scrambled to assemble the puzzle of his resurrection and came up with only two pieces.

The first was that an ancient magic, exquisitely hungry, still carved a hollow in his ribs. So the witch king's spell—if not the man himself—still lived. That meant he could return.

The second, even more disconcerting thing was that the spell had put his body back together but hadn't the decency to clothe him. His naked-ness struck a well-worn chord of fear in his heart. A century he'd spent keeping the secret of his sex from the world at large. Only one had ever known what he hid between his legs.

And now *he* knew. This stranger with the blood of his familiar dripping from his fingers.

Ambrose took a step away from him.

"I wouldn't do that if I were y—"

Too late. A surge of agony stopped Ambrose. It was as if he'd stepped on hot coals, been struck by lightning. A glowing sigil of runes in the soil trapped him where he stood.

He staggered back into the circle but didn't cover himself. He didn't want to give the stranger any leverage, any sign of weakness. Instead, he recovered from the pain of the spell and defaulted to the oldest and most reliable means of disarming powerful, dangerous sorcerers.

He smiled. "You've caught me somewhat off guard. I appreciate the resurrection, though I don't suppose you have a spell to spare for conjuring me some clothes?"

The witch didn't return the smile. If anything, he looked more wary. Mercifully, he wasn't looking at Ambrose's nakedness, but the runes scar-ring an arcane collar around his throat.

"It worked," said the stranger, as if to himself. "You're the Grim Wolf of Bellgrave, back from the dead."

"You have me at a disadvantage," said Ambrose. "But I'd be most pleased to make the acquaintance of the one who resurrected me. To whom do I owe this honor?"

"Emery Vale. I'm the necromancer who tithed a small fortune to resur-rect you." He spoke in melody, but his body didn't dance to it. He held himself in expressive repose, emotion buried in a grave deeper than the one from which Ambrose had risen. "You're welcome, I suppose."

A small fortune and his familiar, Ambrose thought. He looked down on the poor, broken body of the hound. Its tail made a spiral, the long proud snout tipped up toward its master in supplication. The gaping wound in its chest had Ambrose absently touching his own where an enchanted axe had caved his ribs in. A blaze of scar tissue met the calluses of his fingertips.

"A worthwhile sacrifice for your protection," Emery said, following his gaze.

"Is that why you resurrected me? To protect you?"

"That is the idea. Or part of it." He tilted his head. His movements and the gleam of his dark eyes were graceful and opportunistic as a carrion bird, clever and cruel. "I wouldn't say no to a spot of revenge, either. All this assuming you'll comply. I have a pact ready to be signed, if you're keen. If not, I can let the sigil take you back to the grave, but when do the dead ever get a second chance?"

The threat had to be a performance—Emery wouldn't easily discard the thing he'd traded a sacred familiar for. He must be desperate for help and concealing it. That was leverage Ambrose might be able to exploit.

On the other hand, the familiar's murder revealed Emery's unconscionable ruthlessness. Ambrose would have to tread carefully and put on an amiable face indeed if he was to forge an escape.

Fortunately, sweetness came naturally to him.

Before he asked his questions, he scanned their surroundings. A flickering witch light illuminated the scene. No headstone, tomb, or great statue marked the spot. He'd been laid to rest in an unmarked grave in the woods. An entire skeleton had been assembled on the ground, its pearly bones labeled with bits of paper.

Ambrose's heart tripped. Around the skull's brow was a golden circlet with empty settings where rubies once glowed. It was fused with the bone. Still a king, even in death. In the grave, a single casket lay open, the runes that once sealed it all singed and cracked through.

Seeing their resting place desecrated disturbed him less than the lack of monument. Their enemies had cursed them with the worst fate for any man who sought to make himself immortal—that of being forgotten.

The magic in his breast slavered for their punishment. The only thing that sated his ravenous heart was that he and his king had been buried together. He wondered if, in separating their skeletons, the necromancer had mistaken one rib for another, one segment of spine. It seemed to him that a life lived so enmeshed would make it impossible to tell whose bones belonged to whom.

As if in reward for the thought, the arcane collar squeezed gently, like a barely perceptible hand on the nape of his neck.

Affection, hope, and guilt burned in him. The three emotions together made a braid of his insides, tight and twisted.

He's gone. I failed him. But if I'm alive, if his magic is, too, he could find his way back to me. We can be together again.

It was Ambrose's duty to ensure it, and his last hope of redemption.

First, he needed answers.

"How did you find our grave?"

"By accident, many years ago. A dead cicada told me about something strange in the ground. I didn't dig you up, of course. I did my research. But I had an inkling you were here."

"What year is it?"

"2024."

Ambrose reeled. Five *centuries*. That was how long he'd been feeding worms. Every enemy who'd put him there was gone. Again, he looked to the dead hound. "If the tithe for resurrection is your familiar, you only get one opportunity to bring someone back from the dead. Why me and not someone more important to you?"

"You assume anyone is important to me. I told you. I need protection."

"From?"

"Hellebore and Morcant Van Moor." He spoke the names as if grinding them by mortar and pestle.

"Who are they?"

"Other necromancers. You could call Hellebore my rival and Morcant my nemesis, if you want to be dramatic. It hardly matters who they are, only whether you can deal with them. Can you?"

"Not at the moment." Ambrose cast a pointed look toward the sigil at his feet.

"I won't free you from it without assurance you won't strangle me."

"That would be a poor way to express my gratitude to the man who resurrected me," Ambrose said. "I assure you—"

"I want it in writing," Emery interrupted. He drew a scroll from his robes. A honeyed, evergreen smell of magic wafted off the paper.

A pact like that could bind Ambrose permanently to his service. That is, if there weren't already another spell which superseded it . . .

He looked back at his old master's skeleton, searching for the thing that could potentially free him without subjugating himself to Emery. He counted the matchstick bones of his master's right hand, segments of phalange, shrapnel for the wrist, and—

His heart sank. The metacarpal bone of the right index finger was gone.

Emery wasn't smiling when Ambrose's gaze met his, but the light cast him like a grinning skull nonetheless. He drew the bone from his robes and held it up, runes shining on its surface. "Is this what you're looking for?"

Ambrose smiled blithely, though the runes of the arcane collar felt too tight for words, and his mind reeled in search of a means to regain possession of the bone. "I see you're already a step ahead of me. Do you know what it does?"

"It's obvious from the runes on your skeleton and his that some magical pact binds you, but I didn't know if magic so old could hold for several centuries. It's . . . unique." He paused, and in the space of that silence, Ambrose tried to determine a means to avoid what he knew would come, but it was too late. "But no, I don't know what it does," Emery said. **"Tell me."**

The finger bone glowed a faint necrotic green. The runes on Ambrose's neck burned. Prepared as he was, his heart still heaved with the desire to refuse. It didn't matter. The arcane collar squeezed every word from him like pulp from a juiced peach.

"On a finger bone of the right hand of my master were carved the runes of an unbreakable pact. Whomsoever holds it holds me, as the corresponding runes were carved in my spine. It is my leash. My tether. I submit to the one who holds it, obey their every command, can never bring them to harm, and never leave their side."

It had been an expression of his devotion to a man he adored, and now Emery had corrupted that loyalty by stealing it for himself.

This part remained unsaid.

Emery's eyes narrowed. He looked between the glowing runes on the bone and the ones lit green on Ambrose's neck, fading as the compulsion ended. "How does it work?"

Ambrose, scraping the recesses of his newly born mind for an escape plan, hadn't expected such a question. "What do you mean?"

"Magic requires a tithe. This is powerful magic to have survived this long, but I can't see what's been sacrificed, so are you lying?"

"There isn't a surviving soul that can vouch for my character, but it's not in mine to lie," Ambrose said, still affable in spite of his circumstances. It wouldn't do to anger his captor.

It didn't reassure Emery in the least. "One way to know for sure." He pointed the bone at Ambrose. **"Kneel."**

The arcane collar choked obedience from Ambrose. He stumbled to his knees, head bowed in shame rather than deference, the only small rebellion he was permitted.

Emery said, "If this is an act, it's a good one. So if I release you from the sigil, you belong to me?" He didn't appear smug, more vaguely nauseated, as if Ambrose were an inconvenient necessity.

It sickened Ambrose's insatiable magic. He'd belonged in life and death to only *one* man.

Yet, in this perversion of his original pact, he saw an opportunity. Nothing about it prevented him from finding the means to return his master to his rightful spot at Ambrose's side.

"Release me, and I am yours to command." The words tasted rancid.

Emery still looked mistrustful. He appraised the rune bone. "It wouldn't bode well for either of us if someone were to take this from me. I guess that's why the old bastard had it engraved in his skeleton. I don't suppose I could have it transferred to mine?"

"That's beyond my knowledge," Ambrose said, praying it was impossible. "I was the king's guard. I know little of magic. I do know that the process hurts."

"Mm. Don't fancy *that*." Emery tugged at a strand of his hair and tied it in a knot around the finger bone. With a mutter of magic, he tithed the strand. A magic ward or lock, Ambrose assumed. He was not a witch, but he'd been around one long enough to recognize the spell. Emery pocketed Ambrose's tether. "That ought to be enough." After a moment's hesitation, he added, "You could be feigning obedience so I free you, only to turn on me after."

"I've no reason to do that. I'm grateful to have been resurrected in the first place."

Emery didn't respond. Hopefully he wasn't contemplating something more painful or humiliating than kneeling to compel Ambrose into performing as further assurance of the pact's veracity.

"Tell me your name."

"Ambrose."

"Ambrose." He tasted the name, but whether he appreciated its flavor, Ambrose couldn't tell.

There was a moment of hesitation. The pact was indelible. All that remained was to release Ambrose from the sigil.

He saw the play as if watching it on a stage. The necromancer had to bet that the arcane tether would hold once the sigil was gone. It would. That little fossil controlled Ambrose entirely, but it still required a leap of faith for Emery to spit on the sigil and dispel it.

With an expression of distaste, he did. It flared and died. The only illumination now came from the pale witch light. Ambrose took a step. Emery took one backward.

"**Stop**," he commanded.

Ambrose grunted as the collar yanked him still, but in that brief second of freedom, he'd spotted something familiar in the unblooded steel of Emery's scavenger eyes.

Fear.

Ambrose, in life, had been a gentle soul. But he had also been the king's guard, with all the righteousness that defending a king entailed.

This man knew who Ambrose was. He'd read the history, knew the things Ambrose had done.

He had reason to be afraid.

What they had was so far from trust. It was hardly a transaction, the leash a fragile thread restraining Ambrose's instincts.

When the witch king returned, he would snap that leash, and if Emery proved himself a villain, nothing would save him from royal justice.

CHAPTER 2

After a grim silence, Emery waved a hand as if to dismiss the uncomfortable limbo of their new pact. "We should get you some clothes."

The idea of seeing a tailor in Ambrose's current state made his blood run cold. The only credit due his captor was that he hadn't raised issue with Ambrose's masculinity thus far, but would the rest of the world? "I doubt any tailors are awake at this hour."

Emery tilted his head. "Mm. I should warn you, the time you're from . . . Well, the modern world might come as an itty-bitty shock to you."

"Then I'm lucky to have a guide."

He'd meant it, but Emery frowned as though it had been a sarcastic jest. "We'll see. First—" He regarded the corpse of his familiar. "I suppose I could taxidermy her."

Ambrose suppressed his disgust. Slaughtering the familiar for a resurrection had a ruthless pragmatism to it. Stuffing and mounting her like a hunting trophy?

It had been too much to hope the man who'd revived him was sane.

Emery removed something from a pouch at his belt—a fine powder, which he sprinkled over the corpse. With a ripple of magic, it vanished, transported elsewhere. He then gathered the ends of the blanket on which the witch king's bones had lain and disrespectfully bundled it together like a load for laundering. He transported this with the same dust as the familiar.

Ambrose's fist clenched, and the collar squeezed in warning. He could not stand against Emery. Even wanting to triggered rebuke. In truth, it should be a relief that the bones weren't discarded back in the grave. The pact's restrictions ensured Ambrose couldn't return here without Emery. If the remains were needed for any ritual in the witch king's return, there was a better chance of retrieving them from Emery's possession.

Assuming he'd transported them somewhere safe and not into the sea.

"Can't risk you being reported for indecent exposure. Here." Emery shucked his cloak and handed it to Ambrose so he could pretend at decency. He had to wrap the cloak tightly, as it wasn't quite large enough, but it protected his modesty. The thick wool lined with satin was more comfortable than the armor Ambrose donned while protecting his charge.

That comfort was mitigated by traipsing barefoot through the woods. The prickle of pine needles on the soles of his feet stung, but they were a sweet reminder. *I'm back. I survived.*

Emery pulled something from his pocket. A rectangle of black glass that illuminated brightly with the touch of his thumb. He tapped through images of a colorful—diagram? No, a map.

"What manner of magical relic is that?" Ambrose asked.

"It's called a mobile phone."

"I . . . see. And what does it do?"

"A lot of things. Right now, it's showing me where the nearest clothing store is."

Ambrose wrinkled his nose, curious about an artifact whose tithe—its source of power—he couldn't discern. His own abilities were testament to how dangerous that sort could be. How powerful was this witch to hold something like that so casually?

He wanted to ask more but refrained. His ignorance to this world's idiosyncrasies, and his nakedness, left him vulnerable.

Strange light filtered through the woods ahead, warm and too white to be fire. This time of night, that could only mean one thing: magic. Ambrose stiffened, but Emery didn't seem alarmed in the least, marching toward it.

How was Ambrose meant to protect anyone who showed such lackluster caution?

When they emerged from the trees, he understood. Tall lanterns lined the streets of a city, illuminating a world foreign to the one he'd died in. He had to squint against the acidic brightness of the signs lit above shops. Spinning illusions of women in gowns fit for throne rooms danced in window displays. Hulking machines of steel and glass slept on the side of the road. At the late hour, not a soul wandered with the exception of a stray cat.

Ambrose should have heeded Emery's warnings about the drastic changes from his century to this one. "How rich has this city become that it can squander magic to light signs no one is awake to read?"

"Bellgrave? Posh?" Emery scoffed. "It's not magic powering the lights, it's science. Technology." He waved the "mobile phone" in his hand. "None of this requires a tithe, only electricity."

"Magic by other names," Ambrose supplied.

"Sure. If that's easier to understand."

Ambrose tried not to take offense at the condescension. He had a practiced look of naivety, a habit born of years spent protecting himself and his master's secrets. Nobody suspected the muscle could have a keen mind. Inside, however, he flinched.

No, he had never been *particularly* clever, but it would have been kinder not to say so.

"None of these shops appear open."

Emery clicked his tongue. "We can change that."

Curious. Was Emery so renowned he could hail a shop to open at his beck and call? Ambrose followed him toward a shop with colorful clothes on display. He'd never been taught his letters and couldn't read the sign, but it had a magpie incorporated into the design.

"I've heard Wyngrave's has some fetching looks. Or would you prefer something more . . . military?" Emery gave Ambrose a look up and down.

His crow-like expression made Ambrose feel like carrion. He'd never cared much for the aesthetics of clothing, only how utilitarian they'd be. "Whatever you command me to wear will be suitable. So long as it doesn't restrict movement, I'm happy."

Emery's look was unreadable. "Happy. Hm." He reached into the tithe belt at his waist, pulling something gossamer from a pouch and crushing it in his fist. The pane of glass in the window display vanished. Emery trespassed into the darkened store, and Ambrose's assertions about his new master twisted in a new direction.

He was not a witch of wealth, renown, and power. He was a *thief.*

Ambrose stood frozen in the open window.

Emery looked over his shoulder. "Well? Come in! You'll have to try things on. I'm not a wizard when it comes to eyeballing sizes."

"We're stealing?"

"Isn't that obvious?"

"Is theft not still punishable? If you already have enemies, I wouldn't hasten to add the county sheriff and the lord of this city."

"Oh, dear, that isn't quite how this works anymore."

"Theft is no longer unlawful?"

"Oh, it very much is. I didn't expect you to take issue with it, though. According to history, you've done a lot worse."

"My actions were by order of the king. His word was law. By his command, all I did was lawful."

Emery snorted. "So killing people, fine, but a bit of petty larceny? Heaven forbid. Look, I need to charm the cameras to replace our faces. Now, quickly, **come here.**"

Ambrose was less prepared this time, puzzling over what a "camera" was. The collar choked a noise from his throat as it yanked and dragged him forward. He stumbled into the shop, past the spinning mannequins, halting at Emery's side.

Emery gave him a look—half appraising, half guarded—a question in his eyes. He didn't ask it. "Have a look around while I sort security out."

Ambrose didn't know where to begin with the clothes. He could don armor as quickly as he could plait hair, but some of the garments here looked like they required detailed instruction. Emery, tired of his ineptitude, chose for him once finished with the cameras. A new traveling cloak, several pairs of trousers, and shirts that covered the rune collar on his neck. Other essentials like small clothes ("pants," Emery called them) they'd get from a "department store."

The night of crime dragged on. Emery led him on a tour of the town's shops, stealing tithes, potion ingredients, parchment, and, inexplicably, a stuffed squirrel with a squeaker in its bushy tail.

By the time he announced they were ready to head home, the eastern sky blushed with sunrise. Ambrose had slept the dead sleep of centuries but felt weary. Growing a new body, even with the help of a spell, had taken great effort, and he looked forward to whatever passed for a bedroll in this strange world.

Emery didn't lead him to a castle, manor house, or cottage. Using stolen bone powder from the apothecary, he opened a portal and took them to a—

A ruined chapel.

It cowered in the shrubs while the surrounding woods devoured it. Ivy, moss, and lichen turned the old stone green and scaly. All that remained of a stained-glass rose window were colorful teeth around its mouth, and the air smelled thickly damp of a nearby bog. The door, wooden and painted green, looked new. Otherwise, the ruin appeared to have been there since Ambrose's generation—a weary relic clinging to life by fraying fingernails.

He searched the trees for any sign of alternate accommodation, but none was forthcoming. "You live here?"

"I expect you're used to a castle with a roaring fire and servants to dress you. My home has only one of those things."

Ambrose suppressed an honest answer. He'd enjoyed courtier comforts and a warm bedroll when he deserved them, a cold cell when he didn't. The damp autumn air seeped through his new clothes in reminder of the latter.

Emery walked up to the painted door, licked his finger, then drew a symbol over the knob. It unlocked magically, swinging open. Before entering, Emery turned around and held out a hand.

"You'll need to give me something of yours I can tithe so you can pass through my wards."

"I have nothing but the clothes you stole for me."

"Not a possession. A strand of hair will do."

Ambrose ran his fingers through the rough-cut layers of white hair fringing his face. It hadn't returned to its original brown. Necromantic magic had siphoned the color in his past life, and it had stayed that way in this one. He used to have twine to bind some of it off his neck. Perhaps he could find some later.

He pulled out a strand and gave it to Emery, who pressed it against the door. In a shower of sparks, it burnt a waving line into the paint. Ambrose followed him inside, magic trailing its fingers through his hair in recognition as he passed.

Once, he'd viewed magic with childish wonder and reverence. Now, his feelings were complicated. It felt like the caress of a lover whose affections had soured. He shuddered.

Inside, he'd expected it to feel like a crypt, the lair of a man mad enough to raise a several-centuries-old corpse. Instead, an enchanted ward kept the rain from drizzling through a hole in the ceiling, moonlight pouring through instead. The sparks of a spell from Emery warmly lit the room with candles and a fireplace. Untidily stacked bookshelves scaled the walls, and the books that wouldn't fit formed stalagmites surrounding squashy chairs. A lumpy tartan blanket pooled where Emery had once been cocooned.

It was more comfortable than expected, but certain things put Ambrose on edge, too. Through a doorway, he spied a kitchen with steel machines the likes of which he'd never seen. A bed just the right size and shape for a hound lay empty next to the crackling fire. The fire in particular made him avert his eyes, neck sweating with memory.

No one came to greet them, and Emery wore no wedding band. It shouldn't have surprised Ambrose. A man who couldn't love his familiar enough to spare her life wasn't liable to give his heart to a wife, but he looked four and twenty years at least, well past marrying age. Ambrose thought he might have partnered for the stability of heirs, if not for love.

He switched focus to his own purpose here. "I'll search the perimeter for dangers. Do you have a sword to equip me?"

Emery's hawkish stare flicked skeptically from Ambrose's face to his hands, where a soot-stained spell of magic smeared him from fingertips to elbows.

"In the history books, you never needed a weapon."

Ambrose stiffened. "I prefer a sword."

"Sorry to burst that particular bubble, but swords aren't really a thing anymore. It wouldn't serve you well, anyway. Wait until you hear about firearms."

The word turned Ambrose's stomach. Surely the ritual that turned his hands into weapons wasn't a commonplace weapon of this era?

"You don't need to search the perimeter. My wards will inform me if anything crosses the boundary or tries to enter. For now, it's late. We can dive into the details of this arrangement after some rest."

From the charcoal smear of sleeplessness under Emery's eyes, he didn't rest often.

Ambrose wanted answers, but fear of repercussion tempered his tongue. While his suspicions and apprehension rose, he disguised them with an amicable smile and a nod. "Of course, though I'd appreciate knowing the details of what imperils you. Information could spell the difference between victory or failure."

"Mm. The particulars are tricky. I've an idea. A loophole, maybe, but tomorrow. My enemies don't know about this place, anyway. I'm safe here. Mostly."

That wasn't reassuring in the least.

Emery flicked his fingers toward the armchairs and blankets. "Help yourself."

He disappeared into an adjoining chamber, the door closing with the distinct click of a lock and the sniff of magic.

So he didn't trust Ambrose even while holding his tether. It was a mutual feeling.

Now that he was alone, the bone-deep weariness of his resurrection sapped his strength. He melted into the armchair, pulling blankets over himself, disconcerted by the way they smelled of Emery—like sweet Scotch and campfire smoke.

The thought drew his eyes to the fire. With a flare of remembered pain, he looked away. Best not to think about that. Instead, he ought to dissect his new reality and form a plan.

Of a few things he was certain. He needed to find a way to return the witch king to life, he could not trust Emery, and he was wildly out of his depth in an era so temporally far from his own. He would need to learn as much as possible to survive, and that would mean ingratiating himself to his new master. At least temporarily.

Moreover, he would need to find a way to maintain his current form. The witch king had committed to maintaining the illusion of Ambrose's masculine body where most would have flung the word "abomination" at him. Emery wouldn't likely provide such potions for free, but if Ambrose could convince him, or better yet, if Ambrose could find a way to procure such potions for himself—

The books lining the shelves taunted him with all their hidden knowledge. Solutions to his problem could lie in their pages, if only he could read them.

The witch king could have, if he were here.

A pang of grief and longing went through Ambrose, keen as the axe that clove them apart all those years ago. If only Ambrose hadn't been outnumbered, if only he'd fought harder, they'd still be side by side.

My sweet, loyal hound. Not even the vast distance of centuries could tear you from me.

The voice, intimately familiar, was a spectral caress in his mind, so faint he couldn't know for certain if he'd truly heard it, or if it had been a trick of the wind in the eaves and the crackling fire.

The fire.

It drew his eye like the morbid curiosity to look directly at something he knew would haunt him later. It leapt and snapped, snaring him in memory.

A raging forge. The hollow husk that still vaguely resembled a man inside. A hot poker sifting the embers.

He'd hesitated. Of course he'd hesitated.

Then the witch king, who could so rarely risk touching him, not in view of courtiers and lords, laid his soft, un-calloused palm against Ambrose's cheek and said, "I cannot ask this of you."

But that soft touch only steeled Ambrose's resolve. "To protect you, I would do anything."

He jammed his hands deep into the ashes. Hot charcoal crumbled and encased him to the elbows in an agony so intense, his mind went white. He screamed. His flesh melted. Pain transcended reason. One moment, he burned as if every mote of him were aflame. The next, he shuddered in the gripping jaws of cold, his body failing to make sense of what it felt. Does this pain sting, scald, freeze, bruise, lacerate, ache, infect?

His mind hadn't known, so his body had felt it all.

The hungry fire flashed necrotic green as it fed, skin and sacrifice feeding the spell. His blood boiled with magic like hot oil, quickening into the bones of him, transmuting his pain into the kind he could inflict.

But Ambrose had always been loyal. No amount of pain could turn his heart. And the witch king's gentle hand on his cheek, catching his scalding tears, had been its own twisted balm of relief.

Many centuries later, he lay in blankets next to a fire, looking at his permanently ash-stained skin. Hunger, that old dog, licked its lips and curled in his belly. A starving void he'd never quite sated since that day.

He wondered if the abilities that blighted ritual had imbued him with still worked. He feared finding out. For all that they were useful, they'd always left him feeling sick and hungrier than ever.

He'd never regretted it, though. Not when it had made him such an effective guard against all those who would do his king harm. Not when, afterward, he'd spent a week in bed healing, tended to by his king, who applied cooling salves to Ambrose's arms and palms and fingers, intimate as a honeymoon and sensual as a kiss.

The closest they could come to either.

He turned his face from the fire, focusing instead on the aperture in the ceiling through which a window of starry sky winked at him. In spite of the hunger, his leash held in the hand of a stranger, and the fact he was alone, his thoughts turned two words around like a spindling thread of hope.

I survived, I survived, I survived.

CHAPTER 3

Ambrose woke to the disconcerting sound of claws scrabbling against the door of Emery's room.

He never slept deeply, ever alert to the sounds of danger and intruders. He roused at once.

The door was shut, and the sound came from within. He cursed internally. If his new master hadn't dismissed Ambrose's concerns, maybe he wouldn't be trapped in his bedchamber with some strange beast. If he was already dead, that spelled disaster for Ambrose, who could no more read a book than interpret this new world.

He searched the room for a makeshift weapon. If the situation was desperate, he'd resort to using the abilities bestowed on him, but not before exhausting other possibilities. He took the poker from its stand next to the fireplace and crept silently toward the door, where the clawing noise continued, followed by a low whine, then—most inexplicable of all—a shrill squeak.

Emery's voice, indulgent and unafraid, came muffled through the door. "Fine, fine, you impatient cur."

The door opened. A hound half Ambrose's height bounded out. It spotted him and charged, rearing up on its hind legs. Ambrose did the most sensible thing and fell into a fighting stance, but the dog didn't bite, only stood on its hind legs with paws hooked over Ambrose's wrists. With his alarm wearing off, he recognized its white curly hair and long snout. This was Emery's familiar, down to the cleaved chest, now stitched crookedly back together.

Emery stood framed in the door. "Not a dog person, I take it."

The dog cocked its head, eyes pale and cloudy. It was slightly horrifying that Emery could sacrifice the creature then raise its corpse into undead servitude. The spirit of the familiar was gone. Only the shell remained, its empty eyes a pleading echo of the sentience they'd once held. He wasn't sure if this was better or worse than taxidermy.

It turned and loped back to Emery's room before emerging with the stuffed squirrel toy from last night squeaking in its jaws. The hound bowed and wagged its tail. Not an attack, but an attempt to play.

Ambrose was on edge. Understandable, perhaps, given the circumstances, but he'd need to adjust quickly. He took the offered end of the squirrel toy and shook it, crouching down on the floor and ruffling the hound's ears. She growled playfully, giving in to the tug-o'-war, and Ambrose cooed in answer.

Emery watched him with wary disbelief and more than a little judgment. It was becoming a familiar expression. "I stand corrected."

Belatedly, Ambrose answered Emery's question. "I like dogs plenty. I simply didn't expect an undead one."

"Katzica won't hurt you unless you try to harm me."

"I can't harm you."

"I like to have insurance. I've no idea if resurrection left you with all your faculties or weakened the spell binding you."

Ambrose tucked away the memory of the voice last night. He still didn't know if he'd imagined it. "I've taken no leave of my senses."

"Good." It didn't sound as though Emery believed him. "Speaking of resurrection, I don't imagine the spell brought you back with a full belly. If you're hungry, there's—" He paused. "Actually, I'm not sure what food's in the kitchen. Toast, probably."

"My appetite isn't particular." A delicate way of saying that Ambrose could eat just about anything.

"Help yourself. I need to prepare for classes. We leave in fifteen minutes."

Ambrose eyed the unfamiliar shapes in the kitchen. Katzica followed him in, tail wagging, but she couldn't explain what he saw. There was no wood to burn, no stone or iron oven, no hanging herbs or garlic. Like literacy, the culinary arts weren't a competency Ambrose had ever acquired, but he might have been able to muddle his way around a proper kitchen. Here, he hovered amongst the steel machinery, reminded that the steel he knew how to wield best was for killing people. Pulling open cupboards, he found little that could be called food. There was a tin with an unappetizing picture of beans on it.

With no clue how to open it, he gave up and wandered out the front door, searching the shrubs for edible plants. To his relief, much of the flora looked the same as when he'd died. He picked a few dandelion leaves, dock leaves, and even found some primrose in bloom. An overgrown flowerbed in front of the chapel also yielded some mint.

He picked enough for two. Emery would need breakfast as well, and perhaps he'd be more amenable with Ambrose if he proved teachable in the kitchen.

Emery returned, laced into austere black clothes embroidered with white, a bone-colored jewel dangling from one ear. He stopped dead when Ambrose, beaming with pride, offered him a bowl.

"What is that? What are you eating?"

Ambrose stopped mid-chew, looking at the contents of his bowl. "Salad. I made you one as well."

"Those are *weeds*."

"Your kitchen isn't familiar to me," Ambrose said, a touch defensively. "All of these are fresh from the outdoors."

"And I'm to trust you didn't add a bit of nightshade or hemlock for added kick?"

Now Ambrose *was* offended. "I cannot bring you to harm, and even if I could, I wouldn't." Emery might not be a stunning exemplar of honor and justice, but he'd resurrected Ambrose. Unless he proved as heinous as the death of his familiar implied, Ambrose would stay his hand.

Emery blinked very quickly, as if taking a new picture to accompany the image he previously held of Ambrose in his head. "I see. Well, I suppose that's—I'll have to find something for you that isn't—Did you even *wash* the weeds? Never mind. I'll order a takeaway later. For now, we're going to be late." He gestured to the clothes they'd pilfered from shops yesterday. "Wear the gloves and cloak. It's best my peers don't make any connections between your spell scars and your true identity. You'll pose as my cousin visiting from abroad. Probably best if you speak as little as possible."

"Where are we going?"

"To class."

So Emery was only an apprentice. "Which class?"

"All of them? I study magic at Bellgrave under a number of masters."

Ambrose absorbed that. If this world had an entire institution devoted to magical learning, perhaps they'd have a library. If he could find a spell or charm that could read the books to him, perhaps he could piece together enough information to resurrect the witch king.

One thing at a time. "What are my orders if anybody threatens you?"

"They won't. Not in public. You're likely to meet one of them, though, and I wouldn't mind if you frightened her. Just a little."

Her? Ambrose's opinion of Emery dove steeply if he'd taken to menacing women. Yet, he'd called her a *rival*. An enemy. That denoted a certain degree of respect, didn't it?

Combined with Emery's unbothered attitude toward Ambrose's sex, it gave him . . . Hope was too whimsical a word, but it gave him pause.

Emery gave Ambrose a look he was starting to recognize—one of corvid calculation. Those raven eyes flicked to Ambrose's ash-dark hands. "Right now, I'd like a demonstration of your abilities. To see that you still have them after all this time."

"I sense that nothing's changed in that regard."

"All the same . . ." He gestured to a chest serving as a table next to the armchair. "There's a spell book in there. Soft, leather bound, with a metal lock. Retrieve it."

Ambrose's stomach churned. The magic stirred in his bones. It felt heavy, like his whole limb had turned necrotic, requiring amputation to cure.

A complicated snarl of emotion held him in place. He hated the way this magic made him feel, yet it had been a *gift*. An invaluable tool and a symbol of his importance to the witch king.

Emery made a noise of lost patience and raised the bone leash. **"Retrieve the book from the chest."**

Ambrose didn't bother to fight it. Magic seethed through his arm as he plunged it through the wood. He felt its splintering protest as matter yielded reluctantly to magic. It was hard not to drown in memories of the way bodies surrendered wetly, the way bones broke, the way a squeezed heart felt when it stopped beating in his palm.

He shoved the thought away. This was just a box with nothing living inside. His hand brushed the interior, feeling the bindings of books, a worn blanket, a thin chain attached to some amulet, until finally one book stood out against the rest. Velvety leather and a delicate clasp shivered with its own enchantment. He grabbed it and pulled it free.

Sweat beaded on his forehead, not from effort but emotion. Using the power left the smell of rotten meat in his nose.

"Fascinating," Emery said, taking the book from him and giving it a cursory examination for damage. "Any other abilities? The history books sometimes called you a wraith."

Ambrose, rather than submit to the collar, demonstrated by allowing the well of magic inside to swallow him. He vanished.

Emery looked alarmed. **"Come back."**

Ambrose shuddered in the collar's thrall and returned to visibility. "You needn't compel me. I will obey."

"You'll have to tell me how you acquired these abilities. The history books never said." Emery still appeared disconcerted. "But later. I have to get to class."

Ambrose dressed to conceal the arcane collar and his scarred hands. The washroom's advanced plumbing and warm water were yet another source of shock, though a pleasant one.

Afterward, he found Emery at the front door, kneeling in front of Katzica. He murmured to her, rubbing her ears. At the sight of Ambrose, he stood.

"You aren't to tell anyone about her," Emery said.

"Of course," Ambrose answered. He could imagine what other witches might think.

That settled, Emery conjured a portal, and Ambrose followed him into a world of alien familiarity.

Before him, the castle he'd once called home punctured the burlap sky with its turrets. Through the ages, it had endured, its bones so old they'd fossilized into the rocky crags overlooking the sea. Ambrose looked upon the castle's stone walls bleached by sea salt, stained by storms, and felt they were brothers, the bones in him just as ancient and scarred.

But the world around it? Nothing could have made Ambrose feel more foreign.

The paths and the gardens of the castle crawled with people. Not servants and courtiers, but common people, bustling with paper cups and "mobile phones" grasped in their hands, gathering in huge groups with books and machines, and all of them—nearly every last one he could see—performing magic, the ozone of enchantments like an endless rip current.

In Ambrose's time, magic had been a rarity, a talent to make or break kingdoms. Now it was common as a curse word.

A rumbling noise drew his attention. He whirled to see one of those machines—a dragon of steel and glass—roaring straight toward them.

He lashed out instinctively, putting himself between Emery and the beast. He aimed his fist for the glass, magic coalescing in his veins to tear through the pane.

It shattered in a burst of glittering rain, and a scream followed.

Ambrose struggled to make sense of what he saw: inside the belly of the machine was a woman, her hands gripping a wheel, eyes wide with horror.

Of course, she should be afraid—whatever this thing was, it had swallowed her—but she seemed more scared of Ambrose. His blood drummed in his ears along with the throbbing pain in his fist.

He tried to sound reassuring. "Let me help you."

"Help me?!"

"Are you insane?" Emery cut in.

Ambrose couldn't help feeling like the only sane one present. "The steel dragon attacked us. It swallowed a girl."

"That's a *car*," Emery corrected. "It wasn't attacking. It was trying to parallel park." He turned to the girl inside. "Sorry. He's not well."

"He smashed my window!"

Ambrose braced himself for punishment. He didn't understand this world at all, but he understood he'd made a grave error.

Emery pulled something from his tithe belt. He slapped the magic together like he was performing something as mundane as brewing tea. The glass caught in Ambrose's clothes and scattered over the ground floated back into the frame of the "car" and reassembled itself, flashing with heat before it fused into a single pane. The girl inside huffed, gathering her things and flinging open the door on her side, revealing just how little peril she'd really been in. She hurried away from them with the air of someone who didn't have time for nonsense this early in the morning.

Ambrose wished he could be so unbothered. Adrenaline still made his heart beat thunderously. He'd truly thought they'd been in danger. Worse than that, his outburst had attracted attention, the din of the grounds gone eerily quiet as people looked on curiously.

He loathed to think what depths of creative punishment Emery would conjure as recompense for this mistake.

"That was a bit of an overreaction, don't you think?"

Ambrose hated simpering, but Emery had killed his familiar—he could do worse to Ambrose if he didn't beg for pardon. He started to kneel.

"Gravest apologies. It was my mistake, and I'll accept any punishment you deem justifi—"

"Please get up. This is already a scene; let's not make it a pantomime."

Ambrose paused. Exasperation was preferable to the fury he'd anticipated. He straightened. "Yes. You're very gracious, my—" He wasn't sure how to address Emery. "Sir, you never gave me your titles."

"I understand that you might be experiencing a level of culture shock hitherto unbeknownst to mankind," Emery said, "but please try to keep the melodramatics to a minimum. Dragons are extinct, we no longer believe in the divine right of kings, and unless I tell you otherwise, we aren't in danger. My mistake for not clarifying. I did bring you here to protect me, but the threat is far more insidious and subtle than—I cannot believe I am about to say this—*steel dragons*. I unfortunately can't beam information into the withering brain cells left to you after several centuries of breathing grave dirt, but try to keep up. I'm going to conjuration class, not walking into the lion's den."

Ambrose accepted the rebuke with a bowed head and shame curdling in his heart. His name had once been uttered amongst the names of heroes and legendary warriors. He'd been brave bordering on fearless. What was he now?

He said, "It will not happen again."

Emery, still staring at him, said under his breath, "Hell, don't look so woeful. You're the Grim Wolf, but I feel like I've kicked a puppy."

Ambrose perked up and smiled obligingly. "Yes, sir."

"It's Emery. Just Emery." He gestured to the castle Ambrose had once called home and said, "Welcome to Bellgrave."

Ambrose followed Emery into the castle, now a school for witches. While the exterior still looked like an old friend, the inside was just as bizarre as the people and technology populating it. Posters and art projects covered the walls. Little shops and restaurants with fragrant food he didn't recognize pocked each alcove. Strangest of all, ghostly rats scurried through the halls en masse, hanging about darkened corners, up on eaves, sometimes passing through the feet of students, making them shiver.

"Is any of it familiar to you?" Emery said.

"I don't recall the rats," Ambrose answered.

"No, you wouldn't. They're new."

Ambrose might have asked after the story behind them, but everywhere eyes were on them. They didn't stare at Ambrose's spell scars and runes, which were covered. They stared at Emery. More accurately, at the absence of his familiar. They whispered, shying away like a school of herring from a shark.

One particular witch waited in an arched alcove. At a glance, she bore a resemblance to Emery, wearing an expression that looked the way poison tasted, her short hair threaded with white. Her eyes were ice chips, her lips painted the color of wine. A brown stoat, turning white for winter, sat perched on her shoulder, watching their approach.

"So the word going 'round is true," she said. "Emery Vale tithed his own familiar."

"Don't pretend you're surprised, Hellebore," Emery said. "You're not a halfway decent actor, and I expect you're the one who's told everyone."

Ambrose stiffened. Hellebore, Emery's rival, the one Ambrose was meant to protect him from.

"Who's this?" Hellebore said.

"This is my cousin." Emery put deliberate affectation into his voice, the implication clear. *I'm lying. Ask me why.*

Hellebore's glass stare went up and down Ambrose's body. "Does he have a sister?"

Ambrose was not the cleverest of souls, but he wasn't witless enough to miss the sensual twist of her mouth or the implication that she'd find a woman who bore his familial resemblance more attractive. Instead of feeling flattery, it hit him with another cold wash of uncertainty.

His own . . . predilections had been far from acceptable in his time, yet Hellebore displayed hers without a twinge of fear that Emery might wield this information against her. It was not the first clue to make him wonder whether this world had changed in ways he might prefer.

Then Emery made a noise of disgust, and that glimmer of hope winked out. "If he had one, Hells, you'd probably have already fucked her, so let's skip the lechery and move on to proper introductions. Ambrose, meet Hellebore. Hellebore—" He paused, assessing where they were, their surroundings. No passing students could see the intricacies of their interaction in the alcove. When his eyes met Ambrose's, there was a silent order in them. *Scare her.* "Meet Ambrose."

Ambrose deliberated quickly. He was unaccustomed to using his powers against women, and he had no idea if Hellebore deserved Emery's ire. She hadn't threatened them so far. What's more, Emery didn't wish to reveal Ambrose's identity, so he might refrain from using the compulsion charm publicly.

Yet Ambrose had erred once already today. He needed Emery's good-will if he hoped to gain knowledge for the witch king's resurrection.

In the end, obedience was a comforting habit to fall back to.

He took Hellebore's hand to shake. The moment they touched, magic sweated his palm into something ephemeral, and he seized delicate bones in his fist. If he squeezed, they'd splinter. It sickened him like it always had, but it was also gratifying, fortifying, familiar in a way nothing in this world had been, when Hellebore's face waxed with terror, and something inside him feasted on her fear.

CHAPTER 4

Hellebore's stoat hissed and traveled down her arm to sink its teeth into Ambrose's wrist. He didn't flinch. He'd suffered far worse. He held on, the magic glutting itself on the shivers of fragile bones clutched in his fist.

"Let go," said Hellebore. To the untrained, she sounded commanding, but Ambrose felt her shaking. She spoke to Emery instead. "I know you're not about to have him break my hand in broad daylight."

"No, but I wanted you to know he could," Emery said. "You can let her go now."

Ambrose did, his stomach souring. Terrifying his master's enemies had been an old game, one he was good at, and it was hard not to take succor from the victory. But this hunger, when he fed it, left him sick instead of sated.

Emery glanced at his phone. "I'll see you later at the usual time and place."

"You can't bring *him*," said Hellebore.

"Oh? Why ever not?" Emery said with infuriating subtext Ambrose couldn't grasp.

"He'll want an explanation if you're absent, but whatever. On your head be it," Hellebore said.

She left, her stoat tucked into the collar of her shirt with its mouth still stained in Ambrose's blood. He removed the glove to suck his wound clean, then put the glove back on. "Women in this era are different from mine."

A HEX FOR HUNGER

29

"I wouldn't say Hellebore is necessarily a first ambassador for all modern women," Emery replied. "Her company doesn't improve with exposure, either."

"She is the one you require protection from," Ambrose said lightly, keeping the judgment from his tone, but Emery was sharp.

"Not only her, but if we're going to start the gender politics conversation, we might as well rip off this particular plaster. She's a threat. Loath as I am to admit it, she's one of the best witches in this school. Don't underestimate her because she's a woman and you're from a time when that was erroneously considered a personal failing. Need I remind you, you aren't exactly a shining example of patriarchal values yourself."

Ambrose braced himself for Emery's snide denial of his masculinity, but he only said, "I don't know how you achieved transition in your time, but in this one, that usually requires consistent medication. We can discuss the particulars later if necessary."

"You think I'm sick."

"Well, yes. I saw the way you looked while terrifying poor Hellebore. But, no, not because you're—whatever you called yourself in your age."

Abomination? Sodomite? Ambrose pasted on a tentative smile. "A man?"

"Yes."

Well, that was a better response than he'd expected. Still, Ambrose didn't know what to make of this conversation and would prefer not to have it.

The halls were nearly empty. "I believe we're running late."

Emery's class took them to the other side of the castle grounds, to a wing that once contained the armory.

Some relics of the past still remained, hung from the walls like hunting trophies. Ambrose's eyes fell immediately upon the sword mounted above the front podium. It had been a long time since it had licked a whetstone, the blade dull from disuse.

Its tip pointed down at the professor, a man of indeterminate age shuffling papers together. He hummed a tune as he did. Something like a lullaby, haunting and nostalgic. He'd lived long enough to have laugh lines, but his expressions and posture had the vigor of uncanny youth. His hair was the same white as Ambrose's, bleached by necromancy, with a distinct widow's peak. A water deer familiar tiptoed at his heel, hooves tapping a staccato rhythm against the stone floor.

Something about the professor's gait and movements reminded Ambrose of watching someone through a reflection on rippling water rather than in the flesh.

Upon entering the room, his bright gaze struck Ambrose with magnetic curiosity, and Emery gave a chilly nod.

Hellebore arrived, taking a seat at the back next to a demurely pretty girl, whom she slung an arm around, flashing Emery a smile that was half snarl.

"I see we have a new student," said the professor in a voice that didn't need spells to cast a charm. It had the mellow vibrancy of a bard's lyre.

"My cousin, visiting from abroad," Emery lied. "Ambrose."

The professor indulged the lie with a smile. "Pleased to have you, Ambrose. I'm Professor Van Moor. I hope you're enjoying your visit to Bellgrave?"

Ambrose smiled brightly. "The grounds are beautiful."

"They are, aren't they?" He looked at Emery as he said it.

Emery's chilly manner gave the interaction, for all its friendly overtures, an air of enmity Ambrose understood. Bad blood smelled the exact same centuries later.

This must be Emery's nemesis, Morcant.

"There's a lot of material to cover today, so I won't hold us up any longer." The professor manipulated the machine at his podium, and a projection appeared on the white wall behind him. Ambrose couldn't read the words, but there was an illustration accompanying them. It depicted a face he'd know anywhere.

The witch king. Captured in charcoal impressions of a smile so captivating, it had bewitched a nation.

And Ambrose.

"Last class, we covered the witch king's rise to power, how he galvanized a war-torn nation whose magical prowess paled in comparison to the southern provinces, and charmed his way into his predecessor's good graces, to the extent the king named him successor rather than his own son."

Ambrose knew this history, though he hadn't met the witch king until after his coronation. It seemed beyond the possibility of coincidence that Morcant would be covering this in his classes while that king's most loyal servant sat, resurrected, in the audience.

He studied Emery and Morcant for any sign they were aware of this irony, but Emery seemed not to pay the class much mind, and Morcant hardly looked at Ambrose. He had an odd habit of pausing in his lecture to snack on small tomatoes, which he plucked from the vine and popped in his mouth whole. The noise, amplified by his microphone, turned Ambrose's stomach.

He otherwise did nothing to indicate why he and Emery had such enmity, or why he'd taken such an interest in the witch king at such an opportune time. Ambrose would have to ask Emery about this odd "coincidence" later.

"We covered the various theories behind the witch king's success," Morcant continued. "Had the witch king genuinely befriended his predecessor, or ensorcelled him into surrendering his dynasty? As with many things, we can never know for certain. Similarly, we might never know what precisely led to his eventual downfall, but that won't stop us from picking apart the possibilities during today's lesson."

Ambrose's stomach turned. Morcant went on to cover a range of reasoning. The famine that struck poorer regions, leaving people starving and angry with their leaders. The witch king's religious advisers, some of whom felt he abused dark magics. The previous monarch's heirs, who resented the loss of their birthright and mistrusted the witch king's intentions.

All the while, Ambrose listened and thought, *None of those things led to his death. It was me. If I hadn't failed him, he'd still be king.*

As if in answer to the sting of self-flagellation, a familiar voice once again kissed the shell of his ear.

Ambrose. My Ambrose. Don't forget why I gave you that name. You haven't failed me. Not yet. Not while you draw breath.

Ambrose did his best to disguise the effect that voice had on him, but the hair rose on his neck in a pleasant shiver nonetheless. Emery glanced at him curiously.

"Cold," Ambrose murmured, his breath short.

Was that truly the witch king's voice? Or was he going mad?

You are not mad, even if there were once fools in our day who'd call you so. I live, insomuch as I can. We are tied, you and I. So long as you draw breath, I can return. You know this.

How? Ambrose thought desperately. *How can I bring you back?*

We will have to await an opportunity, but it seems this Morcant Van Moor, with all his knowledge, could help. Or, if not the man himself, then the books from which he's learned so much about me.

Ambrose understood, but that presented its own barriers. His illiteracy prevented him from acquiring any knowledge written down. If he could speak to Morcant . . . But Emery would never allow it, and Ambrose couldn't leave Emery's side to do so in private.

Still, the witch king's voice gave him hope. He'd find a way to reunite them. He had to.

Emery's library of books, the devices everyone used to navigate this world, all that power and knowledge was useless to him unless he found a way to access it.

As the lecture ended, and students gathered their things, one student in particular caught Ambrose's eye. He hadn't spent the lecture taking notes like the others. He held his mobile phone and had black things in his ears. When he rose, he used a stick, white with a rubber end, to tap his way up the steps.

He was blind. So how could he read the notes on the slides or see the diagrams?

He must have *some* method. Ambrose attempted to devise an excuse to walk over and ask, but Emery interrupted his thoughts.

"Coffee."

"Pardon?"

"Coffee. I need one."

He made his way toward the exit. Ambrose glanced over his shoulder at the blind boy, but he couldn't very well approach now. He'd need to find an appropriate time when Emery wasn't paying attention.

Professor Van Moor watched them on their way out with the smile of a man indulging his misbehaving pet.

Minutes later, they stood in a queue at a "café"—a cozy, fragrant-smelling place with students curled up in armchairs taking a break between classes. It felt more like a sitting room than a restaurant.

Ambrose waited dutifully at Emery's heel while he ordered.

"A large mocha, please. Want anything?"

Ambrose looked askance to see who Emery was speaking to.

"You. I'm asking you. Do you want anything?"

A strange paralysis rendered him mute. Making decisions for himself, that was new. Moreover, he'd never been asked to choose between a selection of beverages he could not read and had never tried.

Emery gave him a quick, assessing look, then turned back to the woman taking their order. "Make that two."

She stepped away to make the drinks, and Emery muttered, "Coffee wouldn't have made it to our country for another few centuries after you died. I'll warn you, most people hate it their first time."

"Then why do you drink it at all?"

"It grows on you."

"That's very generous of you," Ambrose said, keeping the suspicion from his tone. What did Emery expect in return? "Thank you."

"It's just coffee," Emery said. "You're no good to me starving."

Ambrose's mouth twisted with the irony. He'd never known satiety, not since the witch king's ritual had reforged him.

He decided now was as good a time as any to ask about Morcant's chosen subject for the class. "Is it only a coincidence that your professor is teaching the subject of my king, and you happened to have found our grave?"

Emery's lip quirked. "You could say the lessons served to inspire me to revisit your grave, but the timing is less coincidental than you think." He took two paper cups set on the counter for them. "Morcant has always been fascinated by the witch king. One might even call it an unhealthy obsession."

Ambrose chose not to divulge that he and Morcant had that in common, though he'd actually known the witch king. Intimately.

He accepted the paper cup Emery handed him, warmth seeping through his gloves. There was something comforting about the sensation, the smell.

"Come," Emery said. "We have time before my class to look through the books at the library."

If Ambrose had thought the number of books in Emery's home was impressive, nothing could prepare him for Bellgrave's library. Emery hardly blinked as he tapped a small thick paper he called a "card" on something that let them through a barrier into a room several stories tall, every wall and gallery lined with books. Spines and spines of them patterned the walls like scale mail.

Ambrose considered himself dauntless, but the labyrinth of shelves towering above was quite daunting. Even if he could learn to read, what hope had he of finding what he required in this colossal hoard?

Emery had no such difficulties. He navigated the maze like a hound on familiar hunting grounds. The fine bones of his hands flexed as they hovered over spines, freeing one volume after another and adding it to a pile.

While Emery collected anything he deemed relevant, Ambrose took his first sip of coffee. His brow furrowed. The brew tasted bitterly of nothing he'd ever tried, yet somehow evoked a feeling. An emotion. One Ambrose found more undefinable than the flavor.

Something like serenity, but less lonely. Like a full belly of roasted supper, like sanctuary from a long winter.

Wishful things. The sort Ambrose could only hope to taste temporarily.

"I take it you like it," Emery said.

Ambrose took another sip in answer.

As they prepared to check out, Ambrose spotted a familiar figure at a table, head bent over a device open to a page of text.

The blind student.

As Ambrose tried to invent an excuse to walk over and demand answers, the student stood, packed his things, and used his stick to navigate toward a door with a symbol Ambrose inferred was for the men's lavatory.

"I need to relieve myself."

Emery glanced over his shoulder. "Do the distance limits on your little pact require me to closely supervise?"

"The magic allows me to go two furlongs from your side."

"Then I'll wait here."

Ambrose ducked through the door. He had a moment of panic upon seeing several men with their backs to him, hovering next to privies mounted into the wall at a height for making water while standing. A privilege Ambrose's equipment wouldn't permit him, and which gave him a very real moment of panic before remembering he wasn't actually here to relieve himself.

The student he was after was washing his hands. Ambrose, prone to following instinct over composing a plan, walked straight up to him and said, "I saw that you can read. Can you tell me how?"

The boy's face flushed red with incredulity. "E-excuse me?"

"In the lecture hall and in the library," Ambrose clarified. "I've seen you using machines to read. If you please, explain it to me."

"Here? Are you serious?"

"Yes?"

Behind them, students finished up in a hurry and started to leave. Ambrose frowned. It seemed he'd miscalculated, and a public privy was considered a poor place for conversation.

"Just find a tutorial on the internet," the boy said.

He started to brush past Ambrose.

The witch king's voice came bristling in his ear. *You deserve better than such disrespect. Don't let this chance slip past us.*

Ambrose hated resorting to force, but he didn't see an alternative. He grabbed the boy by the scruff of his shirt and shoved him against the wall.

"Hey! What are you—Don't touch me!"

Ambrose didn't use the power, though he felt its craving like the sizzle of frying goose fat in an iron pan. He pressed a thumb to the sensitive knot in the boy's throat. "Answer my question."

"It's an e-reader?!" The boy choked, and Ambrose loosened his grip. "I use text-to-speech so it reads my textbooks out loud to me on my ear buds." He gestured to the black things in his ears.

"Show me."

With shaking fingers, the boy pawed searchingly through his bag for the "e-reader." The order in which he did things and the commands he gave it were complicated, but Ambrose had spent years memorizing the witch king's commands and executing them flawlessly. He ordered the boy to repeat the process only once and committed everything to memory.

"That's it. Will you let me go now? That hurts."

Ambrose released him, a specter of chagrin haunting him for a moment. Once, he'd never have been the man to threaten an innocent person, but the thought perished quickly. The witch king's return would require every meager tool Ambrose had at his disposal. He'd asked politely, and when that failed, used the method which bore results.

He'd never get anywhere without baring his teeth. This world and his had that in common.

"Tell anybody about this and I'll hunt your family for seven generations," he said, then departed.

CHAPTER 5

They returned to the ruined chapel. Home, Ambrose supposed he should call it, for now. He hoped Emery would seal himself away in his room again, giving Ambrose the opportunity to search out an e-reader and begin his reading endeavors, but Emery stoked a fire, poured himself a generous glass of wine, and sank into an armchair instead. Katzica put her head on his knee.

"Sit, would you?" Emery muttered, annoyed. "No need to stand sentinel. It's some time before my next engagement. Sleep, if you can."

Ambrose sat in the chair opposite but found it hard to doze. The comfort of the sitting room was an illusory sort. A crackle of tension gave it an anxious air.

"Now might be a good time to tell me more about your circumstances and what I can do to protect you," Ambrose said.

"That is the purpose of this engagement," Emery answered. "Easier to show you."

He said nothing more in the intervening hours, and Ambrose found himself too apprehensive to sleep. The clock over the mantel read quarter to three in the morning by the time Emery rose from his chair. He wordlessly went to his chambers and emerged again in a black cloak with the hood drawn up, obscuring his face in shadow. He had a magpie feather in hand.

"I'm going to cast a spell that will render you silent. Can people still feel you when you do that invisibility trick of yours?"

"Yes."

A HEX FOR HUNGER

"Then **be sure not to bump into anybody.**"

The telltale magic curled around Ambrose's throat, though gentler than before. This command had a chaotic element to it; Ambrose could not control other people's movement around him. The magic only ensured he would try to avoid them. "Where are we going?"

"Somewhere you aren't supposed to follow."

That much he'd gathered, but he supposed it was too much to hope for a crumb of detail.

Emery swept the feather across Ambrose's body. The incantation settled uncomfortably over his spell-scorched skin, the witch king's magic disconcerted by the signature of another. When he moved, his feet made no sound.

"Good," said Emery. He put his hands into the folds of his robes. Ambrose thought he could feel those long fingers close around the finger bone of his old master. **"Follow me."**

He transported them back to Bellgrave's grounds, on a trail set into a steep bluff. The path wended like a lightning bolt up the hill, lined with towering headstones twice the height of a man. Emery led the way past ancient graves, cracked and creeping with ivy, their inscriptions illegible even to those who could read, each like doors set into the hill.

A necropolis. A city of the dead, all their houses quiet and closed.

At the top of the hill, Emery broke away from the path, venturing between headstones, which got progressively larger and more dilapidated. The grass crisped underfoot with autumn's frost, but only Emery's steps made a sound.

They came to a grave near the summit, so enormous it seemed less a tomb than a tower, angels carved into columns holding the lintel above the mausoleum door. Candles dimly lit the circle of people gathered there. Among them, Hellebore.

"Where's your cousin?" she asked.

"Sleeping," Emery replied. "Like the rest of us should be."

"Shame. He'd make an interesting initiate."

The word gave Ambrose a clue. He peered at the faces of the others gathered here. Many looked like students, most younger than Emery and Hellebore. One stood out due to the burn scars across his face, though he hung back from the rest. Another, a brown-skinned girl with a coat-hanger build and a cloud of curls framing her face, looked at Emery with mocking contempt.

"Too tired even for our Transcendent Rite, old man?" she said, as if Emery were thirty years her senior and not three. "I'll make you a cup of tea and a bicky; you'll be right as rain."

"The rite isn't momentous enough to stay awake for. I'd sleep through your funeral if I could," Emery bit back.

"Optimistic of you to assume you'll outlive me."

"I'd normally agree with you," Emery said, "if you'd been smart enough to listen. Now I expect stupidity will take you before old age catches me."

Hellebore snorted. "Saoirse will run circles around you."

The repartee gave the clear impression Ambrose was only hearing half the conversation. The majority of the people present were—from their expressions—just as clueless. Saoirse looked pleased by Hellebore's compliment, but the rest of them shifted and stomped their feet against the cold while casting Katzica sidelong looks.

Even amongst peers, Emery was unsettling.

Distantly, a church bell rang thrice, an eerie dirge in the cold, quiet night. On the third ring, the doors to the tomb swung open. Professor Van Moor emerged, dressed in a robe similar to the ones Emery and Hellebore wore, though finer and embroidered at the edges with nightshade and bird bones. Only his pale face was visible in the dark. He smiled.

"Hail, initiates, old and new. It's a perfect Hallow's Eve to welcome you, if a cold one. It's warmer inside, so we shouldn't dawdle. I'm sure you're all eager to get to the important part: your Transcendent Rite."

The words had the effect of drawing the silence taut. Several initiates, particularly the youngest, stood tall and attentive.

"There's a bit of obligatory housekeeping before we can proceed. As you know, the arts and skills for which you've shown unique talent come with an unfortunate caveat. Most witches in our world misunderstand them. Though all magic can pose a danger, the deathly arts are maligned by those who fear anything that reminds them of their own mortality. So, to avoid their small-minded derision, we operate in secrecy."

He folded his hands. When he opened them again, the small skull of a bird lay in his open palm amongst sprigs of rosemary. "To keep ourselves safe, all new initiates must make a pact of secrecy. Take a sprig and hold the skull, then repeat these words. *I swear to tell no soul, living or dead, of the events which transpire within and without these walls that pertain to our esteemed guild. I promise to take its secrets to my grave and keep them long beyond it. Not even the veil could part me from this pact. On this I swear my life."*

The words skated like spider legs over Ambrose's skin. That was no frivolous thing to ask of new initiates. He was temporarily relieved to see many of them looked nervous and hesitant, but then Van Moor, looking sympathetic, said, "I know it's a lot to remember, so you can repeat the words after me," and they were all visibly relieved.

That alarmed Ambrose all the more. What powers did this professor wield, to lure these students into trusting him so thoroughly they would make a pact that killed them if broken?

More intriguing was the notion Emery must have made this same pact when he'd first joined. He didn't seem the trusting sort. Had he not broken it by bringing Ambrose here? The wording of the pact seemed clear. He should have dropped dead by now.

Yet, he hadn't. Ambrose puzzled over it. Though not a witch himself, his time at his king's side had taught him about spellcraft. Such pacts had to be specific, the wording ironclad. As each student stepped toward the professor and took a sprig of rosemary, they repeated the words.

"I swear to tell no soul, living or dead. . ." said the first student.

Ambrose had been alive, died, and brought back. Perhaps the spell considered him neither? On that convenient technicality, he must fall outside the pact's bonds.

Reluctantly, he adjusted his view of Emery. He didn't trust him. He wasn't even sure he liked him. But he was powerful enough to achieve a true resurrection and clever enough to exploit a loophole in this pact.

Ambrose would have to be cleverer still to escape him.

The witch king's voice once again touched his mind with gentle affection. *Your sweet nature could prove boon or bane. If he is so heartless as to be unendeared, then you must meet his brutality with your own.*

Ambrose leaned into the voice as if he could warm himself by it against the frosty night. The magic twisted in his stomach. He didn't want to use it, but if he had to . . .

He loved the witch king more than he hated killing.

The last student to step forward and take a rosemary sprig was Saoirse. She held it in hand and cast a defiant look over her shoulder at Emery. He met her eyes, but his expression was blank.

Saoirse said, "I know the words. I don't need you to repeat them."

Professor Van Moor gave an approving nod. She recited the pact verbatim, missing not a syllable, and the rosemary sprig burst into emerald flames that winked out as fast as they'd come alive. On the skull of the bird were now etched runic names for every pacted soul. The professor tucked it into his sleeve and spread his arms once more.

"You all honor me with your trust. In return, I promise to teach you skills and spells our esteemed school could never bear to impart. Welcome to the Necromancers Guild." His smile shone like silver moonlight on a lake. Ambrose mistrusted most people, and Van Moor was no exception, but smiling like that, he could see why the students took such a shine to him. He looked on them warmly and with pride, stoking the fires of their own desires and ambitions. Each of them felt clever and talented under the focus of that smile.

They'd been selected for this. They were special.

Ambrose recognized it like they were all flickers of his own reflection from a long, long time ago.

"Follow me to your Transcendent Rite," said Van Moor.

He turned and descended the steps of the tomb, and the students—starting with the youngest—followed. Emery took up the rear and paused on the threshold for the barest second. Ambrose spotted a rust-red vial in his hand, produced from within his cloak. He touched his finger to the stone arch, stroking the ward spell with his magic. Then the arcane collar tugged Ambrose forward like Emery had pulled his lead.

They descended into the dark.

CHAPTER 6

Candles drooling thick streams of wax lit the way down the narrow stairs.

Ward magic slicked over Ambrose's shoulders as he passed, and he flinched. It should have rejected him; he wasn't permitted here. Evidently, Emery had Morcant's blood in that vial and had used it to grant Ambrose access. He must have been planning this infiltration for some time.

The death of his familiar, Ambrose's resurrection, the specificity required to bypass the secrecy pact, and now ward magic. He'd been meticulous.

The passage opened into an immense stone chamber, two stories with a gallery and sarcophagi set into the walls. The sarcophagus in the center of the room had a decorative cloth covering it, obscuring the stone face of whomever was interred there. The domed ceiling caught all sounds, from the students' stride to the scuttle and squeak of rodents, and amplified them. Not Ambrose's. He moved as silently as the ghosts of this place.

Something about the room made him itchy, like a loose strand of hair had brushed his skin, invisible to the eye but ominously tangible.

The professor stood behind the altar made of the central sarcophagus and gestured for the new recruits to gather close. Emery and the older initiates formed a halo around him. Ambrose kept to the edge of the room, where he was unlikely to bump anything or anyone but still had a clear view of the proceedings.

It seemed a theatrical setting for an initiation. Ambrose's rites had taken place in far more mundane places. An alleyway, a blacksmith's forge, a bedroom.

"Saoirse, Windsor, Iris, you three have been chosen to join our guild for your show of skill in the art of necromancy, but there is one final test before you can officially join our ranks.

"I would happily take all of you, but I'd be remiss not to first ensure that you have what it takes to perform these spells safely. Though necromancy is not the taboo danger it's often made out to be, all magic can be perilous.

"To this end, I've set a test for you."

He unrolled a fraying bolt of silk over the sarcophagus. Inside were three raw chunks of quartz and three daggers. They'd be for some dark ritual, Ambrose assumed. Blood and flesh made powerful tithes, something his body knew well. He'd given it often and willingly to fuel the witch king's spells.

The generosity of your spirit is part of what drew me to you, Ambrose.

Ambrose flushed with the compliment, glad no one could see.

The students exchanged nervous looks, and the professor noticed. "Please, don't worry. I wouldn't ask you to spill your own blood."

From behind the sarcophagus, he lifted a wire cage. Inside were three rats, chewing desperately at the bars and squeaking. Intelligent creatures, they sensed their days were numbered.

Holding up a chunk of quartz, the professor said, "Stones like these have been used a long time for their magical properties. With the right spell and a gifted witch to cast it, a simple chunk of quartz can become a receptacle for messages, memories, anything a creative witch can think of.

"For your test, I'd like you to turn these simple stones into powerful spell jars. Tithe the rat's souls and use them to magically hollow out the quartz."

The instruction was met with mixed reception. Though Saoirse looked unfazed, the other two initiates shuffled from foot to foot. Ambrose understood their apprehension. It had taken him time to accept that no great feats were accomplished without some blood and sacrifice now and again. The rats would die, but if the students were decisive, it would be over quickly and painlessly.

The professor set the stones equidistant apart on the sarcophagus. "Who'd like to go first?"

Saoirse took up a dagger. "I will."

The professor gave an approving nod. He opened a hatch on the top of the cage. The rats surged toward it in hopes of escape. The professor's hand flexed, bones and knuckles straining, and the rats froze in a squealing rictus. They shimmered with magic. The professor moved his hand, hovering it over the table, and one rat floated into place on its back, limbs pinned by whatever spell the professor wielded against it.

It looked like the sort of anatomist's diagram Ambrose had glimpsed in the witch king's study. The creature screeched, fighting the spell, though it was futile. Saoirse brought the dagger down sharply. The screeching stopped.

That was the easy part. Beads of sweat gleamed on her brow as she drew on her magic to tithe the body and ensnare the spirit, using it like a chisel to carve a hole in the quartz. She held the foggy crystal in her free hand, fingers worrying at the grooves and chips in the stone like she could wear them smooth and immaterial.

It must have been a spirited rat. Her teeth clenched. Her breathing became labored.

The quartz flashed with light, obscured by her hand seizing around it. When she opened her fist, the quartz glowed in her palm like a captured star.

"Excellent," said the professor. "Not that I had any doubt. It's not an easy spell, but you've already proven yourself unusually talented, Saoirse." He gestured for her to place the stone back on the sarcophagus, which she did, then he took the dagger from her, wrapping it in silk. He turned back to the other students. "Who's next?"

Saoirse's performance had steeled the will of the other two. They both carried out the ritual and passed the test, although they took longer, and one of them—Windsor—shook so badly when stabbing his rat that he missed and had to do it again.

Ambrose observed Emery, trying to glean something about his temporary master from his response to the proceedings, but he simply watched dispassionately. Almost bored.

All three new initiates succeeded in creating the spell jars, which shone like a constellation on the sarcophagus. The professor's pride shone brighter still.

"It is a privilege to be able to teach you necromancy, an art that I fear would be forgotten if not for brave hearts like yours willing to trust me with your education. Welcome Saoirse, Windsor, Iris. I won't keep you all any later. The ritual is tiring, and you have classes tomorrow. We'll meet again at the usual time and place. For now, goodnight."

Dismissed, the new initiates and the few older ones headed for the door, Emery among them. Then the professor's voice called over their heads.

"Emery. Hellebore. I'd like a word, please."

Hellebore hadn't moved, perhaps aware she'd be held back. Emery stopped. The other initiates flowed around him like a river, casting him curious looks.

Ambrose hung back in the place he'd hidden the whole time. From here, he could see the professor's face in full, but only a sliver of Emery's. His posture was stiff. Bracing.

Professor Van Moor clasped his hands, worrying at the knuckles. His water deer leaned against his leg. An eerie creature. It didn't seem right for a prey animal to have fangs.

"I blame myself, you know," the professor said. His voice took on a different quality. Quiet. Close. He was no longer a teacher. He spoke to Emery and Hellebore like they were family. "I encouraged this little rivalry. You both have such talent and potential, I thought friendly competition would bring out the best in you. Not the worst."

"I did apologize for putting nettles in his cloak," said Hellebore. "It was just a harmless prank. Not like he doesn't know the spell to soothe skin irritation."

"You took my stock of olive pits to ensure knowing the spell wouldn't matter," Emery bit back. "No amount of dock leaves could offer relief."

The professor held up a hand to halt their bickering. "I'm not interested in which of you is most to blame. Like I said, I mostly blame myself. I taught you the things you know, gave you the tools. But I never thought—" He looked at Emery, a well of disappointment in his eyes. "Your own familiar, Emery. It's not the same as bugs and rats. She was a part of you."

Emery stayed silent throughout the scolding. His head was bowed, but not in shame. Too stiff for that.

"Dare I even ask what you bought with Katzica's soul?"

Ambrose felt exposed, the question pointing a finger at him.

Emery stayed silent. The professor sighed.

"I've informed the faculty, since they'll notice her missing. I told them it was an accident. They're offering to overlook it, given your history, but their sympathy will only extend so far. If you keep this up, they'll expel you, and I don't know if I'll be able to protect you next time."

Emery finally spoke, the words a dim echo of the professor's own words. "Protect me."

"In the interest of your success, I'm only asking you to set aside this feud. We may be mostly in the business of raising the dead, but can we not agree this conflict is best put to rest?"

"Of course, Papa," Hellebore said. "I won't hold a grudge. After all, we're all family here."

So they were related. Both the professor and Hellebore awaited Emery's answer, but the silence stretched, and after a time, Emery gave them one.

"This is no petty grudge. I won't rest until you're buried here."

He said it with all the inflections of a fatal curse.

Hellebore's fists clenched, her temper rising, but the professor didn't match the ire of his child at all. He stepped around the sarcophagus, bridging the gap between him and Emery. With a hand, he reached out as if to grasp him by the shoulder, but Emery flinched away, and the professor's hand swung empty to his side. His eyes pinched with grief—real or feigned, Ambrose didn't know Van Moor well enough to tell—but from the sliver of Emery's face that he could see, nothing but hate was mirrored back.

"Please, Emery," said Van Moor. "You're so close to graduation. It would pain me to see you throw that all away when you showed such promise."

CHAPTER 7

Dawn light crept through the trees, and the fire had burnt to ash by the time Emery and Ambrose returned to the ruined chapel to sleep.

Inside, Emery traipsed to the fireplace, leaning over to assess the scattered wine bottles in search of one that wasn't empty. He shook one, which sloshed fortuitously. He uncorked it, sank into an armchair, and took a long swig. The knot in his throat bobbed thrice. With his other hand, he fished a coin from his pocket and began rolling it across his knuckles in a neat bit of sleight of hand.

Ambrose, having already dropped invisibility, stood warily nearby. In his experience, not much good came from imbibing too much alcohol. He hoped Emery wasn't a mean drunk.

"Sit," said Emery.

Ambrose took his seat gingerly on the sofa opposite.

Emery lounged, one leg up, knee cocked, a slim wrist draped over the chair arm so he could stroke Katzica's ear. "So, you've met him now." He balanced the wine bottle on his knee and tipped it by the neck with one finger on the spout. "Morcant Van Moor. What do you think of him?"

Ambrose reviewed his brief encounter. Morcant put forward the impression of a nurturing, attentive teacher, passionate about his magical specialties and the need to pass it on to his pupils. He also seemed to harbor admiration for the witch king, something which did him credit in Ambrose's view.

However, the pact he employed with his initiates would kill them if they ever broke it. He didn't know why such lengths should be necessary to ensure their secrecy. They'd all submitted to the guild's terms willingly.

"It is difficult to say based on such a brief encounter," Ambrose answered earnestly. "My first impression was neither favorable nor unfavorable."

"That's all?"

Ambrose wasn't sure what Emery wanted from him. "The pact he employs to ensure your secrecy is quite extreme."

Emery's eyes glowed with the embers of the fire. With a flick of his wrist, he dispensed something from his tithe pouch, and the flames roared alive again. Ambrose didn't recoil, but he wanted to.

"You probably think us all idiots for making the vow of secrecy in the first place," Emery said. "Though I suppose you're in no position to judge."

Ambrose bristled at the comparison. He had sworn fealty to a king who promised to make the world better. A king he'd adored.

The witch king's voice was like a calming hand on the nape of his neck. *Do not give in to ire too easily. We cannot afford to alienate him just yet.*

"I had wondered how he earned your trust," Ambrose said.

"That's gracious of you." Emery cast him a suspicious glance, perhaps weighing Ambrose's answer with his body language to glean whether the grace was genuine. Ambrose's curiosity was earnest. Besides the voice in his head, he had nothing to hide.

"He was kind, in the beginning." Emery's gaze drifted to the fire, so that he seemed to stare into a realm unseen. Distantly, he added, "And I was gullible enough to believe his charade."

"You're saying the face he puts forward isn't genuine?"

Emery huffed. "Far from it. I said I'd explain everything to you. It's not the sort of story best told sober, or to sober company. Want a drink?"

Best not to lower your guard near him.

Ambrose had never imbibed in the past. He couldn't risk impairment with the witch king's life in his hands.

"Suit yourself," said Emery. "Morcant Van Moor approached me in my first year. I was top of his class at the time, in contest with Hellebore, who hated me already. He styled himself as a supportive, encouraging mentor back then. He still does, to the students he's interested in. Only after I'd made the vow of secrecy did the mask start to drop.

"It's . . . difficult to recount. The petty things are what started it. He'd belittle my progress. If I made a mistake, he'd say things like, 'If you spent half as much time practicing spellcraft as you did with your nose in those tawdry novels you might make a decent necromancer.' When he offered compliments, they usually had an underhanded meaning.

"So I devoted all my time to practicing. I could execute a spell perfectly, and a difficult one way above my level, and do you know what he'd say then?" Emery sat straighter, the liquid in his half-drunk wine bottle sloshing. He took on an imperious tone and posture to say in Morcant's vacant drawl, "*I guess that will do.*"

Slumping back into the chair, Emery paused, giving Ambrose another assessing look while he sipped his wine. "The first time I spoke back to him, he hexed me so that every bite of food I ate for a week smelled and tasted like rotten eggs. He told me that if I'd been an adept-enough witch to cast the counter spell, I needn't have suffered at all. I did try, but it wasn't an ordinary hex. All the conventional means weren't working. And I *was* casting them correctly. I was."

He said it as if to convince himself. Ambrose didn't know Emery well, but he'd managed a true resurrection spell, something only a skilled enchanter could accomplish. Morcant had sown a seed of doubt, and it had taken root.

Emery continued, "I wanted out. But Morcant made it very clear: This wasn't the sort of guild I could walk away from. The secrecy pact kept my mouth shut, so I tried to find a way to expose Morcant to the other faculty."

That hadn't been wise, but Ambrose didn't say so.

"Most of them think the sun shines out his arsehole," Emery spat. "He runs charities, rubs elbows with the higher administration, always remembers their birthdays and gets them something nice, that sort of thing. But there was one professor—Professor Valenti. He was the only one who asked questions. Why I wasn't sleeping well. Why I was excelling in all of my classes except Van Moor's. I think he suspected something. He'd tell me, 'If there's anything wrong, you should come forward.' He wasn't taken in by Morcant's bullshit like the rest of us, so I figured, I can't tell him. Not with the secrecy pact. But what if I showed him?"

Emery delivered his recollections with an air of telling some sordid story that had nothing to do with him. Ambrose privately thought that, while Morcant's pact was questionable, the punishments Emery outlined were hardly the worst things he could imagine. This sort of discipline and criticism were necessary to improvement. He'd suffered worse in his own education. He certainly wouldn't be able to discuss them as if they were idle gossip.

"He got Professor Valenti fired," Emery said. "Morcant sent e-mails from my address, making it look as though we had some sort of *inappropriate* relationship for a student and professor. Valenti won't—*can't* speak to me. Probably thinks the whole thing was my doing. Rumor spread it was me, so of course, the rest of the faculty keep their distance, too. No one wants to risk the same by association.

"Things spiraled after that. I drank myself stupid most days. Started failing classes. Hellebore was true to her name and made my life hell. With pranks, mostly. A spell so that my dorm always smelled like the inside of a gym bag or my bedsheets always itched. I'd retaliate, and Morcant would intervene. Usually taking her side. I couldn't adequately ward the place because it's technically a publicly held property, so I moved here to get away from it. He failed me on papers I should have got better than passing grades on. He took control of my bank account and gives me a monthly allowance. Enough to buy what I need for school and to stay alive, but never escape. He runs surveillance on my Alakagram account. Any avenue through which I could escape or weasel around the secrecy pact to ask for help, he's cut me off from."

Ambrose frowned. He didn't know what a "bank account" or "Alakagram" were, but he got the point. Emery didn't need an arcane collar to be compelled. Morcant had seized control of his life.

He said, "How?"

Emery, who had been leaning back against his chair to stare at the ceiling, lolled drunkenly forward to look at Ambrose. "How?"

"How did he take control from you?"

"Everything's digital nowadays," Emery said, holding aloft his mobile phone. "He only needed the password. Which I gave him."

"Why?"

Emery's demeanor shifted subtly. Though he could say the rest as if drunkenly rambling about a stranger's life and not his own, this part he sobered for. It raised more of Ambrose's suspicions.

"He has leverage over me," Emery said. "The details don't matter, but if I don't do what he says, he's got the power to put me in prison."

Ambrose thought that a very convenient detail to withhold. Whatever leverage Morcant had, it must be a powerful motivator for Emery to relinquish so much control.

What's more, Emery had drunk the contents of that bottle over the course of a short period. A man who'd locked himself in his bedroom because he didn't trust Ambrose didn't seem the type to imperil himself by drinking and lowering his defenses. While he slouched and mimed the movements of someone partially impaired, he continued idly rolling the coin across his knuckles, occasionally vanishing it up his sleeve. Great manual dexterity for a drunk. Ambrose suspected he was stone cold sober.

Perhaps it was all a performance to throw Ambrose off, but he suspected there was more Emery didn't want him to know.

The story he told painted a clearer picture than Ambrose had twenty-four hours prior, but didn't illuminate how he was meant to help.

"What do you need from me?"

"At first, I thought I could hold out until graduation," Emery said. "Just another year, then I can get the hell out. Move down south or to another country, even. But I eavesdropped on him telling Hellebore he plans on moving to another school, or another institution entirely. Somewhere he can continue the guild with lower risk of getting caught. And I have *no* intention of letting him take me."

"So you don't only require my services to protect you. You want me to help you escape," Ambrose said.

"Escape?" Emery chuckled. "No. I thought you'd caught on by now."

Ambrose waited.

"I wasn't lying to them in that tomb," Emery said. "I want them dead, and I want you to help me."

CHAPTER 8

The words were a gentle squeeze around Ambrose's throat. Magic rumbled within him like a hungry stomach.

Part of him was not surprised by Emery's request, although it chafed at an age-old, unquenched desire of his.

He'd wanted to be a knight, a hero, and in so doing had become a weapon. One who fought righteously, yes, and he could not fault those who wielded him. They were only using him as he was designed. But he couldn't deny how the bloodshed had tainted his self-image.

What did surprise him was Emery's reasoning.

Morcant had punished him for his failures in keeping with teachers and their students. Humiliated him in front of his peers and prevented him from escape, yes, but Emery wanted to *murder* him.

It seemed a very dramatic, out-sized response. One Ambrose wanted no part in.

Emery was studying the fire, its glow outlining a striking profile. The proud arch of his nose and raven sweep of silver-streaked hair curling behind his ears made him distinct in silhouette. Light glimmered off the handsome sweep of a cheek, carved hollows in the masculine bump of his throat.

How treacherous of fate to gift such a cruel heart with a fair face.

Ambrose didn't want to kill anymore.

Then he heard it. The witch king's voice, like drops of rain soothing the flush of emotion.

We might not relish the thought, but the necromancer's death could serve our ultimate purposes—if we play our cards correctly.

How?

Death has adverse effects on my memory. It is difficult to recall the specifics of the spell needed to restore my life, but the tithes will doubtless be costly. If I had my grimoire, I could piece together the rest. For now, sweet wolf, I ask for your patience and your faith.

If there was any chance it could bring them together again . . .

"How do you propose we kill him?"

The wine bottle slipped from Emery's hand. He caught it—narrowly. "You agree to it just like that?"

It wasn't that Ambrose wanted to kill. The magic in him did. He could feel it slavering at the mere notion. But if this could reunite him and the witch king, he'd do most anything.

"You hold the arcane leash," Ambrose said. "And I owe you a debt for resurrecting me."

"Right." Emery reached into the pocket of his cloak and withdrew the pearly bone. "I didn't realize the witch king enthralled you so thoroughly that you ceased to have any opinion of your own."

Ambrose repeated his question before he said something regrettable. "How do you propose we kill him?"

"I want to make it look like an accident," Emery said. "Or natural causes. Anything that won't raise suspicion."

Ambrose clenched his spell-stained hands in the upholstery of the sofa arm. He was grateful he wouldn't have to use them, but the magic bared its teeth. It wanted to feed. "Do you have a plan?"

"I'm working on something, but I don't have all the pieces yet. Something to sleep on."

Ambrose looked up through the aperture in the ceiling at the lightening sky. "It's daybreak."

"Yes, well, that's the guild for you. Calling on us at odd hours of the night. You learn to be opportunistic about naps. I will make up a proper bed for you at some point, but for now, I hope the sofa is comfortable. God knows I've crashed on it countless times myself."

"It's perfectly adequate."

Emery didn't lack for blankets or pillows. Given what he'd said about Morcant taking control of his finances, it was safe to assume everything was either spell-crafted or stolen.

But Ambrose had no intention of sleeping.

Emery disappeared with Katzica into his room.

A HEX FOR HUNGER 53

Ambrose waited for the click of the lock, then started searching the chapel for an "e-reader" and "headphones."

It didn't take long. Though Emery seemed to prefer paper books, he had an e-reader stashed under a stack on the coffee table, earphones discarded in a drawer of miscellaneous cords, among other wires and machine bits Ambrose didn't recognize.

He managed to follow the blind boy's instructions through turning it on and navigating to the library. It read out the titles to him in an inflection-less voice, each more ambiguous than the last. He hadn't the faintest clue what a book called *His Virtuous Vices* or *My Hex Husband* were about, but he could safely assume they weren't historic tomes detailing the witch king's accomplishments.

These titles were interspersed with the instructional variety. *A History of Taboo Witchcraft* and *A Study in Rare Spellcraft* could potentially hold clues to the type of magic tethering his soul to the witch king's, but he doubted they'd be so specific.

No, he needed something pertaining to the witch king himself. Perhaps something which could allude to the location of his grimoire.

He'd nearly flipped through the entire library when the monotonous voice read out a title that had him jerking upright.

Desmond Caepernicus: A History of Terror Under the Tyrant Witch King.

He froze, his finger hovering over the book he'd just selected. He could not recall the last time he'd heard the witch king's name uttered aloud. He'd always been referred to by his titles. Even in private moments of intimacy, Ambrose had never spoken aloud the name this machine had just read in the same toneless voice it used to enunciate titles like *Sensuous Sundries.*

The black cover showed an illuminated script with skulls and poisonous botanicals. Hesitant, he tapped the cover and opened the book to its first page. Apprehension rattled in his chest as the monotone voice read him the publishing details, a foreword from the author forewarning of the difficulty in analyzing the actions and details of a figure from so long ago, and then finally, the contents of the book itself.

He only managed a couple chapters, but the more he listened, the more his apprehension grew.

The title purported to attempt an unbiased portrayal of the witch king's actions, free from judgment, yet it focused heavily on his most controversial and desperate actions. It tiptoed around using modern language and definitions of his relationships, making mention of the undisputed loyalty of those within his inner circle while having no way of knowing for certain what the nature of those relationships were.

It mentioned Ambrose, not by name but reputation. The Grim Wolf of Bellgrave. The witch king's "mad dog."

The author demurred, *It can never be known to what extent the Grim Wolf's actions were his own. Was his depravity an innate feature the witch king merely exploited, or was he a soldier following orders under threat of treason to his king if he disobeyed? While occultists and conspirators theorize he might have been magically subjugated, no historical evidence substantiates the claim. Most accounts describe the Grim Wolf as bloodthirsty, rabid, and all too eager to do his master's bidding, such as this journal entry recorded by Reverand Lewis Tybalt, 1410.*

"Forgive me, Father, for I've seen things from which no prayer or divine blessing could bring reprieve. The witch king, in routing out a traitor seeking sanctuary in the abbey, did send his mad dog, who, being a godless heathen, did not respect the sanctity of our church and set upon the poor wretch to part him from his vitals with his bare hands. Such screams I've never heard. Even at choir, I think I can hear their echo. And once the vile act was done, how should the villain appear? Smiling and satisfied.

A devil desecrated our holy church. For keeping such corruption in his close company, may God have mercy on the witch king's soul, and if it be treason for saying so, may God also have mercy on mine."

Ambrose dropped the e-reader into the blankets, but the voice went on until he yanked the earphones out. He wished to hear no more of that night. He remembered it well enough, but hearing it described by an out-sider stung. Of course, the priest didn't know magic sang through his veins and made his body rejoice in the carnage. No one saw how his heart was sickened for it.

As a young boy, he'd attended a jousting competition in the hopes of laying eyes on the witch king's first knight—Sir Aric, a man whose legend-ary stories had carried even to the ears of peasants and farmer's boys like him.

He had watched Sir Aric unseat his every competitor at the joust, then Ambrose had sneaked into the stables to meet him. Yet, when he'd expressed dreams of becoming a hero just like him, the knight said, "Far nobler to be a farmer."

It left Ambrose confused and disappointed.

On his way home, Ambrose and his family fell afoul of bandits. Ambrose's father, insisting they had nothing, was killed first. His mother begged they spare Ambrose. They killed her, too. He would have died next, if Sir Aric hadn't intervened. He died valiantly with a dagger to the throat from the last bandit after felling all the rest.

That was how, baptized in the blood of his hero, Ambrose met the witch king. He'd cast a spell, stopping the bandit mid-thrust of his blade, taking the dagger from his frozen hands to give to Ambrose.

"He killed my knight, but he killed your parents. You deserve vengeance."

The memory felt wet as running ink at the edges. He couldn't recall if he'd hesitated, whether he'd been afraid, angry, grief-stricken. Time had worn the rough edges of that event smooth. He thought, perhaps, there had been someone else there with the witch king, watching, but he couldn't be sure.

Oddly, the only detail Ambrose *could* recall with clarity was that it had required more force than expected to stab somebody.

Once the act was done, the witch king offered him training as a knight. A sweet gift made bitter by circumstance.

Between avenging his family and killing the traitor in sight of a church's priests and saints, the book's recollections of Ambrose's life made him nauseous.

He'd pledged his devout service to the man who'd rescued him from certain death. Somewhere between that moment and this one, he'd spilled so much blood in defense of his king that it dyed red the purity of those heroic dreams. Everyone he'd killed had been an enemy to the crown, yet . . . in his darkest hours, he'd wondered.

In his quest to be a hero, had he become a villain instead?

This book certainly thought so.

The man you hunted was a traitor. A dangerous apostate. Lives were saved with the sacrifice of his.

I know, thought Ambrose.

But as ever, his soul was the one to bear the bloodstains.

You were loyal and true. No king could have asked for better, but these books were written by the ones who killed me. It serves them to paint us both as villains.

Ambrose let the words soothe his fears, but it crossed his mind that, perhaps, the voice he heard was not the witch king's at all. Perhaps it was only a figment of his deranged mind, pretty lies he told himself. Yet, he couldn't help but hold on to the dying embers of hope.

Perhaps things could be different this time.

CHAPTER 9

In the morning, Emery emerged, slamming open his bedroom door and looking more risen-from-the-dead than Ambrose had after five centuries in the ground.

"Feel rough as a badger's arse," he said.

Ambrose didn't feel much better, really. He'd slept poorly after reading that book. He didn't think Emery had truly been drunk the night before, but he certainly looked hungover now.

Katzica rushed over to greet Ambrose, licking his hand with an alarmingly dry tongue.

"Get dressed," Emery ordered. "We're going for a fry-up. I need to consume something that's ninety percent grease."

It wasn't a command, for Ambrose felt no compulsion to get up with any haste, but he sensed Emery kept the tether on his person. It beat like a second heartbeat in his ears.

He dressed in another smothering turtleneck, and Emery enchanted a portal to a pub in a converted stable yard, with a fresh produce stand squatting outside the open barn doors. Emery picked up a punnet of those small tomatoes, which he called cherry tomatoes, paid the farmer, and flicked coins into the tip jar on their way past.

Inside, the original foundation remained, with stalls made into booths and the tack room now a tap room. The smell of hops and frying fat mercifully replaced the expected stench of manure and hay.

The difference sent a pang through an old, forgotten scar of Ambrose's. He recalled the precise color of his cremello mare, her hide like flaxen wheat as he ran his hand along her flank, darkened with foamy sweat.

He shook the memory aside. He couldn't dwell on that.

Emery sat them in a booth, secluded enough they wouldn't be overheard, and a red-faced youth brought them lists of dishes, which were called menus.

"I haven't cooked in some time. Morcant's curses left me rather without appetite—but it's impossible to turn down the breakfast here."

Ambrose's appetite wasn't much better, soured by memory. Perhaps he could avoid revealing he couldn't read the menu by skipping breakfast altogether.

You must eat. You must stay strong.

Ambrose bowed his head. It was true. The menu's lifelike illustrations helped. They depicted honest fare of eggs, bacon, sausages, and toast.

He ordered the same thing as Emery: a stack of pancakes and bacon.

Once the waiter left, Emery said, "I have a plan." He pushed the punnet of tomatoes into the center of the table. "There are spells that induce heart attacks. I could hex one of these, and *you* chuck it in with Morcant's snacks while invisible."

Ambrose considered the timing of Emery picking up the punnet. "Did you come up with that just now?"

"When else? I woke up ten minutes ago."

"Shouldn't we be more . . ." He chose his words carefully. "Methodical?"

"There are about a thousand different ways to kill someone, but the longer we plan, the longer Morcant has to discover that plan." Emery's lip curled whenever he uttered the professor's name, who, Ambrose noted, he never gave the proper honorifics for. Never *Professor Van Moor*. Always *Morcant*, said as if spitting something out from between his teeth.

The plan struck Ambrose as strange, the same way Emery drinking alcohol in front of someone he didn't trust had. He'd assumed, given the meticulousness necessary to resurrect him, get him through the secrecy pact, and into the guild's quarters, Emery tended toward over-preparation. This spontaneous plan contradicted that assessment of his character, so which was he? Mastermind, or just rash and talented enough to get lucky?

"How will you enchant it?" Ambrose asked.

From his satchel, Emery produced—death would be a mercy—more books.

Emery pushed one toward him. The leathery cover contained dusty, moth-eaten pages. "I brought these along for inspiration. Found them at an antiques store. They look like medical texts, but, you know, for people who definitely shouldn't practice medicine. I'm sure they'll have *something* we can use."

Ambrose nodded airily, leafing through the one in front of him. He pretended to read it, but the letters were no more use to him than spider silk was for sharpening a sword.

On one page, he came upon nude diagrams of a man and woman, as defined by standard medicine, their genitals and bodies all in alignment with who they were.

The images were a kick to the stomach. He'd avoided thinking about his body thus far. The witch king's magic had crafted him a form more comfortable to embody than the lumps and curves his teen years had cursed him with. The witch king's magic still hungered in him. Would it also maintain his body's transformation, partial though it had been?

He doubted it. His body had been maintained by regular potions.

The waiter brought their food. It was a welcome distraction. Ambrose pushed the book away from him and picked up his utensils. The pancakes in front of him were unlike the sort he remembered; these were thick and fluffy, fried golden. He watched Emery drizzle some whiskey-colored syrup over his pancakes and, at a loss, copied him.

The moment he took a bite, he forgot his worries. The pancakes were fluffy and sticky with the sweetest syrup he'd ever tasted. The meat was salty and succulent with dripping fat. Together, the combination made him close his eyes and slump back in his seat, head knocking against the wood panel behind him.

"Should I leave you two alone?" Emery said.

Ambrose flushed, swirling his fork through the sticky sauce on the pancakes. "What is this?"

"Maple syrup."

"Nectar of the gods, more like."

Emery almost smiled. Or his cheeks dimpled, which seemed close. Then he seemed to recover himself, regarding Ambrose with his customary suspicion. "It's made from tree sap, though the trees aren't native here. Yet another thing that wouldn't reach us until a few centuries after you died."

Ambrose was a man lost in time and mostly terrified, unable to read menus and hearing the voice of his dead king in a body that could betray him any moment while at the beck and call of a half-mad and vengeful witch.

But the food . . . The food might make it worthwhile.

Emery had only eaten a few bites himself, but stopped to tap a finger to a page of his book. "Here. An enchantment to make the heart race. Normally used for medical purposes, but under the 'adverse effects,' it warns the spell could stop the heart altogether if made too potent. Let's see, tithes. Hm. Oh. Well, that won't work."

"Why?"

"It requires a tithe of suet from the fat of a rare Tibetan hog, which is strictly regulated since it can also be used in spells for performance enhancement. For, er, sexual purposes. It does mention another tithe here." He scowled. "The third eye of a three-eyed toad. Really? Fat chance of finding *that* at Minty's Mortar and Pestle."

"You live in a bog," Ambrose pointed out.

"Ah, yes. Shall we don our waders and go hunting?"

Ambrose resented the tone of sarcasm. It was only a suggestion.

Emery squinted at him. "Are you pouting?"

"No," Ambrose said, adjusting his expression to something more neutral.

"I didn't know the Grim Wolf of Bellgrave *pouted*."

"Witches in my day harvested tithes from the wild."

Emery slumped back, letting out a groaning exhale. "Well, if we can't find anything else, I suppose we can try. Not as though it's easy to come by tithes with lethal purposes at the average apothecary."

An hour later, Ambrose found himself walking gingerly across peat mats in search of three-eyed toads.

The bog surrounding Emery's ruin reeked of humidity, compost, and mud. It was the sort of bog where decaying plant matter floated and congealed on the water's surface until it was solid enough to walk across. The spongy mats squelched and bounced underfoot, making Ambrose feel as if he were bobbing on a boat at sea. He had to walk with his arms out for balance or avoid pitching over into peat, which, if he sank through, was liable to swallow him. He was a passable swimmer, but he didn't want to test those skills in waters like these.

Worse than the risk of drowning were the midges. Too small to see or hear, he only became aware of them when he felt a prickling bite on his face or hairline—the sensory equivalent of a rough seam on the inside of a shirt or loud chewing. It made Ambrose itchy all over.

As he saw a toad and went waddling after it, grasping it firmly by the legs to hold up and examine for a third eye, he reflected that he had been given worse orders than these, but perhaps none so undignified.

The history books might reflect less darkly on the Grim Wolf of Bellgrave if their authors could see him now.

Emery, not content to simply whisk Ambrose away on the errand, had joined him in the search. Raising his knees high to pull his boots out of mud or shake out the puddles seeping into his socks, Emery resembled a stork with his long, slender limbs held at odd angles to keep his balance.

It tugged at the corners of Ambrose's mouth, to watch him lunge for a toad only to belly flop onto the peat mat with a muffled swear word.

"Don't laugh. It's not as if you've done any better. There's mud on your face."

"And is that nearly a *smile* on yours?" Ambrose didn't think a bit of jest would be too risky. He smeared the mud away, or tried. His sleeve was equally muddy and only served to paint more on.

Emery paused. "I can smile. I smile all the time."

"So your sour look is a choice and not an unfortunate paralysis of the face."

"What have I got to smile about? I'm covered in mud and rotten plant gunk—" He'd gotten up, flicking the aforementioned gunk from his feet with little kicks like a cat with wet paws. "—getting eaten by midges in a stinking bog, searching for a rare amphibious mutant that probably doesn't exist so I can murder the bastard who ruined my life, with an accomplice who'd probably murder me, too, if not for the magic shock collar his own bastard of a master saddled him with."

He is unworthy of you, the witch king muttered darkly.

Ambrose's stomach boiled with a motion not unlike the rippling peat mats. "He is—wasn't a bastard."

"If you say so—Ah!" Emery pointed. "Look at that. There."

Ambrose followed the direction indicated but could make out nothing in the yellowing beige-brown of the bog.

"That toad, there," Emery went on. He'd adopted a hunting stance. It made him look like a squatting toad himself, albeit a far prettier one.

A thought Ambrose squashed like a mosquito.

He stalked toward the spot with Emery. As he got closer, he saw the toad hunkered in the grasses, well camouflaged as a lump of mud. In the center of its forehead was a yellow pustule of an eye.

Emery flexed his fingers and pointed. "You go around and I'll herd it toward you."

Ambrose did as instructed, but when Emery moved, the toad did not head in the direction it was chased. It sprang to the right and made for open water.

"*No!*" Emery shouted. "Get after it!"

Ambrose lunged.

This was his first mistake.

The slippery, rippling peat mats did not offer much traction. He landed a foot short of the toad on a new and weakly patched-together mat, full of holes like honeycomb.

It couldn't hold his weight and buckled.

He nearly took in a lungful of acidic water as the cold shocked his body. Darkness enveloped him as he sank into the bog.

Shock gave way to panic. His eyes stung with silt when he tried to open them. He kicked for the surface but couldn't be sure he'd aimed the right direction, until he hit something slimy and semi-solid.

A peat mat. He was underneath one.

He tried to push up through it, but it was far denser than the one he'd fallen through. He sank his fingers into the muddy underbelly, but it held firmly together.

The second mistake he only recognized in the unsettling, serene quiet of the bog's muddy waters.

Emery hadn't used a compulsion command. The collar hadn't squeezed. It hadn't yanked Ambrose into pursuit. He had, out of idiocy or old habit, obeyed.

Now he was going to drown.

CHAPTER 10

You cannot die here, my Ambrose. Not while you have my magic at your disposal.

Ambrose clenched his eyes shut harder against the silty water.

Of course. He should have thought of it earlier. The hunger in his breast snarled for blood, but the only thing Ambrose sank his fingers through was the sodden underside of the peat mat. He concentrated, let the magic pour through him like water carving out a new gorge.

It allowed his hands to part the dense matter of the peat and tear through to the other side, but when he grasped for anything solid to pull himself out, all he found was more peat, which sank with him.

His lungs burned. The bog was too thick to swim, dragging at his ankles, filling his bones with lead. He kicked and flailed and—

A hand grasped his.

Desperately he kicked, and another hand grasped his arm, pulling him up.

Breaking the surface felt like bursting through the shell of a fruit from the inside. He gasped, blinking the dirty water from his eyes. Emery lay sprawled on his belly across the peat mat, holding Ambrose by both arms.

"Oh, good, you're still breathing. I don't know if you realize, but I only had *one* familiar, so I really can't recreate the spell to bring you back."

Ambrose started to say, "Get me out of here," but ended up coughing and spitting up the muddy water dripping into his mouth.

"Quit flailing. Listen. The peat won't hold your weight unless it's distributed evenly. Try and float on your belly."

Ambrose swallowed his pride and, taking a deep breath to help his buoyancy, allowed his body to rise in the water as if he were going to perform a swimming stroke. Once he was mostly parallel with the surface, Emery shimmied backward. The peat mat sank a little beneath them but held together.

Bit by bit, Ambrose crawled his way out of the bog and, once they were on a solid mat, he rose to his knees.

Emery got up, looking down at his sodden, muddy clothes. "Not the most dignified rescue, but you're alive."

Ambrose looked up at him.

Emery didn't have the same beatific features as his old master. The witch king had been likened to celestial bodies—the sun, the stars. With golden hair, clear blue eyes, and a smile like a blessing, the bards sang that his looks made angels jealous.

Emery was, in all ways, his opposite. Raven hair threaded with gray, eyes like bottomless night, sharp in all the ways the witch king looked soft.

He was no less handsome, and he'd saved Ambrose's life.

He tried to eschew the burgeoning warmth in his chest. Saving him had been the sensible thing to do. He was a valuable tool, and he couldn't serve Emery from the bottom of the bog.

But Emery had also brought him back in the first place, and he was beginning to find it hard not to feel grateful.

"The toad got away," Ambrose said.

As if to answer him, they heard a creaky croak. They turned in unison. Three feet away, the toad sat watching them as though the spectacle of Ambrose nearly drowning had been its day's entertainment.

Emery took a step, but Ambrose said, "Wait."

He had a better method. In hindsight, he was ashamed he hadn't thought of it before.

Drawing on his magic, he donned his invisibility and crept up on the toad, careful not to bounce the peat mat too much. He grasped the creature by the legs.

The plan was to sneak the tomato into Morcant's usual punnet of them during a guild meeting.

A HEX FOR HUNGER

They had considered doing it during classes, so that there would be plenty of witnesses to the accident of poor health. No foul play afoot.

Emery objected to this setting for one reason. Surrounded by other magical faculty, a witch might well be able to stabilize Morcant and send him to hospital before he met his maker, at which point doctors might discover the true source of his heart attack.

In the guild, there would be witnesses, but none who'd have to hand both the tithes and capabilities necessary to rescue Morcant from his fate.

The next meeting took place in the same tomb they'd visited for the Transcendent Rite. Ambrose accompanied Emery invisibly, breathing shallowly in the dusty air of the crypt. He kept to the walls, to the sarcophagi set into alcoves.

He'd tucked the hexed cherry tomato safely in the pocket of his cloak. While on his person, clothes and objects were invisible, but there was a chance someone might see the fruit appear from thin air when he dropped it in the punnet. He would have to act while no one was watching.

Morcant took his place at the central sarcophagus to wax poetic about the final step in the initiates' transformation toward true necromancy. He praised the new initiates on their successful casting of the spell jar, spoke with pride of the powerful witches they were destined to become. "I want you all, during this last rite, to imagine yourselves as you've always dreamed you'd be. Do not focus on your flaws, your weaknesses. Embody the powerful person I know you each to be, and you shall succeed."

Emery, standing with his arms crossed against the wall nearest Ambrose, rolled his eyes.

Ambrose paid less attention to Morcant than to the array of items left out on the sarcophagus. There were three long-stemmed black roses, a flask, three potion bottles containing a clear, sparkling blue liquid, and Morcant's punnet of cherry tomatoes, still dewy from being washed. While Morcant stood behind the sarcophagus, and the initiates in front of it, there wasn't room to safely get close enough. Ambrose would have to bide his time for the perfect moment.

There was a stone door in the back of the crypt, runes carved around its perimeter.

Morcant touched the runes. "This is a corpse door, used to seal in a draugr or revenant. I've dispatched it, of course, so you have nothing to fear. Follow my instruction, and your transformation will be complete. Hellebore will accompany us to assist."

Before entering, he took up a piece of charcoal and asked each initiate to pull the neck of their robes down so he could ink a rune onto their skin, meant to help with their transformation into acolytes. It all struck Ambrose as rather melodramatic and unnecessary. His own transformation had not been given ceremony—it was agony to change and best gotten over with.

Saoirse stepped forward, wearing a dress patterned with pumpkins beneath her cloak. When she pulled the neck down for the rune, Ambrose overheard Morcant say, "Next time, be sure to dress more appropriately."

Saoirse's expression crumpled with brief confusion. She glanced down at her dress, as if to check it was the same one she'd donned that morning. Ambrose did, too, uncertain what was inappropriate about it.

It occurred to him slowly. She was quite a tall girl. Her voice had a resonant timbre, beautiful and unique.

He wondered if they were kin. Souls whose bodies weren't in complete alignment. He sensed, more from Morcant's comment than anything, that it was true, and that this was the true source of his criticism—not that her clothes were too revealing or unprofessional, but that they were feminine.

Ambrose hadn't felt one way or another about Morcant, but in that moment a fury as hot as the forge of his own unmaking burned through him.

No one else had heard. Saoirse swallowed her hurt and confusion, putting it out of her mind to focus on the ritual.

Morcant finished drawing the runes. Three snaking lines with an upside-down triangle drawn through the middle one. Reaching into his tithe belt, he crushed a fistful of briar berries and smeared them across the corpse door. It groaned and moved into a recess in the wall, scraping and making the ground quake, revealing a pitch-black room. Ambrose squinted but could make out nothing.

Morcant took one of the potion bottles and one of the black roses from the sarcophagus. He ignited a witch light in his palm, but the darkness seemed to swallow its glow, a dim aura surrounding him as he led Saoirse and Hellebore inside.

Curiosity piqued, Ambrose wondered if he should follow and observe the ritual, but he couldn't tell how large the tomb was. The risk of bumping into someone in the dark was too great, and that wasn't his purpose in coming here.

Before the door shut, Morcant added, "Hellebore, bring the tomatoes, would you? In case either of us get hungry."

Hellebore fetched the punnet. Ambrose couldn't edge out from his hiding spot to intercept her without squeezing through the crowd of initiates. He couldn't risk it.

The corpse door groaned shut, sealing Morcant, Hellebore, and Saoirse inside.

CHAPTER 11

Emery's lips firmed into a thin line of annoyance as he glanced subtly toward the spot where Ambrose hid. They couldn't do anything except wait for Morcant's return and hope he hadn't eaten the whole punnet in the meantime.

In the quiet that followed, tension coiled.

"How long does it take?" asked Windsor, one of the initiates.

The question was not directed at anyone in particular, but their attention seemed magnetized to Emery, who leaned indolently against the sarcophagus. Even the third years, who'd been through this before, looked to him rather than answer.

"Fifteen minutes, if it goes well. Twenty if not."

That only made Windsor more nervous. "How is it meant to go well? I don't understand what we're supposed to do."

"It's just a meditative exercise," Emery said. "Helps open you to the spirit world. Useful for communicating with ghosts. Witches are bridges between material and ethereal planes anyway. It's innate. Honestly, I fell asleep during mine and still passed."

Windsor didn't look comforted in the least, and the other initiates continued to eye Emery like he was a fox in a coop of chickens.

While they waited, Ambrose risked moving to the side of the sarcophagus Morcant usually gave his speeches from. Emery's enchantment made his passage silent. To avoid being bumped into, he scrunched up to sit on the edge of a sarcophagus set into the wall. It was not a perfect hiding spot. If Morcant strayed too close to the wall, he might bump Ambrose's knees, but with the corpse door just to his right, he was at greater advantage to drop the hexed fruit in with the rest.

The time passed slowly. Finally, the corpse door scraped open, making the other initiates jump. Saoirse emerged, looking clammy-skinned but well.

"Saoirse has passed," Morcant said. "With flying colors, might I add. I hope she'll wear the mark of her official initiation into our guild with pride. There are no more tests for her. All my knowledge, she can count as hers, too."

Saoirse glowed, or perhaps that was the sheen of sweat. Hellebore was nowhere to be seen.

Ambrose strained his neck to see if she hung back in the doorway but she wasn't there.

Perhaps she awaited the next initiate in the tomb. Either way, another chance to place the tomato—which Ambrose was beginning to think of as their murder weapon—had passed.

Frustrated, he squeezed back into the alcove while Morcant passed, picking up the spell objects and leading Windsor through the corpse door.

That only left Iris. Afterward, Ambrose had to hope for an opportunity before the rite finished entirely. He didn't relish discovering the limits of Emery's patience if he failed.

Windsor took the full twenty minutes. Morcant announced he had performed "admirably."

Ambrose had often known, upon entering a room, whether the witch king was calm or agitated based on the quality of the silence alone. The infinitesimal pause before Morcant said "admirable" implied it was anything but. It certainly paled in comparison to his effusive praise of Saoirse.

Windsor had looked relieved until the pronouncement. Now, he looked anxious.

Morcant left with Iris. Ambrose wished he could reconvene with Emery, ask what he should do if the opportunity did not present itself. Could they risk planting the hex near the end of the meeting, when Morcant would be leaving the isolation of the tomb and might find help in time? It was late at night, or early morning. The world would not be awake, but Ambrose didn't like to take the initiative without orders. He couldn't be punished for doing what he'd been told, but that never held true for improvisation.

The tomb wasn't as quiet, with Saoirse and Windsor discussing in low voices how their rite had gone. Ambrose risked emerging to edge around the room to the place Emery stood. He didn't want to startle Emery by touching him, but he also didn't want to risk speaking loudly enough that the cavernous room caught the sound. The charm muffled his footsteps, not his voice.

Emery leaned against the wall, one leg kicked back against it, arms crossed, a finger tapping restlessly against his elbow. Ambrose, hoping to trap the sound between the wall and his body, stood as close as he dared and whispered into Emery's ear.

"If a reliable opportunity does not arise, should I still go through with it?"

Emery didn't jump or shout, but he went rigid with alarm. Goose bumps rose on his neck where Ambrose's breath fell. He turned his head slightly, perhaps testing how close they were, and his nose nearly brushed Ambrose's cheek. He'd be able to tell from his hot breath condensing before him that Ambrose was very near, but he didn't speak. He gave a stiff, barely perceptible nod.

Ambrose shivered, though whether because he still had a job to do or because Emery's closeness was a pocket of heat in the cold tomb, he didn't know. He pushed off the wall, padding silently back to his hiding place.

The corpse door shuddered open again. Morcant declared Iris successful, his praise neither glowing nor underhanded, merely neutral. She looked peevishly at Saoirse, who smirked back. Then, finally, finally, Hellebore emerged.

The punnet of tomatoes was, mercifully, not empty. But it wasn't particularly *full* either.

The moment had come. Ambrose reached into the folds of his cloak and removed the tomato, which he buffed to remove any lint. Not as though Morcant had to worry about consuming dirt, given what would become of him in a moment's time, but it wouldn't do for the plot to fail all because a piece of fluff put him off eating it.

Hellebore walked past. Ambrose had to pull a leg up, now fully crouched like a monk in prayer within the alcove. As she passed his hiding spot, he dropped the hexed tomato in with the rest.

It bounced a little. Hellebore looked, but she didn't notice the extra. Emery had, though. His gaze sharpened, then flitted away.

Hellebore continued to the end of the sarcophagus and put everything down where it had been to begin with.

Morcant said, "It is late, and these rites can be quite tiring. I will not keep you any longer. However, I want to say one last congratulations to the new initiates." The current guild members clapped, except Emery. "I also want to thank our current esteemed guild members for attending." More clapping. "And one last thing before I bid you goodnight; as I said, the rite is tiring, so be sure to eat something and drink lots of water when you get to your dorms. In fact, if you're feeling peckish, feel free to help yourself." He gestured to the punnet of tomatoes.

Ambrose's heart, which had only resumed beating recently, stopped. He shot a glance toward Emery, who looked equally paralyzed.

Perhaps no one would take Morcant up on it. They weren't exactly a common snack.

Saoirse said, "Oh, go on, then."

Emery could give no indication what he wanted Ambrose to do without alerting the others. There was only a split second to react. The tomatoes had rolled around. Ambrose didn't know which was hexed. With perhaps seven tomatoes in there, the chances were low but not negligible. He could wait and hope by chance the girl didn't pick the wrong one, or he could intervene.

Ambrose set his jaw. He'd failed to be the hero he hoped in one era, but—accident or not—he would not play accomplice to the death of a young girl.

As she reached for the punnet, Ambrose lunged from his hiding spot. They were close enough he didn't need to reach far. He knocked the punnet away and sent the cherry tomatoes flying and rolling across the ground. Saoirse yelped. Morcant whipped around, as if expecting someone behind him who'd played a silly prank. Emery was all the way on the other side of the tomb, and Ambrose had recoiled back into the corner.

Shaking his head, Morcant said, "Perhaps your rite was so successful you called a spirit into the tomb. One which hates tomatoes, evidently."

Saoirse laughed nervously, as did the other initiates.

"No matter." Morcant leaned down, picking up one of the least bruised tomatoes. He opened a hip flask and whispered an incantation to clean it. A hygiene spell. "There, good as new," he said, holding it out to Saoirse.

It happened too quickly. There was nothing Ambrose could do.

Saoirse held up her hands. "Thank you. I'm all right."

Morcant shrugged. "Suit yourself."

Then he popped the tomato into his own mouth.

The sickening pop of it between his teeth evoked both nauseated disgust and anxiety as Ambrose prepared, not for the first time, to watch a man die. Provided that tomato had been the hexed one, Morcant's heart would stop.

Morcant swallowed. Everything appeared normal at first. Then he started to choke. He held his chest, coughing into his fist.

Hellebore said, "Dad?"

He coughed again, hoarser this time. Ambrose looked past him to the man responsible. Emery's expression betrayed nothing, watching as if from afar. While Hellebore slapped her father on the back, and the other initiates hovered like flies worrying a fresh carcass, Emery hung back.

Morcant gave one more throat-rending cough, as though trying to expel his very soul, then stopped. He swallowed. Wiped at his mouth. Straightening up, he gave his chest a couple thumps, but otherwise he appeared—to Ambrose's eyes—entirely hale and whole. Fully recovered.

Had it been the incorrect tomato? Had he nearly choked on an unhexed one?

Ambrose didn't know whether to appreciate the irony or suspect it.

"Are you all right?" Hellebore asked.

"I'm fine, I'm fine." Morcant waved her away. "But perhaps these tomatoes are best left to the grave. Go on, everyone, I'll be fine. Hellebore, would you help me clean up?"

The initiates gratefully dispersed. As they filed up the stairs, Ambrose started to pad in that direction as well, but as he did, he noticed Morcant pause while bending to pick up a tomato. He was staring at the sarcophagus Ambrose had been hiding on top of.

Ambrose saw what caught his attention. A dark red smear on the stone, directly on the spot where Ambrose had sat.

Blood.

It took a moment for the spinning gears of his mind to catch up. He was not injured. He hadn't sat in anything. His fears had just caught up to him.

The abilities bestowed upon him by the witch king, they were permanent, but the transformation of his body, apparently, was not.

CHAPTER 12

Logically, Ambrose knew fear of discovery should be his priority. Morcant might realize someone had invisibly observed his guild, and there was no telling what he'd do to an intruder.

Yet the notion of having to spend his second life looking, sounding, and bleeding like a woman felt infinitely worse. Worse than the cold water of the bog, worse than the strangling hold of the arcane collar, his body molting into one he did not recognize made him want to run.

He couldn't run, not far. His leash prevented it. He could go no farther from Emery than two furlongs before pain would wrench him back.

Morcant's voice arrested Emery's progress to the stairs. "What is this?"

Ambrose's fear and shame compounded. He felt like a naive youth, waking to find his bedroll wet with blood, stuffing his smallclothes with rags and trying to hide it from the castle's servants by burning his bedding. The witch king had been furious he'd hidden the truth of his sex from him. He'd punished him, not for being as he was, but for lying about it.

He'd also cast the spell which stopped the hideous effects of puberty from continuing to wreck him. He'd provided the magic which gave Ambrose's body its current shape.

Emery stared at the stain for a long moment, eyes squinting in confusion. "Looks like blood, sir."

"I know it's blood," said Morcant. "I'm asking how it got there."

"How should I know?"

"Because it wasn't there when Hellebore and I entered the tomb with the initiates," Morcant said in a tone of infantilizing condescension. "And it's there now."

"Maybe one of your tomatoes got squashed." In the forced nonchalance of Emery's voice, Ambrose thought he heard a tremor of something else entirely.

Candlelight rendered the gaunt lines of Morcant's face and deep-set eyes into a skull. For the first time, Ambrose glimpsed the version of him Emery loathed.

"Show me your arms," Morcant said.

Emery didn't move.

"Don't make me repeat myself."

"It's not mine."

"Then you won't mind proving it." From his tithe belt, Morcant produced two things: a cat's whisker and a switchblade. "Given the pranks you've pulled on Hellebore with blood tithes, it's fair of me to ask, little rat."

Emery's expression flared with undisguised fury. It was only brief, extinguished when Hellebore snapped, "Just get it over with."

It was more emotion than Ambrose had yet seen on him, and he wasn't sure which of the things Morcant had said specifically triggered that depth of response.

Movements stiff, Emery rolled up both sleeves. The skin beneath was an olive tan unspoiled by wounds or scars.

Morcant took Emery roughly by the arm and drew the blade across his wrist.

Ambrose nearly burst out from hiding. He narrowly suppressed the urge to smash Morcant's skull against the sarcophagus. It consumed him suddenly, without warning, and Ambrose struggled to justify it.

The cut was shallow, and Emery did no more than clench his jaw.

Ambrose stayed his hand, but his blood still pounded. He had to remind himself that *this* was not the master he'd made an oath to protect all those years ago. Clearly, his old habits had been resurrected with him.

Morcant took the cat's whisker and used it to wick the blood from the shallow wound. Holding this over the smear of Ambrose's blood on the sarcophagus, he dropped it, and when the two came together, blue flame engulfed the whisker until it turned to ash.

Morcant made a muttered noise of malcontent or disbelief. "Good of you to tell the truth, for once," he said. "You may go."

Emery turned his back. The instant he did, Morcant gave Hellebore a nod. She took something from her pocket—it looked like a bundle of hair coarsely tied into an odd shape—and pierced it with a needle.

Emery flinched, grasping his stomach, then continued toward the exit.

Though they left at Emery's usual laconic speed, it still felt like they were fleeing.

Transported back to Emery's home, Ambrose couldn't leave his apprehension behind. The danger of discovery had passed, so the fear of his own body took over.

It was a paralyzing fear. It pushed out all thought of the strange spell Hellebore cast as they left. He couldn't think of a plan. He couldn't contemplate going to the bathroom to change, to shower, to stuff his underclothes with rags or whatever magic implement modern people used during their monthly cycles.

These were distant abstracts. In the moment, he only wondered if it would be feasible to remain invisible forever.

Emery looked around for him. Evidently, he expected Ambrose to drop invisibility the moment they were safe from Morcant.

Ambrose felt anything but safe.

The sound of their entry hadn't gone unnoticed. Katzica bounded out of the open bedroom door, greeting Emery with play bows and a wagging tail. Her keen nose picked up on Ambrose, too. She greeted him in the same fashion, mortifying him with the intensity and direction of her sniffing.

"Katzica, come here," Emery called. Obediently, she came to heel. "That was close," he said to the otherwise empty room.

Ambrose remained silent, braced for retribution. The fault for their close call was his.

Emery said, "You can shower first. We'll discuss the botched murder attempt later."

He rummaged through a storage cupboard and took out a pile of towels, which he set on the back of the sofa, then went into the bathroom, where the sound of running water followed. He emerged, saying, "If the temperature's not to your liking, turn the nozzle toward the red for hot and blue for cold, all right? Call on me if you have trouble."

Before Ambrose could digest this act of decency, Emery disappeared into his bedroom, calling Katzica after him.

Ambrose couldn't hold off any longer. He took the towels with him into the wash room. He kept to the security of invisibility as he took his clothes off, but the evidence became visible the moment he shed his pants. He didn't know what to do with them. Stomach turning, he put them in the sink to deal with later.

The sight of blood didn't bother him. What it meant did. He was losing himself.

Drawing back the curtain around the bath, he tested the temperature of the water and jumped at the incandescent warmth of it. Steam billowed from within. He stepped gingerly over the edge of the basin and, after a moment's trepidation, under the stream.

The concept of a hot "shower" did not properly register until he felt the water soaking his hair, sluicing over his shoulders and down his chest, painting his invisible form in rivers and tributaries from the network of scars where the water caught.

The winch of his tight muscles unwound a fraction at a time. The steam opened his lungs to deeper breaths. He closed his eyes.

He hadn't realized until that moment how much he'd begun to enjoy this new world, with its delicious food and peculiar technology, but the water washed him in it anew.

He wanted the witch king to experience this. Sweet maple syrup and hot showers. A softer world. If theirs hadn't been so harsh, maybe things wouldn't have turned out so—

The thought made him suddenly aware of the acute silence in his mind. This would normally be the time for his words of wisdom and comfort, but as Ambrose waited, no voice came to reassure him that this was a minor obstacle on the path to their reunion.

Had something weakened their bond? If this harrowing moment had somehow separated them, he couldn't bear it.

He could only handle one problem at a time, and it seemed he had countless. Mortifying as it was, he would have to ask Emery for help.

He stayed in the shower a long while, until the steam fogged the room and clouded over the mirror. After ensuring he was clean as possible, he wrapped the towel around his waist, glad Emery's preference for black extended to his linens. Wiping away some condensation on the mirror, he took a deep breath and released his clenched hold on invisibility.

He looked the same. His face had not reverted to its softer shapes. His brows were still thick, his cheeks still rough with stubble.

He took a deep breath and opened the door.

At the same time, he heard the front door open and shut. Emery came into sight of the hall, carrying transparent sacks. He froze, looking at Ambrose. Ambrose was too tense and uncertain how to approach the impending conversation to interpret the way Emery's eyes stuck to him. The steam had followed him out of the bathroom, licking his ankles, and he wanted badly to disappear back inside and soak in the shower until the room became so humid he drowned in it.

Instead, he said, "I have a problem."

Emery gave his head a shake. "I noticed."

He plunked the sacks down on the coffee table and began pulling boxes from it. Little blue boxes, square crinkly packets, rattling bottles that looked medicinal, and a bar wrapped in gold leaf.

There were also a few vials of liquid, which Emery set to one side.

"I wasn't sure the delivery boy would find us out here, but he managed. Though I believe he might have thought it all very haunted, because he'd fled by the time I opened the door. Regardless, I wasn't sure of what you'd need, and then I wasn't sure *you'd* be sure of what you'd need, so I bought a bit of everything."

"What is all this?"

Emery let out a pained sigh. "I really should find someone better equipped to explain it, but it's not as though I have friends, and Hellebore—"

"No," Ambrose said with panicked certainty. "Just . . . tell me what you understand."

"I *understand*. I didn't flunk high school biology or anything, but I've not exactly had experience. Look, these—" He pulled open the crinkly packet, which held several padded square envelopes. "Sanitary towels. I believe you stick them in your underwear. These ones have wings, which are apparently superior. These ones are tampons. I'm sure if we put our heads together we can figure out the instructions for inserting one."

Ambrose nearly fainted as Emery ripped one open, turning the purple tube over in his hands like it was a puzzling ancient artifact, before depressing a plunger on one side and shooting a finger of cotton on a string across the coffee table.

"Ah," Emery said. "So you'd put it in first, then do that."

"It goes inside," Ambrose said numbly.

"I think you use the string to pull it out after."

Ambrose's face drained of blood.

"Too much? There were cups, too, but those looked beyond either of us, frankly. These here are just painkillers if you get cramps. Take two." Emery rattled the pill bottle. "And chocolate, because I've heard that helps."

Ambrose, rendered speechless, tried to absorb it all. Emery didn't seem fazed by his body's peculiarities. He was helping, which was a relief. More than a relief. The warming sensation of the hot shower spread through his chest. A balm of gratitude.

Emery didn't have to offer things like pain medication or chocolate, yet he had.

Still, this was not precisely the help Ambrose meant to ask for. He didn't want products to aid him through menstruation. He didn't want to menstruate. Period.

At least this would prevent him from spoiling all his clothes. He didn't really want to see Emery perform demonstrations with the "tampons," again, so Ambrose muttered an awkward thank-you, gathered up the things, and took them into the bathroom with something fresh to wear.

He couldn't contemplate using the tampon after seeing one ejected onto the coffee table, so he opted for the sanitary towel instead, which was at least self-explanatory, though it took him a while to realize he needed to peel the paper off the sticky underside. After taking an age to wash his hands and swallowing down the two pills dry, he sat on the closed lid of the privy and hid.

He didn't feel prepared to see Emery. Something about this act of kindness made him sore, like a bruise he'd acquired mysteriously without remembering the cause.

He also didn't want to find out the hard way he'd used the sanitary towels improperly.

So he lingered, feeling yellow-bellied and ridiculous, until he broke off a piece of chocolate and took a bite.

It broke between his teeth and immediately began to melt against his tongue in a beautiful orchestra of sweet and bitter flavor. It had a similar taste to the mocha he'd had earlier. He had to resist taking a second bite immediately.

He was so enraptured, he almost didn't notice the way his magic, normally a background growl of discontented hunger, was briefly, briefly quiet.

CHAPTER 13

In the morning, sounds from the kitchen implied a rodent had dislodged every metal pot and pan from its hook.

Ambrose went to investigate and found Emery wearing pajamas and a black apron covered in flour. It had writing underneath an embroidered picture of a cockerel. He was in the process of kneading dough by stretching it against the flour-covered counter and occasionally slamming it down with an impact like a tree being felled.

Ambrose got the impression he was taking out some of his rage from yesterday's failure on the yeast.

"What are you making?" Ambrose asked.

Emery leapt out of his skin. Katzica, begging at his heel, hadn't alerted him to Ambrose's presence. "Sweet hell, I need to put a damn bell on you."

Ambrose wasn't trying to be stealthy; he was naturally light-footed.

Emery turned around. "Cinnamon buns. I'm making cinnamon buns for Morcant's stupid charity fundraiser tomorrow, so he can make a stupidly good impression on all the stupid faculty who believe his benevolent saint schtick. All of us in the guild are required to participate. Whatever, ignore the buns." He grabbed a potion bottle of glimmering liquid off the windowsill and held it out to Ambrose. His fingers left dustings of flour on the surface, and an oily, navy-blue decoction sloshed within. A tag had been written and tied to the neck of the bottle, but Ambrose couldn't read it.

"What's this?" he asked, hoping Emery wouldn't point to the label.

"It will help with your hormones," Emery said.

"Whore . . . moans?" Ambrose repeated, trying not to appear as confused and insulted as he felt.

"Hormones. One word. Whatever magic the witch king used, it's no longer effective. Plenty of trans men use this now."

"Trans men."

"That's the word used nowadays. For men like you." Emery rambled, becoming more aggressive with the dough. "Although, there's other language and labels, and I won't decide yours for you. If you want a treatise on modern queer labels, we can check one out of the library. That just seemed the most apt given what little you've shared."

Ambrose didn't really catch the rest. He couldn't stop rolling the word around his mouth like a new flavor, tasting its bitter sweetness with the same reverence as the chocolate.

In his life, there had been whispers of sainted monks who'd been born women and turned into men as acts of God, but there'd never been a name for them. Not that he knew. Some people celebrated them, but most took a darker view of their existence, and it had been safer—given his position—to keep it secret.

To hear that there were entire books devoted to the subject left his heart torn between mourning and celebration.

"I had to brew it myself," Emery said, dusting flour from his hands. "Getting a prescription may be . . . tricky. Given you're, well, *you*. I'm quite adept with potions, though, and the formula is easy. I can't guarantee the taste, but, well—"

Ambrose looked at Emery. A smear of flour painted a white streak on his cheek. His hair was damp from a sweaty night's sleep, sleeves rolled above the elbows, fine-boned fingers flexing and stretching the dough, exertion making the veins stand out on his forearms.

He had a compelling physicality. Built like a fawn—tall and lanky—at once delicate and powerful. He often put forward an inhuman demeanor. Unfeeling.

Now, he looked messy. Real. He spoke idly, as if his generosity was inconsequential.

It was hard not to look a long time and see him anew.

"Thank you." Ambrose tried to sound as grateful as he felt.

Emery paused, looking uncertain. "It was nothing."

He busied himself kneading dough again.

Emery's sweeping penmanship on the potion's label mimicked the swoop of Ambrose's heartbeat as he uncorked the bottle. He wasn't afraid it was poison. Emery needed him. He wasn't afraid it would put him under some thrall. The collar already did that.

He was afraid these moments would make him like Emery.

It was a risk Ambrose deemed worthwhile to ensure his body didn't melt into one he didn't recognize.

He downed the potion. It tasted like bonfire smoke, neither delicious nor repulsive.

"You'll need them weekly." Emery had rolled up the dough and stuffed it in a bowl, covering it with a thin see-through material. He opened the refrigerator, absently searching for something to eat while he talked. "I'll batch-brew them later. For now, I wanted to discuss yesterday. The plan didn't work. The tomato Morcant ate, was it the hexed one?"

"I don't know," Ambrose said.

"Mm, hard to track them rolling across the floor, I suppose. When he choked, I thought maybe—Yet he's hideously alive and well." He pulled an apple from a drawer, rubbing it against his shirt. "I wonder if he has a ward or talisman protecting against hexes and poisons, but he could have just as easily eaten a clean one."

He bit into the apple, and abruptly his expression metamorphosed, the color draining from his face. He rushed to the sink and spat into it, dropping the apple in the process.

It rolled at Ambrose's feet. He picked it up, examining the bitten spot, but there wasn't any hole for a worm or sign of rot.

"What's wrong?"

Emery shuddered, stomach heaving. "I've been hexed."

Abruptly, Ambrose remembered the spell Hellebore cast as they'd left the catacombs last night. He'd been too distracted by the betrayals of his own body to recall, and felt a stab of guilt for not mentioning it sooner.

Rather than admit to it, he said, "Hexed how?"

"That tasted like . . . like—rotten would have been a mercy." He hacked, ran the water in the sink and went to take a drink, only to spit that out, too. "*Everything* tastes vile."

It was beyond vile. If Emery couldn't keep down food or water, the hex would kill him.

"Sod this," Emery said. "He dies tomorrow. We need a plan. Maybe we shouldn't rely too heavily on magic."

Ambrose agreed, but killing Morcant wouldn't remove this hex if the spell had been cast through a focus, like the one Hellebore used. "What do you propose?"

"Making it look like a heart attack didn't work, so let's try making it look like an accident."

Ambrose understood that meant violence, and the hunger, which had been mysteriously quiet since yesterday, roared in his ears like a dam unleashed.

Beneath that, Ambrose had a scheme of his own.

After today, he owed Emery a debt. He was going to find that hexed object Hellebore had and destroy it so Emery need not suffer any longer.

The weather threatened rain on the day Morcant held a charity fundraiser for children with learning disabilities. Tents and stands had been erected in the gardens of Bellgrave's castle grounds, selling crafts, jewelry, and baked goods.

Ambrose hung back invisibly beneath a tree in sight of Morcant, who stood beneath an enormous statue at the center of the garden. It depicted a woman on rearing horseback, her hands gracefully flexed to cast a spell. Ambrose could imagine the hand served as a torch, but for the moment it went unlit.

The sculptor had captured the majesty and regal nature of their subject well, but something about the face of the woman struck a familiar chord for him.

Emery stood next to Ambrose, leaning against a tree.

Over the past day, he'd eaten nothing and managed a few sips of water. He looked sallow and weary for it. Ambrose found it difficult to parse his need to return Emery's generosity with his instinct to protect the one who held his tether, but it unsettled him to see Emery so unwell. He needed to find Hellebore and hope she kept the hex focus on her person.

It was not his only purpose here today. Emery had gone over the plan with him in detail. He was to wait until Morcant gave a speech declaring how much money had been raised, and while he was standing beneath the statue, Ambrose would drop it on his head. He'd need to use his abilities to destabilize the structure and bring it down.

Emery said, "It was a statue of the witch king, once."

Ambrose shot him an incredulous look, then considered the statue again.

He saw the resemblance. The features had shinier areas where they'd been sheared down, and there were parts of the body where it appeared someone had smelted another material over the stone to form a bust. Some areas had been neglected, though, and Ambrose's heart keened at the familiarity of the hands.

"Morcant's always been obsessed with the witch king. I think he fancies himself a successor." Emery's mouth twisted. "Ironic that I found you first. He'd love to have you, instead."

"And who is it now?"

"Hm?"

"The statue."

"Ilonara Thorn. The witch king's killer."

It took monumental willpower not to grab Emery by the arm and demand more information, but Morcant's water deer had clipped around the statue, its doe-eyed stare fixed on Emery. Morcant's gaze soon followed.

"That's my cue," Emery muttered as he turned to go. For a moment, he paused, a hand in his pocket. Ambrose thought he could feel Emery's finger traipse the length of his leash.

Emery hadn't, so far, given him a compulsion order to kill Morcant. They'd discussed the plan, the methods. Was he debating whether to trust Ambrose or use the arcane collar?

Ambrose waited. Hunger rumbled like a distant storm in his gut. Emery pulled his hand out of his pocket and said, "Make sure you don't miss."

He stalked off. He didn't go far enough to strain the tether of magic connecting them, but Ambrose still felt the minor distance as a subtle pull.

A whisper in his ear said, *It doesn't matter whether he orders you or not. We need Morcant dead if we're to be reunited.*

A flood of relief brought Ambrose up short. The witch king had returned.

I never left. I merely did not wish to exacerbate your shame by bearing witness to it. I withdrew for a time, but I am here now.

Ambrose didn't know how to place the feelings that dredged up. The sentiment was not misplaced. Ambrose *hadn't* wanted anyone to see him like that. Or rather, most anyone. The witch king was not just anyone, though; he was the only one entrusted with the knowledge of who Ambrose really was, and so the only one from whom he'd accept comfort.

He was being too sensitive. There were better things to put his mind to.

His duty was to prepare the statue for its collision course with Morcant's skull, but first, he searched for Hellebore.

He found her at Saoirse's stand, where she'd put together handcrafted jewelry using a variety of boldly colored beads, some bearing the aura of magical enchantment.

Saoirse's aura wasn't nearly so bright. She was dressed in plain clothes today, speaking demurely to those who expressed interest in her wares.

Hellebore hip-checked her in greeting. "These look great. Overachiever."

"Thanks, my grandma taught me how to make these." Saoirse's smile flickered brighter, but it was still a pale imitation of her usual.

When the woman making a purchase moved on, Hellebore said, "What's up?"

"What do you mean?"

Ambrose crept closer. Hellebore wore a dress instead of robes today, which might have foiled his hopes of finding the hex focus, but she had a leather satchel over one shoulder.

He'd need the perfect opportunity to search it without her notice. He could phase through it, but if she moved too much, it would be difficult to maintain the magic without giving her *some* sense of his presence.

"I mean that you're quiet lately and dressing like you're going to a funeral, which is *my* thing," Hellebore said.

Ambrose didn't know her well, but he could have sworn the jibe was playful. Friendly rather than cutting.

Saoirse worried her bottom lip between her teeth. "Sorry."

"Don't *sorry* me. What happened?"

"I shouldn't tell you."

"I won't leave you alone until you do. Give me the gossip."

Definitely friendly.

"I don't want to talk shite about your *da*," Saoirse finally admitted.

"Oh, but he's my favorite person to talk shit about." Hellebore's tone sobered, though. "What did he do?"

"Told me my makeup made me look like a whore." She shrugged, as though it didn't bother her, though it clearly did. "Not in so many words, and he was right."

"He damn well was not. He's an arsehole," Hellebore said.

"You're allowed to think so. You're his daughter."

Hellebore frowned. A look of genuine distress fought the usual sardonic smirk she wore. "Here."

She opened the flap of her handbag, and Ambrose saw it. The hex object—a grubby bundle of hair—vibrated with malevolent magic. It was tucked within an inside pocket.

Hellebore rooted through her bag for something else. Ambrose waited until she'd retrieved what she wanted, then darted his hand in after hers. It phased through the material, magic coursing through his body. He thought Hellebore sensed it, as she shivered like someone had walked over her grave.

He focused, grasping the hex object, its aura—wiry and repulsive in texture—clashing with the signature of the witch king. Methodically, he prized it from her bag the way he'd taken the book from Emery's chest.

It came free and vanished into his hand.

Hellebore was handing a slim black tube to Saoirse, saying, "This color will look better on you than me," but Ambrose had already skulked away from their stand, keen to be far from it when Hellebore discovered the stolen hex object.

He aimed to take it straight to Emery. It was easy to find him. He could follow the smell of cinnamon buns, but aside from that, the tether made his proximity feel tangible, like he was the tide drawn toward the pull of the moon.

It unsettled him. This was a sensation he'd only associated with the witch king, feelings reserved for one man. It grated against his sense of loyalty to feel them for another.

Emery was boxing a bun for a patron, smiling as he handed it over. Ambrose had never seen him smile, not with teeth. Though it was a showman's smile, a polite smile, it transformed his demeanor from cantankerous to charming, and almost made it possible to ignore the extra leanness to his face and figure after a day of dehydration.

Ambrose waited until the patron had gone before speaking under his breath. "I'm here."

Emery stiffened. "Shouldn't you be working on the statue?"

"I found the means to remove the hex placed on you."

Emery's expression shifted, then quickly shuttered at the sound of a familiar voice approaching.

Morcant walked with two people, a man and a woman who appeared to be a couple. Modernity had stripped Ambrose of any knowledge of what fashions were reserved for the rich and powerful, but their attitude and body language conveyed well enough that they were influential.

"Georgia makes the most beautiful croissants, Philomena. You must try one," Morcant was saying at a stand two down from Emery's.

"They do look lovely, but my nose is leading me this way," Philomena said. "Something smells like cinnamon."

She drifted toward the scent which had tormented Ambrose all morning. Emery had said they could eat what was left, but the trays were half empty already. Each bun had a beautiful swirl, glazed with icing sugar, charmed to stay warm and glistening.

Morcant's and Emery's eyes met. They looked like feral cats sizing one another up.

Philomena, oblivious to it, said, "These smell incredible."

"They're kept warm by an enchantment. Unfortunately necessary, given the weather we're having." Emery put on the showman's smile from earlier, but a twitching muscle in his jaw betrayed his nerves.

"Very rude of it to rain," Philomena agreed. "And on a day of charity! I tell you, I was going to make a full round of the market before making any decisions, but if I come back and these have run out, I'll have to wear all black in mourning. We'll take two, won't we, dear?"

"As you like, love," said her husband.

"An excellent choice," Morcant said. "Emery was one of my top students. He has an excellent memory for recipes. Never gets them wrong."

Morcant sounded complimentary, but something, perhaps the use of past tense—*Emery* was *one of my top students*—made Emery's smile falter. The tongs shook as he placed each cinnamon bun in a paper box.

"I could hold them here for you, if you wanted to finish your rounds and eat them later? They'll stay fresh and warm, so there's no rush."

"You're a sweetheart," Philomena said. "But it's unbecoming for a woman to walk around a market drooling."

Emery's eyes darted once to Morcant, then he handed over the box.

Before he could accept Philomena's money, Morcant said, "Oh, allow me," and pressed the coins into Emery's hands.

Emery's knuckle bones strained against his skin, his revulsion at the touch tangible.

An invisible battle waged, a deep-sea struggle where only vague ripples on the surface belied the fury of the combatants. Ambrose only understood it vaguely. Morcant had brought these people here to spoil them, to ingratiate himself to them, but he didn't want Emery to earn similar goodwill.

"Oh, you're too kind, you didn't have to do that!" Philomena said.

Her husband said, "We'll get the drinks, then."

Morcant said, "Nonsense, I'm your host today."

Philomena took her first bite of the cinnamon bun.

An expectant pause followed. In theory, it was the silence of those awaiting a verdict on the taste of the bun. In practice, it felt as though Morcant awaited the announcement of his firstborn son while Emery braced for news of a loved one sent to war.

Philomena chewed once, then froze, cheek stuffed. Her complexion went gray. Then she abruptly turned, coughing and spitting onto the grass.

Her husband sputtered, "My dear, what's wrong?" Then he gave a yell of alarm.

The masticated piece of bun Philomena had spat on the ground wriggled unpleasantly. It was writhing with maggots.

CHAPTER 14

Morcant played his part in the pantomime as if critics and accolades awaited him in the wings. Deep concern, genuine shock at the sight of the worms, fighting back nausea, profuse apologies.

All the while, Emery stood stock-still. Only Ambrose, close enough to touch, could see him shaking.

He expected Emery to defend himself, to apologize, to say anything at all, but as Morcant began to rattle off a thousand apologies of his own— "I'm *so* sorry. I'm sure it was some mistake. He's deeply troubled and acts out at times. Please don't blame him, I should have known."—Ambrose could see the futility.

Morcant's theater played out exactly as he'd intended.

It still galled him that Emery didn't fight back. In that moment, he couldn't tell if it was the ravenous enchantment on his soul that yearned to carve Morcant's heart out, or if that anger was all his own. He'd never had a stomach for unfairness.

Such protective instincts. It's why I chose you. But be wary of extending your kindness to those who'd take advantage.

Emery turned to flee, and Ambrose quit the stage to follow.

He'd retreated to a secluded spot, crouched over and heaving into a hedge. Ambrose, who'd seen maggots feasting on far worse things, might have considered it an overreaction, but the hex was probably exacerbating Emery's disgust.

Ambrose looked around. They were alone in a gated portion of the gardens. No one was around to see or overhear them. He dropped invisibility.

"Are you all right?"

Emery let out a wheezing, humorless laugh. "Ah, yes, projectile vomit. The obvious symptom of someone who is truly well."

"Maybe this will help."

He held out the hex object. It was the first time he could properly examine it. Formed from locks of hair tied and knotted together, it made the shape of a man. The hair had been frayed together densely, but the color was quite distinct.

Emery looked up from the hedge. "Is that *my* hair?"

"Hellebore used it to place the hex on you," Ambrose said. "I assumed you might know how to destroy it."

Emery's eyes narrowed. "I didn't ask you to do that."

"No."

"Then why did you?"

"You've been . . . accommodating with me." Ambrose shrugged. "Is it so hard to believe I don't enjoy watching you suffer?"

"Yes. Making people suffer was your whole thing." Emery hawked and spat, wiping his mouth with the back of his wrist. "I don't buy your sweetly acquiescent guard-dog routine for a second."

Ambrose tried not to look hurt, and apparently failed.

"See? That!" Emery said. "Your sad puppy eyes aren't fooling anyone who knows the first thing about your history, so just drop it."

"It's not a mask. I truly—I only did what I had to, back then. I didn't enjoy it."

Emery stared at him as if the force of his gaze could serve as truth serum.

Ambrose squeezed the hex object in his fist. "Would you truly prefer to starve than believe me?"

Emery didn't answer at first, but when Ambrose took a step back, he held a hand out. "Let me see it."

Ambrose handed it over, glad to be rid of its sticky magic.

"I don't even want to know how she got hold of so much of my hair," Emery muttered. Using a match, he burnt a dried petal from his tithe belt until the flame turned blue. Then he set the hex focus alight.

It caught easily. Emery dropped it, the flame devouring it in seconds before winking out, leaving a black stain in the grass.

Immediately, color returned to Emery's cheeks. "I'm starving."

"I wouldn't recommend eating one of your cinnamon buns."

Emery laughed dryly. "I'll have to make more."

"Why didn't you tell someone Morcant hexed the food?"

"Do you honestly think they'd believe me?"

"No, but it makes you look more suspect to stand by and say nothing."

"I look suspect regardless. Protest too much, you're guilty. Not at all, you're guilty. A moderate amount? Too calm, you're guilty." Emery sounded angrier with Ambrose than his situation. "You lived during an era of monarchs and dynasties. Tell me. How often did someone wronged by the witch king ever see justice?"

"The witch king was a just and noble—"

Emery had the audacity to snort. "You believe that?"

"Everything he did, he did for good cause. He was a good king."

"He was a *tyrant*," Emery spat. "He accrued wealth, power, and magic to secure his position against his rivals and hunted anyone who might threaten his reign. He didn't care who he exploited in the process because if any of them became a problem, he had a universal solution: you. He could throw you at anyone who stood against him."

The voice in Ambrose's head hissed, *This liar seeks to turn you against me.*

"They were traitors, criminals, agitators—"

"Fancy words for people who got in his way. You're just proving my point. If it's a peasant's word against your king's, who did you and his councilmen believe, and what happened to you if you disagreed with him?"

"You were not there. I was. I *knew* him. He was my—" Ambrose tasted copper. "—friend."

Emery huffed in disbelief. Shaking his head, he got to his feet. "People that powerful don't have friends. They have victims and sycophants. You were just lucky enough to be the latter."

"I served him willingly, gave my life for him willingly."

"So willing, you bear the brand of his compulsion around your neck and the scars of his spells on your skin?" He snorted derisively. "I suppose it's easier to pretend to love your chains than break them."

Ambrose recoiled. His first instinct was to refute the argument. He'd sworn obedience to the witch king. It had been his gift because he loved the man, believed in his cause and the world he sought to build.

But it was difficult to form the words when the collar felt like an incriminating counterargument choking his conviction.

He knew how it looked. If he'd been such a willing servant, why had the witch king needed the compulsion charm in the first place?

The answer shamed Ambrose too much to speak of it.

Footsteps approached. Ambrose returned to the safety of invisibility just as Hellebore came through the ivy-covered gate. At the sight of Emery's wan complexion and the wet bushes, she said, "Really? They're only maggots. Not like *you* ate any."

"If you're not offering anti-sick elixirs, off you fuck, Hellebore."

"They want you to clear out your stand."

"I'm sure the maggots will sort that out for me."

"He'd go easier on you if you stopped acting like a maggot yourself, you know."

Emery snorted. "Thanks for that sage bit of advice. I see it's worked wonders for you."

Hellebore made a throaty noise of disgust. "Just sort your stand out and get out of here, all right? I don't want to be a crossfire casualty when you piss him off again."

Emery watched her stalk away, his hands clenching and flexing. After a beat, he stuck his hand in his pocket, and a corresponding shiver ran down Ambrose's spine.

A moment of prickling anticipation followed, then Emery said to the vacant space, "**Follow the plan. Kill Morcant Van Moor.**"

Ambrose felt the burn of each rune etched in his neck scald him with the compulsion to do just as he said.

By midafternoon, most of the stands were cleared of goods. Emery disposed of the remaining cinnamon buns.

The compulsion order had effectively diminished the burden of sympathy Ambrose had felt for Emery, but he resented the fact he'd never gotten to try one. He'd lived only a few days of this era, during which he'd partaken of the food, and it was tragic to see the buns at the bottom of a garbage bin. It was almost a relief to wish death on Morcant for petty reasons like wasted food, rather than because he was cruel to Emery, who could be generous but also intolerably mistrustful. Reactive. Haughty. Ambrose didn't understand him, and understood less why he felt foolishly protective of him.

His kindnesses are all conditional. He would do you none if you were not useful to him. Do not let the goodness in your heart blind you to the darkness in his.

Ambrose knew he should accept the truth of the witch king's words. Emery had killed his familiar and plotted to murder his professor after a few punishments and petty humiliations.

A HEX FOR HUNGER

Yet Ambrose sensed there was more to his story.

Morcant ascended the steps leading to the statue with a lit torch in one hand. The heat from the flame cast him and the others in a melting mirage. He spoke to a small group of men and women, all over the age of sixty with similar demeanor and dress to Philomena and her husband, who had, understandably, left. Flanking Morcant was a boy Ambrose recognized from the guild. The third year with numerous facial piercings and a burn scar. Ambrose thought he was called Dalton.

Ambrose had a good view of the proceedings from behind the statue. He stood at the same height as the horse's hocks and could use its leg as a barrier between himself and Morcant's retinue.

The cold stone under his hands grounded him. When the time came, all he had to do was phase through the material and destabilize it. If the whole thing came down, nothing but a miracle could save Morcant.

He would have to ensure no one else was nearby, but he doubted Morcant would share the limelight of his speech.

"We should let you get on with it," an elderly man with a moustache was saying.

"Yes, it is that time, isn't it?" Morcant agreed.

The crowd dispersed, except Dalton, who glanced nervously between Morcant and the torch he held.

Once the faculty members descended the steps, Morcant turned to hand it to him. "Now's the time."

In the torch's light, Dalton looked waxy. He wiped sweaty hands on his pants. "I don't know if I can."

"It's perfectly safe," Morcant said.

Ambrose's arms burned with remembrance. When confronted with fire, he felt the same fear now shining on Dalton's scarred face. The boy reached for the torch once more, but Morcant thrust it toward him, and he startled back like a spooked horse.

While Dalton looked ready to bolt, Ambrose prepared for his moment— he might only get seconds. He sank his hands through the stone leg of the horse. Magic turned his veins to ley lines and poured like acid into the statue, finding the weak points.

He had minimal experience using it this way. Under most circumstances, the matter his magic cleaved apart was more . . . human. The marble took longer to shatter as his magic searched for something meatier to sink its teeth into.

"Don't make a scene," Morcant said. "You want to face your fears, don't you?"

"I do! I just—" The boy's eyes reflected a recollection of pain so searing that the past seemed present. People were beginning to whisper. They could hear the exchange.

Ambrose had to focus hard to push his magic into the weak points of the statue, to eat away through dense marble.

Dalton's open hand made a fist and dropped to his side. Shame made his voice creak. "I can't."

Morcant withdrew the torch. He said, just loud enough that the audience could hear, "Of course. I wouldn't want you to feel uncomfortable." But with his back to the crowd, they couldn't see the sneer painting deep shadows across his face.

Ambrose could. Morcant looked like a revenant in firelight.

The hunger within turned ravenous. Raging. It surged through the marble, destabilizing its weakest attachments.

Dalton fled down the steps to Morcant's parting shot:

"Should have known you didn't have the balls."

Just as the horse's stone testicles broke free, fell, and clipped Morcant's skull with an audible crunch.

CHAPTER 15

Morcant's dropped torch rolled, extinguishing in a puddle with a hiss. Ambrose yanked his hands free of the statue, too stunned to make sense of it. He hadn't managed to topple the whole statue, but had the plan really gone wrong if it still worked?

You must make certain. Reach into his heart and ensure it's not beating.

The collar squeezed so tight, Ambrose nearly let out a gasping cry that could give him away. That was not part of the plan. Murdering Morcant that way would *not* look like an accident. The hunger within still railed against its bonds, slavering to be used exactly as the witch king asked.

But Emery had compelled him to follow the plan, so the collar held him steadfast in place. He couldn't check Morcant for a pulse if he tried.

There'd been cries of alarm, a high shriek. People from the front of the crowd surged forward to check Morcant's body, sprawled like an ink spatter on the steps. Someone knelt next to him and put their fingers to his neck.

Impossibly, he stirred.

How? Ambrose had watched the stone come down on Morcant's head. He'd heard the crunch. Or had it been the sound of the statue coming apart?

No, the sound of bone cracking left an impression.

Yet, Morcant sat up, rubbing his skull. His unbroken skull. Someone helped him to his feet, asking if he was all right.

"Fine, fine. A narrow miss," he said.

"I thought for sure it hit you," someone said.

"A glancing blow." Morcant touched his head again. His fingers came back a little bloody. "Nothing serious."

"Thank heavens."

"I'm parked nearby. I can take you to hospital."

In the commotion, Ambrose searched the crowd for Emery.

He stood back from the crowd, eyes wide. After a searching, horror-stricken moment, he seemed to confirm for himself that, yes, Morcant was indeed still breathing. Then he broke away from the crowd, heading for the park gates.

Ambrose followed. He had to, or the collar would start exacting punishment with a vengeance. Navigating the crowds of people took him on a circuitous route to catch up, and as Emery got farther from him, the distance tore at him like a man on the rack.

He caught up a ways outside the park, far from the fundraiser's attendees. He grasped Emery's wrist and dropped invisibility.

Emery jumped, ripping his hand free. "Stop doing that!"

"Doing what?"

"Sneaking up on me!" Emery shook his hands, as if Ambrose's touch were something disgusting stuck to his skin. "What happened?"

"It hit him. Well—" Ambrose reconsidered his wording. "*They* hit him."

"That wasn't the plan," Emery said. "The plan was the whole statue."

"It didn't work. My abilities have never been put to such use before. But he *was* struck."

"Not hard enough."

"I heard it," Ambrose insisted. "Fifteen, perhaps twenty pounds of pure marble impacted his skull. It cracked."

"You must have imagined it. He's barely bleeding."

"Something more is at work," Ambrose said. "Some magic."

He could see Emery resist believing it. He didn't want to, but before Ambrose could press the subject, Emery shoved him into a bush.

Normally, he'd have been able to avoid losing his balance, but it shocked him so badly he went top over tail into the shrub, landing on the other side of it. He recovered just in time to hear Hellebore's voice.

"Running away from the scene of the crime?"

"What are you talking about?" Emery said.

"You don't expect us to believe you weren't involved in that charade."

From Ambrose's place in the shrubs, he caught glimpses of Hellebore. He'd never seen someone saunter with purpose before. He slipped into invisibility, avoiding any movement that could disturb the hedges and give his hiding place away.

"That," Emery said, "was karma. I'm only sorry it has such poor aim."

"You'll have to convince my father. He's ordered you to come with me."

"Like hell—" Emery's voice cut off as Hellebore grabbed his wrist. He wrenched free, but the burnt-hair smell of a spell lingered on the air. Ambrose couldn't tell what kind, but there was a rune mark on Emery's wrist.

"What's this?" Emery demanded.

"Follow me and you won't have to find out."

She marched in the other direction. Emery hesitated a moment too long and cried out in pain, grasping his chest. Hellebore kept moving, and he jerked along after her.

Ambrose knew that spell. He'd lived most of his life under it, albeit his own leash was a whole lot longer.

His heart hammered. If Hellebore used a portal to drag Emery somewhere Ambrose couldn't follow, his own tether would choke the life out of him.

He rushed to pursue them. Sure enough, Hellebore dragged Emery through a gate into a secluded garden where no one would see her open a portal to the necropolis. Emery dragged his heels, grunting in pain, aware this would spell disaster for them. The moment he stepped through, the tether would register Ambrose as miles away from him and exact its punishment.

Ambrose had the hair of a second. He broke into a run. Hellebore stepped through the portal. Emery let out a yell, nearly doubling over from the tearing pain of that temporary separation, and Ambrose, knowing he would feel the same in but a second, crowded against Emery's back, wrapped an arm around his waist, and carried them both over the threshold.

During a fraction of a moment, Emery was on one side of the portal, and Ambrose the other. The way the tether tore at him—he imagined many of his victims had felt the same as he rent them apart. A wave of nausea hit him, sickly hot and shivering with cold at the same time.

Then they were through, and the feeling evaporated. The portal shut behind them. Ambrose released Emery. Too soon, apparently, because he collapsed to his knees in the grass.

They'd emerged next to the tomb leading into the guild's headquarters. Ambrose had never seen it in daylight hours. With the sun in golden descent, it looked too peaceful for what haunted the earth's bowels.

Gasping for air and heaving himself up by a tombstone, Emery said, "Are you being paid? Because you're a professional bitch, Hellebore."

"Oh, buck up. I've had period cramps more painful than what you just went through."

Ambrose would rate the pain on a similar level, personally, but watching the interaction from the safety of invisibility, he couldn't comment. He found it strange that Hellebore knew how to use magic so similar to the charm placed on himself. It wasn't commonplace magic, or hadn't been in his time.

Emery said, "I thought Morcant would be on his way to hospital."

"He is. But he thinks you're a flight risk, so he wants you locked up until he's cleared to leave."

"He wasn't even knocked unconscious. Why bother with hospitals? Why bother with me? He's fine."

"Miracles aside, he knows you're behind that little accident."

"He's paranoid."

Emery sounded flippant, but Ambrose sensed his unease. Neither of their murder attempts had gone well. The first hadn't even looked like a murder attempt, while the second hadn't looked enough like an accident to dissuade Morcant from suspecting Emery.

Hellebore opened the mausoleum door and headed down the steps into the crypt. The wards must have prevented her from opening a portal directly inside.

Emery kept to her heels with a glance over his shoulder to check Ambrose still followed. The tiny glimmer of fear in his dark eyes triggered an instinctive response. Ambrose reached out and touched Emery's elbow to reassure him he was still there.

Remember. He is still your enemy, not your charge.

Ambrose retracted his hand, feeling foolish. It was true. Emery had stolen him from the witch king, did not care for him, was only using him, and hadn't even trusted him to carry out their plan without a compulsion order. He'd killed his familiar and now wished to kill his mentor.

How had this foolish impulse to protect him arisen in the first place? It had to be nothing but deeply ingrained habit or the by-product of Emery holding his leash—

His leash.

If Hellebore searched Emery before locking him up, she would find it.

A HEX FOR HUNGER 99

The thought of her holding it was intolerable. The thought of her or—worse—Morcant seizing the power to command him . . .

Dread chilled him more than the cool air of the crypt.

Hellebore led them through labyrinthine catacombs the guild meetings never ventured into, stopping in a dank chamber where several metal cells waited, unoccupied.

"Here we are," Hellebore said, bored. "Want me to bring you water? A snack? A smutty novel? You'll be here a while."

"I'll entertain myself with the magic of my imagination, something you'd benefit from rather than mindlessly following Morcant's orders."

"Have it your way. Give me your tithe belt and turn out your pockets."

Emery stiffened.

"Don't dawdle," Hellebore said.

As Emery removed the tithe belt beneath his cloak and handed it over, Ambrose racked his brain for some way he could intervene without revealing his presence—a risk they couldn't take. It would ruin their plot if Morcant knew Emery had found a way to secret an accomplice into the depths of their guild.

The only solution he scrounged up could go wrong a thousand different ways, but he had little alternative. Heart in his throat, he moved silently behind Emery and, at the same time that Emery put his hands in his pockets, Ambrose shoved his own in alongside.

There was an awkward moment's pause, the second in which something about the brush of skin and Emery's caught breath turned the anxiety in Ambrose's stomach into a nervous flutter.

He couldn't seize the leash from Emery—it went against the pact he was sworn to—but Emery could *give* it to him.

Too late, he recognized the futility. Emery hadn't trusted him to kill Morcant uncompelled. He wouldn't trust Ambrose to hold the leash on the good faith he'd return it.

But he had to trust Ambrose more than he trusted *Hellebore*.

Ambrose waited, so close a wave of Emery's hair fluttered with his breath. So close he could smell the woodsy spice of a scented oil Emery used on his skin.

He thought, *Please, trust me.*

At the same time, he didn't know if Emery *should*. The hunger—that insatiable appetite Ambrose could never quite slake—purred at the thought of taking the leash and holding it in confidence. Not for Emery, but for the witch king.

Emery's fingers closed around the bone, palming it in his fist. He slowly withdrew his hands, the pockets pinched to turn inside out. Ambrose withdrew his hands, too, his thumb against the sprinting pulse in Emery's wrist, but Emery didn't relinquish the leash, and Ambrose's hands left empty.

CHAPTER 16

Hellebore regarded the turned-out pockets with a roll of her eyes. "What's in your hand?"

Ambrose thought, *You'd better have a plan for this.* Emery couldn't cast a spell. Hellebore had all his tithes in that belt.

Emery raised his hands in surrender and opened them, palms facing her.

They were empty. Even Ambrose, close as he was, hadn't seen its vanishing. If there was magic for concealing an object that could be cast using the ephemeral dust on the air, he'd never heard of it.

"Good boy," Hellebore said. "Now get in your cage."

A bolt of anger brought Ambrose a step closer to her. He couldn't count the number of guardsmen and pretentious associates of the witch king who'd used those words against him in cold disparagement. As if he was a domesticated animal, just the witch king's mad dog and not his—

Ambrose swallowed his pride and stayed stock-still. He stood between the two now. If Hellebore came closer to Emery, she'd encounter the barrier of his body.

A foolish move, after they'd taken such pains to maintain his secret.

She tilted her head, still wearing the impudent smirk on her darkly painted lips, but her arms raised with goose flesh. She couldn't see Ambrose, but she could sense a threat.

He quietly backed away. It wasn't worth it.

Emery got in the cage. "Don't lose the key."

"It'd be a mercy if I did." A flash of regret passed over Hellebore's face, too fleeting to be sure it had been there at all. "He's really angry with you. You're safer in here, I think."

She left with a passing promise to return with water. Ambrose waited until even the echoes of her footsteps faded into silence.

Emery stood against the back wall of the cage, arms crossed. He affected an air of nonchalance, but Ambrose had been pressed close enough to feel a pulse fast as hummingbird wings in the delicate skin of Emery's wrist. He was rattled.

"Where did you hide it?" Ambrose asked.

Emery gave his hand a flick, and the finger bone slipped from his open sleeve into the palm of his hand. If Ambrose hadn't watched closely, he'd have missed it.

"Sleight of hand. The sort of magic they can't stop me from performing with hexes, counterspells, and talismans."

Ambrose should have known. He'd watched Emery perform the same trick with a coin while drinking a whole bottle of wine. "You could have trusted me to protect you."

"Can I?" He sang it like a sardonic melody. "If that's so, I suppose I can trust you to break me out of here?"

Ambrose looked at the iron lock to Emery's cell. If he could break a statue, he could break that.

The question, now, was whether he wanted to.

A conflict had been playing out in his mind for the past few days. A tug-of-war between his instincts to protect Emery and the wiser goal to get free of him. He would play along with the murder plot. It was the witch king's wish, and he didn't feel too guilty over Morcant.

But a second voice had joined the first in his head, its whispers so distant they seemed imaginary. They asked a far more frightening question.

What if the voice he heard, the one he thought belonged to the witch king, the one guiding him to murder Morcant, was an illusion? A simple disease of a mind addled by centuries of death and the pains of resurrection? It could be real, or it could be a habitual echo from a man who left an indelible imprint on Ambrose's life. He didn't have answers, and didn't know which prospect he found most distressing: that he felt compelled to protect a man he couldn't trust or that his king was never coming back.

I'm as real as you are. We are two sides of the same coin. I could no more be parted from you than the sun from the sky.

He had to hope that was true. For now, he had a choice between voluntarily freeing Emery, or refusing, at which point Emery would compel him to do so anyway.

To most it was not a choice at all, but to Ambrose, who'd been given so few choices in life, this one was weighty. Significant. Emery's raven eyes watched intensely. He held too still, the knot in his throat bobbing on a swallow, betraying his false calm. His fingers tightened around the leash.

Ambrose couldn't fight his nature. He wrapped a hand around the cage's lock, iron turning to bruised fruit flesh, pulped in his fist. His magic couldn't slake its thirst on metal like it could meat. Ambrose had to ignore the way it made his stomach roil as the tumblers of the lock, succumbing to his power, disintegrated into ash and shrapnel.

The door opened.

Emery didn't move. The effect of his dark eyes, now wide in quizzical uncertainty, made Ambrose's heart skip, youthful hope peering through the cracks in Emery's scavenger facade.

It died in a flash. "Trying to get on my good side?"

He pushed off the wall to brush past, but Ambrose put out an arm to block the door. Emery stopped short. His chest rose in a held breath against the barrier of Ambrose's forearm.

"I don't like being compelled," Ambrose said. "I'd rather choose to help you."

"And why would you want to help me?"

Ambrose didn't know. Each guess felt like grasping a heart in his hands, hoping each beat would bring answers, only to squeeze too hard and watch as it all leaked out between his fingers.

The only thing, the truest thing, felt too personal to tell. *I didn't like watching them starve you.*

Ambrose knew what it was like to be hungry. He didn't like to think about the source of his hunger. He didn't want to think about what Emery had said to him in the park, either, but it echoed in his ears.

I suppose it's easier to pretend to love your chains than break them.

"I don't trust you. Whether I use the collar or not, what difference does it make?" Emery said.

"I can't break my chains, but I can hope you won't use them to yoke me to your will."

Emery's gaze searched his expression until Ambrose began to feel undressed by it.

Finally, he said, "Have it your way."

It felt a bit like blinding sunlight off snow in winter. Not warm nor comfortable, but tentatively hopeful of summers to come.

Back at the chapel ruin, Emery buzzed around the walls of the building to check and double-check his wards. Ambrose shadowed him, watching the dense woods for signs of Morcant or Hellebore.

"Do they know where you live?"

"Of course not." Emery spat to dispel a waning ward and redraw its rune. He roughly rolled the leg of his trousers to the knee and drew corresponding runes on his skin. "I converted the ruin and portal to and from school to protect myself from their surveillance." He cast the spell, wincing as it took a tithe of flesh.

"Blood is stronger," Ambrose said.

"Yes, well, I don't fancy carving myself up today."

Ambrose shrugged, rolling up his sleeves. Emery regarded him like a mutated carp he'd fished from the bog.

"It's just blood. My body will make more," Ambrose said.

He thought it was sensible, but Emery pointed at the ladder of scars on Ambrose's arm and said, "The witch king harvested from you whenever he required, like some kind of vampire?"

"I offered."

Emery's dark stare held a sudden comprehension that made Ambrose feel more naked than the night of his resurrection. "Like you offered to let me out of that cage."

Rattled and trying not to show it, Ambrose lowered his sleeve, deeply offended enough to take the offer off the table.

It didn't faze Emery. He finished repairing the wards and paced into the chapel, putting a new log on the waning embers of the last fire and speaking as he worked.

"He's likely aware I'm trying to kill him in earnest now. He probably believed all my threats were just hot air before."

Ambrose hovered over Emery as he stoked the fire. "What do you think he'll do?"

"Up his defenses. Protect himself more thoroughly." He paused a moment, then gave the embers an aggressive stab with the poker. "Punish me."

"How?"

Emery's gaze flickered to Ambrose's arms, now covered. "His

punishments may seem nothing compared to yours. They're creative. Meant to inflict suffering without leaving scars. Not the visible kind, anyway."

"Like the hunger Hellebore hexed you with."

"Yeah . . . like that one," Emery said.

An unwelcome thought crept up on Ambrose. It occurred to him how similar his own spells felt. Punishing. *Hungry.* There was something in that, though he didn't know what.

"We need to act quickly. Whatever chance we get, we probably won't get a second one," Emery murmured.

"Given how poorly our plans have gone, what makes you believe improvisation will go any better? How are we to make it look like an accident?"

"No. No improvising, and no more making it look like an accident." He tapped his fingers against his lower lip. At his heel, Katzica nudged him, wagging her tail anxiously. He hardly noticed her, too absorbed in the panic of rectifying his situation. "Maybe I've been approaching this the wrong way. I resurrected you. Doesn't it make the most sense to play to your strengths?"

A queer mix of yearning and repulsion stewed in Ambrose's gut. The spell stains on his hands felt tacky with the memory of blood. "You mean—?"

"It's what you're known for, isn't it?" Emery raised the poker, the hot end of it burning like a coal. He stared into it. "I'd put this through his eye if I had the stomach for it, but I've never—" He set the poker down in its stand, one finger still tilting it by the handle. "If I faltered at the crucial moment, I doubt Morcant would afford me another opportunity."

Ambrose startled as a dry nose pressed into his palm. Katzica gazed up at him, the pale cataracts of her eyes unseeing. Her white fur still bore the rusty stains from where Emery cut her open.

Had he been about to say that he'd never killed anyone before? Did Katzica not count? Or was it a charade? A means to lure Ambrose into making the killing blow, so that if things went wrong, he'd be the one to blame?

"There will be an inquest into his murder," Ambrose said. "How do you plan to avoid suspicion?"

"It's only a murder investigation if they find the body."

CHAPTER 17

They went through two logs on the fire discussing the new plan. Though it was not so intricate as those previous, Emery couldn't stop from repeating their roles and combing over the details several times.

He would agree to meet Morcant under the guise of fear and contrition. Once they had him alone, Emery would keep him distracted and talking until the time was right. Ambrose would strike, and if luck was on their side, Morcant would join the specters of his beloved tomb.

It was crude in its simplicity, but in Ambrose's experience, murder was rarely elegant.

After brainstorming various ways it could go wrong and how they could circumvent those (increasingly unlikely) events, Emery penned a note on a torn scrap of paper, apologizing to Morcant and requesting they meet. Ambrose couldn't read it, but Emery did so aloud, asking whether it sounded too sycophantic. It had to be believable.

"Perhaps make it more petulant," Ambrose said.

"Are you saying I'm petulant?"

"I see no benefit in answering that."

To his surprise, the ghost of a smile tickled Emery's face as he edited the note. After staring at it an interminable time, he threw it on the fire.

Ambrose raised an eyebrow. "Shouldn't you have sent it to him?"

"I just did." He rubbed his temples. "Not by conventional means, though."

He didn't elaborate further, just continued rubbing his head.

"Headache?" Ambrose asked.

"Morcant. He uses the rune we got at initiation to send us untraceable messages. A boon for us in this case, since it leaves no paper trail. Police won't know I'm the last person he spoke to. He's agreed to meet to discuss what happened. *Neutral territory*, he proposes. *Somewhere private.* I need to suggest a place. Somewhere no one can observe us but won't raise his suspicions."

Ambrose scowled. "Will he not aim to harm you?"

"Oh, undoubtedly. He'll want to punish me for the *mild concussion* he got after getting knocked in the head by a pair of stone horse bollocks."

"I still don't understand how he survived that encounter."

"That's something I've been considering," Emery said. "If you believe he got a solid smack, yet came out of it no worse for wear, we could be dealing with a powerful defensive charm. An armor enchantment, maybe."

Ambrose wasn't used to being taken seriously. It was an agreeable change. "The witch king used such enchantments, in my time."

"Did he? Well, then Morcant definitely would. He adores the witch king. Idolizes him. I swear, he'd bring the bastard back just to suck his dick."

Ambrose experienced a multitude of emotions at once—humor, anger, jealousy, disgust—in the span of five seconds, all of them most likely playing out on his face. It took an incalculable amount of willpower to master himself. Not because, he found upon inspection of his feelings, he had any true animosity for Emery's slight to the witch king, who'd been called worse than "bastard" before, but because the idea of the witch king doing anything sexual with *Morcant* was about as appealing as a moldy breakfast.

"Is Morcant—" Ambrose spat the words out like they tasted sour. "Inclined toward men?"

"God, no. Or, I don't actually know. I'd be offended if he was one of ours, though."

"Ours?"

"Queer," Emery elaborated. "Gay. Homosexual. Sodomites, I guess, was the word people favored in your time."

Ambrose felt heat climb up his throat and into his cheeks. He'd never, not once, been identified as such. "I never said—I'm n—How can you tell?"

"You were buried together." A sad look flitted across Emery's eyes, then took flight, gone. "Unless I'm mistaken, and he only viewed you as property."

Ambrose flinched. "No, we—" He felt tongue-tied. Never had he given voice to the secret feelings between him and his king. They'd gone their entire lives performing an elaborate dance to disguise it, even from themselves. Like the faithful's belief in divinity, they'd known what they had was more than the devotion of a knight to his liege king.

Ambrose had never been religious, though, and in his more shameful moments he'd wondered whether the love between them was shared or a figment of his imagination.

After all, they'd never . . . consummated those feelings.

You were the only one who knew my heart. That which keeps to the shadows for safety is no less real for being hard to see.

Ambrose cast aside his doubts. He couldn't allow Emery's prying to crack his regard for the witch king.

There was one element of the conversation he turned over with more fondness. *One of ours. A homosexual.*

"You're not mistaken." Ambrose couldn't keep the quiet awe from his voice. "It was not acceptable, in my time. I'm not used to it out in the open. "

Emery had many hard lines to his face. The high cheeks drawn to a pointed chin, the steep slope of his forehead leading to the high arch of his nose, the sharp sneer of his mouth. Ambrose might never have known all those edges could look soft.

"It's different now," Emery said. "Not all better, but not like it was for you."

The delight that inspired almost made Ambrose smile. "It will take getting used to."

"Just wait until you meet a drag queen. But we're getting distracted. Morcant. We need to meet him, find a way to strip him of his defenses, and kill him. I don't suppose your ability to pierce inanimate and animate objects alike includes enchanted armor?"

Ambrose unconsciously touched his chest, where a blaze of scar tissue marked the place an enchanted axe had cloven him from his past life. He shook his head. "I wouldn't put faith in an untested theory."

"Then we will need to disarm him."

"Is there a spell you could cast that would counter his defenses?"

"Yes, but even if I could gather the tithes in time, casting a spell right in front of Morcant is risky. He could retaliate too quickly, counter my own spell, or flee the moment he sees me casting. No, I need something subtler. A trap of some kind. Something I could prepare before Morcant arrives."

Ambrose nodded. "Like the sigil."

"Hm?"

"The sigil you used to trap me after resurrecting me."

Emery's eyes lit up. Clicking his fingers, he marched back to the living room and started seizing books off of shelves until he had a stack he could bury himself in.

It took time to design the sigil which could both ensnare Morcant and disarm him of defensive charms, but Emery proved an adept spell crafter. He drew and redrew variations on paper before he was satisfied enough to draw the final one on the floor of his living room.

"I need to test that it works," Emery said. "Come here."

Ambrose rose from the chair, offering his arm.

Emery stared at him. "Just like that?"

Ambrose shrugged. "Do I have reason to hesitate?"

"It's bizarre that you trust me to cast spells on you so readily. I didn't think the Grim Wolf of Bellgrave would be so . . . amenable."

It wasn't that Ambrose didn't feel a degree of wariness around spell magic. "I'm sure I've endured far worse than whatever flesh tithe you need of me now."

"I'm not taking a flesh tithe!" Emery said, horrified.

"Then I have even less reason to fear."

Emery made a noise of disbelief, but he stepped forward. Ambrose offered up his bare arms, but the smoky ash stains of spell magic covered him from his fingertips to the ditch of his elbows, so Emery had to draw on his biceps.

Abruptly, he felt it was a mistake to comply. Not for the reasons Emery expected, but because it brought a measure of tactility to their interaction he hadn't prepared for.

Emery wrapped one hand around Ambrose's arm and used the other to draw. The warm, firm pressure of his fingertips and the brush of knuckles as the charcoal scratched across his skin felt oddly intense. All of Ambrose's nerves awakened to the sensation of touch that wasn't aimed to harm.

"I've been wondering." Emery cleared his throat like something was stuck in it. "This spell—Your abilities. It's remarkable that even after resurrection, the spell sustains itself. What did the witch king tithe for it?"

Ambrose clenched the answer behind his teeth. He didn't want to recall the pain of that spell's making, and sank further into the soothing sense of Emery drawing on him instead. His answer came out strained. "He burned the body of a hanged man whose death no one would mourn. I was forged in his ashes."

Emery, to his consternation, stopped drawing and said, "What?"

Ambrose needed that sensation as an anchor to the present. Slipping into memory never went well, but he answered all the same, like that could quench the flame devouring him. "I had to put my hands in the forge while the witch king cast this on me."

"Is that why you're so nervous around fire?"

"I'm not nervous around fire."

"I see how you look at the fireplace."

Ambrose hadn't realized Emery watched him closely enough to pick up on these things. It unnerved and . . . flattered him. Deeply contradictory feelings. "Perhaps they do awaken memories, yes."

Emery brushed a thumb over the smoking tendrils of spell magic, and Ambrose tried to disguise a shiver. "It's a barbaric spell."

The contradictory feelings continued. Ambrose found he took offense and agreed in equal measure. "It was necessary."

"Hm. Still doesn't explain how the spell endured so long without further tithes to feed it. Is there any other component? Something you have to do in order to get the spell to work?"

Ambrose shook his head. He had never tithed anything. The spell lived on in him, an unquenchable, infinite hunger. Much like the witch king himself, whose voice he still heard. If the two were linked, he couldn't betray his king by telling Emery. "I can't cast magic the way witches can. The spell changed me. That's all I know."

Emery sobered. "I imagine it hurt."

He'd looked up as he said it, meeting Ambrose's eyes. Firelight cast Emery's a treacle shade of brown. He mostly looked at Ambrose with guarded disdain, sometimes tinged with fear. He looked open now. Like he was sketching Ambrose anew in his mind, a sigil with a different shape to its history and purpose.

Ambrose had to look away. "It was like no agony I've known before or since."

Emery didn't reply out loud, but his touch, which had already been gentle, was even more so. He finished drawing on one arm and moved to the other, conveniently able to capture Ambrose's gaze once more as he said, "This one won't hurt. Promise."

It kindled a feeling in Ambrose he was too afraid to name.

Emery placed his hands over each of Ambrose's biceps and subtly squeezed. The spell settled over him like a blanket. So soft, it could not be armor, yet it was. Warm and protective.

Emery sucked in a sharp breath. "Done." He stepped away, brushing a knuckle over his brow. It left a streak of charcoal in its wake, and Ambrose had the inane thought he should scrub it away.

You are too loyal for these foolish thoughts, sweet wolf. He is unworthy to hold the bone that binds you.

Ambrose's insides gave a sick swoop of guilt. He'd been so starved of touch in his past life, just the act of Emery drawing on him had awakened a different sort of appetite, but these thoughts and feelings were nothing but the mirage of an oasis to a parched man.

"Now to see if it works. Step into the center of the sigil." Emery cleared his throat again. "Please."

Ambrose walked up to the very edge. The sigil had a series of concentric circles around a triangle, with many runes written around the perimeter, making an intricate circle of its own to encompass the whole. The uneven stone floor hadn't offered the most flawless surface, but Emery had managed a near-perfect drawing, free of smudges or broken, jagged lines. He was an adept witch.

It was not Ambrose's first time playing test subject. Not all of the witch king's experiments had gone well. Spells backfired. Sometimes in humorous ways, like stripping Ambrose of his trousers, leaving him standing in his tunic and nothing more. Sometimes less humorous, like when it had struck him ill and set him vomiting for the span of three days.

It was the cost of learning. Yet, Ambrose found that the perfectionism of Emery's sigil made it easier to trust the spell would behave as intended.

He stepped into the center. In that instant, the warm embrace of armor fell away, leaving a windswept cold in its place. He tried to leave the circle, but beams of light sprang up to imprison him there.

It worked.

CHAPTER 18

It was the dead of night when they received word from Morcant that he would come to Emery's meeting place—a vacant patch of wilderness on the opposite side of the bog.

They had already trudged out of the ruin and found the perfect place to draw the sigil at the edge of the bog. Days without rain had turned the mud hard and chalky, perfect for drawing in, and they'd scattered dead leaves to camouflage it from view.

Ambrose lay in wait in the tree line. He maintained invisibility, though darkness shrouded him just as well.

Magic boiled, slick as oil in his veins, eager to catch fire, awaiting a target to devour. The sensation contrasted sharply with the caress of Emery's spell.

The softness of his touch as he'd cast it made Ambrose forget temporarily the madness of the course he'd set them on. Morcant was not a particularly good man, but Ambrose still didn't know that he deserved the recompense Emery intended to exact. Nor did he relish being the executioner.

Oh, he enjoyed it in the moment—the brief satiety once the magic achieved its destructive purposes—but later, it left him sick like a drunk come dawn. *Remember, you aren't doing this for him. You're doing it for us.*

It was cold comfort. He hoped Morcant might fall into the bog and drown, saving them the trouble.

Instead, he was late.

Ambrose suspected that was by design. Emery paced to and fro near the sigil, checking his phone for the time, his witch light bobbing dutifully after him. He shouldn't let his fear show so plainly.

A HEX FOR HUNGER 113

A portal finally opened. Morcant stepped through.

He bore no signs of harm, no bandages on his head or visible bruises to his face. The witch light cast him in monstrous, moving shadows as he emerged on the far side of Emery.

Opposite where they needed him to stand.

Emery said, "I wasn't sure you were coming."

Morcant shrugged lazily. "I didn't know whether your correspondence was genuine, or if I'd be walking into another poorly constructed trap."

"I wanted to—apologize." After a beat of hesitation, Emery took a step toward Morcant. He had to try and herd the conversation toward the sigil.

"Wonders never cease. There *is* a first time for everything." Morcant didn't sound convinced.

"Profusely," Emery amended through gritted teeth. His performance would win no awards. "I was—frustrated after your punishment. I lashed out." As he spoke, he got closer. There were two horse strides between them.

"You were always prone to fits of emotion," Morcant agreed. "I thought you might master them in time. But I still haven't heard an apology."

"I'm sorry."

"You tried to murder me."

"*So* sorry," Emery said.

Morcant was close enough to reach out and grasp Emery by the throat. Ambrose wrestled with the dread pitting his stomach and the instruction to stay hidden until the time came, but the sight of Emery in close proximity to this man who meant him ill riled his protective instincts.

Emery passed Morcant, as if too agitated to stand still. Positioned there, he could perhaps encourage Morcant to take a few steps back toward the sigil. "I didn't think. I was desperate to avoid further punishment, and nothing I did ever seemed enough, so I thought this was the only way. It was foolish."

"Unbelievably so." Morcant remained steadfast despite Emery stepping closer than could be comfortable. "But even at your most unpredictable, I didn't think you'd be so quick to add a second murder to the blood on your hands."

Ambrose held his breath. He was attempting to goad Emery by bringing up Katzica.

"That wasn't—!" Emery's throat clenched, as if he'd taken what he was about to say and swallowed it. "It doesn't matter. I won't make excuses. I'm sorry."

"I do not believe you, nor do I accept your apology."

Morcant moved, but in the wrong direction. He lay a hand on Emery's shoulder, the knuckle bones prominent as the teeth of a saw, his fingers devilishly long. The cords of Emery's neck stood out as if the touch had cut him.

If Morcant made another threatening move, Ambrose would have to rush out of hiding. He could try and shove him into the sigil by brute force, but if he failed, Morcant would teleport to safety, and the entire ruse would be for nothing.

So Ambrose waited, muscles taut as bowstrings.

"I might change my mind if you tell me something," Morcant said. "Only if you're honest. I can always tell when you're lying."

"What do you want to know?"

Morcant leaned in. He spoke softly, but in the dead of night his words were clearly audible. "How *did* you destroy that statue?"

Emery's back straightened. "Pardon?"

"I took the liberty of a quick detour on my way here." As Morcant spoke, he walked a half circle around Emery, turning his back to the boy who wanted him dead and coming fortuitously close to the sigil. "After inspecting the statue for tampering, I found a spell signature. It wasn't yours."

Emery took a step forward. "That's not possible."

Morcant reeled around to hiss, "I told you to be honest."

"I don't know what you mean. If not my signature, then whose?"

Ambrose thought, if they survived this encounter, he would have to teach Emery to be a better liar. He usually spoke with rhythmic affectation, like his words were lyrics to a song. When he lied, he became uncharacteristically poker-faced, as if hoping Morcant would interpret his calm as a sign of sincerity.

They'd gotten very close to where Ambrose hid, a few steps away from the sigil.

The witch king's voice took on an eager tone. *Close. Closer.*

Ambrose's magic reared like a chained predator. The more it hungered, the more Ambrose feared its use. Something about its voracious appetite and Morcant's questions and the eager voice in his head beset him with doubt.

None of their other plans had worked. Why should this be different?

"Don't play stupid, Emery," Morcant said. He walked toward the tree line, toward Ambrose, who shuddered with the convulsive desire of his magic to feed. "You have done many stupid things, particularly this year, but you were my prize student for a reason. I know you've found yourself an accomplice. And that 'cousin' you brought to frighten Hellebore isn't a witch, but he did *something* to her when he shook her hand, so . . ." Facing the trees, only Ambrose saw Morcant's sharp smile before it vanished as he turned to face his pupil. "Was it him? Or have you found a witch foolish enough to join this fool's errand? Name them."

His footsteps disturbed the leaf litter. He stood only a scant breath away from the perimeter of the sigil. Ambrose could see the dark trench of its design in the flickering witch light. One step backward, that's all they needed. Ambrose couldn't pull him into the sigil without stepping into it himself.

"I promise you, I don't know what you mean." Emery took a harried step forward, trying to herd Morcant backward.

Morcant didn't budge. "Don't *lie*."

As he said it, he thrust a hand out, fingers clenching around some tithe.

Emery crumpled to his knees, clutching his throat and gasping. Ambrose nearly bolted, his restraint held by a thread.

"That spell will only let you breathe if you tell the truth," Morcant said. "While every lie will make you suffocate faster."

"I didn't—" The loud wheeze of air punched from Emery's lungs unnerved all the singing insects and wildlife of the bog into silence. Ambrose's instincts sang for them, buzzing in his head. He needed to intervene, but Emery occupied the most advantageous spot from which to shove Morcant directly into the sigil, right in front of him.

Still, Ambrose took a step out from hiding.

His magic hummed in his ears.

He didn't touch Morcant.

Not yet.

"Your accomplice must be a powerful witch to have avoided my notice thus far, and the signature matched none of your guild siblings, so *who*?"

The spell let up long enough for Emery to spit out a crumb of truth. "He's not a witch—Agh!"

A strangled cry followed. Not from the truth-telling curse wrenching his throat closed, but from something purer and simpler.

Pain.

It set Ambrose's teeth on edge all the more. Spells like that one required living tithes, so where had Morcant kept the small creature he'd just killed to make Emery suffer?

Ambrose couldn't bear the cruelty anymore. He'd never had a stomach for it, and he knew Emery was far from a saint, but in the warm embrace of his magic that night, he'd seen a softer side to the man than before. One which Ambrose felt compelled—by no charm except his own gentled heart—to protect.

Emery bowed over his stomach, head between his knees, moaning when the spell gave him breath enough to vocalize his pain. Low enough to the ground that Ambrose could stand over him.

"You are going to tell me which fool you've coerced into assisting you," Morcant said.

Ambrose took a step closer.

"You will cease these futile attempts to kill me and accept my leadership or continue to suffer the consequences. If you behave reasonably, I can be benevolent, so I will ask you again. One last time."

Ambrose stood over Emery. His body was not enough to block the effects of the spell, but—

"Who is your accomplice?" Morcant demanded.

"I am," said Ambrose, and he shoved Morcant with all his strength into the cage of the sigil.

CHAPTER 19

Morcant, caught unawares, stumbled back. The lines of the sigil ignited with acidic green fire. They flared brightly before dimming to a glow, rays of light like an aurora forming a prison. Morcant lunged for the edge and hit that magical barrier, letting out a seething hiss as the recoil of punishing magic held him in place.

The voice of the witch king bayed in Ambrose's ears. *Yes! You've done it! Now, kill him. Kill him!*

Ambrose dropped invisibility the moment he'd made physical contact. No use hiding now. The only man who knew his secret was about to die.

Morcant seemed not to realize as much. He composed himself and said, "Ah, Emery's 'cousin.' Pray tell, who are you, really?"

Ambrose ignored him, looking back at Emery. The second the trap had sprung, it had broken the hold on Morcant's spell. Emery sucked in desperate breaths, looking up from his position kneeling in the grass. Not at Morcant, but Ambrose.

Ambrose had diverted from their plan to protect Emery. He'd acted without orders.

A sinuous tension embroidered the space between their shared gaze.

He held out a hand to help Emery to his feet. Emery hesitated, then took it. He had mud on his forehead and under his nails, face drawn from pain, but he didn't let go right away. His hand lingered and squeezed in a silent communication of gratitude.

"Ah." Morcant's voice snaked uninvited between them. "You've found yourself a lover to play bodyguard?"

Ambrose's face heated. Emery withdrew his hand. Violet bruises bloomed against his throat where the spell had choked him. It looked like a vile mockery of the arcane collar Ambrose bore. His magic longed to turn around and tear Morcant asunder, and Ambrose—in spite of all his reservations—was starting to see the appeal, but a practical curiosity nipped at the heels of that hostility.

Why wasn't Morcant trying harder to escape? He didn't reach for his tithe belt, didn't rail against his prison anymore, hadn't even sounded bothered when discussing Emery's attempts to murder him in the first place.

He wasn't afraid.

He should be, the witch king growled.

Emery said, "His identity is the least of your concerns."

Morcant raised an eyebrow, detecting a clue in Emery's tone. "*Should* I know him?"

"You should know he's going to kill you now."

Morcant had the audacity to chuckle. "He's no witch, and he has no weapon."

"I'd ask him to give you a demonstration, but I have something to say to you first."

"You were never good at games, Emery, and this one bores me."

"You can't belittle me anymore. Once, those words hurt. You knew they did. That was the point, wasn't it? Win me over with praise, kindness, and adulation for the skills few people appreciated, so that when you reprimanded me, humiliated me, punished me, I'd believe I must have deserved it, because why would someone who'd once been so kind suddenly be so cruel?"

"Didn't you deserve it?" Morcant's expression had a phantasmal edge, bathed in the sigil's aurora. "The art of necromancy demands nothing short of perfection. I couldn't allow you to endanger anyone else with your negligence."

Ambrose narrowed his eyes. Anyone *else*? What was Morcant on about?

Emery bristled. "*My* negligence? You *tricked* us."

"I gave you a choice."

"An uninformed—"

"I will take no responsibility for your regret."

Emery let out a snarl of frustration. "*Fuck* you. And *fuck* this. I'm not speaking with you to justify myself, I'm doing this for my own catharsis. I have one last question. Just one before you die."

"I don't see why I should be compelled under threat of death to be truthful, but I'll humor you. Ask."

Ambrose observed the exchange with his heart ticking an uncanny beat. Something about Emery's demeanor unnerved him. Much of the time, he behaved in perfect control of his emotions, chilly with apathy, yet Morcant always seemed to know the perfect thing to prick him into a reaction.

There was more to their history. Something Ambrose was missing.

"*Why?*" Emery clenched his fists so hard they shook. "Why are you doing this? I can't bring myself to believe you're just that sick and sadistic, that there's no *practical* reason why you'd trap new kids each year, so tell me. What are we to you? What the hell do you get out of it?"

Morcant had the sort of face that was once handsome and still would be when rendered in paintings, but a soulless sheen to his eyes and the smile he wore rendered him a ghoul.

"You'll soon find out," he said.

A cold chill rinsed Ambrose's bones. What did he mean by that?

Emery looked close to shouting again, but instead he unclenched his fists and took a shuddering breath. "Fine. I don't know why I thought I'd get any closure from you. The only peace I'll find is with you rotting underground."

"I'm eager to see how you plan on accomplishing that."

Emery hardly met Ambrose's eye. His brow pinched together. "Ambrose?"

The impatient, hungry magic slavered like a starved hound at that one, simple questioning expression of his name. Ambrose understood the order to kill was implicit, but he'd expected . . . something more. An execution order. A jerk of the arcane collar, even though Emery had agreed not to use it.

It felt like both a curse and a gift to have the choice left in his hands, to reach willingly into the sigil, into Morcant's chest, all because Emery and the witch king wanted him to.

Do it. Kill him.

He approached the sigil.

Morcant didn't shrink away. He waited, expectant. As Ambrose rolled up his sleeves, his eyes gleamed.

"Interesting." He stared greedily at the stain of magic reaching for Ambrose's elbows.

You will rend soul from shell. Carve the flesh from the peel and leave him pitted like devoured fruit.

Ambrose suppressed a shudder. He'd never heard the witch king's voice sound that way, so feral and vicious. Hunger made his extremities numb. Nothing about this felt right.

In the space of his hesitation, Morcant said, "This is rather anticlimactic."

"What are you waiting for?" Emery asked.

Ambrose didn't know, but the whole situation itched like a parasite below the skin, unseen but deeply felt. Morcant didn't move, didn't try to flee. He wasn't afraid. Why wasn't he afraid?

He will be! the voice shrilled, a toothy edge to it. *He will fear us when he is hollow and empty, and we will dine well on the harrowing of his wretched heart. Kill him. Kill him. Kill him now.*

"I—" Ambrose said.

Kill him.

"Ambrose." A hint of the fear that should have been Morcant's crept into Emery's voice. *"Please."*

Kill him.

Ambrose stared into Morcant's pale blue eyes. Nothing like the undiluted sea of color the witch king's had been, yet still alike. A phantom familiarity that put him ill at ease.

He wished the act hadn't fallen to him at all. His dreams of heroism had decayed slowly in the witch king's service. He wasn't a fool. He knew he'd done terrible deeds under that oath he'd sworn. He did them for a king he'd believed had grander purposes. He did them for a king he'd trusted, and a man he'd . . .

Loved.

Maybe none of that absolved him, but he'd kept his oath. Once the fetid blood stained his hands, what noble attribute could he cling to, aside from his loyalty?

He still didn't want his second life to follow in the footsteps of his first.

Kill him!

Ambrose lifted a hand. Hesitated.

Morcant smirked. "It seems your assassin's courage has failed him. Well—"

"Ambrose, do it," Emery pleaded.

"This has all been very entertaining, but I'm quite tired, so . . ." Morcant finally, finally reached for his tithe belt. Perhaps to cast some counterspell on the sigil. Perhaps to lash out at his captors.

Don't let him escape!

Ambrose gritted his teeth and lunged.

At the same time, Emery said, "**Kill him!**"

A hot needle of magic carved the words into Ambrose's neck. The collar cinched tighter than a corset. The compulsion jerked him forward an extra step than intended. His hand found the resistance of Morcant's ribs and rendered them soft as rotten fruit. The magic plunged forward, devouring, sinking its teeth to the gums, tearing, shredding. It lapped for blood, but something was wrong.

Every bite tasted dry as sawdust. There was nothing substantial to swallow, no meat to the magic's feast. Whatever it normally dined on, Morcant's table lay barren.

They were eye to eye. Morcant stared down at Ambrose's arm half buried in his chest, at the blood seeping from the wound. Pain colored his face, of course, but surprise, too. For the first time that night, Morcant's smile fell away. The expression which replaced it was no less unsettling.

Awe.

He looked into Ambrose's face and said, "Grim . . . Wolf."

Ambrose wrenched his hand free. Blood and viscera followed like Morcant's chest was a burst gourd. Ambrose staggered away as the corpse crumpled to the ground. It made a heavy sound hitting the packed earth. The sigil, sensing no more life within, faded and dispelled into sparks like fireflies, winking out into the night.

Silence followed.

It seemed inconceivable the necromancer was dead.

It was dark. It was quiet. Ambrose's stomach lurched with a terrible starvation. He didn't know how the magic worked, but it had been different tonight than in his past life. It normally made him feel briefly sated to use it this way. Tonight, it felt as though his magic had sought to feed upon Morcant—his soul, his life, whatever it was the magic found nourishing— and found nothing there.

He didn't understand what had changed, but he understood what he felt when he looked at Emery.

Betrayal.

"He's dead," Emery said, relieved. "You did it. You killed him."

"You made me," Ambrose said.

The self-reproof lasted a flinching second before Emery's expression hardened. "You hesitated. He was trying to escape."

"I had him."

"This was my last chance."

"I *had* him," Ambrose repeated. The venom in his own voice surprised him. Whether he murdered the man under compulsion, or at the behest of the voice in his head, or because he'd decided it was the right thing to do, what did it matter?

Resurrection hadn't bought him any redemption. Before Morcant, Ambrose owed a debt of blood to many people. What was one more?

None of this bothered him so much as the fact he'd trusted Emery not to use the collar, and he had anyway.

Emery's expression shuttered. "It's done. Now, we need to deal with the body."

CHAPTER 20

It rained as they went about their grim business.

While Emery prepared a spell to clean all traces of blood, Ambrose tied heavy stones to Morcant's limbs and dumped his corpse in the bog. It sank into the murky depths, peat and mulch making it impossible to see to the bottom.

He returned to find Emery scuffing out the sigil. The rain would wash away the rest until the earth looked as though no one had ever disturbed it, and no one had ever died here.

In awkward silence, they returned home. A penetrating cold from the rain and the taint of their deed left Ambrose craving a shower, but he didn't know if he wanted to be alone or dreaded it.

He couldn't go about life in clothes covered in blood and bog grime. He stripped out of his shirt, and Emery said, "Bring it here."

He crouched by the fire, stoking it to life. In its glow, he didn't look relieved any longer. Only tired. He stripped his shirt off, though it only had a few drops of arterial spray. Underneath, he had the body of a fawn, long-limbed and delicate with ribs showing. The firelight gave him a fragile look, like filigree gold.

He threw his clothes on the fire and held out a hand for Ambrose's, too.

Ambrose gave the wadded shirt over and watched it catch and curl. The cotton smelled like paper burning. His pants would have to go, too, but he waited. It didn't feel like a moment for vulnerability.

Perhaps Emery shared the sentiment. "Leave the rest of your clothes in the bathroom when you're finished washing. I'd like to be alone."

Ambrose thought he detected the barest hint of guilt in his words. While leaving, he saw Emery reach for a bottle of wine.

It irked him. Emery hadn't been the one to punch a hole in Morcant's chest. Why did he get to drink the memory away, while Ambrose marinated in it?

Something else bothered him more. Now they'd closed the business of ending Morcant, what use did Emery have for him? As the one with blood on his hands, the only thing he'd be now was a loose end.

He dumped his stained clothes on the tile floor of the bathroom and gratefully stepped into the steaming water. Perhaps it could scald away the feeling of Morcant's guts congealing around his fist. The hot water did bring some serenity, but in the space of that calm, something else made itself known.

The hunger.

There was good reason Ambrose hated using his abilities to kill. Every time he did, the magic fed. Upon the death, or perhaps the pain. He didn't know. All he knew was this strange spell feasted on *something* when he killed, and though it would gorge itself, it was never quite sated. He would feel satisfaction only temporarily, then the hunger would return, worse than before.

Not this time. There was no satiety, only emaciation. Whatever it dined on, it had found Morcant's table wanting.

When he finished washing, he wrapped himself in a towel. From the hall, he could hear the fire crackling but no sounds from the living room. Curiosity compelled him to check.

Emery lay curled up on the sofa in pajama bottoms, knees tucked to his chest, his fingers still half wrapped around the neck of a wine bottle. He'd passed out, shivering. Evidently the fire and wine were not enough to warm him. In his other hand, cradled to his chest, he gripped something else.

The arcane tether.

It gleamed pearly white in the firelight, but something was wrapped around it. Something Ambrose could not make sense of.

A silky pink ribbon had been tied in a bow around the bone.

The whole tableau was surreal and confusing. Why had Emery done that? Did he use it to tie the bone to his pocket? Why not use a spell? Why use something so . . . pretty? It was like seeing a wild boar in a bonnet.

As Ambrose watched, Emery nuzzled into the sofa cushions, sighed, and the clench of his fist loosened. The bone slipped from his fingers. The

A HEX FOR HUNGER 125

hollow tap of it hitting the floor made Ambrose's heart plunge, not for fear of it breaking, but for the opportunity it presented.

The laws of his pact forbade him from trying to take the leash from his master. It also forbade him from harming the witch king, which made interfering with the leash impossible, since it had been quite *attached* to the witch king at the time. That he'd even added a pact pertaining to theft might have been ludicrous, but the witch king had seen enough injuries in war to know that possessing all ten fingers was a luxury.

This insurance had still pricked at Ambrose's pride. The witch king had nothing to fear from him.

Now, seeing the bone lying there on the floor, he wondered if the pact held when he wasn't taking it off Emery's person.

If he took it, he'd be free. To do what, he didn't know. He was not a citizen of this time, world, country. He had no idea how to survive it, let alone integrate with it.

But if he left, he wouldn't have to wait and discover what Emery planned to do with him now that his usefulness had expired.

Yet he found himself thinking of their breakfast at the stables, the chocolate he'd bought to ease Ambrose through a trying moment, and—he blanched with self-reproach—the soft touch of his hands over Ambrose's spell-scarred arms. The way his magic felt like an embrace.

He ground his teeth. Emery had killed his familiar then forced Ambrose to kill his enemy for him. Ambrose should not—could not—feel fondness for this man.

He crept closer. The fire crackled and snapped. Emery stirred but didn't wake as Ambrose knelt next to the sofa. This close, the runes engraving the length of the bone were clearly visible. They glowed the same green as his collar.

He reached for it.

Yes, take it. Take it and kill him.

Ambrose stopped short of touching it. His blood ran cold.

Had he heard that right? The witch king had been fixated on killing Morcant. He'd never fixed his malice on Emery before.

Morcant was an inadequate tithe for the spell to return me. Emery forced your hand. He's vulnerable. He won't even feel it.

Stricken, Ambrose looked into Emery's sleeping face. With his eyes closed, his lashes swept over his cheeks like strokes of ink, slumber easing all the tension from his expression, he looked beguilingly innocent. He shivered from the cold. Ambrose shivered a little, too.

Emery's was the peaceful repose that begged for a blanket tucked around his shoulders, a press of lips to his brow, not a dagger in the back.

Ambrose could barely stomach killing Morcant. He surely couldn't stomach this.

If he took hold of the leash, that fragile little piece of bone, what would happen? Would he grasp his freedom, or would the last vapors of the witch king breathing within him use it to compel him?

If that happened, he'd be forced to kill Emery.

No, thought Ambrose. *I may not owe him my loyalty, but I owe him more than this.*

All that you owe, you owe to me.

Ambrose had acted of his own volition to *protect* Emery that night. He could contemplate fleeing, but not this. Perhaps the leash was better off in Emery's hands.

The voice burned with vitriol. *You swore an oath to me, to protect and serve me. This witch stole you from me. He will prevent you returning to my side, where you belong, unless you end his life.*

"I can't."

Ambrose only realized he'd spoken aloud when Emery's eyes flew open. He startled back, propped half upright on his hands like an animal ready to bolt. In doing so, he released the bottle of wine. It rang against the floor and rolled, clinking to a stop against the bone. Emery looked down at it, then up at Ambrose, eyes filled with—

Terror.

Ambrose didn't know what possessed him to act as he did. He should have lunged for the bone and taken it. He should have seized his independence as soon as the opportunity presented itself.

Perhaps the fear of the witch king's wrath held him back.

Perhaps he was out of practice at acting in his own interests.

But more likely he hated to see Emery's peaceful expression replaced by fear, knowing he was the one who caused it.

Instead of taking the bone, he straightened and reached behind Emery for the blanket folded over the arm of the sofa. He swept it over him, tucking it around his shoulders the way he'd wanted to when he'd first seen him asleep.

"You looked cold," he said.

Not anymore. Now, he looked flushed and confused.

A HEX FOR HUNGER 127

Ambrose didn't wish to interrogate how foolish he'd been or the way his heart thundered.

"Goodnight," he said.

"Wait."

Ambrose had been halfway to the opposite chair, to bed down and avoid thinking about this night altogether, but he paused.

"I have something for you," Emery said.

He led Ambrose down the hall. It appeared longer. Aside from trips to the toilet, Ambrose had never ventured past the first door, but he swore Emery's had been the second door at the end.

Now there were three doors.

"I wasn't about to leave you sleeping on the sofa every night," Emery said. He thrust open the second door. "It isn't much, but I figured you'll sleep better with your own room."

Ambrose stepped cautiously past him.

He didn't know what he'd expected, but not this.

The chamber was a magical addition. A canopy bed with sheer gauzy drapes dominating the center, with a rustic painted dresser on one side and an illustration of butterflies on the wall. A lit candle on the bedside gave it a quaint warmth.

"I had no idea how you'd want it decorated, but it should be more comfortable."

Emery's flippancy covered a layer of awkwardness. It took powerful magic to transform space like this, yet he seemed uncertain if the generosity would be taken well. He stole most of the tithes he used, but it was still an extravagance by Ambrose's measure.

He didn't know why Emery would give it to him, let alone feel ashamed on the basis of its decor. He'd only been wondering whether Emery planned on disposing of him moments ago.

This implied the opposite, and Ambrose didn't know how to feel about it.

"Are you a throw rug sort of person?" Emery carried on. "Do you have artistic preferences? Colors? Honestly, I went with white because of your hair." He didn't know what he preferred. The hunger occupied so much space within him, he wondered if it had left him enough space to know himself.

Through a tight throat, he said, "Thank you."

128 ALISTAIR REEVES

"Er. You're welcome. I'll see you in the morning."

Ambrose waited for the sound of Emery's washing to end before venturing to the living room, collecting the e-reader and headphones he'd been ferreting under the cushions of the sofa, and taking them to his new room.

Once changed into his sleep clothes, he allowed himself the strange and exquisite pleasure of running his fingers over the bed's plush coverlet. He got in, sheets caressing his skin, cool but warming to his touch.

Such a simple thing, getting into bed, yet he couldn't remember the last time he'd done so. It felt sinful to enjoy the comfort alone.

He couldn't meditate on those feelings long. It was too confusing to wonder why something that felt so good should also make him so unsettled.

He turned the e-reader on and navigated to the place he'd left off. If he found information that could restore the witch king to his life and former power without killing Emery, that might stave off the sneaking anxiety.

In browsing for his intended book, he accidentally tapped on the wrong one.

It was something Emery must have already begun, because it picked up mid-chapter, where he'd left off.

It was a dreadful idea to follow Henry into the wine cellar alone, but damn it all, that scandalous wink he threw over his shoulder was irresistible.

Ambrose froze. What was this book about? How was a wink scandalous? He'd certainly never seen such a thing before.

The book continued, *"Henry, we shouldn't,"* whispered Simon. *"If the gentleman and ladies of the ton were to find us this way—"*

"I cannot help how I feel for you," Henry insisted. *"Can you?"*

"But isn't it wrong? Between two men."

"If this is wrong," Henry said, his lips a brand against Simon's throat, *"then I don't want to be right."*

Heat bloomed in Ambrose's cheeks. He prepared to tap frantically out of this book to find another. Instead, he paused, finger hovering over the screen as the voice droned on, its unenthusiastic tone at odds with the sensuous direction the story took.

Transfixed, he couldn't bring himself to silence it.

This book was about two men. Two men in love. Two men *having sex*.

It would have been burned in his time, and the people who wrote it—it didn't bear thinking what would have happened to them.

Yet Emery had it on an electronic device he'd never attempted to hide. He'd said this era was better for men like them. Not perfect, but better.

Ambrose put the e-reader down. He sank into bed and, with a queer combination of hope and pleasure fluttering in his stomach, continued to listen long into the night while thinking about the way Emery's breath had caught when Ambrose's hands smoothed the blanket over his shoulders.

CHAPTER 21

Ambrose woke to the sounds of clinking from the kitchen.

He rose to find Emery, looking bright-eyed and at ease, frying eggs, bacon, and sausages in a pan.

Aside from the cinnamon buns, he'd never used the kitchen, ordering "takeaways" instead. Ambrose had no complaints. Eating (and listening to novels about emotionally repressed homosexuals) were amongst his favorite things about this new world, but it wasn't terribly in character for him.

"There you are. I made breakfast."

"You cook?"

"Why the tone of surprise?"

"You've never cooked. You baked, but it was under duress."

"I'll have you know, I'm very good in the kitchen! Or I used to be. Nothing like a hex that makes everything taste like sewer water to put you off your appetite. But today's a new day."

He slid a plate of food across the counter toward Ambrose.

Ambrose took it. "You seem . . . happy."

"It's been known to happen."

"Last night, you didn't seem happy." Ambrose really hoped Emery bought the whole *You looked cold* thing. He didn't want to revisit the witch king's order to execute Emery, not when Ambrose seemed to have finally endeared himself to the witch, and not when his usefulness to that witch had expired.

"Yes, well, it was a lot to take in. But I woke up this morning and thought, I'll never see that bastard again. I don't have to walk on eggshells through all

A HEX FOR HUNGER 131

my classes. I don't have to worry about what sadistic punishment he'll come up with in response to an imagined slight. So yes, I'm . . ." He paused, twirling the spatula around in the air. "Relieved. Free. I'm happy he's dead."

"And Hellebore?"

"Oh, she's a pain in the arse, but everything she did, she did at his whim. We'll have to make sure she doesn't find the body, but I don't think she'll want police snooping around any more than he would have."

Ambrose hadn't taken a bite of his food yet. He feared asking the one thing he really wished to know. *And me? What happens to me now?*

Emery waved at him with the spatula. "Don't wait for me. Get stuck in, or it'll go cold."

"I—" Should he ask? It wasn't likely Emery would reveal his plans if he had any. "Thank you."

Emery waited. Ambrose got the sense he was waiting for approval. In spite of his worries, he took a savoring bite of bacon, closing his eyes briefly.

He really hoped Emery had no nefarious plans for him, because he would sorely miss the food.

Emery looked pleased by his response. "So. It's a Saturday, and most people get to have a lie-in on Saturdays, but Morcant would drag us out of bed before the sun rose for our guild meetings. I think he did it deliberately to ensure we never slept well. Everyone will think the meeting is still running. I think we should attend for the sake of appearances. Pretend to be shocked when he doesn't turn up."

Ambrose paused. What Emery had said replayed in his mind, something which made Ambrose tentatively hopeful. "May I speak honestly?"

Emery's brow scrunched. "Er, yes? Do you not usually?"

"No. I mean, yes, I do. It's just that you're not terribly convincing at pretend."

Some egg fell from Emery's fork. "I beg your pardon?"

"Last night, when you were lying to Morcant, he could tell."

"Well, yes . . . He always could. I thought he had some lie-detection spell. Are you saying it's because I'm a bad liar?"

Ambrose smiled sheepishly and shrugged.

"How bad?"

"Dreadful."

It felt oddly thrilling to say it. Not only because he'd never dream of saying something so bold to the witch king, but because the conversation served to inadvertently assuage Ambrose's fears.

If Emery was planning to get rid of him, he wasn't an adept-enough liar to hide it.

Emery stared at him for a moment, then laughed. Ambrose dropped his fork in surprise. He'd never seen Emery smile so brightly. It lit him up. He had *dimples*.

"What?" Emery said.

"You're—" *Beautiful.* Ambrose could have bit through his tongue to stop himself saying it. The witch king's voice was eerily silent, but that itself felt like condemnation. "It's rare to see you smile, is all," Ambrose said.

"Well, that hasn't helped my ability to lie, apparently! Are you doling out any lessons on maintaining a poker face?" At Ambrose's confused look, he added, "It's a game where you— Nevermind. It means not betraying your emotions on your face."

"Ah, then this 'poker face' wouldn't serve you. It is not in your character to appear unreadable. You might not smile often, but you're normally quite animated. You speak with your hands, your face is very expressive. Like this." Ambrose attempted an impression of Emery's mannerisms.

Emery choked. "You could just call me a faggot, and I'd get the picture."

Which resulted in an educating moment for Ambrose on the history of the word, both its horrifying usage and the fact Emery had adopted it in defiance of its derogatory meanings.

He seemed genuinely light-hearted and relieved, and there was no point in ruining it by brooding over the witch king's orders.

Besides, he wished to bask in the first time he'd seen Emery truly smile a little longer.

The initiates did not look well when Emery and Ambrose first arrived at the mausoleum. Ambrose invisibly observed from the corner, as usual, and they all looked exhausted.

Saoirse in particular.

She yawned, and the rest of the guild caught it. They all shifted uneasily from foot to foot, battling between the need for sleep and the tension in the air.

Morcant always arrived early. He wasn't here. Neither was Hellebore.

"Maybe he's still in hospital," Saoirse said.

The other initiates nodded tentatively. They'd all been at the fundraiser.

When Ambrose had first seen Saoirse, she dressed in eclectically feminine styles—earrings shaped like ladybirds, dresses in mushroom patterns, boots with brightly colored laces. Today, she wore trousers and a slouching shirt that barely fit her.

It could have been argued that the early hour left her too tired to put in the usual effort, but she'd dressed plainly at the fundraiser, too. Ambrose remembered the remark from Morcant about her "inappropriate" dress. It had burrowed beneath her skin and taken root. He hoped, now Morcant was gone, she could get back to the girl she'd been.

She approached Emery and said under her breath, "Did you really have something to do with it?"

"With what?"

"The accident yesterday, obviously."

"I haven't developed telepathic powers, last I checked."

"Hellebore seemed fairly convinced."

"Hellebore's not fanciful enough to believe in telepathy."

Saoirse gave him a withering look.

"Where *is* Hellebore?" he went on, diverting the conversation. "Morcant might be in hospital, but surely she'd let you know if the meeting was off, seeing as you're her favorite."

He said it in a deprecating tone, but Saoirse didn't seem to think it a slight. "She left the dorms this morning in a rush. She didn't tell me why. So you really don't know what's going on?"

"Not the foggiest."

"And that accident yesterday wasn't you?"

"Nope."

She stared at him, studying his expression. He'd done a better job lying this time, but Ambrose thought he may be laying the attitude on thick.

Footsteps pounded down the stairs, and everybody straightened in anticipation of who would arrive.

Hellebore rushed into the tomb and, upon seeing Emery, charged toward him. Her messy bun tumbled loosely from its ties, and she wore no makeup. Without lipstick, she'd gone from vampire to near-cherubic.

At least in appearance. Her personality was another matter.

"He's not here?" she demanded.

No one needed to ask who she meant. The other initiates murmured confirmation, but she hadn't directed the question at them.

Emery said, "Not yet."

"Where is he?" Hellebore said.

"*I* don't keep his itinerary on me. That's your forte."

Sarcasm was a more comfortable mask for him. *That's better*, thought Ambrose.

"We all know his itinerary for today includes our guild meetings at five in the morning. It's five-sixteen, and he isn't here. He usually meets me before we arrive, but he didn't come. I rang him and heard nothing back. I took a portal home and can't find him."

"Well, it was rude of him to drag us all out of bed if he isn't going to show."

Hellebore advanced on him. Ambrose, standing only a pace to Emery's left, felt the force of her anger as if its presence had density.

"I know you did something at the fundraiser yesterday. Then you weaseled your way out of punishment somehow, and now I can't find him. That's *not good*. I know you have something to do with it, so just tell me."

Ambrose didn't like her intensity or the direction of her questions. Her anger had taken a subtle sidestep in an alien direction, sprung up from a different source than the one he'd assumed.

He couldn't place why. She just seemed off.

Emery held up his hands in a helpless gesture of confusion. "I may have played a little prank yesterday, but last I heard he'd been sent to hospital." He smirked. "Did you check there?"

"You infuriating piece of—" She reeled an arm back to punch him.

Ambrose lunged to intervene, but Hellebore hit the wall behind Emery's head. Ambrose wrestled his impulse under control just in time. He couldn't reveal himself now. It would put them beyond suspicion, tantamount to a confession.

Emery had flinched away from her, his back pressed flat to the wall.

"Please just tell me what happened," she said. Some of her anger bled into fear. She spoke so low, Ambrose barely heard. "We can sort it out, but if we don't, we'll be dead when he finds us."

It struck Ambrose what had bothered him so about Hellebore's demeanor. She wasn't afraid her father was missing, or hurt, or maybe even dead. She was afraid of what he'd do to them. She believed entirely that Emery had tried to kill Morcant only yesterday, but she was utterly convinced of her father's safe return.

Emery started to say, "How many times can I say I don't know before you—"

He stopped short.

At first, Ambrose didn't know why, but then he heard it, too.

Footsteps. Slow, echoing footsteps on the stairs.

Emery's face drained of color. Everyone looked to the doorway, to the shoes appearing on the declining steps, the black robes noticeably free of peat and blood, the gaunt face.

"Apologies for my lateness," said Morcant.

Frigid dread pooled in Ambrose's half-beating heart.

It made sense now. The way his magic could not feed on Morcant's demise like the countless deaths wrought before. Why Hellebore had been so convinced of his return. The reason he had not, even in the dying moments of his last breath, been afraid.

Morcant Van Moor was immortal.

CHAPTER 22

During Ambrose's service to the witch king, the witch king had died twice.

Once, it had been poison. At a feast with an allied prince, the witch king had taken ill. He ordered Ambrose to take him to his chamber and ensure no one, not even the physicians, was allowed in. After an agony of hours, he'd finally passed. Ambrose had knelt by his deathbed until morning, waiting. Eventually, sunny life returned to the pallid gray of the witch king's face. Vigor returned to his body, once locked in rigor mortis. When he'd sat up, he'd asked for a glass of water, then asked who had done it.

There had been no evidence. The cooks claimed no knowledge. Ambrose had been ordered to dispatch them all for their negligence. The prince insisted he'd had nothing to do with it, that he would never.

The witch king went to war with him anyway.

The second time had been more difficult to hide: a fatal wound to the neck on the battlefield. Ambrose had to drag his king into a tent under the guise he'd still been breathing and physically force the medics to leave for their own good. If they'd witnessed him return from death, he would have had them killed.

Instead, people began to think Ambrose had some magical ability to heal. He'd been observed healing admirably from scrapes himself, though he'd never been so invulnerable as the rumors claimed. It meant they did not know the witch king was immortal, but that had another adverse effect: They saw Ambrose as the key to the king's vitality, and didn't know just how right they were.

So long as you live, so will I.

It appeared Morcant's idolatry of the witch king had gone much further than they'd known. He'd found a way to cheat death, too.

Emery didn't move, didn't speak. He abandoned his liar's facade and stared, uncomprehending, eyes wide.

"Dad," said Hellebore. She did an admirable job subduing her feelings, but Ambrose could see her shaking.

"You both look as though you've seen a ghost," Morcant said. "Which is appropriate for today's lesson. We'll be taking a little field trip. Give me a moment."

He reached for his tithe belt, but he wasn't wearing it. Probably because the acidic bog had destroyed its contents.

Ambrose couldn't quite believe he planned on moving forward with their lesson as usual. He kept waiting for some punishment, or for Morcant to call him out from his invisible hiding place.

Grim Wolf, he'd said before dying.

"I appear to have misplaced my tithe belt. Would you lend me some bone powder, Hellebore?"

At the sound of her name, she jerked into motion, fumbling a liberal amount into her father's palm.

Emery still hadn't moved, watching Morcant as though he was a mirage. He couldn't say anything, couldn't ask the question they both wished to know.

How did you do it? How are you here?

Morcant went up the steps. Portals couldn't be opened within the mausoleum's wards, so he waited until he got to the top. He tossed the bone powder in the doorway, blocking the one exit from the mausoleum. "Come now, we have to make up for lost time."

The other initiates obediently filed through the portal. Hellebore lingered a moment longer until her father nodded, and she went through.

Emery hadn't moved. The narrow stairway would force him to squeeze past Morcant, a nearness that felt perilous.

They didn't know what he had planned, but it wouldn't be pleasant.

Portals didn't transmit sound, so none of the other initiates heard Morcant say, "Feel free to bring your little pet."

Emery stayed at the foot of the stairs, frozen in place. Ambrose, invisible behind him, didn't wish for the other students to see him, nor did he want Emery to feel alone.

He touched Emery's hand, balled into a fist. Emery jerked at first, surprised, then relaxed into his touch. Low in his ear, Ambrose said, "If you want me to kill him again, it can be done."

"I wouldn't," said Morcant, the tunnel capturing the sound of Ambrose's voice. "It would only be temporary, and things would get awfully messy if I had to raise assault charges against you. Very difficult to finish your education from behind bars."

"What are you going to do to me?" Emery said softly.

"I'm teaching a lesson, as usual. We'll see if you learn it." He paused, tilting his head. "I'm not going to kill you, if that's what you're worried about. That wouldn't teach you anything."

They had little choice. With the only exit blocked, their best hope was to portal somewhere else the moment they emerged on the other side.

"After you," Morcant said.

Emery hesitated, then released Ambrose's hand and started up the steps. The passage wasn't wide enough to walk two abreast, so Ambrose kept as close to his back as possible. Morcant ushered them through.

Ambrose, preparing for the momentary pain of separation the portal would cause, didn't notice Morcant slapping a hand to the back of Emery's neck until it was too late. Emery let out a yell of pain. Ambrose could do nothing from his disadvantaged position on the lower step, but he could see the mark left behind on Emery's neck. A rune glowed like cinders there.

"Just to ensure you don't try to run," Morcant said. "You'll only be able to use my portals, not your own. The spell will wear off after an hour."

Emery rubbed the back of his neck, the mark fading from an ember glow to sooty black.

Ambrose's heart hammered. They would have to endure whatever punishment Morcant had devised.

Ambrose had once wondered why Morcant tolerated Emery's impunity so often when he seemed perfectly capable of getting Emery imprisoned or expelled, considering both his wealth of power and his ability to manipulate the perceptions of the faculty.

Now, he saw that it was a game, the aim of which was to control Emery completely.

These thoughts frayed the weave of Ambrose's convictions, as his mind drew unerring parallels to someone else he'd known.

Emery said, "Fine."

A HEX FOR HUNGER

139

Morcant put his back to the wall to let Emery pass. Just as Emery reached the portal, Ambrose wound an arm around his waist. They passed through as one, the momentary tear at Ambrose's collar barely making him wince. They stumbled out the other side into a graveyard.

Ambrose didn't remove his arm right away. He whispered quickly, "Tell me what I can do to protect you."

Emery's heart beat so hard Ambrose could feel it through his back where they were pressed together. "Just don't let him kill me?"

The tremor in his voice made Ambrose ache. He'd always had a weakness for those who entrusted him with their protection. What's more, Emery hadn't compelled him. He wasn't being ordered. He was being asked.

His chest felt like an oven, hot and hard to breathe.

"I can do that."

He released Emery just as Morcant came through the portal behind them.

"Initiates," Morcant said. "Today we will be practicing the simple art of spirit summoning. Though these spells aren't terribly complex, they do require a degree of . . . shall we call it sensitivity? To the arcane, occult, and otherworldly. This sensitivity can atrophy with disuse, so consider this exercising the muscle. Now, follow me."

The necropolis where the guild held their vigils had weathered untold centuries, but here the graves shone with polish, some with detailed portraits above lengthy inscriptions. Aside from a few older plots, most seemed well-kept, the gardens of aster and autumn crocus tidy and free of leaf litter.

Morcant approached a tombstone with fresh flowers laid in front of it. He'd already prepared the spot. Silk covered the gravestone like a funeral shroud, with a candle and a parcel of leaves and twine placed on top of it.

"This exercise will be old hat for our veteran guild members, so . . . Emery. Care to give our newest students a demonstration?"

Emery narrowed his eyes at the tableau. Ambrose understood his skepticism. As punishments went, this one was suspiciously benign.

"Well?" Morcant prompted.

Emery swallowed and took a step forward. Ambrose couldn't follow him through the crowd of initiates to the grave plot, not without bumping into someone. He edged around the perimeter.

Morcant produced a matchbox and held it out. Emery took it like it might be a stinging nettle, but nothing happened. He struck a match and lit the candle, then ignited the string of the wrapped parcel.

"Dried hawthorn leaves, marigold petals, and wild blackberries," Morcant explained. "Burn these to thin the veil between this world and the next. The tithes are helpful, but not required. All that is truly required comes from within the witch. Magical theory disputes what, in lieu of physical tithes, allows some witches an easier time communicating with the dead than others. A popular theory is that witches with more empathy and love draw spirits to them like moths to flame. But we'll likely never know for certain."

If that were true, Morcant would be incapable. Ambrose studied the students' faces, wondering what they made of all this. Saoirse listened intently, her expression studious, but a little confusion flickered in her face whenever she glanced at Hellebore, who hadn't spoken and looked nearly as uncomfortable as Emery.

The others' faces ranged from confused to exhausted. None of them offered Ambrose an answer to what Morcant intended to do.

"Go ahead, Emery," Morcant said. "Show them how it's done."

The parcel's twine acted like a wick, carrying the flame to the dried herbs within. They caught faster than the leaves woven to encase them, which were still a lively green. It burned like a lantern, glowing from within, the scent making Ambrose's throat itch. In the amber light, a track of sweat ran from Emery's temple to his jaw.

He took a step back from the grave. When he opened his hands, fingers bent into claw shapes as if trying to dredge the earth, the air chilled. Ambrose had to breathe shallowly to avoid making visible clouds of vapor with every exhale.

Emery gritted his teeth, concentrating. A few wisps of ghostly light filtered up from the earth like motes of dust, drifting and converging into mist. Emery paled in their spectral glow.

"It does not normally take so long," Morcant said. "You're out of practice."

"Or getting old," Saoirse jibed. She looked to Hellebore, expecting her to carry on their usual banter, but she seemed in no mood, watching everything with her arms crossed. Not her usual, confident posture but defensive, warding against what was to come.

"Or he's stalling," Morcant said.

Emery clamped his eyes shut and twisted his neck, as if weathering a wave of pain. A few specks of light seemed to drift like rain from the spirit mist, watering the grave. He was losing his grasp on it.

"I hope you haven't developed a sudden phobia of ghosts," Morcant said. "That would be unfortunate for a necromancer."

The initiates tittered nervously. Emery's fingers made the tense, crooked shapes of spider legs as he rallied his concentration. A few more motes of light joined the rest.

Morcant looked like a smug predator watching its prey take one delicate step after another toward an ambush. Ambrose edged closer, ready to intervene if Morcant tried to cast a spell.

"Or," Morcant said, "could it be you're afraid of what this particular spirit has to say?"

"What?" Emery gasped between clenched teeth.

The mist shifted and resolved into a vaguely human shape, completely transparent except for the place its heart would be, and a sound that was half moan, half speech filled the graveyard.

"Y-you!?"

Morcant moved with swift subtlety. His hand vanished into a sleeve. Ambrose didn't know what spell he'd prepared, but he knew he wouldn't let it reach its target.

He ran to place himself between Morcant and Emery, making no attempt to disguise the sound of his footsteps.

The other students startled, the word "ghost" whispered between them, then they shrieked as a gale-force wind blasted through them.

Something shiny had collapsed in Morcant's clenched fist. Ambrose staggered to a stop, bracing against the wind. The students wearing hats held them on, robes flapping. Emery's candle guttered and fell from the tombstone, taking the silk and herbs with it.

A wind spell? Had he done it to interrupt Emery's concentration?

It hadn't worked. Emery still dragged at the ephemeral scraps of spirit, the assembled glow hanging in the air before him, but something made the initiates stir. A hush fell over them. Ambrose followed their gazes to the tombstone's inscription, revealed when the silk shroud had been blown away.

He knew the moment Emery's focus had diverted long enough to read it, because the air suddenly warmed with his lost concentration.

The assembled dust of the spirit scattered to the wind.

Emery stared at the grave. He looked stricken, worse than he had upon seeing Morcant walk down those steps, hale and whole.

Ambrose didn't understand the nature of the war unfolding before him, and he couldn't read the inscription himself, but he was sure of one thing.

142   ALISTAIR REEVES

Emery had *known* whoever was buried here.

"Can't do it?" Morcant said. "That's disappointing, when you were once my best and brightest."

Without warning, Emery lunged at him.

CHAPTER 23

Ambrose staggered out of Emery's path, shock temporarily overcoming his instincts to intervene. He'd been so focused on preventing Morcant from harming Emery, it hadn't occurred to him that they might end up in a scenario where it was the other way around.

Emery's fist snapped Morcant's head around. He righted himself quickly, wiping at the blood on his lip.

Emery panted, a tripwire ready to snap, and Morcant said, "Why, you little rat."

Emery threw himself at Morcant again with a snarling cry of rage. They collided bodily, the force taking them to the ground. A lock of hair hung madly loose over Emery's forehead as his hands found purchase around Morcant's throat.

It was pointless to choke the man to death, they both knew it, but nothing rational piloted Emery's body. Animal rage, fear—they demanded an outlet and found it by squeezing the air from Morcant's lungs.

Morcant scrabbled for something in his robes. Hellebore rushed in, preparing to cast some spell as he rolled, managing to pin Emery under him. He withdrew something glinting and sharp from his pocket.

Ambrose didn't have the time to assess the risk in revealing himself. The sight of the knife spurred him into motion. He dragged Morcant off just as he lashed out with the knife, nicking Emery's arm. A shallow cut. Ambrose threw Morcant to the grass. Emery, still not returned to his senses, lunged after him, but Ambrose caught him by the shoulders. He fought against the restraint, his whole body shuddering.

The altercation only lasted the space of some seconds, but it must have looked inexplicably strange to the spectators—as if an invisible force had thrown Morcant aside and frozen Emery in place.

The initiates wore identical looks of horror and alarm. In any other circumstances, it would have given Ambrose away, except they were in a graveyard for the express purpose of summoning spirits.

"Was that a ghost?"

"Can't be. Poltergeist?"

Convenient. It wouldn't hold up to scrutiny if Ambrose continued this way.

Morcant spat blood into the grass. "Neither. It was the wind. As Emery just artfully demonstrated, he's out of practice at even the most basic spells and must resort to cruder tools, like his fists."

Emery breathed harshly, his chest rising and falling under Ambrose's arm, but he wasn't looking at Morcant anymore. He looked at the gravestone.

"Fucking bastard," he said under his breath, but the fires of his rage had extinguished, leaving a wretched despair in their ashes.

The initiates all whispered back and forth, their voices like wind through the leaves. Ambrose caught snatches of conversation.

"Craig Kendrick. Who's that?"

"Student. Went missing."

"Turned up dead, though. Real gruesome."

"Did Emery know him or something?"

"Don't think so."

Emery had never mentioned a Craig Kendrick, but that didn't mean they hadn't known each other. Had they been friends?

Or more than friends. Craig was a boy's name.

Ambrose convinced himself that the twist in his stomach was solely due to the cruelty of tricking Emery into speaking with the spirit of a dead lover, and not because Emery having a lover made him jealous.

"What do you want me to do with him?" Hellebore helped her father up by the elbow and awaited instruction—not with eager zeal but grim anticipation.

Ambrose bristled, awaiting Morcant's verdict.

"Nothing," Morcant said. "Let him go."

Hellebore blinked. "What? Really?"

"He is troubled. Punishing him will only make it worse. I have tried teaching, I have tried compassion. Neither worked, so now I will try

A HEX FOR HUNGER
145

patience." He looked at Emery with a glittering sadness in his eyes. "I understand you've had challenging relationships with teachers before."

"Stop," said Emery in a raw voice.

"But I wish you wouldn't use us as scapegoats for your anger toward him. We aren't responsible for the way you feel. Certainly not the way you act. It's a shame you behave this way, when you showed such promise."

He turned away, wiping at his lip. It wasn't even swollen, healed already, but under the blood and in the dark, the others wouldn't notice. "You may go, but I expect an apology when you return."

Emery had been holding his breath. Ambrose felt the moment it all rushed out of him in a derisive laugh, hollow and hopeless.

Morcant marched off into the graveyard. The other initiates followed dutifully, casting Emery wary looks like he might snap on them next. The last to go was Hellebore.

"Pathetic," she muttered.

The word lacked heat, but it burned Emery all the same. His eyes were sleeplessly bruised. Harrowed and humiliated, he hung his head to look away from them.

This was the true punishment. Morcant had rigged the spirit summoning to make it more difficult and used the pain of some buried history to goad Emery into a reaction, alienating him from his peers, making him look violent, dangerous.

Now, whatever judgments Morcant passed down would appear justified. The other students would believe he deserved it.

Ambrose had expected something more physical, like the spell that choked the truth from Emery, or the one that made all his food taste vile, but he was beginning to understand that Morcant's weapons were not all made of spells or steel. He'd found tools that cut the spirit, wounded the heart, and confused the mind. He'd tormented Emery where no one watched, then made him look unreasonable. Reactionary. Crazy.

Ambrose's heart hammered. His mind turned to a buried memory of a horse's flaxen hide shivering under his hands, just before—

It wasn't the same, he told himself, casting the recollection aside.

Out from under Morcant's scrutiny, all of Emery's strength fled him. He slackened, his weight sinking against Ambrose.

"Tell me what you need."

"I need to go home."

They had to walk until the rune placed on Emery's neck faded. Ambrose offered to carry him, but Emery refused. Too proud, though the fight with Morcant had taken its toll. He needed Ambrose's arm for support, his body warming the expanse of Ambrose's ribs.

They struggled a half mile before Morcant's spell wore off. Looking very ill, Emery took them the rest of the way home through a portal.

Once safely within the wards, his strength failed him entirely. Ambrose caught him on his way to the floor.

"I can walk."

Ambrose lifted him in spite of his protests. He laid Emery on the sofa and pulled a blanket over him.

"Where are your bandages?" The cut on Emery's arm still bled.

"Bathroom cabinet, underneath the sink."

Ambrose had to rummage through bottles and rolls of paper towel until he found a green box containing bandages. He returned to the sofa and sat on the edge, holding out his hand. Emery looked like a starving stray animal being offered food. Wary, yet wanting.

Slowly, he held it out. Ambrose took it and examined the cut. He could see no signs of poison or infection setting in, and it was mercifully shallow. He took the roll of bandages from the open box at his feet.

Emery said, "There's disinfectant."

He indicated a tube of paste like the kind he'd taught Ambrose to use when cleaning his teeth. Ambrose squeezed a little ointment onto the cut, cleaning it gingerly, then began winding the bandage around it. His knuckles grazed the pulse flickering in Emery's wrist, and Emery met his eyes for a scant second. It was only a fleeting look, but all Ambrose's awareness gathered in his fingertips where they touched.

Emery withdrew his arm. "Thanks."

Ambrose swallowed. The moment felt more dangerous than the tip of a sword under his throat.

He really couldn't feel this way. Not about him.

He got up to leave, and his heart didn't skip—couldn't skip—when Emery grasped his wrist and said, "Stay?"

Ambrose hesitated. If he weighed Emery's faults against his virtues, it would not be difficult to tell which way the scale tipped. He had appointed Ambrose a comfortable, personal chamber of his own. He'd given him good food. He'd rescued Ambrose from drowning.

A HEX FOR HUNGER 147

He'd also killed his familiar, ensnared Ambrose, and used him to murder a dangerous witch who'd now proven himself immortal. After the scene in the graveyard, it was clear he'd been withholding information. A boy called Craig Kendrick had died, and it had something to do with Emery, or Morcant wouldn't have chosen this particular punishment.

The other kindnesses mattered little against the weight of all that.

So why did his heart flutter when Emery held his wrist and asked him to stay?

Why did he sit on the edge of the sofa?

Why did he flip his wrist so he could urge Emery to release it and hold his hand instead?

The cushions sank with his weight, and Emery sank with it, closer to him.

He had to ask. "Who was Craig Kendrick?"

Emery took his hand away. It was a dance back and forth between begging for comfort and being too proud to accept it. "Would you believe me if I said I didn't really know?"

"No."

"Well, it's true. I didn't know him." Emery sucked in a breath. "He was a student here who went missing at the beginning of my first term at Bellgrave. He didn't have many surviving relatives, apparently. Bit of a loner." Emery snorted. "Perfect target, really."

"For Morcant?"

Emery pulled his knees to his chest, picking at a frayed cuticle. "They found his body in late autumn. Somehow, the mortician's log got leaked. They couldn't figure an exact time of death, but they knew he'd been kept for weeks, at least from the day he disappeared. He was thinner when they found him, first of all. Like he'd been starved. And his hair was longer."

Ambrose recalled the cells in the catacombs. "Did they know how he was killed?"

"It was hard to miss. He had a massive stab wound. A through and through, back to chest, but it was practically the length of his spine. *Stab* wound. Some of his insides were cut clean through, but the knife would have to be wide as his torso was long to make a wound like that."

"Magic?"

"No. There were hints of magic, but no concrete signature. It had been cleaned of anything traceable. They found a chunk of metal in his chest." Emery's expression darkened. "Tip of the knife broke off, probably."

Ambrose absorbed that. He'd never seen anything similar during his time with the witch king, but then, the witch king had rarely used magic or knives. Only Ambrose.

He shook the thought away. The witch king hadn't *used* him. He'd served voluntarily.

"What does all that have to do with you?" he asked.

"Do you really have to ask?"

"I want to know."

"Why?"

"It is easier to protect someone I can trust, and who trusts me." It was only half of the truth. *I want to know you. I want to trust you.* He shouldn't, but he did.

"And if what I tell you makes you trust me less, or at least think less of me?"

"Knowing you're withholding things from me makes both those true."

The night sky through the hole in the ceiling was too velvet dark for stars or moonshine to light Emery's features, the shadows carving his face with dread.

"The rats," he said finally. "The ones we sacrifice in our initiation ritual."

"What about them?"

"They weren't rats."

CHAPTER 24

Ambrose took a moment to comprehend what Emery meant. The rats weren't rats.

Craig Kendrick turned up dead with a stab wound as if from a massive dagger.

A massive dagger, or else he had been transfigured very small at the time of the killing blow.

"They're human?" Ambrose asked.

Emery nodded.

"All of them?"

"He never said. But I think so."

"Where does he get his victims from? Surely a slew of deaths and disappearances from the same area draws notice."

"I think Craig Kendrick was an anomaly. I can't be certain, but I think Morcant tried to recruit him, but he got wise to what Morcant was up to and became a loose end. The others? I have no idea. I think . . . I think he tries to find the sort of people few will report missing." He swallowed. "Could have been me."

Ambrose had never ventured to ask after Emery's family. By now, it seemed clear he didn't have any. He waited for Emery to say more, and when he didn't, decided to leave it for now. He didn't like to pry, or to be the one pried open.

"Did you know?"

"At the time? Of course not. I thought it was a rat. I didn't want to kill an animal, either."

Ambrose paused, a recollection floating to the surface in his mind. "All the ghosts of rats in the castle, you said they were new."

Emery's mouth twisted ruefully. "Call it a desperate act of a guilty conscience. I tried to bring the rat back. Didn't realize the grounds were beset by a plague, once upon a time. Perhaps I . . . overdid the spell."

Ambrose tilted his head, trying to envision that youthful version of Emery. The one so aggrieved by the death of a supposed rat, he raised an entire castle of rats from the dead. The image was so at odds with the Emery of today, who'd tithed his familiar and tried to murder his mentor.

But then, Ambrose didn't recognize the man he'd become when compared to the idealistic boy he'd once been, either.

"Why did you?"

"He was still putting on his kindly mentor face at the time. Told me, so long as I was quick, it would be painless."

The witch king had said the same of Emery.

We are not the same.

Emery continued, "Afterwards, when no one else was around? That was the first time he dropped the act. Told me it hurt him to see me upset, and it was unfair to care more about the rat's pain than his." Emery screwed up his face. "The mental gymnastics were spectacular, but I couldn't see what was happening while in the middle of it. When someone's only ever been kind, the first time they're not, you still think the kind version is the true one. I trusted him, so . . ." A helpless shrug.

Ambrose shifted uncomfortably. His mind jumped to the witch king gifting him a filly. "When did you find out the rat was a boy?"

"There was a professor who tried to help me. Do you remember? After getting him fired and destroying my reputation, Morcant told me the truth. If I tried to bring anyone else into our business, he still had the murder weapon. All the evidence he'd need to have me put away."

"He might have revealed as much to all his students tonight if you'd successfully raised Craig's spirit," Ambrose murmured. "Did nobody investigate or think to ask the ghost who killed him?"

Emery shook his head and launched into an explanation. Most spirits hardly remembered anything about their lives or how they died. Certain objects of significance or music could trigger a memory, but they seldom remembered *everything*. Poltergeists were slightly different, anchored to the world of the living and retaining their original personalities, but most spirits were like the threads from an unwoven tapestry. They could be rewoven, but rarely. The threads retained echoes of emotions they experienced in life, hence why some were more reactive and aggressive while others were peaceful.

Ambrose understood, but it still raised certain questions. "I see why the ghost might not threaten his secrets, but you can. You've involved me. That's proof enough the secrecy pact is fallible. So, if Morcant can have you imprisoned for murder, why risk your continued interference?"

"I didn't know." Emery pressed his knuckles to a rising headache. "Not until tonight."

Ambrose waited.

"What does he have to fear from me?" Emery asked. "He's immortal."

Ambrose knew all too well how fallible immortality could be. Morcant's overconfidence could prove an advantage to them. "He isn't invulnerable. Whatever spell he's used, it can be undone. We just need to determine how he's achieved immortality in the first place."

"I don't know where to start. I don't even know whether I have any right to ask for your help." Emery wet his lips and looked away, some of his hair falling into his eyes. "It's hard to trust someone who's done the things you have, but I started thinking last night that I . . . haven't been the most trustworthy, either. Or kind." His expression crumpled, as if pained. "But you're the only hope I have."

Ambrose had been associated with many things in his time. Power, justice, and retribution, he'd thought. Fear, doom, and carnage, according to history. A living nightmare.

Never hope.

Katzica, lying on the rug by the fire, lifted her head from her paws and whined.

Emery groaned and rubbed his head. "I really don't feel well. I'm freezing. Are you?"

"The evening's exhausted you. You should rest. I'll start a fire."

As he piled two logs on and lit a wax ball of kindling beneath them, Emery's labored breaths filled the quiet room. He didn't sound well at all.

"Should I bring my blankets in here?" Ambrose asked.

"What?"

"I'll sleep in the armchair, if you don't wish to be alone." Never mind that Ambrose had no intention of letting him sleep on his own when his breathing sounded like that.

"Don't be daft. We have beds."

Ambrose wouldn't risk separate rooms in case Emery's health worsened, and they *certainly* couldn't share a bed. "I am used to the floor."

Emery had started to move. Or tried to. He got to his feet and swayed. "Wait. I can't feel—"

His knees crumpled beneath him. Ambrose narrowly caught him to soften the fall, but something was wrong.

Panic laced Emery's voice. "I can't move my legs."

"What?"

"I can't stand."

Ambrose swore. His eyes darted to the bandage on Emery's arm. Had the knife been dipped in a slow-acting paralysis agent?

Katzica stood and let out a low growl, padding toward the door. Outside, footsteps approached.

"The wards." Emery's voice was hoarse. "Oh hell, the wards."

"What?"

"They have my blood." Emery looked at his bandaged arm. "They have my blood, they can get through."

Emery's hand had no strength or control to grip Ambrose's as he tried to get to his feet.

"I'll carry you."

"Too late for that. They'll know you're here. You have to hide. You have to sneak up on them."

"What about you?"

Katzica growled more viciously as the steps got closer and the door handle turned. They'd run out of time.

Emery's expression flared with panic. **"Hide!"**

The magic hit like a thunderclap. Ambrose fought, but the arcane collar throttled him into obedience. Invisibility cloaked him. Though he saw the sense in hiding when a deftly cast hex could spell disaster for them both, it chafed his instincts to leave Emery helpless. The collar dragged him into a sheltered cove of books from which he could see the whole room—Emery, collapsed and still tangled in robes and blankets, and the entrance hallway.

The front door cracked open.

Katzica lunged at the intruder, but they were faster. A spell slithered like an intoxicating scent into the hound's nose, and she reverted to the tail-wagging domesticity of her breed, even trotting alongside the witch who'd charmed her.

Hellebore stalked into the room. She wore leather gloves over her hands and a black cloak, the hood of which she swept off as she entered. Her eyes skipped over Emery and searched the shadows. "Where's your new friend?"

"Ambrose—hngh!" Emery's speech truncated with a grunt of pain. Hellebore's stoat familiar had raced across the floor and bitten Emery's ankle. At the same time, Hellebore snapped her fingers, the sulfuric scent of a spell poisoning the air. Her familiar's teeth must have been laced with a tithe, because when Emery opened his mouth, no sound followed.

"Sorry, I forgot I don't care," she said. "You'll find it harder to give him orders when you can't speak. Seeing as he's not your friend, just the servant you resurrected to do your bidding, I doubt he'll come to your rescue. But we'll see."

The words itched like a persistent bug bite. They'd once been true. Were they any longer? Had he and Emery not grown closer?

He waited. Better to show himself when she lowered her guard, believing he'd left Emery to her mercy. They didn't know why Hellebore had come, or what Morcant was planning, but this could be their opportunity to find out.

Hellebore circled Emery like a scavenger. Her familiar climbed up her leg to perch on her shoulder, while she stopped at the fire, staring into its light with an unreadable expression. "Why couldn't you just leave well enough alone?"

Emery couldn't answer, but it seemed Hellebore didn't wish for one. She carried on.

"You can't fight him. You definitely can't *kill* him. Everything you try gets us punished. If you'd just followed along, I wouldn't have to—" She broke off, throat constricting around a swallow. Then she reached into her robes and drew out a dagger identical to the ones used in killing the rats for Morcant's ritual.

It had a petal-shaped blade, rusty stains still tarnishing it, and from this distance, Ambrose could see the tip was chipped.

They found a chunk of metal in his chest, though. Tip of the knife broke off, probably.

It was the dagger Emery used to unwittingly kill Craig Kendrick.

Emery's eyes widened. Slouched on the floor, his legs trembled but didn't move with his efforts to rise.

Hellebore said, "Now that you know my dad's secret, he wants me to deal with you."

Emery stilled. He managed a fearful grunt in his throat, but nothing more.

Hellebore turned from the fire and looked at the empty wine bottles scattered across the floor, kicking one. It rung glassily across the stone. "You made it way too easy for him, you know. Drinking yourself stupid. Lashing out at him in front of the other guild members. Falling behind in classes after all that business with the professor."

Emery managed a noise again, this one furious and indignant.

"I know you weren't sleeping with him. Shit, you're not *that* lonely, desperate, and stupid. But everyone else believes it. It won't be hard for them to believe you killed yourself, either."

Ambrose's heart stopped. The fog around Morcant's schemes cleared. Painting Emery as troubled by hexing his pastries with maggots at the charity event, goading him into lashing out in the graveyard in front of his peers—humiliation hadn't been the end goal. It gave everyone the impression Emery's sanity held on by a thread, and now Morcant could cut that thread himself and frame it as a suicide.

Born of a guilty mind, they'd say, when their spells found Emery's blood on the dagger along with Craig Kendrick's.

Ambrose's magic gurgled hungrily at the thought, and the witch king's voice insinuated its way into his mind soon after.

Let him fall. Let her kill him.

Ambrose shuddered. He couldn't bring himself to kill Emery. Could he really stand by and watch Hellebore do it for him?

Emery's face drained of color as Hellebore knelt next to him, her grip white-knuckled on the dagger's handle. Her expression soured.

"I hated you, you know. Every time you got yourself in trouble, I got dragged in. It was my responsibility to keep you in line. I hated you, but not *this much*." She reached for his arm. The dagger shook in her other hand as she pressed it to Emery's vein. "I hate you most of all for this. Because goddammit, Emery, I never, *ever* wanted to kill anyone else. You weren't the only one distraught when you found out about the rats, but did you ever ask? We could have been friends. Could have handled it together." Her voice quavered. "So fuck you."

Emery had enough movement to clench the fist not held by Hellebore. His big, dark eyes searched the shadows for Ambrose, a silent plea in their depths.

Ambrose liked to think he knew his strengths. In his youth, he'd been especially tall for his sex and liked challenging the boys to wrestling competitions, where they would tell him boys were stronger than girls. When he gloatingly won, he could say, "Guess I'm a boy."

He'd prided himself on his strength. Strength and loyalty—the two virtues he clung to.

He did not feel very strong looking into Emery's eyes and being begged wordlessly for help while the witch king ordered him not to. He didn't feel loyal with his heart torn between his oath and this boy he'd only known a fortnight.

Hellebore tilted her head, interpreting correctly the desperate plea in Emery's eyes. "Waiting on the Grim Wolf to save you? If he was going to, I think he would have by now. I wondered if maybe you'd befriended him enough that he'd help you, but I guess we have our answer."

The stricken look of grief on Emery's face carved a hole in Ambrose's heart.

He turns your head in so little time? When you are nothing but a tool at his disposal, when he barters his own survival by risking yours and mine.

Ambrose winced, and his magic licked its lips.

Let her kill him. Is his death not a worthwhile price for the reward of our reunion?

Guilt gnawed on Ambrose's insides. Letting Emery die, failing the witch king, both brought him shame. The former should be easier. He should hate Emery for using the compulsion when he'd said he wouldn't, for dragging him into this cult's business. He shouldn't trust a man who'd murdered a boy and his own familiar.

In his early days of knighthood, Ambrose had viewed the world in idyllic colors, tarnished only by people like the bandits who killed his family. The witch king had rescued him from death and given him the tools and training to become a hero in his own right. A person with the strength to save others rather than requiring passive rescue.

Or so he'd believed . . .

The events of the past days had resurrected memories he wished he could have left in the grave. Memories that forced him to question whether all his years of service to the witch king had really been so virtuous as he'd romanticized them to be.

He'd believed they acted in pursuit of a better future. He'd clung to that belief because abandoning it would mean reconciling with all the things he'd done in service of that belief. Ambrose could not pinpoint the moment he'd realized his heroic aims had been twisted to villainous means, but it was too late now. He couldn't cleanse his sins any more than the moon could make daylight.

That he'd never broken his oath, this was the only virtue left to his rotten name, which even the annals of history had erased in favor of his dread title. *Grim Wolf.*

He'd loved and stayed loyal to the bitter end. He could not abandon his king now.

So he stood and watched as Hellebore pressed the knife to Emery's wrist.

CHAPTER 25

Scarlet bloomed along the dagger's edge, and Emery, who should not have been able to move at all, bolted into sudden motion.

He knocked the dagger flying with his free hand, then swiped the blood from his arm and cast a spell that flung Hellebore back into a pile of books. He made a desperate bid for the dagger, stumbling clumsily under the effects of the paralysis agent. Ambrose didn't know how it had worn off or if Emery had used a spell to clear his system, but Hellebore had all her strength, and her familiar reacted even more quickly. She sprang after him, and the stoat sank its teeth into Emery's wrist just as he reached the dagger.

He recoiled. Hellebore took advantage of his pause, seizing his robes, pinning him to the floor. He rolled to dislodge her. In the ensuing struggle, one of them kicked the dagger. It spun, coming to a stop with its chipped end pointed unerringly at the spot in which Ambrose hid.

They clawed at each other, punching and kicking, attempting to pin the other down. The desperate speed of their exchanged blows left no time to search for the right tithe to cast a spell, nor the time to think of the right one. Hellebore bade her familiar keep back, worried he'd be crushed. He perched on the arm of the sofa, poised to intervene if she needed him.

The scuffle brought them closer to the fire, throwing wild, leaping shadows across the floor, stretching in a macabre dance.

Emery let out a winded gasp. Hellebore, shorter but stronger, had finally got the upper hand as she pinned him with a knee in his stomach. His fist landed a disorienting blow to her head, but it didn't dislodge her. She got her fingers around his throat and pushed his head toward the fire.

Yes, whispered the witch king in anticipation. Ambrose felt his magic rise to the threat of encroaching death like a stray dog scenting raw meat.

He's no saint, Ambrose reminded himself. *He's done horrible things, too. You don't owe him a rescue.*

Yet every bone in his body felt as though they splintered with the effort to hold still and not intervene.

Hellebore's expression twisted with the effort to push Emery's face toward the fire. Ambrose's spell scars burned with the memory of their making. He knew what it felt like to burn.

It was too much.

He thought, *I can't watch this.*

You must! You pledged yourself to me. *You are loyal to* me. *What virtues will you have left if you break your oath? Let him* die.

"Stop *fighting*," Hellebore gritted out. "What do you have to fight for anyway? Your reputation is ruined. He's never going to let you graduate. He got rid of your only ally and killed your familiar."

Ambrose's heart stopped.

He looked at Katzica, soulless and empty, wagging her tail as she watched someone try to kill her witch.

Emery hadn't killed her?

Why would he let Ambrose believe it if it wasn't true? Ambrose racked his mind for any clue he could have picked up on, anything at all, and only recalled the moment with Morcant in the bog.

Even at your most unpredictable, I didn't think you'd be so quick to add a second murder to the blood on your hands.

Ambrose thought the first had been Katzica.

Now he knew it was Craig Kendrick.

Emery hadn't killed either of them, not really. Morcant had been the architect of their fates, and Emery the implement, a circumstance with which Ambrose empathized too keenly.

Why Emery concealed the truth mattered less than the truth itself. He was not the villain of this tale, he was the victim, and Ambrose had misjudged him horribly.

Now he was about to die thinking Ambrose hadn't cared enough to come to his rescue.

Emery managed to let out a noise—not quite a word, the spell still gagging him, but a sound so tragically sad and scared, it spurred Ambrose to action.

A HEX FOR HUNGER 159

He couldn't stand by. He couldn't watch Emery die. Not like this.

But when he went to move, the collar shackled him in place.

He tried again, but his body refused to obey his orders. A frisson of real horror went through him.

The last order Emery gave him was to hide. He'd offered none to follow. Ambrose couldn't help, not even if he wanted to.

Emery didn't realize the folly of his first command, and while Hellebore's spell rendered him mute, he couldn't give a second one.

The thought of standing by while Hellebore killed him was intolerable, but the thought of him dying with the belief Ambrose hadn't cared? Hadn't tried to help?

He struggled against his bonds. They lashed out with punishing echoes of the pain incurred when the collar had been cast upon him. His muscles screamed, pain running molten to the marrow of his bones. He couldn't even speak. The order to *hide* was all-encompassing. He couldn't move, couldn't reveal himself, couldn't do anything to help. Fighting it was fruitless. The collar squeezed until he could hardly breathe.

"What do you have left to fight for anyway?" Hellebore said, tears shining in her eyes as she pushed and pushed and Emery's resistance held for a moment, then his eyes softened, and he surrendered.

Ambrose nearly shut his eyes against it.

The fire licked at Emery's hair. The scent of it burning fumed through the room, and with it a burst of magic. It sucked Emery under like a riptide, dispelling the hex that held him mute.

"Ambrose, **help**—*please!*"

His magical chains snapped. Ambrose broke free, charging across the room. Hellebore whirled around to see him closing in on her but had no time to reach for a tithe. He seized her by her robes and tossed her across the floor. Her back hit the sofa, breath gushing from her lungs in a whoosh. She scrambled back, but Ambrose was already upon her, grasping her throat in his hands.

The magic bared its teeth against her bare neck, and the witch king's reticent murmur greeted Ambrose like an unwelcome wind in winter. *If you cannot kill the boy, the girl will do for now.*

Ambrose recoiled. In the heat of the moment, he didn't know why.

No! the witch king howled.

Hellebore scrambled to her feet, snatched powder from her tithe belt, and opened a portal. Her stoat rushed to her side, snuffling her neck where

Ambrose's fingers had been. Her eyes were wild, dark, and terrified as she cast one baleful look over her shoulder before vanishing through, closing the window behind her.

The ruin fell quiet, except for their harried breathing.

You've ruined it. My chance at resurrection, squandered. Where is your loyalty? Where is your love for your king? I did not think it so weak that it could die alongside you and stay buried after you rose.

Ambrose flinched under the admonishment, a bone-deep ache setting in. He didn't know why he'd hesitated to kill Hellebore. He had far less affection for her than Emery. The witch king wanting Morcant dead, then Emery, then—reluctantly—Hellebore, it tasted like the subtle bitterness of a poison-laced drink.

Emery coughed, the smoky air still thick with the scent of burnt hair. Ambrose jolted from his thoughts and knelt beside him, but Emery nearly backpedaled into the fire, afraid.

"I won't hurt you." Though the witch king still growled that he should.

"Why didn't you intervene sooner?"

Ambrose winced. "You ordered me to hide. Until you told me otherwise, I could do nothing else."

Emery's head snapped to the side as if he'd struck himself. "Shit."

With shame, Ambrose added, "Though I was slow to try . . ."

He couldn't tell if Emery's expression looked mistrustful or just plain hurt.

"Why?"

Katzica, no longer ensorcelled, sheepishly tucked her head under Emery's elbow and gave his chin an apologetic lick.

"Because I thought you'd killed her," Ambrose said. "Your own familiar. I thought you hid more from me. I didn't know if I could . . ."

"Trust me," Emery finished for him. He stroked Katzica's floppy ears, giving her a smile that looked more like a frown. "I suppose neither of us are given to trust easily."

"What really happened to her?" Ambrose asked.

"She tried to protect me."

Ambrose waited for more.

"After the professor who tried to help me was dismissed, Morcant sought to punish me. I was still living in the dorms. It was easy for him to hex my food whenever he wanted to. Only, Katzica often sneaked a bite to test them for poisons herself. I told her not to, but—" He looked away and pretended he wasn't disguising tears in the crook of his elbow. The crack in his voice gave them away. "It probably would have only made me sick, but it killed her."

Ambrose looked around them at the empty wine bottles. He remembered his first night, watching Emery drink in front of a man he didn't trust. An idea came to him.

"Is that how you broke through the paralysis agent Morcant cut you with? You haven't been drinking wine. You've been inuring yourself."

"Mm. I'd take microdoses of anything I thought Morcant might use against me. Clearly, I didn't do a good enough job with paralysis poisons. I'll have to up my dosage of those."

Katzica whined, licking his chin. Ambrose regarded the hound. She'd loved her witch dearly to continue miming behaviors she'd perform in life to comfort him. She'd protected him with the same devotion Ambrose had the witch king, and died for it. Only Emery had mourned her fiercely and desperately enough he couldn't quite let her go. He'd raised her, just as he'd raised all the rats in Bellgrave. "You don't like hurting things," Ambrose murmured.

"I know it sounds ridiculous given how many times I've tried to kill Morcant."

Ambrose didn't answer but privately recalled how, in his first year of killing for the witch king, he'd taken ill so badly the physicians thought he wouldn't survive, and the witch king's attempts to heal him only served to make him sicker.

"I don't want to kill anyone," Emery said. "I just don't know how else I'll ever be free of him if I don't." Emery gave Ambrose a searching, uncertain look. "For a second, I thought you would kill Hellebore. But you didn't."

"No. I didn't." He still wasn't sure what that meant for him or the witch king. He chewed the inside of his cheek before finally asking what had plagued him since Hellebore first revealed it. "Why didn't you tell me the truth about Craig Kendrick? About Katzica?"

Outside, the insects sang more quietly, and even the fire crackled with softer intensity. A vein pulsing rapidly in Emery's throat was the only sign the question distressed him. Finally, he said, "I was afraid of you, you know."

Ambrose didn't see how that was an answer.

"Morcant had us read plenty of history books about you. They depict you as the bloodthirsty right hand of the witch king. I thought you liked killing, and that you'd kill me if not for this." He pulled the finger bone from his pocket and held it up between them, a pale sliver in the dark room. "Then I met you, and you seemed so—*sweet*. A little overzealous when you were protecting me, but good-spirited. I didn't expect it. Didn't trust it, either. But I should have known the history books only had half the story. You don't like hurting people either, do you?"

Ambrose might have felt less vulnerable if he'd been carved open with a scalpel. "Only when it's necessary."

"If I'd known that . . ." Emery gave a mirthless laugh. "I didn't tell you the truth about Katzica because I was afraid of you, and thought it would be better if you were afraid of me, too. I thought you'd hesitate before betraying me if you thought I was just as ruthless as your former master. But as you've so sensitively pointed out before, I'm a terrible actor."

That was not a wholly terrible quality if it meant his lies were easily spotted. Ambrose felt a dash of self-reproach that he hadn't realized the truth about Katzica sooner, but it had been his very first impression of Emery, before getting to know him.

"You're not afraid of me anymore," Ambrose murmured.

Emery flushed. "Well. I figured, if you hesitated to kill someone like *Morcant*, of all people, you might not be as gleefully murdery as the history books say." He hugged his knees, leaning forward so their faces were much closer than before. "I'm sorry I forced you to."

"I would have done it anyway."

"I know. So I'm doubly sorry. Looking back, I treated you abhorrently. Condescending. Controlling." He huffed a dry laugh. "No different from how Morcant treated me." Then his voice got very quiet. "I don't want to become like him."

He sounded afraid. Perhaps it was easy, when treated cruelly, to become cruel yourself. Ambrose studied the inky black of his hands and tried not to consider how that might apply to him, but it was becoming difficult to ignore all these nagging comparisons.

"You aren't anything like him," he said.

Emery looked at him. He wet his lips. Ambrose found himself enraptured by the sheen left on his mouth, the smoldering flames reflected in his dark eyes. His voice came out hoarse when he said, "I want to promise you something."

"What?"

"I'll never use the compulsion again."

Ambrose's heart gave a weakly hopeful knock against his sternum.

"I don't expect you to believe me," Emery went on. "I'd break the spell if I knew how. Maybe we can figure that out, but for now—" He reached into his robes and drew out the tether, holding it out in his open palm. It still had the ridiculous pink ribbon tied in a bow around it. "I want to give you this."

Ambrose's breathing came shallow and heady as he looked at that fragile bit of bone laid across Emery's open hand, innocuous and innocent. As if he were offering to let Ambrose borrow a quill or a pint of milk.

He reached out. His fingertip only barely brushed the bone when the command blazed through him.

Kill Emery.

And the collar gave an alarming jerk.

CHAPTER 26

When Ambrose had completed his training, the witch king rewarded him with the gift of a mare with a coat of flaxen gold called Primrose.

"The Two Roses" they'd been called, as they'd gone into battle together. She had been a magnificent steed, soft to his heel, trusting of his every direction. She'd been particularly fond of strawberries.

He'd reared her himself and ridden her for five years, until the day he erred. In maneuvering her away from an assailant's oncoming spear, he'd left the witch king open to attack. Ambrose had dismounted quickly enough to dispatch the attacker himself, but to protect his horse over his king had been a grave transgression. One the witch king couldn't forgive.

He'd ordered Ambrose to kill Primrose. She'd been so trusting as he ran his hand along her flank one last time.

Emery looked just as open and trusting as he offered Ambrose the tether.

The collar choked, urging Ambrose to reach out and rend him apart, just as he had with Primrose.

It pained me to see you mourn her, but we could never afford the privileges of even one mistake. Just as we cannot afford your hesitation now. Kill him.

Ambrose recoiled. Whether because the witch king was not fully realized enough for the compulsion to work, or because Emery still held the tether preventing Ambrose from harming him, Ambrose couldn't tell.

He snatched his hand back as though the bone had burned him. His magic came to a boil in his blood, and the witch king's voice screamed.

No! Take it, you must take it! It is mine. *It is* ours.

"Ambrose?" Emery looked worried. "What is it?"

Ambrose shuddered.

During the altercation with Hellebore, he'd struggled between his duty to resurrect the witch king and his growing desire to protect Emery. He still did not know how to reconcile the two, but deep in the marrow of his bones, he understood that if he took the tether for himself, he might not have the choice. It soured Ambrose's longing for a reunion, if it came at the cost of Emery's life and what was left of Ambrose's soul.

Emery slowly curled a fist around the bone and withdrew it. "Ambrose?"

"It's nothing."

A gradual metamorphosis happened in the subtleties of Emery's expression, a softness which deepened the lines around his mouth, the heaviness of his brows. "Sometimes, I think I can trust you to protect me from Morcant. Other times, I'm not sure I trust you to protect me from yourself."

Ambrose cringed. The witch king's voice railed and screamed like a gale, furious he'd surrendered another opportunity. The half-starved magic seemed to turn inward for sustenance, turning its teeth on Ambrose for lack of outside nourishment.

He couldn't tell Emery that the bloodlust was not his own. *It isn't me, just my dead master who insists that killing you will bring him back.* If he tried to explain the witch king's voice, the way his spirit seemed to linger within his very marrow, Emery would think him mad and mistrust him all the more.

He wanted to tell Emery *something*, though. They stood on the precipice of something deeper than the strained bargain they'd struck from the moment Ambrose rose from the grave, and if the magic hungered for death, Ambrose was *starved* for whatever scrap of trust and friendship he could savor.

"You once asked me how my magic works. How it sustains itself without a constant supply of tithes." He held up his arm, flexing his inky fingers. "I don't know for certain, but it always feels . . . hungry. Hungriest when I'm about to kill someone, and most sated directly after, though not for long. More often I feel sick, as if I overindulged."

"So the magic takes tithes from the people you kill? A cycle of sacrifice to sustain itself?"

"Perhaps. The witch king never explained it in full. I am likely too dull-minded to understand magical theory in detail."

"You seem anything but dull-minded to me."

"I am no great witch."

Emery studied him, a wary edge to his tone. "Are you telling me the magic lusts for my blood?"

Ambrose nodded. It was at least half the truth.

"But you cannot act upon it while I hold the arcane leash?"

Ambrose nodded again.

"And am I right in saying . . . you don't *want* to do as the magic bids you?" Emery suddenly seemed fragile as a mayfly. "You don't want to kill me?"

"I want to protect you." This, at least, was true.

Emery looked momentarily overcome, dipping his chin to avoid Ambrose's eyes. The firelight on the angles of his face painted him in the strokes of a fallen angel, and suddenly it was not the urge to kill Ambrose had to wrestle down, but the urge to run his thumb down the steep line of Emery's cheek bone to the dimples around his mouth.

"I want to believe you," Emery said.

"I understand why you might not," Ambrose said. He gestured to the arcane leash still clutched in Emery's fist. "When that is the only thing between us and self-destruction."

Emery let out a dry laugh. He twirled the arcane leash. "Well. It certainly complicates things, doesn't it?"

"What can be done about it?"

"I could research a means to undo the spell which binds you, but if it's tied to your magic, it would leave you without your abilities."

"That seems . . . unwise while Morcant is still alive."

"Should I hide it?"

Ambrose hesitated before putting words to the truth in his heart. "I'd prefer it in your hands over anyone else's."

He thought he heard a quiet hiss in the recesses of his mind and knew he might pay for this later.

Emery looked touched. "All right." His eyes sharpened with resolve. "What about this? I will be its custodian for now, but only until we find a way to remove its curse without leaving you vulnerable, and under the condition I never use it against you."

In spite of old instincts which scoffed at the notion Emery would keep his word, Ambrose's heart gave a hopeful, dangerous leap.

This thing between them, it wasn't trust. Emery had used Ambrose before. Ambrose still heard the voice of his old master ordering him to kill

A HEX FOR HUNGER 167

Emery. The leash was a thin boundary between them. Ambrose could not bite the hand that held it without suffering the collar's choke, and Emery couldn't trust that his attack dog's teeth wouldn't turn against him if he loosened his grip.

No, what they had wasn't trust, but if the stalemate of their mutually assured destruction was the closest thing to trust Ambrose could have, he would gorge himself on it. If a tenuous accord was the only substitute for intimacy he could find, he'd feast. Even as he thought, *You will break your promise. Everyone always does*; a bloom of tender affection unfurled in his heart, and he hungered for it more desperately than his magic lusted for blood.

"Agreed?" said Emery, holding out a hand to shake.

His skin was fine as silk under Ambrose's calluses. "Agreed."

Before they could contemplate what to do about Morcant, they had to reinstate the wards protecting Emery's home.

"They have my blood, so mine won't work anymore," Emery said.

He'd changed into practical clothes for walking the perimeter of the ruin—an oversized cable-knit jumper, rubber boots, and jeans, which clung to his long legs in a manner Ambrose deliberately did not notice.

"I could steal something powerful from the apothecary, but they won't have anything with the same longevity as flesh-and-blood tithes. Perhaps I can reinforce it with—"

"You could use mine," Ambrose interrupted.

Emery scowled, shaking his head. "No."

Ambrose rolled up his sleeves anyway.

"It's quite a lot of blood," Emery protested. "And it never ceases to unsettle me that you offer it up so willingly."

"I'm accustomed to it."

"That is exactly why it unsettles me."

Ambrose held out his arm, but Emery pushed it away. "It's not something I'd ask of anyone."

"You're not asking, I'm offering."

"I had to smear mine around the entire perimeter. It took a while. I went through, like, six pints of sports drink—*oh Christ.*"

Emery had a small switch-knife on his tithe belt used for harvesting plant cuttings, and Ambrose had seized it to unflinchingly draw a line over the thin skin of his wrist. Blood welled, dripping around his arm in a scarlet bracelet.

"Ambrose!" Emery took his arm, crushing something from his tithe belt over it in a wisp of silvery spell magic. "You could have at least let me sterilize the knife first."

"We were wasting time when Morcant could find you any moment."

"Fine. Okay. All right, well, come here," Emery said. He gently daubed the blood already dripping from the cut onto two fingers and inscribed runes onto the walls of his ruin, but as he cast the first of them, his brow scrunched.

"What?" Ambrose said.

"That's only one ward, and it's far stronger than mine were."

"Because I gave it to you," Ambrose said. "Gifted tithes make for stronger magic."

Emery drew another symbol on the next wall. "How do you know that?"

"The witch king taught me."

Emery went oddly silent at that.

In the end, he only needed one ward per wall. With the ruin protected, they retreated inside, and Emery went to get the box of bandages and antiseptic, which was getting a great deal of use lately. He sat Ambrose down at the kitchen table and pressed a clean compress to the wound to staunch the bleeding.

"You didn't have to cut so deep."

"You said you needed a lot."

"Before I knew there was some old-world magic about gifts that would make your blood more powerful than mine." While he applied pressure to the compress, his thumb found a raised snarl of scar tissue already there. He thoughtlessly brushed along the seam of flesh.

Ambrose studied the floor. The moment stirred reminders of similar encounters with the witch king, where tending one another's wounds after battle were the only times they were permitted to touch one another without arousing suspicion.

Emery's touch was different. Less inhibited. Curious. "Were all of these for the witch king?"

"Most."

"The rest?"

"Battles."

Emery checked the cut and found it had clotted enough to stop bleeding. "He was more monstrous to you than Morcant was to me."

A HEX FOR HUNGER
169

"That isn't true." Ambrose rushed to his king's defense. "All that I suffered, I did in service of a cause we both believe in."

Emery raised an eyebrow. "And that is?"

"A better world."

Emery laughed dryly. His fingers had once again found a lattice of scars just beneath Ambrose's elbow. "And you trusted someone who did this to know what a better world would look like?"

All Ambrose's accustomed protests—about the need to sacrifice, the nobility of service to a higher power than oneself—died when Emery crunched the shed skin of a snake in his fist to draw on a spell, which glowed between his fingers like a caged star. He smoothed his open palm over the cut, healing it partially like waves wearing smooth a trench in the sand. He paused, still holding Ambrose's arm in that frustratingly tender grip. "You still care for him, don't you?"

Emery had aimed the question precisely. It pinned Ambrose in place. He'd seen evidence this world tolerated people like him far better than his era ever had, but it was another thing to express out loud something he'd kept secret until the day he'd died—a complicated bond between him and a man he'd given all his devotion and received an axe to the heart for, a bond which felt anathema to the feelings evoked by the idle brush of Emery's thumb over his scars.

In the end, he could only speak the closest approximation of the truth. "He is my king."

Emery's nod contained its own hidden feelings.

They prepared for sleep in weary silence. Before Emery closed his bedroom door, he lingered, as if reluctant to be alone.

Ambrose felt the same, afraid of what he might face in the solitude of his room, which was not solitude at all when he shared his head with another.

He hadn't the chance to ask if Emery desired company before he said goodnight and hurriedly shut his door.

Ambrose sequestered himself in his own room. Alone. Before he got changed into sleep clothes, before he got into bed, he waited.

The witch king's presence made the air thin and hard to breathe. He existed within and without, impossible to ignore.

Into the silence, Ambrose whispered, "I'm sorry."

You've forsaken me, your king.

"No."

You've cast me aside in favor of another.

"*No!*"

Don't lie, the witch king hissed, his presence so thick in Ambrose's throat it was difficult to speak through it. *I feel how your heart warms to a morsel of comfort or a kind word from him. You have thrown away two opportunities to save me instead of him.*

Ambrose shuddered with a wave of memory. Prostrating himself at the witch king's feet to beg his forgiveness, promising he'd never endanger his life again, vowing to do whatever it took to restore the king's trust in him.

"That trust is broken," the king had said. "Only one thing can restore it."

And Ambrose had said, "Anything. I will do anything."

He had been kneeling when the witch king carved the runes into his spine with magic and a white-hot needle. There'd been no medicine to dull the pain, but he didn't think one existed which could inoculate him against such a unique agony. It sutured his soul into the lining of the witch king's will, and he had chewed the inside of his cheek and suffered it with the constant reminder that it was less than he deserved.

His reward might have felt worth it, if not for what had come after. Once the runes were carved into the very bones of him and his flesh knitted back together, the witch king smeared his lips with Ambrose's blood and sealed the spell with a kiss to the nape of his neck.

Sometimes, if Ambrose closed his eyes, he could remember the warmth of that kiss spreading through the bones of him. Their first and only one.

When he'd risen with the collar freshly inked around his throat, the witch king gave him his first compulsion order.

Ambrose didn't even remember what the witch king's voice sounded like. He hardly remembered what his own body had felt like at the time.

He did remember the coarse sheen of Primrose's fur as he ran a hand over her flank, still foamy from battle.

Her ribs had caved to his magic like any other.

He'd been sick for days afterward, and the witch king had tended to him like a lover, while Ambrose rotted in the oubliette of his pain, guilt, shame, and grief.

He'd blamed himself entirely, at the time.

Watching Emery fight back, suffering with the guilt of killing Craig Kendrick but not the *blame*, which he put solely on Morcant's shoulders— it opened a door in the attic of Ambrose's mind which he'd long kept shut.

Even now, you turn your back on me, the witch king said, his voice a well of pain and resentment.

"No," Ambrose insisted. He had many difficult and conflicted feelings about his history, feelings he could not sort through in an evening, but he was still assured of a few things. Among them, a deep-set belief that the witch king's vision of a kinder world had been a dream worth realizing, and that he would never have done the things he had if he didn't think they were necessary.

Now, Ambrose had to prove to him they no longer were.

He still loved him too much not to try. He wanted the witch king to know the comforts of chocolate and a hot shower and a world that didn't force them to hide who they were.

He pushed away the vivid sensation of Primrose's shivering hide carved open by the magic's appetite and replaced it with a different one—the yearning for more than the pragmatic touch of tending wounds and tightening one another's vambraces. The sweet agony of kissing his king's ring instead of his lips.

"I will bring you back, but not like this. Not by killing a man who doesn't deserve it. There has to be another way. With your magic, there must be. If any witch could defeat death, it would be you."

A long, unsettling silence followed. The room had been alive with the sound of wind whistling through the eaves and rain on the windowpane, but even these sounds seemed muted, leaving only Ambrose's heartbeat to thunder.

Finally the witch king said, *We will need my remains and my grimoire.*

Relief unwinched all the taut muscles of Ambrose's body. He seized upon the idea immediately. Emery had magically ferried away the witch king's skeleton somewhere. Perhaps he'd be willing to return it. And the grimoire—that might prove difficult, but there had been so many books in the library, surely they could find one which gave a hint as to its location.

He went to sleep with these ideas spinning in his head. The collar felt looser. The future, brighter.

Fate had other plans for him, though. The next morning, Emery fell ill.

CHAPTER 27

The first clue that Emery wasn't well: He didn't emerge from his bedroom when the clock struck noon.

Ambrose had slept fitfully. He'd made himself toast and listened with one ear to the book about Henry and Simon while the other ear waited for sounds from Emery's room. None came, not even the click of Katzica's claws on the floor.

Silence preyed on Ambrose's worst fears. Surely if anyone had broken the wards or hurt Emery, he would have heard? He wanted to check in but had never been given permission to enter Emery's bed chamber.

Once the sun reached midday, he couldn't staunch his worry any longer and knocked on the door.

A grunt of surprise followed, then a groan. "It's open."

Ambrose cracked the door. The curtains were drawn, but in a thin shaft of light, Katzica could be made out curled up on the end of the bed beside a lumpy shape in the blankets. Emery's voice issued from within.

"You can come in."

Ambrose stepped gingerly over the threshold. If he'd thought the living room a mess, it didn't compare to Emery's bedroom. Hardly a foot of floor space was not occupied by stacks of books, odd magical artifacts, trinkets, tithes, and potion bottles. A footpath snaked between the chaos. Most strange were the wardrobes, one of which had the large doors common for clothing storage, another peppered with a grid of different-sized drawers, all with different knobs, the wood a mosaic of myriad colors in flaking paint.

A HEX FOR HUNGER 173

Ambrose couldn't see Emery's face and followed one path toward the bed. His heart lurched a little seeing two empty potion bottles on the nightstand.

"Are you well?"

"Feel like I got hit by a bus." Emery's face emerged, cocooned in the blanket. "Must have caught something hanging out in graveyards an' soggy bogs every night the past week."

Ambrose's heart picked up speed. "Have the potions helped?"

"One of 'em was to counter hexes. Not that they usually work. Morcant crafts his to be impervious."

"And the other?"

"Painkillers. My head is caning, but I don't think he hexed me. This isn't his style. Probably just a cold."

Just, Ambrose thought with mounting alarm. He'd suffered a cold and nearly perished. He leaned close to press his hand to Emery's forehead and found it stifling and clammy.

"You're feverish. Have you any spells to cure this?"

"There's no cure for a cold, silly." He sounded delirious.

Ambrose bit his tongue to keep the hysteria from tinging his voice. He could protect Emery from violent spells and witches, but illness? It was little wonder he'd come down with something, given the stress, sleepless nights, and lingering effects of Morcant's various punishments. The consequences if he succumbed to sickness now, though?

Together, they stood a chance against Morcant, but not with Emery one feverish step from the grave. Ambrose hadn't damaged his standing with the witch king by refusing to kill Emery only to let him die of an ailment immediately after.

Colds had felled warriors and kings. He needed to find a way to bring Emery's body back to healthy equilibrium, balance his humors, something.

Blearily, Emery looked at the clock on his nightstand, then bolted up. "Shit, I didn't think it was *that* late."

"You should rest."

Emery swung his legs over the edge of the bed and started pulling on fluffy slippers. "I've got to go to the library. Find any books on immortality they might have."

Ambrose grasped his shoulder. "You should *sleep*."

"But—"

"You're ill." Ambrose pushed him back into bed insistently, bearing him back until he lay against the pillows. "Let me care for you."

Never mind he hadn't a clue how to do that. Emery had stopped fighting at least. Rather, he'd stopped moving altogether, staring at Ambrose wide-eyed, flushing to his neck and chest.

Abruptly, Ambrose realized his position—looming over Emery and pinning him to the mattress.

Afraid of intimidating him, Ambrose lurched back. "I'll find something to help." He retreated from the bedroom and went out into the hall. "Get some rest. I'll be back."

He shut the door, trying to think back to his own illness.

The physicians had used all manner of tincture and poultice to try and break his fevers, but the most effective means had been bloodletting with leeches, and he was quite conveniently located in a bog.

There were two issues. Leaving the sanctuary of the wards was one. The collar was the second. It would only let him go so far from Emery's side.

He had to attempt it. Taking a mason jar from the kitchen and donning his cloak, he ventured out into the cold, damp air, closing the door silently behind him so he didn't disturb Emery.

He didn't get far before something caught his notice. Around the side wall, planks of wood and a gleam of dark iron peeked out from the moss and ivy. Upon closer inspection, it was a cellar door, smelling damp and rotted from disuse.

A bog seemed a poor place for a cellar, but then, it seemed a poor place for the chapel, so perhaps this spot hadn't always been part of the wetlands. Either way, he'd seen no doors inside that could lead here.

It didn't look as though Emery used it with any frequency, yet something about the door called to him.

Wonderingly, he knelt and reached for the iron padlock chaining the doors shut, startling at the unnatural heat of the metal. Magic laced its fingers with his. It had a familiar touch—like the peace of escaping a storm into a place of sanctuary.

Emery's magic. His signature was unmistakable.

Ambrose flexed his hand. With his abilities, he could break the lock easily, but the presence of the spell bothered him. It begged the question: What had Emery hidden down there, and from whom?

It got under his skin. The new, delicate trust between them could fracture easily under the weight of one heavy secret.

A HEX FOR HUNGER

175

This could be where he hid my remains, the witch king breathed.

Ambrose had the same thought, but now was not the time. He needed to do something about Emery's fever.

You may not get another opportunity to search this place unobserved. Is my resurrection so much less important? He will not perish in the space of a few minutes.

Guilt gnawed at him. He'd refused his king's orders twice already, and exploring the cellar shouldn't take long.

Careful to be quiet, he gripped the padlock in his fist and let magic burn its way through the interior like lit oil. It snapped open. He wouldn't be able to lock it again, so only a cursory inspection would make it appear untouched. But if Emery came down here . . .

He'd have to cross that bridge when he came to it.

The doors creaked open no matter how delicately he moved them. The stairs descended into a hungry black mouth. His arms broke out in gooseflesh as, with every step, the temperature dropped by a degree. The cavernous echo of his footfall accompanied a constant percussion of water dripping, which he discovered the source of when he got to the bottom stair and a frigid flood soaked him to the ankles.

Without a torch, the only light provided came through the open cellar door. In its wan glow was a sodden pile of firewood and some ancient barrels, but mostly cracked stone and water. It looked empty and unused, except—

The air smelled of damp and algae, but some other fragrance accompanied it. An unplaceable wintery aura of snow and spruce.

They're here. My bones are here.

Ambrose's gaze snagged on a pile of moldering blankets in the corner.

He recalled that first night of his resurrection: Emery had bundled the witch king's skeleton up like a load of laundry and cast a spell to transport it elsewhere.

He waded across to it. The closer he came, the more the chill aura of magic enveloped him. With reverent caution, he unfolded the soggy blanket, but no matter how delicately he moved, the bones within clacked together.

Careful!

Ambrose didn't want to risk dropping any into the foul water, so he bundled the blankets up in his arms, climbed the steps out of the cellar, and laid them out on a bare patch of earth.

Most of the bones were all jumbled together, but the skull stood out with its golden circlet, divested of its rubies and sheen by grave robbers and long centuries. Looking at its graying teeth and black sockets, he struggled to remember the sunlight of the witch king's smile or the blue of his eyes.

"What do I do with them?" he whispered.

You must find one in particular. The seventh vertebrae of the neck.

"How will I be able to tell which one?"

He needn't have asked. As he touched the bones to sort through them, his thumb brushed one so cold it felt as though it burned him.

Yes, that one! It bears a mark.

Ambrose had to use the corner of the blanket to hold it. Through the fabric, the cold seeped through, seeking to freeze his blood. On the backward protrusion was a mark—not like the engravings of the arcane tether. It glowed like frigid breath on the air.

Through intuition, he suspected only he could see it, or Emery might not have discarded it in the first place.

"What's to be done with it now?" Ambrose asked.

As yet? Nothing. This spell requires a phrase to unlock it, a phrase only written in my grimoire.

"You don't remember the phrase by rote?" That was not like the witch king.

Spirit memories are fallible, but I have one foot in the grave and one on the other side with you. It is not forgetfulness which keeps me from using the spell now, but a requirement in its creation. Do you remember how we gave up our names?

Ambrose did. It had felt momentous as a marriage, at the time. They'd written one another's names on old vellum, sealed in twine made from the hair of anyone who'd known them. They'd burnt on an aspen wood fire, and in that instant, Ambrose had forgotten the girl's name he'd been given at birth. He'd wanted nothing more than to be parted from it, and there was old magic which claimed power over those whose names you knew, so the witch king wanted to be rid of his, too. *Once we have the phrase from the grimoire, invoking our names and using the enchantment from my corpse will resurrect me.*

That explained why he hadn't wished to use this spell in the first place. It was a great deal more complicated, and opened him up to vulnerabilities by reclaiming his true name.

But the history books had already written his true name in their pages. Someone had found it. In all likelihood, it had been Ilonara Thorn, the woman who'd killed him and replaced his statue in the park. The security of sundering his name was long gone.

"What should I do with this in the meantime?" Ambrose asked, holding up the vertebrae.

Keep it safe and on your person until the opportunity arises.

The spell attached to the bone made him shiver, but he preferred this to the alternative. He tore a piece of cloth to wrap it with and tucked it obediently in his trouser pocket, where he could feel it through two layers of fabric.

The witch king instructed him to return the rest of his remains where he'd found them, and so Ambrose descended back into the cellar to do just that. After crawling out and closing the door, he placed the broken padlock so that it looked just as it had when he first stumbled across it.

He tried not to acknowledge how eager he was to return to his original task, not yet ready to confront why hunting for leeches in a bog had become preferable to resurrecting his king.

He roamed farther into the woods, testing the distance of his tether carefully. Still within sight of the ruin, he sensed it straining. For a moment, he stopped and held his chest, for the way the leash pulled felt a lot like heartache.

By then he'd come to the edge of the bog.

He didn't wish to go far enough that he might fall through a peat mat again, so he kept to the shallows, swirling through algae and leaf litter in search of leeches.

Eventually, he recognized the futility of searching with his eyes rather than using the more obvious method of fishing for them via bait. He took his shoes and socks off at shore and, gritting his teeth against the cold and awful sensation of mud and silt between his toes, stepped into the bog barefoot. After going a few steps, he lifted a foot. Sure enough, a slimy, sluglike body clung to his ankle. He filled the jar with water and pried the leech off into the jar, then continued his search.

The task was grim, so his mind wandered. He'd spent a good deal of time in this bog by now, but the last time, it had been to bury Morcant. He wondered how the necromancer had looked crawling out of the water, choking up lungfuls of mud and peat. How did it work to return when your body had been so thoroughly maimed and drowned? He'd only seen the witch king revived twice, and neither from deaths so . . . final.

They would need to uncover the exact mechanics of Morcant's immortality if they held a hope of defeating him, but somehow Ambrose doubted he would have employed the same spells as the witch king. He may have idolized him, but the witch king *had* died in the end. Morcant would want a more secure means to eternal life.

He peeled another leech from his big toe and stuck it in the jar with the rest. Fortunately, a life of bloodshed left him immune to squeamishness, but as he peeled the engorged parasite from his skin, he considered the blood it contained. Blood made for powerful tithes.

How much more powerful a tithe would an entire human sacrifice make?

Morcant must have made use of Craig Kendrick's death somehow, and all the sacrifices that came after. It didn't take a distant leap to assume that might have something to do with his immortality.

It was a good place to start looking, provided Emery survived his fever.

With that thought, Ambrose headed back, but as he paused to pick up his discarded socks and boots, he felt the disconcerting touch of someone's gaze upon him.

He paused. Holding still, he scanned the trees for anyone hidden. Then he heard a low hiss.

He whirled and beheld the creature menacing him—

A goose.

It was not like any goose he'd seen, with its brown plumage, black head, and white cheeks. He'd also never seen a goose look so serpentlike, arcing its long neck as if preparing to strike.

Then it lowered its head, spread its wings, and charged.

Ambrose had faced bandits, assassins, and legendary warriors, but all of them had shown him due respect as an opponent. There was something far more alarming about a creature so small charging fearlessly toward him. He had no wish to fight it and find out this world had venomous bird snakes, so he scooped up his boots and ran.

It gave chase, flapping, honking, and hissing.

The ruin was within sight, but the goose had the advantage of flight. Ambrose let out a yell and ducked as great wings beat around his head. When he righted himself, still running, he spotted movement in the window of the ruined chapel.

Emery held open his curtains, staring in bewilderment at Ambrose fleeing the monster. The monster in question must not be deadly, or else it was very cruel of Emery to laugh so hard. And while he was *ill*.

Ambrose ran round to the front door, where the goose harassed his ankles. Feinting a kick toward it, he sneaked through the door and slammed it behind him.

Emery's laughter rang through the ruin like the chapel's lost bell brought to life. He stood in the entryway, still ensconced in his blankets and looking halfway to tears.

"What—" he said between gasps for air. "What were you doing?"

"Your world has snake geese."

"What? That's just a goose."

"I assure you, it is not."

"It's a *North Kadian* goose."

"It's a menace."

"Well," Emery choked, "that part's true."

Ambrose might have felt very foolish, but he'd never heard Emery laugh so heartily before. Hearing it felt like basking in ticklish sunlight, and he found he didn't mind embarrassing himself a little to bring Emery joy.

"You should be resting."

"I was until I heard goose honks and someone running. What were you doing?"

Ambrose held up the jar. "We have to balance your humors if you're to survive the fever." He sloshed the murky water around. "Leeches can aid you in that regard."

"Leeches!?"

"They're effective."

"Absolutely not."

A note of real worry wormed its way into Ambrose's voice. "They look unappealing, but I'm sure I'd have died without them when I fell ill, and we can't allow your fever to worsen or—"

Emery's morphing expression stopped him. For a moment, he looked dumbfounded, then his face cracked with a smile Ambrose had never seen before. Teasing and endeared.

"I think I prefer paracetamol." His smile turned sheepish. "Sorry. I keep forgetting how much has changed for you. Colds aren't as deadly as they used to be, so I promise you, the leeches are unnecessary. But it's kind of you to worry."

Ambrose did feel foolish. He'd stood barefoot in a bog and been assailed by a goose for no purpose besides Emery's amusement.

180   ALISTAIR REEVES

Yet he found Emery's amusement prize enough.

Emery looked at his muddy feet. "Please tell me you didn't catch them by—"

"Yes," Ambrose said, skipping over it to the more important bit. "And it gave me an idea of how Morcant might be achieving his immortality."

CHAPTER 28

Ambrose explained, while sitting on the edge of the bathtub and washing his feet, how he'd come to the conclusion Morcant's immortality could be linked to the humans sacrificed by his guild in their initiation rites.

Emery looked disheartened but not surprised. "I had a similar thought last night."

"Oh?"

"Remember that moment before you killed him in the bog? I asked him what it was all for—the cult, the rats, trapping us. He said I'd soon find out. We found out." He wrung the blankets in his hands, which he still wore around his shoulders. "It's all so tidy. Without dirtying his hands, he gains immortality and the leverage to control us. I don't relish the thought. If it's true, it means I helped make him immortal. But to find out how it works . . ."

His eyes lit up with an idea, then he disappeared out the door. Ambrose dried off, followed, and found Emery on his belly, reaching under the sofa.

From beneath it, he retrieved the dagger Hellebore tried to kill him with.

Ambrose had forgotten about it in the turmoil. "He can't use it as evidence against you now."

"I'm more interested in whether we can ascertain any spell placed on it related to his immortality."

Emery went to his bedroom to gather tithes from the chest of drawers with different-colored knobs. An array of smells wafted from its cabinets, filling the air with the fume of old tea, dusty and herbal. He seemed to have a sorting system determined by the different styled knobs and paintings on each drawer. After gathering some poppy seeds, an oak leaf, and the feather of a jaybird, Emery shuffled out to the kitchen, where the dagger used to kill Craig Kendrick lay wrapped in a cloth on the table.

After laying the spell ingredients around the dagger, Emery unwrapped it.

"Perhaps you should wait until you're well," Ambrose said. "Spells can be draining."

"Now you've put the thought in my head, I have to know."

He sat down for it, crossing his legs. After steeling his resolve, he swiped a hand across the tithes. They burst into dust like dandelion seeds. Emery opened his hand, as if waiting for a bird to eat out of his palm, and the swirling particles of the spell landed there, seeping into his skin and leaving a stream of rune marks. Emery held them up to read, then sighed with disappointment.

"That would have been too easy."

"What did it say?"

"The only spell cast through the dagger was the one I performed to create the spell jar. If there is no evidence of any spell cast, I'd assume Morcant cleansed it to cover his tracks, but that's not the case if my spell's aura is still there."

"Perhaps the spell jar was the objective after all?" Ambrose said.

"Seems a waste of a human sacrifice for a measly spell jar."

"What could he use it for?"

"Anything. I suppose you could pack quite a lot of spells into a jar made with a human sacrifice, but that still seems a gratuitous waste of a tithe like that, and besides, I don't see how it would make him immortal." He worried his bottom lip between his teeth, a deep furrow between his brows as he thought. "There's every possibility he did use the sacrifice as a tithe, but through a different vehicle than the dagger. We could test the sarcophagus in the mausoleum where the sacrifices are made, but let's face it, it's unlikely he'd leave evidence lying around."

Ambrose had hoped for a better clue than this, but it offered him an opportunity to ask the questions he otherwise didn't know how to broach.

"There is somewhere else we might find answers . . ."

Emery perked up, eyes bright and inquisitive.

He almost never looked that way at Ambrose. Not before the night they'd killed Morcant. Since then, Emery had opened up little by little. Trusted him more and more.

Ambrose needed to tread carefully if he meant to keep that trust. "The witch king was immortal himself."

Emery's mouth fell open a little. "And you think Morcant might have used the same method?"

Ambrose shook his head. "Not precisely the same one, but it stands to reason, given his . . . affinity for the witch king, he might have derived inspiration."

"How did he do it? The witch king. Did he tell you?"

"Not . . . entirely." He took a steadying breath. It felt dangerous to divulge this. Emery had made clear his low regard of the witch king, so Ambrose didn't know how revealing this information might go. Would Emery view the strength of Ambrose's bond to his king as a threat and rescind his newly gifted trust? Would he take steps to prevent the witch king's return, thwarting Ambrose's quest for redemption?

Fortunately, Ambrose knew so little, and nothing particularly damning. At least, not yet. "He didn't share with me the specifics of the spell or how it worked, only the result. His immortality was tied to me. So long as I lived, so, too, would he."

Emery stared, a frown slowly invading his expression, thoughtful and puzzled. "That . . . but that shouldn't work."

"I saw for myself that it did."

"But it's so—so—"

"What?"

"Fallible!" Emery got up, sniffling but too agitated to sit still. "He threw you into danger all the time. Unless you were invulnerable, he endangered his own immortality every time he put you at risk."

"He did equip me with considerable powers to ensure I wasn't easily slain."

"But you *were* slain, and so was *he*. Was there an added layer to the spell? Some other caveat or contingency in the event something happened to you?"

Ambrose shrugged helplessly. This wasn't the direction he'd expected the conversation to go. "Not to my knowledge."

"It shouldn't work," Emery repeated. "It . . . it just shouldn't work."

"That was the thrust of my raising the subject," Ambrose said, hopeful he could redirect things. "If we can discover more about my king's methods, perhaps we'll uncover a path to Morcant's."

"How do we accomplish that? He died centuries ago."

"He had a grimoire," Ambrose said. "A book in which he wrote all the recipes for spells of his own invention. If we can find it, perhaps it will hold the answer."

As he spoke, Emery's expression dimmed, the eager hope guttering in his eyes.

"What's wrong?" Ambrose asked.

He expected Emery to tell him the grimoire had been destroyed, burnt, lost, or locked away where no one could possibly retrieve it.

Instead, he said, "Morcant has it."

It became clear after some explanation why Morcant possessing the grimoire was only a marginal improvement on it having been lost or destroyed.

Early on, when Emery first tried to free himself from the shackles of Morcant's pact, he'd attempted to find Morcant's home and rummage through it in search of the daggers from the initiation rite.

It hadn't taken much snooping through school offices and files to find an address, but he'd gone and found the house desolate with only the whiff of having been magically kept clean, a pile of letters inside.

Evidently, Morcant had two residences—one he used for all his official correspondences and professor work, another where he actually lived.

Finding his abode would prove no simple task if he had the place warded the way Emery did. They would have to be very sly or very lucky to find it.

The next-best place to search, and the only one available to them, was his office at school.

Ambrose didn't like it.

"I have classes I need to attend anyway," Emery said.

"Morcant will be there."

"Exactly. While he's teaching, I at least know where he is and where he's not. If we want to snoop around, the best time would be while he's occupied teaching." When Ambrose still looked doubtful, he added, "It's a public place. He won't attack me in broad daylight. Not directly."

A HEX FOR HUNGER   185

Though Ambrose saw the sense in it, he had no desire to repeat the events of last night. It had sparked a particular anxiety to watch without the capacity to intervene.

But they had few other avenues. "If you're certain."

So, by the power of "paracetamol" and a pocket full of tissues, Emery went to class. Ambrose no longer accompanied him invisibly. He posed to everyone, once more, as Emery's cousin, except for Morcant and Hellebore, to whom he posed as a threat.

After one uneventful class, Emery led them to Morcant's lecture hall.

"We'll check he's teaching first," Emery said under his breath. "Make sure he hasn't caught the same cold as me and pulled a sicky. Do immortals catch colds?"

Ambrose didn't know, but it was safer to check. They paused just outside the door to the lecture hall. Morcant's crisp voice drifted past, speaking to an eager first year at the podium. They peered inside to confirm Hellebore was there, too, scanning the backs of the students' heads. None had her boyish sable cut, nor the curly blonde of her girlfriend.

"Fancy seeing you so soon."

Ambrose had mastered himself enough not to jump at the sound of Hellebore's voice directly behind them. He did step in front of Emery, though. Hellebore's stoat familiar glared at him from her shoulder, daring him to try anything.

"Oh, call off your dog, Emery. It's not as if I'd do anything *here*."

Ambrose bristled, but before he could snap at her, Emery said, "He's not a dog, Hellebore. He has a name."

"Fido?" Hellebore guessed.

Emery looked up at Ambrose. "Would you like to reintroduce yourself?"

"No," Ambrose replied, which was apparently funny, because Emery cracked a smile.

One Ambrose found difficult not to reciprocate.

Hellebore smiled, too, though not nicely. "I see. He's not your dog because you're the one eating out of his hand?"

Emery's smile vanished. "You don't get to revert back to banter after trying to kill me."

She ignored him, pointing a finger between them. "I did wonder how you roped him into all this. Very risky, though, betting your familiar and your final hope on a medieval knight whose only historical account of sexuality is the subtext of being unfailingly loyal and buried with his old master. Lucky you."

186   ALISTAIR REEVES

Ambrose felt like he'd swallowed swamp water. Hellebore knowing anything about his sexual appetites was beyond uncomfortable. Inferring those appetites hungered for Emery in particular?

He was not ready to confront that, and certainly not with her.

"Speaking of getting lucky," Emery said, "where is that angelic ingenue you always have hanging off your arm? I didn't see her in the lecture hall."

For a brief second, Hellebore's haughty demeanor shattered, flinty eyes going suspiciously shiny. "It was only a fling. She's far too innocent for anything long-term."

Replaying the moment pain flashed across her face, Ambrose wondered if the limp didn't disguise a broken limb. On the surface, she looked as well manicured as topiary—not a smudge to her lipstick, not a chip in the obsidian paint of her nails—but she'd been shaken when Morcant went missing. A hint of that frantic energy remained.

"That's a pity. I thought she'd be good for you," Emery said.

"Then you don't know me very well." To end the conversation, she gestured to the lecture hall doors. "After you."

"Actually, I'm not feeling well." Accompanied by a lingering sniffle, Emery didn't have to fake it. "I'm going home. Let me know if I miss anything good."

"I'm not sharing my notes."

"God forbid you be charitable." Emery performed a curtsy. *Sarcastically.*

Hellebore went into the classroom, and they went the opposite way down the hall.

"We'll have to be quick," Emery said. "In case Hellebore has any suspicions and rats us out."

Morcant's office was down a long corridor in the eastern wing of the castle's upper floor. Some doors were open enough to see other professors sitting at their desks, grading papers and preparing lectures. Morcant's office was at the very end.

Emery paused and put an ear to the door, listening, but it was silent. The spell to unlock its brassy knob worked easily.

Emery whispered, "Well, we're not likely to find anything extraordinary in an office he doesn't ward against lock spells, but might as well try."

Morcant's office was austere and seemingly benign. Ambrose hadn't expected ebony shelves, bloodred drapes, and pens fashioned from

A HEX FOR HUNGER

187

animal bones—it made sense to maintain a professional air to his peers, after all—but it didn't even hold the pretense of a personality. Instead, it had the clean air of a functional place oft used but unloved, liminal in its purpose.

Emery sighed, clearly sharing Ambrose's thoughts. They weren't going to find anything here.

"I'll check the notes on his desk, you have a look through those bookshelves."

That brought Ambrose up short. Faced with all the spines of Morcant's library, he realized how useless he'd be, because he couldn't read a single one. If any had crucial information, even a clue, he'd have to hope it came in the form of a picture or false interior with a powerful relic hidden inside.

He'd concealed his lack of literacy from Emery this entire time. He hadn't been able to conceal the reality of his gender, his sexuality, or his history as the witch king's sword—all secrets which made him feel vulnerable.

Yet, of all of them, *this* scared him worst of all.

Your mind was never keen enough to sharpen for literacy. A sharp sword was all you required.

Ambrose flinched. After his promises and apologies, the witch king still resented him.

Though he didn't relish the notion of revealing his deficiency to Emery, he couldn't abide standing here and *pretending* to help.

"I can't read them," Ambrose said.

Emery didn't look up from the desk. "Are they in a different language?"

"No, I mean I can't read." Ambrose tried not to let shame bow his spine, but his posture became more defensive regardless. "At all."

Emery's brows creased over his big brown eyes. "Really?"

"I was never taught. I'm sorry." Ambrose cast around for anything to look at except Emery's face, which he couldn't read, either.

Emery put down the sheaf of paper he'd been leafing through and crossed the room. He scanned the rows of books while Ambrose awaited judgment.

"Would you like to learn?"

Ambrose startled. "Could you?"

"Not, like, *here this instant*, but at home," Emery said.

"I'll be of little use to you here."

"Keep watch for anyone coming. And——" He paused briefly before spitting out the rest. "Keep me company."

Ambrose brightened with relief. Habit had prepared him for scorn, derision, punishment—never compassion or generosity. These lighter feelings weighed on him more heavily for their unfamiliarity, but they also made him unbearably fond of Emery.

He was going to learn to read . . .

Ambrose kept watch while Emery went through everything on Morcant's desk, his search becoming more frenzied the longer he didn't find anything. Finally, while flipping through a thick notebook, he said, "Aha!"

Ambrose looked up. "What is it?"

"Nothing. That's the sound I hoped I would make in earnest when I came across anything remotely useful, but this is his diary keeping his entire schedule and a list of errands from the past year, and I can't find anything worthwhile. It's just grocery lists and a lecture itinerary. He doesn't even write down our guild meetings. Definitely nothing about a grimoire."

They couldn't surrender with nothing. "Does he have any recent or future engagements?"

Emery flipped a page. "He wrote a reminder to buy blue morpho butterfly wings at the apothecary. They're used in transmutation spells, but that could be for anything. Oh, wait . . . He has an appointment listed this Wednesday. 'One a.m. at the Mavon Bridge.' It doesn't say who with."

"That's late for an engagement."

Emery nodded. "Unless he attends secret raves. Not like it could be a doctor's appointment, though, he'd never *need* one."

"We could follow him."

It wasn't the strongest lead, having no obvious connection to Morcant's immortality, but they were running out of time before his lecture ended.

The clock struck noon as they left the deserted office corridor and joined the throngs of students leaving their classes. Ambrose couldn't quite believe they'd managed it without getting caught, but as they approached the gate leading out of the castle grounds, a familiar figure awaited them.

Emery stopped short.

"You missed class today. I'm glad I caught you."

Morcant waited in the portcullis. As he strode toward them, Emery's hand brushed Ambrose's briefly. Whether by accident or because he sought reassurance, Ambrose didn't know. He stepped in front of Emery anyway.

A HEX FOR HUNGER   189

"We were just heading home." Emery didn't bother saying he was ill.

"I'd like a word before you do."

"I have nothing to say to you."

"I didn't mean you," Morcant said. "It's your charming friend I'd like to talk to."

CHAPTER 29

Emery went rigid next to Ambrose. "What could you possibly have to—"

"Alone," Morcant clarified. He gestured toward the gardens of the inner courtyard.

Ambrose couldn't summon any surprise that a man obsessed with the witch king would relish an opportunity to speak with his resurrected guard. That didn't mean Ambrose had to humor the request.

"I have nothing to say to you, either."

"Really? Not even a little curious?"

"No."

"Good chat," Emery said.

He took Ambrose's hand and made to brush past Morcant. Ambrose experienced an abrupt shift of his focus from the threat in front of him to the warm contact of Emery's hand in his, so he didn't notice Morcant moving to intercept them until he nearly collided bodily with the man.

"I'd rather not use my authority as professor to report some of your recent behavior, but if you don't at least honor me with a conversation, I won't have much choice."

Emery froze, fingers clenching briefly. Ambrose reluctantly extricated himself—he wouldn't allow Morcant to further sully Emery's reputation just to avoid talking. They were in public, on castle grounds. It was perhaps the safest opportunity to have this discussion, and maybe he could glean information from it, such as the whereabouts of the witch king's grimoire.

Emery released him, and Ambrose faced Morcant, who studied him with undiluted surgical interest.

"It's fascinating, to see you in the flesh. Unprecedented, really."

"He isn't a lab rat," Emery said heatedly. "He's not yours to dissect and play with."

"He isn't yours, either."

"That's not what I meant."

"He was the witch king's," Morcant finished, his gaze barely flicking to acknowledge Emery before fixing with strange gravity on Ambrose. "I wonder if he still is."

Ambrose bristled. By questioning his loyalty, Morcant had undressed his dilemma: his growing fondness for Emery and his oath to the witch king competing for dominion. He didn't want that inner conflict playing out in front of Morcant—not when Ambrose hadn't the time to parse his own feelings, and not when it could weaken his position in this conversation. Morcant wanted something out of this. He wouldn't bother otherwise. Ambrose needed to know what that something was and prevent him taking it.

Still, his words got under Ambrose's skin. *He was the witch king's. I wonder if he still is.*

Ambrose's magic stirred, and the voice of the witch king purred in his ear.

Listen to him.

Ambrose relented. "You can have your conversation, but I doubt very much you'll get what you want from it."

Emery was looking at him, his (unfairly pretty) eyes large and dark with worry. "Ambrose . . ."

"Very good," Morcant said, and gestured toward the courtyard once more. "After you."

Ambrose's desire to reassure Emery warred with his instincts to conceal his fondness from Morcant, who'd doubtlessly exploit it. In the end, he only gave the witch a stiff nod as he passed.

Each step drew his leash tighter. He felt the distance more acutely than when he'd ventured into the bog in search of leeches. Morcant chose a secluded bench, sat, and gestured to the spot beside him. The weather had cooled, so aside from students using the courtyard as a thoroughfare, none stopped or lingered long enough to overhear them.

From here, Emery was still visible, leaning against the stone wall of the portcullis and watching warily.

192   ALISTAIR REEVES

Ambrose quickly came up with a plan of approach. The history books claimed he was a bloodthirsty dog of the witch king, a mindless weapon that bent to his whims. It would be best to behave accordingly and give Morcant no indication he had a mind of his own. Once he understood what Morcant was after—information about the witch king's immortality, no doubt—he could focus on keeping him from it, or perhaps leverage it to learn more about the witch king's grimoire.

Morcant cast a charm to prevent eavesdropping and said, "So. You have a name. *Ambrose.* Appropriate. I assume the witch king gave it to you?"

He had helped. The name Ambrose had surrendered in the spell hadn't suited him, but he didn't wish to tell Morcant so much. "What do you want?"

"To ask you questions. It's rare to expend so much passion and energy researching figures of ancient history, and then find yourself with the opportunity to speak to one of them."

"You're not merely sating your curiosity," Ambrose said. "You want something."

Morcant's smile leaned to one side. "Can't it be both? I will get to the point, I promise you, but first, there is something I'm dying to know— Why do you serve Emery?"

Ambrose refused to give Morcant anything too close to the quick, preferring a safer facet of the truth. "I'm indebted to him for resurrecting me. I will repay that debt."

"So it is merely transactional."

"Yes," he lied.

Morcant's stare bored through him. One of his eyes was a slightly different color—paler, glassy. For a flash, Ambrose thought he saw the shadow of a rune in the depths of his pupil, and wondered if the eye was enchanted. Could he see through magical illusions? Could he see through lies?

"It has nothing to do with these—" Morcant raised a hand to Ambrose's neck. "—these fascinating marks?"

He made to touch them.

Ambrose grabbed Morcant's wrist in a bone-crunching grip.

"Did I touch a sore spot?" Morcant said.

Ambrose squeezed, allowing the magic to seep hungrily through.

Morcant winced. "You know by now, threatening me is pointless."

"I can't kill you," Ambrose allowed, "but I can hurt you."

He released Morcant forcefully, and Morcant put respectful distance back between them. Ambrose concealed the nausea of using his abilities with a thick swallow.

He'd been a fool to assume Morcant only wanted to know about the witch king's immortality, rather than the witch king's unique spells, of which Ambrose was a living demonstration.

In his periphery, Emery moved away from the wall, clearly debating whether to intervene. After a quelling look from Ambrose, he relaxed. Barely.

"I assume from your reaction that I'm correct, then. I wondered if it was a trick of memory—I did *die* shortly after I saw it used for the first time—but it seemed the collar compelled you to obey Emery's order to kill me."

Ambrose could think of nothing worse than information about his pact in Morcant's hands, but he also couldn't summon any plausible deniability to bolster a lie, so—

"He's promised never to use it and to help break it," Ambrose said.

"Oh, I don't care what sort of ethical quibbles Emery's self-flagellating over. I'm more interested in how the collar *works*. How the spell is cast, how the magic persists long after the witch king's death."

"Fortunately for me, I don't know."

"And you wouldn't tell me if you did."

Ambrose smiled.

"Well, since you aren't inclined to volunteer anything, allow me to lay out my theory," Morcant said. "I have a lot of them, you understand, but this one relates to your famed loyalty.

"By the time the witch king was assassinated and deposed, he had no remaining allegiances, no loyal followers, none but you. You, who never wavered. You followed his orders to the letter, even when it made people fear and abhor you.

"Why were you different? I had so many theories, but having met you, I've narrowed it down to two."

Ambrose debated leaving. He didn't know what Morcant was driving at yet, but his instincts told him he wouldn't like it.

But he needed information.

"The first theory is perhaps the most obvious," Morcant said. "The witch king controlled you through magic. Your abilities were legendary, and I couldn't imagine him imparting such power without a safeguard to ensure you never turned that power against him. This first theory seemed, until recently, the most probable. Now that I've met you, I think I might favor the second."

"And what's that?"

"You loved him."

Ambrose felt no different from Morcant's rats, pinned to a sarcophagus beneath the point of a dagger, heart and soul expunged for his dark purpose. Inexplicably, he glanced toward Emery waiting in the portcullis.

He couldn't hide the truth of it. He'd loved the witch king, and he might have given it away minutes prior to this conversation.

He's the witch king's. I wonder if he still is.

He should have refuted it. Now he felt as though, between the witch king and Emery, he had two weaknesses while Morcant had none.

Morcant continued, "If I were you, and I had been placed under a restrictive contract, forced to obey my master's every command, I'd start to chafe against that control. I'd want to rebel. The most logical explanation is you never did because you submitted to your master willingly. Because you loved him." His eyes narrowed. "Perhaps you still do."

"It's a pretty theory," Ambrose said. He wouldn't confirm or deny either. "It still doesn't explain what you want from me."

"I want to know what you want. Freedom? No . . . If all you wanted was someone powerful enough to break your chains, you'd have jumped at the opportunity to speak with me. So it must be . . ." His mouth formed an *O* of understanding as the reason came to him. "You want to bring him back."

The witch king's spirit seemed to rise like mist around them, as if summoned by that wish verbalized.

Ambrose tried to disguise his discomfort, but Morcant's eyes gleamed, the paler one flashing. "I can help you."

An unlikely ally, the witch king murmured, and Ambrose feared his shrewdly considering tone.

"Why would you help me?" Ambrose asked, hoping they could finally come to the crux of Morcant's purpose here. He wanted something. He'd dug into Ambrose's desires and come away with a bargaining chip. Now Ambrose waited to see what he'd use it for.

Morcant turned his head to look at Emery and said ominously, "He trusts you."

Ambrose felt a chill. "He trusts I will honor our transaction."

Morcant's smile was an oil slick, prismatic in all the colors of malevolence it hid when the light struck it just so. "The way he looks at you, I'd say it's something more."

How did Emery look at him? Ambrose wished he knew, and wished it hadn't been so transparent Morcant could use it for leverage.

"You've gleaned from a single look that he harbors enough affection to make me an effective tool against him?"

"His greatest weakness is that he's lonely. He's mistrustful but not guarded enough. Not by half. He yearns for companionship, and I think he'd risk anything for yours."

Ambrose concealed the way his heart fluttered at the thought.

"Let me be plain," Morcant went on. "Emery's more a threat to himself than me, but I tire of cleaning up every mess he spills. I want you to help me rein him in."

Ambrose didn't like the destination of this conversation—one he'd only glimpsed in the distance, but which now resolved before him. "And I'm to do that . . . how, exactly?"

"Tell me how that charming necklace of yours works," Morcant said.

Ambrose's blood ran cold.

Unintelligible whispers blew through his mind like a fell wind. The witch king stirred, agitated.

The image of Emery bound in the manacle of the arcane collar made Ambrose sick. Emery could not even pretend at obeisance. To have it forced upon him would erode who he was, his identity—

For a split second, Ambrose wondered if that was what had become of him, too.

"If I help you, what will you give me in return?

"Your master's grimoire."

Though this was precisely the thing Ambrose had been angling for, it seemed too perfect that Morcant offered it right away. Too neat. "You have it? Where?"

"It would be a waste to tell you."

"You want me to trust you on your word?"

"If it holds secrets to the witch king's resurrection, isn't that worth the risk of a little trust?"

"If you have it, why do you need me to understand the arcane collar?"

"Aside from a few journal entries, which are too cryptic to count as recipes for spells, the grimoire is mostly written in cipher. You could be the key to decrypting it."

Ambrose might have laughed. Emery had promised to teach him his letters not an hour ago.

"I will happily share it with you and bring your master back, if that is indeed your wish," Morcant continued. "It would be a relief to finally have an equal among witches."

Equal.

The witch king's spirit rattled like a serpent's tail, incensed by the comparison, his desire to return warring with the desire to squash this pretender.

Ambrose almost liked the idea of letting Morcant perish in his hubris, but not at the expense of Emery's freedom.

He decided to try and leverage something more. "I don't trust you. Perhaps if you were inclined to impart some of that knowledge you prize so deeply."

"Of which variety?"

"The immortal variety. How you achieved it, if not by the same means as my master."

Morcant smiled devilishly. "A good magician never reveals his secrets."

"So it has nothing to do with your initiates, the rats, and sacrifices like Craig Kendrick."

The smile vanished. "An arcane collar for Emery in exchange for your king's return. I'll give you nothing more."

"Why do you tolerate him when it would be so easy to avoid the risk he poses altogether by having him arrested? It makes no sense unless he serves some other purpose."

"He's already served his purpose," Morcant said, but with a wary edge that hadn't been there before. "And he will never allow you to bring the witch king back. He has the talent, but his spirit is too soft."

"You keep recruiting each year, even though increased numbers may only attract more attention to your guild," Ambrose pressed. "You must be getting something worth the risk."

"Do you agree to my terms or not?" Morcant demanded.

CHAPTER 30

The tether pulled Ambrose's heart and his focus toward the portcullis, where Emery still waited, arms crossed, watching.

He yearns for companionship, and I think he'd risk anything for yours.

Ambrose had tried to suppress the desirous thoughts that crossed his mind—preoccupations with tucking silvered hair behind Emery's ears, or with the way his fingers mapped Ambrose's scars. The notion that Emery might have those same thoughts about him hadn't occurred to him before.

He was still loyal to the witch king, but he could no longer deny Emery had stolen some of that devotion for himself while Ambrose wasn't looking.

What if the witch king wanted him to accept Morcant's bargain? His lingering spirit fumed, hating Morcant, desiring nothing less than to owe this imposter his life. Yet he hesitated before discarding a tool that could be used.

Ambrose felt like a man on the rack, bones breaking as he was torn between the thing he wanted and the oath he'd upheld to his grave.

Finally, the witch king's voice broke into his mind. *He is arrogant and untrustworthy. My grimoire is not his to barter with. We will retrieve it ourselves, and when I return, he will pay for his impunity. Refuse him.*

Ambrose nearly let out the breath he'd been holding in a rush of relief. He stood, preparing to walk away.

"I'll let you consider it," Morcant said.

"There is nothing to consider," said Ambrose. "My loyalty would be worthless if it was so easily bought."

There was a smirk in Morcant's voice. "Loyalty to whom, I wonder?"

Ambrose ignored him. He made his way across the courtyard. Emery straightened up from where he'd been leaning against the wall, taking a rushed few steps forward. The tether loosened its pull, saturating the reunion with a sense of relief.

Emery fell into step with him. "What did he want?"

"He wanted me to explain the arcane collar," Ambrose said. "So he can put one on you."

Emery blanched. "In exchange for what?"

Ambrose stopped, suffused with a feeling like sunshine. "You aren't going to ask me whether I refused him?"

Emery heard the smile in his voice and looked charmingly flustered. "Well, I didn't think you would. You're—You're very straightforward and don't strike me as the backstabbing type."

As they left the courtyard, Ambrose clung to the giddy feeling.

It was the first time he felt certain that Emery did trust him.

They spent the afternoon in the library, where Emery started to teach Ambrose how to write.

After collecting a pile of books, Emery took him to a quiet corner with a window overlooking the surrounding moors and large squishy pillows Emery called beanbag chairs. "We'll start by teaching you to write your name."

It turned out this was putting the cart before the horse. Emery wrote the capital letter "A" on a piece of parchment and, handing over the pen, asked Ambrose to copy it. Ambrose wrapped his fist around the pen to do just that, but found his hand obscured the paper, and he couldn't control the shapes his pen made with the grace Emery did.

"You've never held a pen?" Emery said incredulously.

A stab of frustration and embarrassment went through Ambrose, that something so basic should be so difficult for him.

But then Emery flinched with self-reproach and said, "Sorry, that was unkind. Here."

With a shy, exquisitely gentle touch, he arranged Ambrose's fingers around the pen, curling the middle beneath the index and thumb. A feeling just as downy and soft made Ambrose's heart skip.

For the rest of the lesson, he found himself transfixed by the long graceful bones and veins carving the back of Emery's hands. The expressive way he wrote his letters, like each one was the step to a dance. The way he

A HEX FOR HUNGER 199

inserted several fingers between different pages of a book to hold his place, the curves of the paper reminiscent of certain human anatomy.

His embarrassment gave way to a different feeling altogether. A bone-deep craving for the brief moments Emery leaned close to look over his work and nod with approval.

He said. "That's your name."

Ambrose tilted his head. His own letters stumbled across the page, but they still felt momentous. "I always thought I'd be too dim-witted for writing."

"Whatever gave you that idea?"

Ambrose didn't speak. The answer felt like an admission.

Emery's smile dimmed. "Or should I have asked, who?"

"A sword only needs a sharp edge, not a sharp mind," Ambrose said, but as it left his mouth, he felt like the words were damning his king instead of defending him.

A scowl deepened the lines around Emery's mouth. "He didn't treat you very well."

"He treated me better than anyone."

"That speaks more lowly of everyone than it speaks highly of him."

Ambrose tried to quell his frustration, but it leaked into his voice. "When I said I was a man, nobody believed me, and he gave me a body to convince them. He gave me a purpose. He kept me in his company."

"In chains," Emery said, and when that halted Ambrose, he bit his lip and fell quiet, too. After a beat, he lifted one lithe hand to brush Ambrose's hair aside and touch the marks on his neck.

Morcant had, an hour ago, tried to do the same. Ambrose's response now could not be more different.

On the outside, he held still, but inside he quaked while fearfully certain Emery could feel it.

The touch ignited his blood. He had to fight not to lean into those hands he'd spent the past hour admiring.

"You hate it when I speak ill of him," Emery said. "But you hate Morcant. Are they really any different?"

Ambrose had done everything in his power not to acknowledge those parallels. They painted his history in overcast hues, poisoned the romantic tales he'd told himself about a guard's tragic love for a king who could never marry him. They'd understood that helping one another remove their armor was as close to undressing as they'd come, that tasting wine for him was as good as a kiss.

He had grown used to treating every crumb of stolen affection as a feast.

Compared to that, the touch of Emery's fingers tracing the inky marks on his neck was an overindulgence.

"Why do you defend him?"

Ambrose fought to keep his breath steady. "I swore an oath to do so until the day I died."

"And you did. You died. So did he. He's still dead. You should be free of him."

Ambrose could practically hear the witch king's teeth grinding together. His magic sharpened its claws, but Ambrose? He could hardly breathe for the desire to taste the freedom Emery offered.

Taking in the soft part of Emery's lips, perhaps it wasn't only freedom he'd like to taste.

They were bent over the papers on the table, faces close. Old instincts made Ambrose prickle with fear. In his time, looking at another man this way spelled danger. Just the thought of kissing in public caused the hair on the nape of his neck to rise in anticipation of a noose. He had to resist the urge to search over his shoulder for onlookers. He wasn't doing anything wrong—

Except he *was*, but not because they were both men. He couldn't kiss Emery when his heart was promised to another.

I never knew you could stray so easily.

Ambrose sucked in a breath and withdrew.

The open look in Emery's eyes shuttered. "S-sorry. Let's practice the other letters."

Emery cleared his throat and tried to brush past the awkwardness by returning to his writing lessons, but Ambrose struggled to concentrate as the witch king continued to admonish him.

Treacherous. How brittle your loyalty has become. If your devotion to me were true, you'd have killed him already.

Ambrose felt the guilt and self-loathing a thousandfold, as he always did, but something else accompanied them. A new feeling, one he could barely name let alone acknowledge.

Anger.

The night of Morcant's clandestine meeting at the bridge, it didn't have the decency to rain properly, instead opting for the dismal, misty damp that penetrated your clothes with cold.

A HEX FOR HUNGER 201

Ambrose accompanied Emery along the bank, queued with house boats and sleeping moorhens. Emery had devised a clever spell that made them both invisible to everyone except each other, allowing them the silent communication of raised eyebrows and pointed fingers. More importantly, it prevented them from getting separated.

Emery smoothed the wrinkles from the slip of paper he'd written the address on, eyeing the oxidized copper numbers on the restaurant's red brick. Ambrose was still muddling through memorization of his letters and their phonemes, but numbers he found easier. He felt a slight thrill that he could read this one. A two and seven.

"Twenty-seven," he said.

Emery gave an approving smile. "This is the place. Now we find a spot to wait."

The restaurant was at the corner of the pier and a canal, which slunk its way deeper into the city. The bridge, where Morcant's meeting would take place, crossed the canal, tall lanterns lighting its stone arch. Emery found a spot beneath the restaurant's trellised canopy, sheltered from the rain. A low wall with flower beds fenced in the outdoor seating area and provided cover. The tables left little space in between, and Ambrose debated where to stand. The memory of sitting close on library cushions while watching Emery's hands make elegantly slanting letters across parchment, listening to the rasp of the pen and the thunder of his own heartbeat, was still too fresh.

Emery liberated him from the decision, crowding next to him behind the walled flower bed. Rain dripped helpfully down Ambrose's back, distracting from the brush of their elbows.

"Who do you think he's meeting?" he asked.

"Honestly? No idea. It can't be a common errand if it's happening at one in the bloody morning."

They fell quiet at the sound of someone's approach. Two figures crossed the bridge from its opposite side to stand in the lantern's spotlight.

"He's late," Morcant said. His water deer's hooves tapped against the planks next to him, her large eyes watching the dark keenly.

Hellebore didn't answer. She turned her back to Morcant, leaning her elbows on the bridge's rail to stare into the dark water of the canal.

"Sulking is unbecoming of a woman," Morcant said.

"I'm not sulking. I'm angry with you."

"It's hardly my fault that girl broke things off, but I did say she wasn't worth your time."

Hellebore let out a dry laugh. "I know I didn't give her the clap, yet she seemed *extremely* convinced I'm the only one it could have come from. I know she didn't fool around on me."

Morcant's expression wrinkled. "Well, one of you did, or we wouldn't be having this repugnant conversation."

"Jude isn't like that. You hexed her."

"I never laid a finger on her." Morcant adopted a tone of parental concern. "I warned you. Love can blind you to the obvious. Clearly she wasn't as faithful as she seemed, only a convincing liar."

Hellebore didn't look at him, but from this vantage, Ambrose could see her face. Hurt cut across it, a sliver of doubt wedged in her resolve. Her stoat familiar, cuddled into her hood like a scarf, licked her cheek.

After watching her stand over Emery with a dagger, Ambrose couldn't scrounge an excess of sympathy, but he felt a twinge of it. Less for Hellebore's heartbreak than for the confusion Morcant cultivated in her. How long could you live with lies and illusions before they disfigured your reality so completely, they might as well have been true?

How long before they disfigured who you were, as well?

Being Morcant's daughter did not appear to afford her special treatment, nor had it inoculated her to his venom.

Footsteps sounded, and another figure cut hastily toward the bridge from a narrow side street. He walked with a cane and wore a loose-fitting long coat. A hood covered his head, but as he approached the bridge, a shaft of light banished the shadows on his face. He had a trim graying beard on a mouth deeply lined with grim apprehension.

He wasn't familiar to Ambrose, but Emery tensed with recognition.

"Professor Valenti," said Morcant.

"It's just Mr. Valenti now. Thanks to you."

Ambrose remembered in a rush—the professor Emery had gone to for help, the one who'd suspected Morcant, the one who'd lost his job to rumors of an inappropriate relationship with a student.

This was him.

CHAPTER 31

I assure you, I never believed those rumors," Morcant said. "I was one of the few who defended your character. You've always been a decent sort."

"Mm-hm." Valenti didn't sound convinced. "So you just asked me here in the dead of night to clear the air?"

"Well, given your reputation, you can't blame me for wishing to distance our association for now, but that is only temporary. I asked you here for quite the opposite purpose. I hated to see you thrown out unfairly and hoped, between us, we could prove you were falsely accused."

Valenti didn't have an answer to that immediately. It was apparent he hadn't expected this; what he had expected, Ambrose could only speculate. Perhaps he'd come for closure, perhaps for curiosity's sake, or maybe for the vindication of telling Morcant what sort of spiky object he could insert in himself.

"Why would you do that?" Valenti said finally.

"I'd love to tell you it's out of the goodness of my heart, but I'm afraid it's more selfish than that. Emery . . ." Morcant paused, letting the name hang in the air a second longer. "I don't wish to speak ill of a troubled student, but I believe I'm to be the next target of his manipulations."

Emery wrung his hands, fingers knotted together like tangled skeins of yarn. Ambrose repressed the urge to reach over and steady them.

"Emery was a good kid," Valenti said.

"He was a very good student, I agree, but he is troubled."

"Troubled, but not the way you *mean*."

"He abused alcohol and raised the specters of a plague of rats," Morcant said, as if gently pointing out the food Valenti had stuck in his teeth. "He's barely passing several classes; these points are all academic."

Stubbornly, Valenti would not be moved. "I don't believe he sent those messages."

"They came from his e-mail address."

"He never said anything like that to me before. Not in person, let alone over e-mail. My *university* e-mail. He's a smart kid. Too smart for that."

"Precisely. He's intelligent enough to know this would be a foolproof way to indict you. The faculty would be too paranoid about the potential scandal to look at things any more deeply, so they rushed to the most expedient means of sweeping the problem under the rug: getting rid of you."

"But what does that accomplish for Emery?" Valenti demanded.

"Who's to say what rewards are concocted from a deranged mind's deranged actions?" Morcant said, but his annoyance was like a hangnail caught in the smooth fabric of his facade. It unraveled and snagged, more conspicuous because of how confident he normally appeared. His familiar gave some of it away, too, stomping its hooves.

Valenti directed his questions at more lethal avenues. "What has you so convinced Emery did this maliciously, and that you're his next target?"

"His behavior has escalated," Morcant said. "He's made several attempts on my life now. One nearly succeeded."

Emery's nails had begun to leave crescent divots in the skin of his arm where he gripped himself, and Ambrose couldn't resist it any longer. He reached over and pried Emery's fingers free, squeezing his hand.

Emery looked at him, shocked. Ambrose hoped his gaze conveyed a silent entreaty to stay calm, that he was not alone.

Emery looked back toward the bridge, but he also leaned ever so slightly closer.

Valenti narrowed his eyes. "What evidence do you have?"

"Will my hospital records do?" Morcant pressed.

"*No.* If e-mails can be falsified, so can hospital records, and so far you've given me nothing concrete connected to Emery himself. Did anyone think to check if his e-mail had been hacked, or if it was sent from an IP other than his own?"

Morcant glared at Valenti. "There's no need to be aggressive. I'm trying to help you."

A HEX FOR HUNGER 205

"Help me? Then help me understand. Emery is a student who moved here quite recently, had no support from family or scholarships, yet seemed, in spite of all that, quite all right before he started taking your class. You, on the other hand, are a well-established professor, well connected to the college's faculty, enmeshed in charities and local politics, with plenty of friends in high places who trust you. It would be easy for you to manipulate the scenario I found myself in, and equally simple to reach out to those more powerful rather than meeting with a social pariah in the dead of night. And why have you brought your daughter along?" He gestured to Hellebore.

She'd stayed out of the conversation, leaning back against the rail of the bridge until that moment. She straightened and stepped forward.

Morcant let out an annoyed sigh. "You know, you could have had your job back, but I can't abide a man of learning who asks so many inane questions."

With the flick of his wrist, he cast a spell, and Valenti vanished. His cane clattered to the cobblestones as something iridescent and blue disintegrated in the palm of Morcant's hand.

Blue morpho butterfly wings had been on his shopping list. Emery had said they were used in transmutation spells.

It appeared as though Valenti had vanished, but as Morcant said, "Hellebore," and she ran across the bridge toward them, Ambrose caught sight of a small skittering shadow.

A rat. Morcant had transformed Valenti into a rat.

He ran straight toward the place they hid, aiming to lose his pursuer amongst the planters and picnic tables of the restaurant. He vanished briefly from view, then scaled the wall and appeared in the flower bed right in front of them.

Hellebore cast a spell, and Valenti froze in place.

She was rushing toward them, and Ambrose suppressed the instinct to run. The wall was between them, and they were invisible. They just had to be quiet.

Hellebore stopped practically face-to-face with them, but her attention was solely on the paralyzed rat. She picked him up, then yowled. He'd sunk his teeth into her finger.

"What is it?" Morcant snapped impatiently. He hadn't moved from the bridge.

"He bit me." Hellebore now held Valenti by the tail. He twitched but could hardly move otherwise.

206   ALISTAIR REEVES

Ambrose's heart rabbited in his chest. What would they do with Valenti now? Emery seemed to be thinking along the same lines, clenching Ambrose's hand in his.

"Your paralysis spells need work." Morcant opened a portal. "Come."

Hellebore trudged after him. Emery jolted into motion, dragging Ambrose along and mouthing the words, *We have to follow them.*

There wasn't time to debate. The enchantment made their footsteps eerily silent as they ran toward the bridge. Morcant was already through, turning to beckon Hellebore after him.

She crossed through the portal. They had seconds and very little space. If they tripped over one another and fell into Hellebore—Ambrose, rather than risk it, swung Emery over his shoulder. He wasn't that much shorter, but he was thin, light, and surprised enough to withhold a protest.

Ambrose stepped through after Hellebore moments before the portal closed. He backpedaled a few paces to put distance between them. Panting, he looked around to regain his bearings.

They were in a garden. To their backs was a terraced house, narrow, and stretching up three stories. It had the leaning look of a cake with too many layers. Around them, the garden hosted a slew of plants that could be used for tithes, many the dangerous variety. They had labels with skulls on them.

Was this Morcant's home?

Emery wiggled to be put down. Heat climbed up Ambrose's neck and cheeks as Emery slid to the ground—a long slide down Ambrose's body.

They retreated to a crab apple tree, which offered a degree of shelter from the drizzle. Invisibility did not feel safe enough at this proximity to two people who'd surely try to kill them if they were found out. Once behind the tree, Emery didn't step away or put distance between them. His hand had lowered, curled around Ambrose's bicep, keeping him close. For safety, if the tense line of Emery's spine and the vein throbbing in his neck were any indication.

He put his back to the tree trunk and looked around it at Morcant.

A shed hunkered between bushes, its face so covered in ivy that its door looked like the mouth of a green cave. Morcant went inside and emerged with a small cage.

Valenti, still hanging by his tail, gave a spasm of horror, but could do no more to escape.

Hellebore put him inside the cage and closed the door. "What are you going to do with him now? People will notice he's missing."

"Nobody is going to shed a tear over a man accused of abusing his students."

That was quite rich coming from a man who actually *was* abusing his students.

"This could be bad," Hellebore insisted. "You're not picking up a bum off the street. People knew this guy. He could—"

"When he turns up dead in a year, I'll doctor the body to make it look like a suicide. Nobody will bat an eye. I'll be even more powerful by then. A year or two after that, we'll move on from Bellgrave and find another haunt, so stop worrying."

In a year. He planned to have another initiate sacrifice Valenti. Still, Morcant's arrogance bordered on hubris, believing himself not only immortal but untouchable.

He took the cage with Valenti's shivering rat body in the bottom and stowed it in the shed. He closed the door, securing it shut with a chain and padlock, then instructed Hellebore to tithe a strand of hair for an enchanted lock.

Ambrose held his breath as the two witches headed back toward the house, passing a few feet from the tree where he and Emery hid. Though the fear of discovery made his heart beat hard, it beat harder still when Emery subtly ducked his head against Ambrose's chest to hide.

The back door creaked open and slammed shut. As they waited to ensure neither enemy returned, the rain came down more heavily. It dripped from the tip of Emery's nose and hair. He shivered, still tucked against Ambrose like a stray cat seeking shelter, one hand wrapped around Ambrose's arm.

His grip loosened, the touch changing in quality.

Did Ambrose imagine that Emery's heartbeat followed the rhythm of his? Was that color in his cheeks from the cold, or something else? Did the rain taste fresher when it was kissed from the lips of a man holding on to him like Ambrose was the only sanctuary after years of storm?

It's only a side effect of the adrenaline, he thought desperately.

He was lying to himself.

Infidel.

The witch king's voice sounded unusually far away. It wasn't the time for kissing, but for the past week Ambrose could think of little else.

Emery's wet lashes dipped as he took a bold glance at Ambrose's lips. It seemed to take effort for him to say, "You can. If you want to."

Ambrose's blood buzzed in his ears. "I can—what?"

"You know." Emery squeezed his bicep. He searched Ambrose's gaze, found all that apprehension and mistook the cause for something else. "How did this go for you? In your time."

"It didn't," Ambrose said.

Emery's breathing was deliberately even. "Never?"

Ambrose hummed an affirmative, remembering the way the witch king had sealed a compulsion charm to his neck with a kiss to his nape, and decided it hardly counted.

There was nothing even to the cadence of Emery's breaths now. "Would you like me to be the first?"

Yes, Ambrose thought.

At the same time, the witch king snarled, *No!*

Guilt formed a garrote around Ambrose's throat, silencing the thing he most wanted to say. He hoped his feelings were plain on his face, because he couldn't voice them. He had spent a lifetime promised to one man, a man who still lived even if he didn't breathe or inhabit a body, a man he was trying to save. A man who had helped and hurt him in equal measure. Despite it, Ambrose forever clung to one thing: He was loyal. He was true. He couldn't willingly turn his back on the man who'd rescued him, trained him, put a sword in his hand and his soul inside a body that fit perfectly.

That he had such complicated feelings failed to diminish the strength of his yearning for Emery.

When he couldn't speak, the candle of hope in Emery's eyes guttered. "Ah." He started to pull away.

"Command me," Ambrose said.

Emery froze. He looked incredulous. "What?"

"Use the collar. Command me."

Ambrose couldn't articulate the reason he asked. It took several logical leaps, and it made little sense, but it was the only way that absolved him of this guilt. If Emery forced his hand, he didn't have to live with the stain of treachery. He'd been ordered, compelled, he couldn't resist. He could enjoy the touch of a man he'd found himself so enchanted by without consciously betraying his king.

He didn't expect Emery to understand. Half of him anticipated disgust, rejection, and he'd deserve it. Being torn between a desire he shouldn't have and the responsibility he'd long upheld was not a conundrum he'd found himself in before.

Would Emery understand intuitively what he was really asking?

Emery's expression softened. He shifted an inch closer. Tentatively, as if reaching toward an animal with a history of biting, he touched the inky marks circling Ambrose's neck, leaving a trail of sensitivity. There was a moment where he seemed to contemplate the power beneath his fingertips, how easily the magic could make Ambrose do as he wished. He looked into Ambrose's eyes and didn't move from that pose for as long as it took their breaths to sync.

Then he whispered, "Kiss me."

Don't.

Ambrose had already bent his head. At first it was the barest graze of lips. The numbing cold should have made it intangible, but that gentle touch made him *burn*. He melted into it, heart rabbiting in his chest. It was too much to take and too little after an era spent starved of affection.

Then Emery tipped forward as if in a trance, their bodies pressed flush against one another, and the tether in Emery's pocket burned against Ambrose's hip.

Kill him.

Ambrose's throat closed in the collar's squeeze, and his hands rose, itching for Emery's neck.

No, he thought forcefully.

He wrenched away, and Emery's eyes startled open.

Treacherous ingrate. If only I'd known your heart could be so callow.

He'd managed to break the compulsion, but the strength of it frightened him. If he'd held it in his bare hand, would he have been incapable of breaking the hold? Did Emery's possession of it not protect him over the one who'd made it?

Then Ambrose came to an altogether new realization.

He'd felt the tug of the arcane collar just now. He hadn't before the kiss.

Emery hadn't compelled him. He'd *asked.*

And Ambrose's answer had been *yes.*

"Ambrose?" Emery looked wide-eyed and worried.

"We should get out of here," Ambrose said.

Emery looked confused, trying to catch up. "Wait, I shouldn't have—If you weren't ready. If I moved too fast, I'm sorry."

Ambrose shook his head adamantly; he had been more than ready.

Emery waited for more, and when he didn't get it, put together a fractured version of the mask he normally wore, with cracks so wide it was easy to see through. "Ambrose, I can't pretend to know your mind, and I suspect the witch king wasn't always good to you. I don't know what hold he still has over you to make you think that a forced kiss is the only kind you can have, but I thought it was—I thought we were—"

He broke off, looking lost and leaving Ambrose to fill in the blanks of those broken off sentiments.

I thought it was . . . real.

I thought we were . . . falling for each other.

But how could either be true? When a third voice intruded to say, *If he knew your heart, he'd hate you for it.*

Ambrose didn't know how to explain the muddy labyrinth of his thoughts.

He'd sworn an oath.

He'd broken it.

He loved the witch king.

And . . . hated him.

He wanted to be free. He wanted to fall in love. He was fairly sure that was happening regardless.

He wasn't so sure a wretch like him deserved to have those feelings returned. Especially not by a boy he'd nearly been compelled to kill twice.

"You did nothing wrong," Ambrose said, voice rough. "It is I who erred. In any case, we shouldn't linger here."

"Okay." Emery shored up the cracks in his broken mask, and this time, managed something serviceable. "We have to get Professor Valenti first. We can't let them keep him."

Ambrose tried to reorient himself by looking away from Emery altogether. "If we do, they'll know we were here."

"He could help us. Plus, what can they do to me that they haven't already tried? At least I have—" He cut himself short.

"You have me," Ambrose confirmed. *This* he could not leave in doubt. "I'll protect you."

Emery took a shaky breath, rainwater spraying from his lips. "You can't just say tha—Never mind, come on."

They went to the shed and examined the lock. It was copper colored, lighter than the one from the mausoleum or Emery's cellar. Emery took a tithe from his belt and swiped it across the padlock to undo Hellebore's spell, but it failed to crack open the lock. Ambrose called upon his magic, but withdrew his hand with a hiss when the enchantment burned him. It had clearly been designed to reject any magical interference.

"Shit. Should have known they'd use something more secure. We need the key," Emery said.

Ambrose glanced back at the house. "We aren't going in there."

"Then we need something more powerful to open it. Maybe old magic could work. I remember Morcant talking about it. Something about how telling a secret could release something locked away."

"A secret?"

"Something you've never told anyone before." Emery looked at Ambrose with a sardonic twist to his mouth. "So if you've been hiding anything from me, now would be the time."

A conniption of anxiety seized Ambrose at the very thought. How many things was he hiding? The fact he heard the voice of his dead master in his head, or that the search for the grimoire and those intimate moments Emery spent teaching him to read had been in service of Ambrose's ultimate goal of resurrecting the witch king?

Or the other secrets. The ones Ambrose could hardly admit to himself. Like the fact he didn't want anything as much as he wanted to kiss Emery again.

The very thought of admitting it out loud had him searching the garden until his gaze landed on the pile of firewood against the shed and a log with an axe embedded in it.

He hefted the axe, marched over to the door, wound up, and swung its blade into the chains securing the lock. They broke in one go, slinking to the ground in coils, mercifully muffled by the pouring rain.

"Oh." Emery was staring. Not at the broken chains, but at Ambrose's arms. "That's . . . that's effective, too."

Ambrose flushed.

He would have to decide what to do about his hoard of secrets eventually, but for now, he could only nurse the glowing embers of affection in private, where reality couldn't dampen them.

CHAPTER 32

The inside of the shed smelled damp and oily. Shutting the door behind them, they couldn't see well and didn't want to risk a witch light in case Morcant spotted it from a window, but they could hear faint squeaking from Valenti. Ambrose fumbled in the dark, his hands falling upon the cool metal of a spade, clay plant pots—

He touched the metal grating of a cage, and a squeak of alarm followed.

"I think I have him."

"Good. Let me just—" Emery took a pinch of powder from his tithe belt and tossed it into the air, but nothing happened. The warm spark of his magic fizzled out like a weak flame doused in rain. "Shit. Something's preventing me from using magic. Some sort of ward? Maybe that's why I couldn't unlock the door. Clearly it allows Morcant and Hellebore to cast spells, but no one else."

"Will it extend past his land?"

"We need to get away from here anyway. Once past the property line, I'll try again, but . . ."

Ambrose understood. They had to sneak past the house. While invisible, it shouldn't be an issue unless Morcant had any traps or detection charms around it.

"We could climb over the fence," Ambrose said.

"*You* could. I'll break my neck. It's eight feet tall. Not all of us are built like a brick shithouse."

Ambrose assumed from the tenor of Emery's voice he should take that as a compliment. "You don't have any tithes for a spell?"

"That could make me leap great distances or fall from great heights? No, I forgot to pack my magical parkour kit."

Valenti squeaked more despairingly.

Ambrose didn't know what parkour was, but it hardly mattered. "The alternative is going through the house."

Emery let out a low groan, looking at the fence. "I know. I'll just say goodbye to my ankles, shall I? Here. Could you give me a boost?"

They set Valenti's cage on the grass. Ambrose got down on one knee in at Emery's feet. Emery looked down at him, a pinch of worry in his brow, but Ambrose felt a stirring of something else.

On his knees, with Emery's belt at eye level, he was very glad for the cold camouflaging the color to his cheeks.

Emery put his foot into Ambrose's laced hands and a steadying grip on Ambrose's shoulder. Ambrose stood, hefting him the remaining few feet to the top of the fence, but he let out a pained yelp when he touched the edge and recoiled. Balance lost, his free foot nearly kicked Ambrose in the chest. Ambrose still managed to catch him around the waist so that his fall was less a crash than a gentle tumble.

"There's—I think the fence has a spell trap." Emery opened his clenched fists to reveal a red weal across the flat of his palms, and Ambrose was seized by the ridiculous urge to punch the offending fence, which would only lead to more injured hands, but none of his urges lately were sensible.

Unfaithful cur. This foolish infatuation will be the death of us both.

Ambrose released Emery, taking a few distancing steps back. "Could a flesh or blood tithe get us through?"

"It's a trap rather than a ward. I don't know what spell Morcant used and can't craft one to undo it."

"Then how do we escape?"

The entire back garden was fenced in, and the house itself was part of a terrace with no means to sneak to the front without going through the house itself.

"It seems naive to hope Morcant's *home* isn't more heavily warded than the fence," Ambrose reasoned.

"Yes, but—" Emery reached into his tithe belt and produced a vial of something rusty red. The same one he'd produced to get Ambrose through the mausoleum wards during that first guild meeting. "*Those* sorts of wards I can break through."

Ambrose didn't like it, but they had no other option. "Stay close."

214 ALISTAIR REEVES

Emery picked up Valenti's cage. "No squeaking."

Valenti squeaked once in confirmation, and they made their way toward the back door, which was accessed through a glass house filled with plants too delicate for the seasonal cold.

The glass house wasn't warded, but as they got closer to the back door, the damp air shivered with the aura of magic, like a sign proclaiming "No Trespassers." The door itself had two panes of stained glass offering a bleak view inside, but aside from the distant glow of light in another room, they couldn't make out Morcant or Hellebore.

Emery uncorked the vial. The blood inside had nearly dried to nothing. He had to, flinching in disgust, insert his pinky finger and try to scrape the remainder with his nail. He smudged some on the door and the forbidding aura of the ward converted into something more welcoming.

They had to hope that stealth and invisibility would be enough to get them through unnoticed.

The door clicked open quietly under Emery's cautious hand. He peeked through the crack before opening it fully upon a dark kitchen.

Ambrose expected something macabre—animals hung to dry over the sink instead of herbs, eyeballs in preserve jars, the lair of a villain.

It looked like an ordinary kitchen, complete with tea-stained mugs left in the sink and a bowl of fruit bearing overly freckly bananas. It was quaintly suburban, nothing like the mausoleum and dark fashions with which Morcant styled himself.

The door from the kitchen led down a hall with unlit sconces on the walls. Ambrose could see the rail of a stairway and the front door. It was a straight shot from here to get out, except sounds came from an adjoining room, and candlelight bathed the floor in a gold halo.

There was nothing for it but to try. Though the spell covered the sound of their passage, they still stepped lightly.

The candlelight came from an archway into a sitting room. Stylistically, it matched Ambrose's expectations better, with walls painted a green so dark it was nearly black. Curios, many of them taxidermized, stared out from bookshelves. Gold fixtures on the furniture caught the light like gleaming eyes.

Morcant lounged in an armchair by the unlit fireplace with a book in his lap.

They couldn't escape while he was within sight of the front door opening. Ambrose wondered if they might have to venture upstairs and go out through a window when Morcant abruptly shouted, "Hellebore!"

A thump from above them, then stomping on the staircase. She stopped there, glaring over the railing at her father. "What?"

"I've been considering, perhaps you were correct about Professor Valenti."

In the cage Emery held, the rat went very still.

"It's a long time to wait for the next initiation rite, and a waste of magic and resources keeping him contained. Perhaps it's best to dispose of him quickly."

Hellebore stiffened. "That wouldn't be my first suggestion."

Morcant rolled his eyes. "We can't free him."

She remained silent.

"I'd have thought you'd gotten over this squeamishness by now," Morcant said. "But you find new ways to disappoint me."

"That's easy for you to say, when you aren't the one getting your hands bloody."

Morcant's expression flashed, and in the candlelight the wine-aged handsomeness of his face transformed into something fermented and rotten. "What did you say?"

Flinching, Hellebore said, "What do you want me to do?"

Morcant eventually subsided into his chair, appeased for now. But as he slid back into a relaxed posture, his eyes swept over the spot Emery and Ambrose stood. The anticipation of being seen made Ambrose's skin crawl, but Morcant had gone back to his book.

He said, "I don't want you to do anything yet. When the time comes, you'll make a spell jar of him like the rest."

"But the second half of the ritual?"

"Can wait."

Ambrose and Emery exchanged looks. The second half of the ritual—when Morcant took the new initiates into the tomb.

Ambrose had completely forgotten about it, too fixated on the more suspicious part where they sacrificed humans transfigured into rats.

What really went on behind that corpse door in the crypt?

Hellebore, though she dressed in dark clothes and held a candle of family resemblance to her father, looked out of place standing in the stairwell, at a loss for words.

Eventually she said, "I'm heading back to my dormitory soon. Is that all?"

"I'll call on you when you're needed."

She retreated up the stairs. Emery and Ambrose waited in the silence, unsure whether to make a break for the door or wait until Morcant left. Before they came to a decision, Morcant rose from his chair, went to the bookshelf, and tugged on something behind a mummified hand on a plinth. The bookshelf swung inward, revealing a secret staircase leading below the house. Morcant disappeared down it.

Whatever lay down those steps, he wanted it kept safe. It was the most logical place to keep anything secret or dangerous, like the spell making him immortal. Or the grimoire.

Ambrose's temptation to follow was tempered by the very real danger of getting caught or trapped down there. It would be better to investigate only if they needed to, and only when Morcant wasn't present.

Just as he met Emery's eye and gave a quiet shake of his head, Morcant reappeared. He'd donned a traveling cloak for the rain. Turning his back to them, he touched that spot on the shelf behind the mummified hand, and the bookcase slid shut once more.

Then he turned and walked toward them.

Emery started to take several steps back, and Ambrose put his arm around his back to stop him from colliding with a side table. They held their breath as Morcant swept past them, coming close enough that the hem of his cloak brushed past their shins. He took his keys from a hook by the door and left, locking it behind him.

In the ensuing silence, Emery let out his breath and cast Ambrose another questioning look.

Morcant's lair was theirs to explore. For how long, they didn't know, but it was the best opportunity they could hope for.

Ambrose nodded.

They crept to the shelf. It took some cautious pawing before they found the hidden switch on the back. The shelf slid aside. Wooden steps descended steeply into darkness, with only a faint glow of green witch light at the bottom to guide them.

Before they lost their nerve, they followed it down.

CHAPTER 33

The room beyond the secret door was cool and dark except for the dramatic cast of necrotic green witch light bouncing from two wall sconces around an arched doorway. As Ambrose and Emery passed through it, the sconces flared, setting off a chain of them down the hall. They banished the dark, illuminating a long tunnel with many doors—each of them old, formed by planks of wood with an iron ring in the center.

Cautiously, they approached the first, pushing it open. The room beyond looked half library, half laboratory. Strange tithes kept in jars of yellow liquid lined the shelves, alongside potion bottles with congealing contents. Some of the books had disconcertingly beige covers, as if bound in human skin.

The hideous collection drew them in.

"One of those could be the witch king's grimoire," Emery said.

If an artifact of the witch king's was present, Ambrose thought he'd sense it like he'd sensed the skeleton in the cellar.

He felt nothing, but they searched anyway.

Many of the spines were unmarked, so they had to pull the books from the shelf to read the covers. Emery touched them without disguising his disgust.

"They look like human skin because they *are* human skin, aren't they?"

Ambrose nodded. The witch king's grimoire had been the same. Bound in the flesh of a man who'd been struck by lightning, the branching shapes still burnt into the leather. Ambrose had resented the times he had to touch it. The book still prickled with echoes of pain.

I sense your disdain for my magic, even as it made you who you are.

Chastised, Ambrose tried to suppress his revulsion for the books. The longer he'd been around Emery, whose balmy magic soothed rather than stung, the more difficult it became not to let his disconcertion with the latter show.

He did a terrible job of keeping his feelings from his face, because Emery said, "What's wrong?"

"I'd rather be reading about Henry and Simon," Ambrose blurted, and the second it was out, he blushed in mortification.

"Who?" Emery asked.

"Nothing."

"Wait, Henry and Simon as in . . . as in, the characters from—Oh, I can't even remember the title."

"*Ruthless Temptations,*" Ambrose said sullenly.

Emery's mouth hung open. "But you're only just learning to read."

"I had a blind student in your class instruct me in the spellcraft of text-to-speech."

"Oh." Emery pulled his lips between his teeth, but it didn't hide his pleased smile. "You don't have to be embarrassed. I have those books because I like them, obviously."

Ambrose's heart still raced. Being caught reading rude books felt like he'd been caught naked, though it presented an opportunity to learn more. "They wink a lot in those books."

"Er, I suppose they do."

"It was not common practice in my era. I'm not sure anyone save rapscallions winked. Is that how modern seduction works?"

Emery snorted. "I don't know if I've ever winked."

"I don't know if I can," Ambrose countered.

"Sure you can. You just close one eye." Emery faced him, winking to demonstrate. "Like that."

Ambrose had to concentrate. He closed one eye, but evidently not smoothly, because Emery started laughing.

"Quicker. And not so . . . emphatically."

Ambrose tried again.

"And not while making that face."

Ambrose was hopeless, but he didn't mind the practice if it made Emery laugh.

A HEX FOR HUNGER   219

"I can get you more books with more homosexual winking if you'd like," Emery offered.

That sounded like a terrible euphemism, but Ambrose warmed to the idea. "I'd like that. There were never any homosexual winking books in my time. At least, none that I knew."

"What was it like for you back then?"

"For those who could partake? Clandestine. It has its appeal in fiction, but in my experience the constant threat of death if your romantic entanglements are exposed made them more . . ." He'd been about to say *damaging*. "Difficult," he said instead.

"Oh . . . Is that why you acted so horrified when we—?" He trailed off. "You don't have to answer."

If there had ever been a perfect moment for an apology, Ambrose might never have guessed it would take place in this wretched library.

"I'm sorry for the way I reacted."

Emery flinched, taking the wrong meaning from the apology.

"I'm not apologizing for kissing you," Ambrose said quickly.

Emery stopped. They gazed at one another for the length of three heartbeats, until Ambrose summoned his courage.

"You—*the kiss* meant a great deal to me. I'm sorry if it seemed otherwise, I *wanted* to kiss you, but there are reasons I—can't. Shouldn't."

Won't, said the voice in his ear.

Emery set the book he held on the table and slowly made his way across the room to stand in front of Ambrose.

"Because of the witch king," he guessed, still guarded, but softer than before.

Ambrose couldn't keep this secret any longer. It was making him ill, but he didn't know a comprehensive way to explain. "There are things I've hidden from you. Or myself. Or both. About the witch king, my oath. Things I need to tell you before we can—I can—"

"Hey." Emery cupped his cheek. He seemed shocked he'd done so, but a second later his thumb soothed a line across one cheek bone. "It's all right. He's dead."

Don't tell him.

Ambrose had to wrench the words through the choking circle of the collar's grip. Emery was standing close enough that the compulsion held some power over Ambrose, but not enough.

"The witch king isn't dead."

Emery's hand stilled. "What?"

"He isn't dead. Not entirely. In life, he performed a ritual that connected us somehow. He could not die so long as I lived. Now you've resurrected me, and I—I hear his voice."

"Why didn't you tell me this before?"

Stop this. Kill him.

Ambrose bit the inside of his cheek to distract from the molten pain the collar inflicted upon him. "I'll explain everything, but for now, I really need you to step back and keep the tether far away from me."

No! Choke him, break him, do not disobey me.

Emery, wide-eyed and confused, took three steps back and fished the slim bone from his pocket. He held it up. "How far?"

Sweat had broken out on Ambrose's forehead, but the collar loosened. Runes glowed faintly with residual power along the pearly length of the bone, still trying to inflict its commands, but the compulsion held no power.

Emery's face dawned with horror. "He was trying to control you."

"Yes."

"What did he want you to do?"

"He wants me to kill you."

Even in the dark, Emery's face paled. The way he pulled back further tugged at Ambrose's heart. He didn't think he could bear it if Emery feared him like he had at the start.

"Why?" Emery asked.

"I suspect he believes it would restore his power. Perhaps revive him. He tried to do the same by ordering me to kill Morcant, but it failed. Presumably because Morcant cannot die. Now it fails because I refuse to do as he asks, but with that in my hands . . ." He looked at the tether and shuddered. "I think the only reason I'm able to refuse is because, while you have it in your possession, I am bound to protect and never harm you. But it belonged to the witch king first. It is his. And so am I." The words tasted more bitter than they ever had.

Emery's face fell. "What do you even mean by that?"

He meant that he'd been loyal for a lifetime and didn't know if he could break free now. He meant that the magic needed to be fed, or he feared it might consume him instead. He meant that the witch king's love was the only kind he'd ever known, and that he still couldn't quite

A HEX FOR HUNGER   221

reconcile how meager it had been. Scraps were luxurious when you were starving.

Mostly, he meant he didn't know who he was anymore, if not the witch king's faithful servant. He'd sacrificed the hero for the wolf.

Carefully, Emery tucked the finger bone into the inner pocket of his robes. He took a few cautious steps forward. Ambrose let him, though his instincts screamed *retreat*. But Emery ensured no contact with the tether when he leaned forward to touch his arm, trailing it to the wrist, encouraging Ambrose to unfist his hands. His nails had bit into his palms. Through the pins and needles, Emery's fingers tucked silkily between each of Ambrose's, reminding him of the way he'd held his place between pages in books at the library. Ambrose knew he'd need no such bookmark to recall with clarity this moment, with his heart tripping and Emery looking at him earnestly.

"I won't let that happen," he said. "You've protected me all this time. I'll do the same for you. We'll find a way to free you of him."

No!

The witch king's rage blazed hotter than it ever had. Ambrose feared it. Still felt a sting of guilt over it. But he'd spent a lifetime serving a man who loved him with the unfelt heat of a distant star, where even the small affection of Emery holding his hand filled his chest with the scorch of summer's sun.

They had a task, so the rest of this conversation would have to wait.

Of the many books they scoured, the witch king's grimoire was not among them, so they ventured down the hall to further doors.

Valenti squeaked piteously and jumped at every noise. Emery couldn't turn him back without the correct tithe, but he seemed all too glad to remain small and protected within his cage.

One door opened into a darkly decorated office—complete with a mummified bat mounted on the wall. Another, a room filled with taxidermy and pickled animals. But the others were . . . different.

One led to a second library, but not like the last they'd explored. This was Bellgrave's public library—galleries of books several stories tall. Looking in had the effect of watching an underwater world through aquarium glass. All the sounds on the other side were muffled. Poking their heads in, the dripping damp from the hall fell away, resolving into the shrouded papery quiet of all libraries.

"They're portals," Emery realized. "These doors are portals to other places."

"Why not just use a regular portal? Why make them permanent?" Ambrose asked.

"These must go to places where regular portals can't function, like the castle. I imagine we won't be able to get back the other way without a secret tithe or enchantment."

Ambrose regarded the library through this particular door. "He couldn't have hidden the witch king's grimoire amongst the school's collection, could he?"

"I reckon it'd be easier than becoming immortal. He could have spelled it to look like some dry textbook."

They couldn't check every tome in the place; it would take them the better part of a year. Besides, it didn't strike Ambrose as plausible that a man like Morcant would keep something he prized so highly somewhere so public.

"Then we keep looking."

The other doors led to stranger places still. A stale apothecary through one. A half-drowned pier through another, the salt smell of the sea whispering to them.

None were so strange as the last.

Through it was a bedroom.

It was not a usual bedroom. The walls were windowless stone. The only light came from a series of thick candles on a dresser, which had burnt so long and been replaced so often that they formed a mountain of wax, dripping into the cracks of the wood, sealing the drawers shut. Next to it was a toy chest, closed with a rusty padlock. There was a chart—some sort of yearly calendar—on the wall above, the days either crossed out in red or given a green tick. There was only one tick in a grid of red.

Besides the dresser, the only furniture was a bed and rocking chair. Seated in it was an elderly woman, who rocked back and forth, humming.

They could only hear the humming distantly through the thin veil of the portal, but it had a haunting lyricism and familiarity to it. Ambrose couldn't place it, but Emery did.

"That's the tune Morcant sings before classes."

Before Ambrose could ask who she might be, Emery stepped through the door. Valenti's squeak of alarm was cut off abruptly by the portal.

"Emery!"

Ambrose missed his wrist by a scant inch. Wincing at the pain of his tether and cursing Emery's rash behavior, he leapt through after him.

A HEX FOR HUNGER

223

The temperature shifted from cold to colder. Ambrose looked behind himself to see the portal gone, a door hewn from stone and etched full of marks in its place.

It looked familiar, but Ambrose couldn't place it, too afraid it was their only way out of here.

Emery had gone to stand next to the woman's chair, looking at her with a deep crease between his brows. She continued to rock, but she'd stopped humming, making the soft clink of chains more noticeable. An iron manacle covered in runes bound one of her ankles, anchored by a clasp drilled into the floor.

Without looking up to acknowledge them, she spoke in a voice dry as kindling. "Add more logs to the fire, Morcant, it's freezing."

"I'm not Morcant," Emery murmured.

She did look up, then. Her eyes had the milky film of thick cataracts. "Well, who are you, then? Hm? Police? What did he do this time?"

Emery frowned. "We're his students."

"Students? My boy, a professor?" She scoffed and waved a hand. "Don't pull my leg. If he's done something awful, never fear. I'll handle it." She leaned forward in her chair, a knobby finger tapping thoughtfully. "I've a switch here, somewhere."

"Who are you?" Emery asked.

"His mother, unfortunately."

Emery cast Ambrose a look. The tableau was strange and tragic. From the way she spoke of her son, and from the way he'd kept her here, there was no love lost between them.

She could know something, but it was difficult to tell how much of her mind was still intact.

"Did Morcant do something wrong?" Emery asked.

"He is something wrong. They say apples don't fall far from the tree, but have they ever heard of an apple tree bearing lemons?"

"Why do you say that?"

"Cried and cried and cried as a babe, didn't he? No matter what I did or how much I fed him. Cried, and then when he was older, couldn't go a night without soiling his sheets. Never had no friends, never talked about nothing except his silly books, never stopped being a baby. No amount of discipline set him right. No matter how many little animals he'd kill to try and make himself hard, he was always *soft*. Troubled."

A shiver skated its bony fingers up Ambrose's spine. Those were familiar words. Words Morcant often used to describe Emery.

"What sort of books did he read?" Emery asked, hedging toward the grimoire.

"Fairy tales. Horse shit."

"Anything on magic?"

"Oh, yes, magic this, magic that. Said he would show me and become a powerful sorcerer one day." She opened her hands, gesturing to her dank chamber. "I don't see any sorcerers here."

"But was there any book he particularly liked?"

"Mm, great, big ruddy thing with an ugly cover."

"Do you know where he kept it?"

She lifted a gnarled finger and pointed at Ambrose.

Not at Ambrose, but the door behind him.

They turned to look at it. In that instant, Ambrose knew where he'd seen it before. It was the corpse door from the mausoleum.

He exchanged a wary look with Emery. They'd been looking for the grimoire, but discovering what occurred during the second half of the initiation rite could also lead them to answers about the source of Morcant's immortality. It was difficult not to see walking into a tomb and walking into a trap as disparate things, though.

Emery ran a finger along the runes engraved in the stone slab. Nothing but magic could cajole it into opening, but in spite of Ambrose's suspicions it would have protections against standard spells, Emery tithed yew bark in a hopeful whisper, and the door rumbled aside.

The chamber beyond was black as pitch.

The moment it opened, the witch king stirred, his spirit like the rustling of leaves. Something else stirred, too—a deep, old magic that swarmed to Ambrose like wasps to wine.

It's here, the witch king whispered. *It's here!*

Ambrose's heart thumped. *The grimoire.*

Emery conjured a witch light. It hovered above his palm, but the darkness had density, and it only carved a thinly veiled path before them.

Before they ventured in, they paused, looking back at the woman bent in her rocking chair.

She'd ceased paying attention to them, unfazed by the opening of a door. The chains still rattled at her ankles, but she didn't fight to free herself. She went back to humming that same tune Morcant did before class.

A HEX FOR HUNGER 225

Ambrose didn't know what should be done about her. Did anyone know she lived down here? It was cruel to keep anyone in these conditions, but cruelty seemed to run in the family. Morcant kept his own mother in this abhorrent state, but he'd suffered her contempt from the moment he'd been born.

Ambrose found it difficult to dredge up much compassion for either, then wondered if he, too, deserved no sympathy. Hadn't he done horrible things in service of his king?

If you let your heart bleed for everyone, they'll exsanguinate you in short order. Our priority must *be the grimoire.*

Emery said, "I wonder if Hellebore knows."

"If we free her, Morcant will know we've been here. Those runes on the manacles could be set to alert him, and there's no helping her if we get caught."

Emery nodded. Resolved, he went to stand before Morcant's mother, one hand clutched in a fist to his chest.

"Wretched little rat," she murmured, looking at Valenti.

Emery said, "We'll come back for you later," and reached out to squeeze her shoulder, but his hand passed straight through.

He recoiled, bumping into Ambrose in his haste to get away.

"Wretched little rat," she said again.

"She's a ghost," Emery said, rubbing his chilled fingers. "Morcant chained her spirit down here."

CHAPTER 34

The revelation twisted Ambrose's insides in knots, but it reaffirmed their desperate need to do what they'd come for and leave. Morcant didn't settle for punishing those he loathed in life alone; he punished them after death, too.

Emery rubbed his hands together vigorously to warm them against the chill of the ghost. "Let's get this over with."

The corpse door was blackly unwelcoming as they passed through. Emery's witch light offered five feet of visibility and no more, so they walked slowly.

All the while, the grimoire called to Ambrose, melodic and dangerous as siren song.

The first thing they came to was an open sarcophagus made of stone. It was empty.

"Just when I think things can't get any more cursed," Emery murmured. "This is the sarcophagus we all sat in during the second half of the initiation rite."

Sure enough, the dried remains of black roses littered the bottom of the sarcophagus. Ambrose tried not to appear overly condescending, but that seemed the point at which anyone sensible might have politely withdrawn their candidacy from the guild.

Emery read his expression too well. "I *know*. Not my finest hour in decision-making, but I thought it was just edgy ambience, not human sacrifice magic."

A HEX FOR HUNGER   227

They inspected it for a false bottom, but aside from the dark, rusty spray of blood on one side, it hid nothing.

They investigated the room further, finding a second corpse door. This one was the same size and shape as the one Morcant and his students entered through for the rite. Emery opened it with a spell, and sure enough, the room where the rats were sacrificed was on the other side. A torch of necrotic green fire burnt eternally in a sconce, carving through the darkness better than the witch light. As they turned, its beam glinted off something on the opposite wall.

Emery gripped Ambrose's arm. Squinting, he understood.

An array of weapons were mounted on display, with a line of identical daggers at the top—a banner of them like wallpaper, with one missing from the far left.

They were the daggers used to kill the rats. Ambrose counted six, excluding the one still hidden in the chapel ruin after Hellebore's attempt to murder Emery with it. Each was affixed to the wall by hooks stinking of ward magic. It would be no easy feat to simply remove them, even if you ventured in to find them.

"When you went looking for them, did you not search the mausoleum first?" Ambrose asked.

"I did, but I couldn't open the corpse door, no matter what charms I used. Maybe it could only be unlocked from this side?"

Something else stole Ambrose's attention.

Below the daggers were many other weapons: swords, maces, a halberd, and—

An axe.

It still glowed faintly with an enchantment, making the blaze of scar tissue along his sternum burn with memory.

Without realizing it, he'd taken several steps toward it.

"Those are all the daggers from the initiation rite," Emery said. "All of them, except mine."

Ambrose heard him distantly, his ears ringing the closer he got to the axe. As if entranced, he found himself a foot from it. The haft bore a chorus of carved runes, its killing edge still keen enough to separate a man's head from his neck. Without knowing why, he reached up to touch it.

"What is it?"

Emery had appeared at his elbow, a crease of concern between his brows.

The weapon seemed to whisper as Ambrose ran a thumb along its edge. He wouldn't have to apply much pressure to draw blood. He felt the cold wind of the spell's signature lingering there. He'd always wondered which of the witch king's enemies had cast it. Ilonara Thorn, maybe?

It had been effective. It had shattered his enchanted armor, sundered the spell which made him heal quickly, bursting apart every protection the witch king imbued him with like teeth scattering from a shattered skull. The only mercy lay in how efficiently it had ended him.

"This is the axe that killed me," Ambrose said.

Emery looked stunned. After a second he said, "I forget sometimes you died at all. Feels like you've always been here." He flushed as though he'd said something revealing. "It must have been awful."

"Not really. It was over so quickly, I hardly remember."

"Was there anything after that?"

"Hm?"

"An afterlife."

Ambrose shook his head. "If there is a heaven, they'd never admit a soul as stained as mine."

An ephemeral feeling flickered past Emery's half-lidded eyes. After a beat, he touched Ambrose's shoulder, one finger grazing the arcane collar. "Those weren't your actions."

"He did not always compel me."

"What's the difference, when you know disobedience means your death?"

Ambrose didn't think he was clever enough to find his way to the bottom of that philosophy. All he knew was that he wanted to do better than that, now he had a second chance to.

"The grimoire is in here somewhere. Let's keep searching."

"We haven't checked this side."

"I think it's this way."

Emery's silence held weight, but he followed.

Ambrose listened for the song, now louder and as physical as taste or touch. The witch light shone over more sarcophagi set into the wall, and Ambrose felt along the cold stone until he came to one that was warm. The tinny ringing in his ears hit a fever pitch.

"It's in here."

"How do you know?" Emery sounded cautious.

"His magic is in my blood. I think it calls to its own."

A HEX FOR HUNGER 229

Emery shivered, looking mistrustfully at the sarcophagus. "Can you open it?"

"I won't have to."

Using his powers for destruction was easy, but retrieving something this way took effort. Nevertheless, the magic answered his call eagerly, flooding his fingertips. He thrust his arm into the sarcophagus, stone melting around his arm like butter. He grimaced as his hand first encountered the dusty bones inside. He cast around until his knuckles brushed coarse leather and old paper.

That's it, my sweet wolf. You've found it.

Magic and the witch king's spirit both coursed through him. He felt like a fragile vase overstuffed with water and soil, packed too tightly for anything else to grow. Abruptly, his head felt as if it might split.

"I almost have it," he said.

Take it!

Emery looked concerned. "Can you pull it out?"

"I think so."

You must!

A bead of sweat trickled down Ambrose's temple. The worry line between Emery's brows deepened.

"Ambrose, I could craft a spell."

Don't listen to him!

"Ambrose!"

Emery reached a hand out to stop him, comfort him, perhaps both, just as Ambrose let out a pained snarl and wrenched the book free from the tomb. It tumbled to the floor from his numb fingers as he let go of his control of the magic. It flooded back into the reservoir of his heart and made every beat feel labored, made his blood feel thick as mud.

You've done it. Good! I can finally return. You can reunite us at last.

"Ambrose. Ambrose, are you all right?" Emery asked.

Ambrose held his aching head and shuddered as Emery tried to pull his hand back to see the harm.

He couldn't take it—the sweetly gentle way Emery asked after his well-being while the witch king rejoiced in spite of his pain.

Reading his mind, the witch king's voice turned bitter. *You've suffered worse pains than these, and I can heal all the moment you return me to this world.*

It was true, and perhaps Ambrose was being too sensitive, but he couldn't help leaning into Emery's cool palm against his forehead.

"You're burning up. You didn't have to do that."

Ambrose didn't know how to explain, but he did. Retrieving the book was penance for the way his once-pure desire to resurrect the witch king had been polluted by a fresh and intoxicating longing to indulge in Emery's attention. He didn't know if Emery felt this, too. The need to be near. To touch. To kiss. And not like a friend kissing his friend's cheek in farewell, but a kiss that said, "Hello," and then made itself at home, but he couldn't indulge any of it without suffering this harrowing guilt that he'd betrayed the one man who'd ever loved him.

He could not even hide these craven wants from the witch king.

He jerked away from Emery's touch. "I'm fine. The book?"

Emery looked lost, uncertain, but his witch light flew to hover a foot above the grimoire. Its fall left a track in the dust. Ambrose stooped to pick it up. It was thicker than his forearm and had a supernatural weight to it, as if the magic of its pages had their own density.

Open it.

The spine made the sound of splintered bones as it fell open.

I remember. I remember now. Page three hundred and thirty-two.

Ambrose had only just learned his numbers, but he'd been getting better with them. He liked numbers. They were solid, immovable. He flipped to the correct page.

It was littered with scrawlings, forming a halo around a singular phrase. Ambrose squinted, but he couldn't understand it. It didn't seem like English.

Emery looked over his shoulder. "*Em ruoved regnuh tel.* What does that mean?"

Say it. Wear my spine like a wedding ring and say the words and my true name. And yours.

Ambrose shuddered. He had all the pieces now. He could bring the witch king back from the dead but chafed at the idea he needed to invoke his old name in order to do it. That was his name no longer.

It was not the only thing contributing to his resistance. After all this time spent trying to resurrect his king, too many doubts clouded his judgment to go through with it immediately.

He wanted to tell Emery.

He wanted Emery to tell him not to.

Do not fail me when we've come this far!

Emery said, "Now we have it, maybe it can help with more than killing Morcant. There could be a way to break the hold of the witch king's magic on you, too."

"Or to bring him back."

He just said it. His mind was fuzzy and muddled from the effects of the spell, and he didn't want to lie anymore. In the moment, revealing the truth felt akin to exorcising himself of the witch king's soul.

Emery's expression turned stormy. Confused. "Bring him back? Why?"

Ambrose had been telling himself a thousand reasons, but the moment Emery asked, none seemed to suffice.

"Why the hell would you want to bring him back?"

"He's my—"

"King. Yes, I know. You say that all the time, but it's starting to sound like a deflection, and I want to understand because it makes no sense."

The witch king growled, *Don't listen to him.*

"We were—He was my—" Ambrose struggled to articulate the complex braid of guilt, loyalty, and love that made up his attachment.

"Is this why you really wanted the grimoire? Have you been lying to me this whole time?"

"No! Yes. I don't know!"

Emery looked stricken. "He was a tyrant, he was terrible. And all this time you wanted to find the grimoire, it wasn't to help me defeat Morcant, it was to bring back the witch king? Why?"

"Because I thought I loved him!"

At the same time, Emery screamed, "He killed you!"

In the cavernous ceiling of the tomb, both phrases echoed. A chorus of *I loved him, I loved him, I loved him* and *he killed you, he killed you, he killed you.*

Ambrose whispered, "What do you mean?"

He lies.

"He didn't kill me. A rebel killed me with *that* axe, we were just—"

"An enchanted axe. An axe specifically charmed to defeat you?" Emery gestured to the one on the wall, its glow a damning indictment.

If it had been a labor for Ambrose's heart to beat after using his magic, it was an agony now.

He stared at the axe. It had cut through his chest, but his heart only felt truly broken in that moment.

"He didn't. He wouldn't."

Of course. Never. This is a farce. "I thought you knew." Emery's voice broke, all his anger draining away. "It's in every history book."

"I can't read them!" Because the witch king never taught him.

"I thought you knew," Emery said again. His jaw worked, his expression flitting between confused and horrified. "I thought you knew, and all your complicated feelings about him were because you were still grappling with that betrayal. It was over five centuries ago, but you've only been alive six weeks. I thought you were still—processing. I thought you must have known the moment rebels showed up with an axe purpose-built to destroy you."

Ambrose, for the first time since his body had been reshaped to fit him, left it behind. His fingers went lax. The book fell and hit the floor with a cacophonous thud.

Even as he didn't want to believe it was true, he knew it was. Loyalty had blinded him so thoroughly, he'd never even considered it.

It made no sense. *So long as you live, so do I.* Why destroy the key to his immortality?

Unless that, too, had been a lie . . .

Emery's expression was sour with self-reproach, but it softened as he took in Ambrose's defeated posture. Slowly, he walked over. Ambrose didn't realize a tear had left a track down his cheek until Emery swiped it away with a thumb.

"I'm sorry," he said.

"Why are you sorry?" Ambrose asked.

"I should have known it's—complicated. Accepting the truth."

Ambrose gave him a questioning look.

"It took me a long time to realize the Morcant who encouraged and mentored me was the same man abusing me."

Ambrose had never applied that word to himself before, but as Emery's hand settled solidly on the back of his neck—not in a gesture of possessive control, but to tip their heads together in empathetic commiseration—he finally admitted it.

The witch king had hurt him in countless ways before enchanting the axe that ended his life.

That betrayal had been the last, but far from the first.

It did not take more than a pair of doe eyes to convince you of this heresy against me. What good is your loyalty, now you turn your back on the only man who could ever love you?

"We should get out of here," Emery said.

Ambrose nodded, eager to be away from the dead silence, where the witch king's voice sounded so loud.

Emery picked up the grimoire from the floor, slapping dust from its cover and tucking it under his arm. Ambrose let him take it. He didn't want to touch it.

They headed for the door which led out through the mausoleum.

Green light flashed. Their eyes had no time to adjust from the dark. Everything was blindingly bright as lightning rocketed up Ambrose's body. Beside him, Emery screamed and recoiled from the doorway.

Ambrose squinted with his arm over his eyes until his vision adjusted. The light had come from the floor, where a sigil had been drawn around the entire tomb, trapping them within.

"I must express my gratitude. You've both inspired me greatly with that little spell."

Morcant appeared in the doorway. With a smug gesture, he indicated the sigil glowing underfoot. His fingers were dark and wet as if dipped in blood—from drawing the sigil, or for some other spell? With one thumb, he drew a line across his neck, staring at the arcane collar. "And for that one."

Emery said, "How can he see us?"

"Did you think, after you ambushed me in the bog, I wouldn't find some means to see through invisibility spells?" Morcant tutted. "I wondered if Ambrose noticed during our little chat, but perhaps I gave him too much credit."

Ambrose's mouth went dry. During their chat in the courtyard, Morcant's eye had an unusual sheen, a slightly paler blue than the other. Ambrose had wondered if it could see through his lies.

In a manner of speaking, it could.

CHAPTER 35

Morcant was only a couple paces from the edge of the sigil.

Ambrose lunged, reaching as far as his arm could stretch, using his momentum to press through the searing pain of the sigil's prison. His magic, already agitated after retrieving the grimoire, answered his call readily.

But before he could reach Morcant's heart, the necromancer snapped his fingers. The still-damp blood on them ignited, and a spell struck Ambrose aside and pinned him to the back wall.

"You've really helped to solve all my problems," Morcant said as he took one step inside the sigil.

Emery backed away, reaching for his tithe belt, but Morcant snapped his fingers again. The wall next to Ambrose shuddered where Emery impacted stone, air punched from his lungs in an audible gasp. Ambrose wrenched viciously against his bonds, distraught to see Emery hurt, but the spelled runes on his wrists glowed fiercely orange, and it felt as if a hot iron burnt more into his neck and wrists.

The grimoire and Valenti's cage rang against the floor where they'd been dropped, Valenti screeching in terror.

"You represented all my problems, so it's only just that you helped solve them," Morcant finished.

"What are you talking about?" Emery spat. Crimson speckled his upper lip where his nose had spouted blood from his impact with the wall.

"Patience, and I'll explain," Morcant said in the even tones of a teacher as he stooped to pick up the grimoire. Valenti, in the cage next to it, cowered away from Morcant's dripping fingers.

A HEX FOR HUNGER   235

"This grimoire is a prize. Your old master was a most brilliant sorcerer, far ahead of his time. He understood old magic long lost to the modern witch."

An hour before this moment, Ambrose might have agreed. Now, his mind echoed over and over like his skull was a drum: *He killed me, he killed me, I loved him, and he killed me.*

Morcant drew close to Emery and put a hand in his pocket. Ambrose strained to free himself, but it was fruitless. Morcant withdrew his tether with a look of satisfied curiosity.

"It is no small feat that a spell he cast centuries ago still holds power today without a solitary tithe to sustain it—or not any tithe insofar as our understanding of the word goes.

"The grimoire contains journal entries, musings, and wondering of the witch king's genius. Take this one." He flipped the book open to an excerpt he'd returned to often, from the way his hands knew the precise place to split the pages, leaving bloody stains on its edges. He read aloud, "*There is weakness and power inherent in hunger—the unfed mouth and the hand offering scraps. What spells could be cast from an unsatisfied appetite?*" He paused, smiling to himself. "*There isn't much a man won't do when he is hungry.*"

As if in answer, the hollow pit of magic made of Ambrose's insides howled to be fed, but he didn't understand the connection between the witch king's words and the spell imbuing him with these awful abilities.

Morcant mirrored Ambrose's thoughts. "These musings I could read, but not understand. He never outlines his conclusions or spell recipes. I said they were enciphered. A white lie, since they might as well be. I thought, perhaps, by letting you find it, you'd hold the key to decrypting it. You, who knew him so . . . intimately."

The word caught on the points of Morcant's teeth so it came out serrated and ready to cause a ragged wound.

Ambrose stung with it. How long had the relationship he'd bled and died for been anything except romantic? That final betrayal had rewritten his history, repainted it from rose to blood red.

"Now, I don't need you to decrypt it," Morcant said. "Your little spat gave me all the insight I needed."

"How?" Emery asked.

Ambrose cast back through recent memory for anything they'd said which could reveal the answer, but drew a blank. His confession about bringing the witch king back, the truth about the enchanted axe, Ambrose

236   ALISTAIR REEVES

reckoning with that betrayal. How did any of it reveal the secrets of the spell chaining Ambrose to the witch king's will?

"I could explain it to you," Morcant said, "but I've always found my students learn better by demonstration."

He bent to pick up Valenti's cage.

Valenti's shivering made the metal rattle. With another snap of Morcant's fingers, the rat froze. He tipped the tiny gray body onto the floor before stepping back to cast a spell transfiguring him back into a human.

Valenti had only spent a few hours in the rat's body, but those hours might have been an age for how transformed he still was. Fear hollowed out his eyes, and livid bruises marred his face from his rough treatment in Morcant's custody. With the same spell used to bind Ambrose and Emery, he was yanked up to stand on the edge of the open sarcophagus at the center of the room.

With a flourish, Morcant conjured a noose.

"The first tithe is perhaps the simplest, and the one you already knew—the body of a hanged man whom nobody will miss or mourn."

Valenti whimpered, "Please don't do this."

Morcant cast a spell to render him silent. The tomb filled with harsh, stifled sobs instead.

"You're fucking sick," Emery said. "It won't work. He was the only professor who tried to help me. I'll miss him."

"You can't miss someone who wasn't there when you needed him most."

Emery's mouth shut with a click of his teeth. Ambrose felt as though he could hear Emery's thoughts, feel what he felt. All those years he'd suffered under Morcant, and Valenti had given up on him in the end just like the other faculty had. Valenti's expression crumpled, defeated. He'd cared enough to try, but against Morcant, that hadn't been enough.

"This second part is hardly simple, but the most obvious."

Morcant went to the wall of weapons and selected a knife—not one of the daggers used in his initiation rite, but a slim finger of a blade, as common in appearance as a letter opener. He stopped in front of Emery, the point of the knife aimed at his chin. Ambrose renewed his efforts to struggle free, and the binding spell burnt a new collar around his neck in recompense.

Morcant said, "The spell needs anchoring between the subject and the one who controls him. I've already taken the liberties with my own and, I regret to say, even with anesthetic, this part hurt."

A HEX FOR HUNGER

237

"You haven't anaesthetized me," Emery said.

"I know."

The spell binding Emery turned him and ground him face-first into the wall. Morcant held the point of the knife against the bump of spine at the base of Emery's neck. His muscles shivered with the effort to free himself, but apart from a scream of pain, those efforts bore nothing.

Ambrose's throat went raw. His snarls for Morcant to stop, the viciousness of his impotent threats, dissolved into pathetic pleas as he watched what had been done to him done unto Emery. The experiences bled together. His mind and body echoed with the remembered pain of having runes carved into his bones as Emery screamed and screamed and screamed.

Emery tried to use the blood trickling down his arm onto his hand to draw a rune on the wall. To free himself, perhaps. Morcant snapped, and more bindings held Emery's wrists.

Ambrose could do nothing to protect him or throw Morcant off him. His helplessness was intolerable.

You did this. It is because of you that he suffers.

Ambrose didn't know if that was the witch king's voice or his own.

Morcant finished his foul work and flicked the knife, casting off a spray of blood on the floor. He sealed the wound in Emery's neck with a spell. By then, blood hung like a hood on the back of his shirt, his olive skin gone wan and sweaty in the sigil's light. Morcant cleaned it with a rag and began writing runes with charcoal, enclosing Emery's neck in a collar to match the one Ambrose wore.

"Don't." Ambrose's voice was hoarse.

Morcant said, "I am almost finished, and then I won't have to suffer the insolence of either of you."

He had to turn Emery once more to draw the rest of the runes on his throat. When he finished, the dark marks looked as much like a noose as the one hanging around Valenti's head.

Ambrose couldn't let this happen. The notion of Emery enthralled to Morcant made him ill. There had to be some way to escape.

There is.

Ambrose shuddered as the witch king's voice flicked like a forked tongue in his ear.

Morcant did something inexplicable, something which Ambrose hadn't recalled being a part of his own enslavement. He turned to Ambrose and roughly cut his shirt open from neck to sternum.

His gaze stuck to the blaze of scar tissue. "Fitting," he said. Then he drew a simple symbol over Ambrose's heart, where the axe had split him open all those years ago.

There'd never been a third person in the spell binding him to the witch king. What was this rune for?

Morcant smiled. "You still don't understand, do you?"

He turned his back on them and gave Valenti his full attention. The enchanted noose tightened. "No matter. I'm sure it will dawn on you." He slowly raised his fist in the air, and as he did the noose drew taut, hefting Valenti onto his toes. "I have all that I need."

Once Valenti died, his life would be tithed. The spell would be cast. Emery would be Morcant's thrall.

Unless you intervene now.

What could Ambrose possibly do?

You have the key in your pocket.

The vertebra. Ambrose used his limited movement to reach for it. It was tangled in the scrap of fabric. He had to wriggle it free, and when a frigid splinter of pain went through his finger from touching it, he knew he'd managed.

Put it on.

Adrenaline flashed ice cold and white hot through his veins. The witch king had betrayed him. The witch king had killed him. The witch king had lied to him. How could Ambrose trust him now?

Put it on. Speak my name and the words from the grimoire. Em ruoved regnuh tel.

He couldn't trust the witch king. Morcant wanted Emery enthralled, but the witch king wanted him dead.

Neither of you are any value to me ensorcelled or dead.

The noose drew a choked noise from Valenti as it lifted him off his feet.

I will dispatch this problem for you.

The room went silent as Valenti suffocated.

You only have to trust me now as you once did.

Ambrose didn't trust him.

He also had no other choice.

Valenti's face turned vivid red.

Do it.

Ambrose put his finger through the ring of bone in his pocket and screamed, "Amelia, em ruoved regnuh tel, Desmond Caepernicus!"

His old name made his tongue feel rough as sand, as though he'd burnt it. The boldness of his words brought Morcant up short. The noose loosened in his lapsed attention. Valenti drew in a desperate wheezing breath.

At the same time, Ambrose felt the bone melt around his finger and seep beneath his skin to fuse within him, to leak into his blood like poison, sweeping through his body. It quested within like a hound flushing out a fox. It lodged in his throat and latched on to his spine. His own bones rattled, all the ligaments and muscles and connections shaking loose the bit of bone that had been inscribed all those centuries ago, and the witch king's bone, that segment of his spine, fitted into the place left behind like a key clicking into a lock.

"What is this?" Morcant demanded.

"Ambrose?" Emery sounded scared, confused. "Ambrose!"

Ambrose shuddered. He couldn't answer. Something stuck in his throat, huge and hard to breathe around. He coughed violently until he spat it out on the floor in a spray of saliva and esophageal gore.

It was a bone just like the one he'd put on his finger a moment before, only this one was not the witch king's vertebra. It was his.

He tried to draw in a much-needed breath, but his body didn't obey. The breath he drew instead was even, calm, relieved. Something cold and powerful and hungry—of course, of course it was hungry—flooded his body in place of any control he had over it. It wore his skin like a jacket, moved him like a puppet. It snapped the bonds of Morcant's spell as if they'd been fraying threads rather than steel. It puppeted Ambrose upright and away from the wall and rolled his shoulders back.

The witch king said in Ambrose's voice, "That's better."

CHAPTER 36

Morcant's expression changed, confusion replaced with—fear?

He hadn't looked afraid when he'd been about to die the first time, but now, in this moment, whatever he saw as Ambrose's fist sank through his chest a second time did scare him.

Ambrose himself was only distantly aware of the magic fizzling through his veins or Morcant's hot blood in his hands.

His body slumped to the ground, lifeless, but not for long. Immortality would knit him back together in time.

Ambrose's panicked thoughts raced to catch up. *My body is not my own. He's possessed me. He's going to force me to—*

With its caster gone, the enchanted noose vanished, and Valenti fell into the sarcophagus, holding his throat as he caught his breath. The spell holding Emery released him, too. He sank to his knees. They shook as he tried to regain his feet.

He tried to find a tithe to defend himself, but the brutality of Morcant's spell left him weak. "Ambrose?" His voice was tinged with doubt.

"I am not Ambrose," the witch king said.

Comprehension dawned in Emery's eyes, and Ambrose hated it.

The witch king could not return without a body, a vessel.

Morcant's hadn't sufficed. His immortality prevented him from ever truly leaving his body empty for occupation.

In lieu of an empty vessel, Ambrose's had been enchanted large enough to share, so the witch king's soul had a place to bide its time until a vessel became available.

Or was emptied out for him.

The words from the grimoire, the bit of vertebrae retrieved from the witch king's remains, neither had been a means to resurrect the witch king from the dead. They had been a safeguard. A contingency plan.

Since Ambrose hadn't been willing to kill someone—to empty their body for the witch king—he had taken possession of Ambrose and would do it himself.

Morcant had taken the tether off Emery. It was on the floor next to his cooling corpse. There was nothing to prevent the witch king from killing him now.

Emery's already wan face drained completely as the witch king, wielding Ambrose's body as the weapon it was, advanced upon him.

Run, Ambrose tried to scream, but his voice had been stolen from him.

Emery scrambled back against the wall. His limbs were weak and uncoordinated from blood loss, but he grabbed a fistful of bone powder to cast a portal.

The witch king seized his wrist in a crushing grip, and the bone powder drifted like snow to the floor, what remained in his grip creating a portal too small to fit through.

No, not him, Ambrose pleaded. *Take anyone but him.*

"He is the only one who will do."

Emery said, "Ambrose, please, if you're in there—"

Get away from me, Ambrose wanted to shout. *Cast a portal, escape, anything.*

"—fight him!" Emery screamed.

Ambrose tried, but whatever control he'd had over himself had been forfeited along with the shrapnel of his spine he'd spat out on the floor.

The witch king drew back a fist. Magic coalesced in his fingers like the point of a dagger aimed at Emery's heart. This time, it was aimed not only to kill but to supplant one soul with another. Emery's for the witch king's. Ambrose thought he could feel the witch king's spirit gathering, turning his fingers icy numb.

Ambrose could hardly forgive himself all the sins he'd committed, but he'd never wash the stains of Emery's blood from his hands. Rail and fight and thrash as he did, he was as powerless as he'd been when the collar compelled him. The witch king's spirit gathered in his hand, turning his fingers icy and numb.

He struck out.

Valenti screamed, "Stop!"

Ambrose had been too transfixed by horror and hadn't heard the professor move.

Nor had the witch king. Valenti threw himself in front of Emery, and the witch king's fist dug out a different heart from the one he'd aimed for.

The hungry magic forged a path within Valenti, even as the witch king's spirit railed against its new host, howling in Ambrose's voice. Valenti's strangled death mewl morphed into the snarl Ambrose had been making as the witch king was dragged from one vessel to another.

Ambrose regained control with a disorienting sense of vertigo. It felt like the moment Emery had dredged him out of the bog.

The witch king stumbled upright in Valenti's body, power and magic enshrouding him in a cloak of mist and fog.

Emery took advantage of the momentary lapse in the witch king's control. He seized Ambrose by the hand and scraped enough of the bone powder off the floor to widen the portal.

Shimmering on the other side were the shattered teeth of the ruin's rose window, the evergreen hue of its freshly painted door.

Ambrose tripped as he lunged toward it—tripped over the grimoire. Instinctively, he picked it up before stumbling through after Emery.

The portal closed, but they didn't stop moving until they were through the front door and inside. Ambrose's breathing sounded wounded and loud as he went into the kitchen and seized a knife from the utensil drawer.

"What are you doing?" Emery wheezed. "Ambrose, stop!"

Ambrose had already drawn the knife across the back of his arm. "Renew the wards. Make them steadfast. Make sure he cannot follow us here."

"They were just renewed the other day."

"He's been with us, been inside me this whole time. He's been here. Make them stronger."

He felt a surge of gratitude when Emery didn't argue further. He gathered tithes, the most powerful ones he'd stolen, from the wardrobe in his bedroom. He daubed them in Ambrose's blood, writing runes across the inside of the door, the lintels of the windows, even climbing the library ladder to the hole in the ruin's ceiling to reinforce the protections of their only sanctuary against their enemies.

Enemies. Plural. They now had two.

Reality settled in.

Morcant had nearly ensnared Emery in an arcane collar just like Ambrose's.

The only way to escape had been to follow the witch king's lead.

The witch king had dispatched Morcant and then nearly done the same with Emery, intent on using him for a vessel.

Instead, he'd gotten Valenti.

Once the wards were secure, Ambrose stared at Emery, still drenched in a cape of his own blood, still with charcoal smears of runes on his neck. Ambrose wanted to wash them away. They were heinous. A possessing claim over Emery's soul that he couldn't abide.

But his own hands had nearly killed Emery tonight, and he didn't feel they were clean enough to wash Emery of anything.

His voice came out a raw croak. "I'm sorry."

Emery's wide, dark eyes were guarded as a prey animal's. "Did you know?"

Ambrose flinched. He hated seeing that look on Emery's face, so similar to the way he'd looked when they first met.

He's afraid of me, and he should be. I am wretched.

The witch king no longer inhabited his head, but those were his words. Would he ever be free of the witch king, or had spending so much time in sick company made him contagious?

"Did you know?" Emery repeated, insistent.

"Know what?"

"That the witch king could take control of you like that."

Ambrose divulged everything the witch king had told him. He'd guarded the secrets for so long, made his loyalty to the witch king such a tenet of his personality, he thought the shame of telling all would crush him for all the ways it implicated Ambrose as much as his king.

Instead, it felt like a bloodletting. An unburdening.

He explained the quest for the witch king's skeleton and his grimoire, how it was meant to bring him back without bloodshed. He felt foolish for having believed it, but in the crypt, he'd only discovered the king was a liar moments before he'd been forced to make a choice in a moment of desperation.

The betrayal still felt as raw as an infected wound. A betrayal Emery must feel, too, learning what Ambrose had hidden from him.

"You wanted to bring him back."

"Yes."

"You did bring him back."

"I—"

"You chose him."

Why did hearing that make Ambrose's heart break?

"I hear his voice," Ambrose said. "*All the time.*"

Emery's frosted expression melted just a little. "How do I know I can trust you? How do I know he's not still there?"

Ambrose shook his head, helpless. "I don't know. If you had the tether—"

"This tether?" Emery opened his hand, two bones rattling together in his palm.

The finger bone and the vertebra.

"I grabbed them on my way through the portal. I figured they were better in our hands than theirs. I know you can't harm me while I hold this, but . . . Ambrose, we have to break this pact you're under."

Once, Ambrose would have felt a mountain of guilt for wanting to sever ties with the witch king, but the day had been filled with revelations. It felt less like his resurrection had spat him out into a different era, and more like the events in that tomb had. Before he'd known the witch king had killed him, and after.

"Whatever it takes to be free of him. I'll do it."

Emery still looked guarded, but he also looked hopeful. "We'll find a way, but first . . . I think now the adrenaline's worn off, I might . . ."

His face paled. Ambrose narrowly caught him before he sank to the floor in a dead faint. Given how much blood he'd lost, it was a wonder he'd stayed conscious as long as he had.

He came to quickly, eyelashes fluttering. "Knew that would happen."

"We need to get you washed and into some clean clothes," Ambrose said.

Emery tried to stand on his own.

"Let me help you," Ambrose said.

Emery avoided his eyes. "I'm fine."

Ambrose's heart sank. What must Emery see, when he looked at Ambrose now? The witch king, armed with Ambrose's body, stealing into it like a burglar.

He didn't want to push. "I'll boil some water."

"Bring the grimoire, too."

A HEX FOR HUNGER 245

Emery sat gingerly on the edge of the sofa, taking the grimoire and wearily opening it to the first page.

When Ambrose returned once more with a bowl of boiled water, cooled to a comfortable temperature with a cloth to soak, Emery was weakly undressing, halfway out of his shirt. Once free of it, his hair settled in a sweaty cloud around his face. He looked at the bowl of hot water and, brows scrunched in mild embarrassment, turned so Ambrose could wash his back.

"Feels wrong to make you do this. Like you're my servant."

Ambrose's knuckles brushed bare skin, feverish and clammy, as he soaked the warm cloth over it to loosen the blood. It had made a river of his spine.

"Serving someone felt sacred to me, until I discovered the person I served was . . ." He cleared his throat, gently rubbing clean a rune from Emery's neck. "I do not think you will make me regret caring for you like this."

Those words and the warm cloth wiping him clean seemed to give Emery a measure of comfort, relief, or both. His taut shoulders unwound a fraction.

But he still gripped the tether in one hand like a lifeline.

He returned to the grimoire in his lap. "We have two immortal necromancers to reckon with now. Let's hope this holds some answers."

As he read, he turned the bones over in his fingers. It made Ambrose shiver. That was a piece of his spine, a part of him that shouldn't have been possible to remove. It filled him with revulsion and not an insignificant amount of self-loathing that the witch king's vertebra now replaced his.

"Do these have anything to do with his immortality?" Emery asked. "Or were they only a means to give him more control over you in the event his resurrection didn't go to plan?"

"All the witch king ever told me was that he could not die so long as I lived."

"That gave him a certain level of invulnerability, but it's not immortality. It should have ended when you died, and why would he betray you, then?" He tapped the rune engraved—tiny as a grain of rice—onto the knob of the vertebra.

"You don't think his immortality had anything to do with me."

"I think the spell he cast on you has something to do with it, but you don't have to be alive for it to work." Emery wouldn't meet his eyes. "It's hard to take at face value anything he told you."

"Or anything I tell you."

Emery winced. "So long as he can control you . . ."

He doesn't trust me anymore.

Why would he, you craven deserter?

Ambrose set his wounded feelings and the echoes of his old master's voice aside.

"He was buried for centuries. Something must have happened that went against his plan, or he'd have returned from the dead like Morcant, right?" Emery hummed. "The coffin I found you in. It was covered in runes and powerful wards. Maybe they kept his body locked up and decaying too badly for him to return."

That did sound plausible.

Emery closed his fist around the bone. "How it is made is how it can be unmade. That is the basic principle of magic like this. If nothing else, we should try to reverse the effects of the spell that allowed him to possess you." He scanned the pages of the grimoire thoughtfully. "He doesn't outline the recipe, but you lived through it. If you can walk me through the steps. We can perform them in reverse."

Ambrose held out his hand. Emery clutched the bone more tightly before reluctantly placing it in Ambrose's open palm, carefully and without touching him.

"There was some phrase you said?"

Ambrose nodded. "It was in the grimoire. Page three hundred and thirty-two."

Emery flipped to it. "Here. *Em ruoved regnuh tel.*"

"I had to put the vertebra on my finger like a ring and say that, along with our old names, and it . . . melted into me, replaced my spine with a piece of his."

Emery's guarded expression flickered. "Did it hurt?"

To put it lightly. The spell might have allowed bones to morph and phase through his body without permanent harm, but it certainly didn't feel *good.* "It was unpleasant."

Emery looked uncertain whether they should continue.

"Whatever it takes to be rid of him," Ambrose said.

A HEX FOR HUNGER 247

Emery nodded stiffly. Ambrose took a deep breath and slid the smooth gray bone over his finger. Clearing his throat, he said the enchanted phrase along with the witch king's true name, "*Amelia, em ruoved regnuh tel, Desmond Caepernicus.*"

Nothing happened.

They waited a moment longer.

"Did I say it wrong?"

"No." Emery's expression turned inward. He grabbed a quill and ink from the side table and, without ceremony, wrote across the top page of the grimoire.

Once, Ambrose might have seen it as desecration of the witch king's property—graffiti on a priceless relic. Now it seemed appropriate, like drawing a moustache on a portrait of someone loathsome. Like saying the king's true name instead of his title, for all that it tasted thorny on his tongue.

Emery finished writing, his mouth twisted in disapproval.

Ambrose could hardly read right side up, let alone upside down. "What is that?"

"I thought, maybe to reverse the spell, we have to say the phrase in reverse."

"And?"

"It reads, *Let hunger devour me.*"

Ambrose shuddered. There was that word again. *Hunger.* It was at the center of this spell, the magic all twisted up in the very bones of him. It was another piece of the puzzle; he just didn't know *how.*

Emery's expression pinched with sympathy. "If you need a minute . . ."

"Desmond Caepernicus, *let hunger devour me* . . ." Ambrose paused. "Ambrose."

Like last time, the vertebra squeezed around his finger as if aiming to sever it. It melted under the skin, traveling up his arm, gritty as pins and needles. His back arched as his bones ground together. The vertebra phased through nerves and muscle and sinew. Once more, he found himself choking before hacking up the piece of spine, wet and bloody.

The rune on it still glowed. The magic was as active as ever.

Emery frowned. "Was there anything else the witch king did to cast the spell?"

The memory came back to Ambrose, and his cheeks heated with a mix of shame and uncertainty. "He . . . He sealed it by kissing the back of my neck." Ambrose rubbed the bump of his spine, still bruised and sore. "There."

Emery's mouth fell open. It shut with a click. "Oh. All right. Well."

"You don't have to."

Emery got up in answer, taking a seat behind Ambrose. He had to push aside some of Ambrose's hair, tickling the back of his neck. Ambrose tried not to shiver or show just how much he appreciated even the most practical, least affectionate of touches.

It still felt intimate. It still felt like being saved when Emery's warm lips kissed apart the spell.

Ambrose felt it break. The magic loosened its hold, a shackle come undone.

But only one. He knew beyond a shadow of a doubt there would be more. The witch king had layered his spells to make them indestructible, and this would be far from the exception.

"Did it work?" Emery asked, close enough his breath could be felt.

Ambrose opened his palm. The bone no longer glowed with the mark of its enchantment. The rune carved there was no more. "I don't think he can possess me any longer," Ambrose said. "But the compulsion collar, his immortality . . ."

"What else went into the spell?"

The ash-stained skin of Ambrose's hands was the only reminder required. "Fire."

Before Emery could register that, Katzica jumped to her feet and let out a low growl.

She snuffled along the floor before stopping with her noise pointed at the window. The curtains were drawn, so Ambrose couldn't see anything out there, but then a noise came.

A heavy thump. Another. The shelves shook.

Emery said, "Something's trying to get into the cellar."

Ambrose remembered the remains of the witch king's skeleton moldering down there. Dread washed over him. "Or out of it."

CHAPTER 37

Where are you going?" Emery asked.

Ambrose donned his cloak, already heading for the door. "If the witch king wants those bones back, they probably benefit him in some way. I can't let him have them."

"We."

"What?"

Thump.

The cellar wasn't locked. Ambrose had broken in. Whatever made those noises was too weak to push them open from within. It was colliding with the doors with each attempt.

Emery pulled up the hood on his own cloak. "*We* can't let him have them. And if undoing the spell requires the flaming husk of a hanged man who'll not be missed, then the witch king's remains are as good as any." He gave Ambrose a searching look. "Will you miss him?"

Thump. Thump.

"No," Ambrose said, his throat hoarse. He hated that it needed to be said. His hand held the door handle, but he didn't turn it. "I don't want to risk him hurting you. You should stay within the wards."

Emery narrowed his eyes. Ambrose could practically read his thoughts. He wanted to trust that Ambrose was protecting him, but what if this was part of a conspiracy to aid the witch king?

Thump. Thump. Thump.

"He wants *you*," Ambrose said. "He wants your body. I don't know why, but this could be a ruse to draw you outside the protection of the wards." He chewed his lip, heart thundering. "If you don't trust me, watch from the open door, from the window, but please don't cross the wards."

Emery hesitated. Was it self-reproach in his eyes or just more mistrust?

The next thump was thunderous, the sound of wood splintering apart. Emery said, "Take Katzica."

Ambrose bolted out the door, Katzica stalking by his heels, her hackles high. The wards and the cozy warmth of the ruin leaked away as they stepped foot into the damp woods.

"Here." Emery was backlit like a stained-glass angel in the doorway of his home. He cast the spell for a witch light, which floated from his open palm to hover over Ambrose's.

"Thank you."

"Just deal with it and come back."

Cryptic noises issued from around the corner, where the cellar door had broken open. Something rattled and hissed through the dried leaves as it crawled over the forest floor. Ambrose raised the witch light high as he turned the corner.

The doors to the cellar were blown wide open, some of the wood splintered in places.

On the ground were the scattered bones of the witch king. They rattled and twitched, crawling over each other like insects feeding on fresh carrion, reassembling into a skeleton.

It righted itself, held together by magic. It turned its hollow sockets on Ambrose, the crown fused to its skull glinting in the light from the ruin's window, where Emery had come to watch. His face blanched at the sight.

Katzica issued a warning growl as the skeleton took its first hobbling steps toward the tree line.

Ambrose shouted to Emery, "Get me something to contain the bones."

Emery nodded and vanished out of sight.

The skeleton took another halting step, less precarious than the first. A third.

Before it could reach the trees, Ambrose rushed it. He seized its femur and rained heavy blows down on its crowned skull. Katzica snarled and snapped the wrist bones in her jaws. They came apart, littering the ground with pale debris.

The shambling creature clawed at him, bony fingers leaving welts across his shoulder, but he didn't stop. He struck over and over, dissolving the skeleton into a mess of bones, which tried to reassemble, though Katzica broke the ulna between her teeth, and Ambrose smashed through several ribs.

Emery reappeared with an old blanket. He shoved it through the broken pane of the window. Ambrose set to work bundling all the witch king's bones within it. Katzica helped, but it was no simple task, as they kept moving of their own volition, trying to reach the man they belonged to.

A fever had come over Ambrose. A single-minded, teeth-gritting determination to be done with this. He didn't want to be haunted by the witch king any longer. He wanted an exorcism. He wanted to be free.

Once he was sure he had them all, he held the ends of the blanket together. Emery had produced a skein of rope to tie it shut. Ambrose took the sack of bones around the ruin to the front, where a tree had a low-hanging branch he could hurl the rope over. He tied it there and searched the forest floor for stones. While he worked, Katzica paced the tree line, ears back, hackles raised. The shadows felt thicker than they should be, but if something sinister approached, it gave him all the more reason to dispose of the remains as quickly as possible.

He made a ring of stones on the ground beneath the sack.

Emery looked a mix of things. Concerned foremost among them, but no longer mistrustful. He disappeared and reappeared with matches and a dark black stone.

"I can't find an accelerant, but I can use this as a tithe for a spell. It will work just as well."

"Good."

As Ambrose turned back to the bundle of bones on the ground, Katzica began to growl and hedge away from the deep shadows of the wood, where an even darker shadow emerged.

No, surely not. Surely he couldn't have found them here so quickly.

"Have you really no love left for me?" said the figure emerging from the wood. "My sweet wolf?"

As he emerged into the light, it was not the witch king's face, but Valenti's. His voice was strange. A reedy version of the old professor's, distorted and braided with that of the soul inhabiting the body.

The wards should have prevented him from coming here. They should have shielded the ruin from scrying spells.

"How did you find us here?" Ambrose asked.

"If death could not separate us, do you think any distance or ward could keep us apart?" the witch king said, his voice somber. "We are twin souls, you and I."

"He's lying," Emery spat from within the safety of the ruin. "He was drawn here by his own remains. He can probably sense them through the wards."

"Can I?" The witch king's expressions looked alien on Valenti's features. In spite of the power with which he spoke and held himself, a frailty weighed upon him. His return, and to an incompatible vessel, had not come without its challenges. "And you'd believe this thief over the one who loves you?"

Ambrose had never heard the word *love* from him aloud before. Once, it would have made his heart soar. Now, it broke it.

He drew a match from the packet Emery had given him. He said, "You killed me."

"I killed us both," answered the witch king.

Ambrose hesitated before he struck the match.

"Don't listen," Emery said. "He's just trying to manipulate you."

The witch king's rasping took on a compelling edge. "We were born to an era where love like ours was answered, not with wedding bells, but a death knell."

"You were a king. You had the power to change that," Emery snarled.

"In *law*, but not in the minds of the lords, not in the minds of the people who believed my sodomy was to blame for miscarriages and failed crops." The witch king took a step closer.

Ambrose held his ground and put the match's end to the striker. He would need Emery's spell to accelerate the flames, and Emery would have to cross the wards to cast it.

The witch king continued, "I knew, after all my efforts failed, that no matter how much power I accrued, it could never hold a candle to the power of *time*. Ours was a love that would have to wait for a world that didn't hate us."

"He's lying," Emery said.

"You're lying," Ambrose echoed. "We didn't die in each other's arms. You sent rebels with an enchanted axe."

"I had to set the stage for our resurrection. I had loyalists prepared to pass down the knowledge through generations, to bring us back when the time was right." In Valenti's eyes was a facsimile of love.

A HEX FOR HUNGER

253

Perhaps the fog had lifted after discovering how he'd died, or perhaps it was only that he'd seen more fondness in Emery's face than had ever shown in the witch king's, but he could see beyond the mask now, and the only genuine emotion there was contempt.

"*Think* about it. We can finally be together in earnest! After all these years . . ." The witch king wearing Valenti's skin took another step closer and reached out a hand.

There was something *in his hand.*

A fistful of bloody nettles.

"Don't you fucking touch him!" Emery snarled.

He burst through the wards with a spell kindled in his palm.

Ambrose struck the match.

The witch king lashed out with a spell of his own.

The nettles burst into inky shadow, springing from his palm to slither around Emery's throat, twisting around his wrists and pinning him to the wall of the ruin. Emery's spell winked out, as did Ambrose's match when it hit the writhing sack of bones. Emery tried to cast the spell once again, but nothing happened.

Whatever the witch king had done had dampened Emery's magic. He lunged past, hands outstretched like claws. His aim had never been Ambrose. It was, as before, to ensnare Emery. He counted on it taking Ambrose by surprise.

It didn't. As the witch king made to bolt past him, Ambrose grabbed him by the head with both hands and twisted until he heard the snap of bone.

The spell binding Emery weakened, and he pulled free, the body collapsing between them. The forest made no sound, but Ambrose heard a rushing in his ears, his heartbeat roaring fast and hard enough to bruise ribs. He took the body by an arm and leg, then swung it atop the sack of bones, which had ceased their writhing the moment the witch king's neck had broken.

He felt bad for Valenti. This had been *his* body once, before the witch king killed him, then claimed and corrupted it. Valenti was gone, for no reason deeper or more meaningful than because he'd tried to protect a student.

In all the centuries since his death, there still was no justice for heroes or the people who tried to be. Perhaps the old stories told about heroes were misguided fables. You couldn't wield a sword for justice. Swords were only made for one thing.

"Ambrose," Emery said.

"We need to burn the bones and the body," Ambrose said. "Quickly."

"My magic isn't back yet."

"There must be a counterspell. *Something*."

Emery looked torn between searching for that something and staying with Ambrose, but he went inside and returned a few moments later with a pouch.

"Bat guano," Emery explained. "Makes a powerful tithe, but it's also flammable, so . . ." He emptied it onto the pile. "And this . . ." In his other hand, he held the witch king's vertebra and finger bone.

A well of emotion made Ambrose's throat too tight for words. It seemed fitting that fire, which had unmade him, could unmake the witch king, too.

"Do you want to do the honors?" Emery held the bones out to him.

Ambrose took them. He struck a second match, and this time when it fell, it caught. The sack charred. Valenti's hair curled. The flames spread, devouring with a stomach-pitting hunger Ambrose felt deep in his bones. The fire reached a roar, and still he held the tether and the vertebra clenched in his right palm, digging into his skin. The smell of the witch king's magic burning was rancid, but he had to watch. He had to know.

Side by side, they stood vigil while the fire turned the bones to glowing coals. Ambrose startled when warm fingers pried apart his clenched fist. Emery met his eyes, his own gleaming in the firelight with more compassion and understanding than Ambrose deserved.

"I know it's not much, but I'm here."

After an evening of guarded looks and flinching from him, Emery's closeness meant everything. It gave Ambrose the courage to loosen his grip on the bones and, heart in his throat, toss them onto the pyre.

He watched the tether blacken and begin to glow from within, until the heat expanding in its hollow marrow splintered it apart. It snapped and popped, sparks leaping into the air, and the runes along its length finally, finally went black.

Ambrose didn't know why he felt like crying. It should have been an exultant moment.

Free. Was he, at last, free?

He looked at his arms, still stained by the witch king's magic, and found it hard to believe the man would ever really be dead. He lived on in Ambrose's every gnarled scar, every craven impulse to bow his head to

A HEX FOR HUNGER 255

someone who might hurt him if he disobeyed, in the guarded look with which Emery had fixed him after that moment in the tomb.

Emery wasn't looking at him like that anymore.

For now, it was enough, but the ever-present, starving magic polluting his body still rumbled like a distant storm.

Emery, watching him, did something inexplicable. He turned and bound Ambrose up in his arms. Shock made Ambrose freeze. The crooked arch of Emery's nose pressed into his neck, his arms squeezing as if he could wring the poison out of him.

There was a scaffold of strength holding Ambrose together, one which had weathered so many floods, he'd thought it indestructible.

Emery's embrace made it all crumble.

"I'll never be free of him."

"You will," Emery said. "We both will."

"He's in my head, he's in my blood, his magic has a hold of me."

"We'll break its hold, Ambrose. Hey. Look at me."

Ambrose did look at him, and found none of the earlier mistrust lingered. Emery's eyes were dark and open and glimmering with empathy, because he knew what it was to be haunted by someone like the witch king. Someone who warped your sense of self, twisted your reality, made you feel as though your suffering was both inconsequential and your own fault.

"You have me," Emery said.

CHAPTER 38

With the witch king's magic still simmering in Ambrose's blood, they returned to the grimoire for answers.

"Morcant said it had something to do with hunger," Emery said, skimming through pages at an enviable speed. "And something we said to each other in that crypt gave him the key to what it all meant. Here!" He read aloud from a journal entry, his frown deepening as he did. "*I have thought long about the sort of spells which might last more than a lifetime. What kind of magic has the power to endure? I was reminded of a poem I read from a mad bard's tale of a wolf who devoured her pups to stave off starvation during a long winter:*

The Perfect Hunter
I watched a she-wolf sup on her pups
Winter killed her prey with cold so
She ate each one in a bite
small and milk-starved,
Starved.
Winter
a better predator than
wolves, but still it
cowers to spring.
What hunts the hunter?
It is hunger, hunger
That hunts, haunts the hunter
None of us ever stop being

hungry
for long."

Emery stopped, brows drawn together. "Most of the hexes Morcant placed on me soured my appetite or made it impossible to eat. Things that starved me in some way. I wonder if he was experimenting with the power of hunger the witch king speaks of here. Did the witch king do anything like that to you?"

Ambrose shook his head. He'd never been denied meals. He needed to be fit for battle at any moment.

"None of Morcant's hexes did what he wanted," Emery said. "Still, if hunger is the tithe powering the witch king's connection to you, and his immortality, maybe satiety is the only thing that can dispel it. So what if I . . . feed you?"

"Feed me?"

"Yeah, like, cook food for you."

"We've eaten together before."

"Mostly takeaways because we have so little time. And I've never fed you . . . by hand? I don't know, old magic is strange! It doesn't operate by the normal rules of standard tithes. I wonder if the spell is fed rather than starved, it will undo this . . . hunger hex." He flushed and couldn't meet Ambrose's eyes. "Sounds stupid, now I've said it out loud. It wouldn't be that simple."

Ambrose shared the sentiment. As they'd talked, as he'd considered all the pain they'd been put through and what they faced, he'd come to an unpleasant conclusion. While they still had several leads concerning Morcant's immortality—the second half of the ritual, the grimoire, the things they'd seen in Morcant's home—Ambrose's circumstances had always felt inescapable, because the witch king's power had always been tied to Ambrose.

So it stood to reason that to destroy one, you had to destroy the other.

He didn't know if it was because he'd already died once, or because his loyalty no longer had anyplace else to go, but he'd already committed to saving Emery over himself.

With the magic still chewing through him, he couldn't bring himself to believe the witch king was truly dead. Perhaps the only way to kill him was the one that had worked right up until the moment of Ambrose's resurrection: burying them both in a warded coffin.

He didn't say so. It seemed cruel to taint their progress with his cynicism. "We have to eat anyway. It's worth a try."

258   ALISTAIR REEVES

Emery had what they needed delivered. It was a strange reversal of the usual shopping ingredients—tithes of inedible dried animal and plant parts ground by pestle and mortar into boiling cauldrons—but it had a similar air of spellcraft to it as Emery stuffed bulbs of garlic and lemon wedges into a chicken with sprigs of rosemary in the roasting pan.

"Nothing fills you up properly like a roast," Emery said.

"Can I do anything to help?" Ambrose asked.

"No, no. Eating and being fed are two separate things. And anyway . . . I used to like cooking. Especially for someone else." His cheeks flushed. "It's different when you're sharing a meal. There are studies on the potency of potions, and the ones you buy at a shop are never as effective as something handcrafted for you personally."

Ambrose hadn't known that, but he thought of the hormone potions Emery brewed for him, and something crackled in his heart like sparks from a fire.

There were advantages to watching Emery cook rather than participating—while he peeled parsnips and chopped potatoes, Ambrose could admire him unobserved.

Perhaps, when he learned his letters properly and could write without the hindrance of amateur skill, he would compose poetry about the depths of Emery's eyes, or the way his silvering hair looked like ribbons of witch light, or the constellation of moles on his tan skin.

He felt like a thief, capturing Emery's image in his mind and stealing it away in his heart.

As things stood, he couldn't come up with an adequate comparison to his favorite feature: Emery's profile. The steep slope of his forehead led to the proud arch of his nose. It reminded him of a raven or a hawk. He'd felt that nose buried in the crook of his neck when they'd embraced earlier. An embrace he hadn't expected or deserved after the things he'd hidden from Emery.

Yet Emery had understood.

Sometimes it seemed as though he understood Ambrose's relationship to the witch king better than Ambrose himself.

It took two hours, then the table was set and Emery carved a drumstick onto Ambrose's plate. He'd made some sort of pastry cup in a muffin tin in the oven, which he piled a little of everything into. Chicken, mashed potato, bits of parsnip and carrot, a glossing of gravy.

A HEX FOR HUNGER 259

Emery scooted his chair closer to Ambrose, holding up this edible cup containing elements of the entire roast feast. "In hindsight, I could have chosen something less messy, but we're committed now."

He held it to Ambrose's lips for him to take a bite. He had not exaggerated—there were far more graceful things he could have chosen. A strawberry, a chocolate dessert, one of those frozen lollies he'd dug out of the back of the freezer. (Literally dug. It had been frozen to the wall and required a butter-knife-turned-ice-pick to unearth.)

As Ambrose took a bite of the roast confection, he couldn't bring himself to care how messy it was. It tasted amazing—hearty and filled with flavor. The citrusy garlic of the chicken skin and the buttery mash mixed with the honey-glazed vegetables in an enchantment of tastes.

Emery laughed, and Ambrose chuckled, too, not caring that he probably looked undignified with gravy dripping down his chin. Emery used his thumb to wipe it and sucked the digit clean. Ambrose's laughter dimmed, his gaze glued to Emery's lips wrapped around his thumb, not unlike the way they wrapped around his words.

Emery realized the effect he'd had. It struck fear in Ambrose's heart to be so unmasked in the desires he kept trying to suppress.

But did he have to suppress them any longer? The spell leashing him might still live, but Ambrose's loyalty to the witch king was as dead as the bones that had been rotting in Emery's cellar.

Emery leaned closer. His thumb, still shiny and wet, traced Ambrose's lower lip rather than his chin. "Is this okay?"

The witch king's magic was still a ravenous flood. He shouldn't risk this sort of intimacy if he could still be a danger to Emery.

What's more, their enemies were cruel, but it would be crueler still to lead Emery into a romance doomed to end whenever they finally came to the conclusion that the only way to kill the witch king was to kill Ambrose, too.

Emery waited for an answer, his gaze tender. Ambrose held his breath and resisted begging. He *wanted* this. He shouldn't surrender to it, but he'd waited so long to be wanted back that Emery's thumb parting his lips broke his resolve.

He gave the barest nod.

Emery leaned in, but their lips didn't meet. The kiss hovered between them.

"Okay?" Emery asked again.

This nod could be felt in the bump of their noses together. Then Emery's smiling lips finally met his.

They first connected clumsily, but in that fumbled moment, Emery reached up and guided him with a gentle hand at the hinge of his jaw, and his mouth opened up, and the taste of Emery did not compare with any of the flavors this new world had taught him.

He made a noise. Muffled. Keening. He'd tried to keep it low and disguised but couldn't. He pushed closer. Kissed harder, sucking on Emery's lower lip. The chair legs snarled across the tile floor as Emery moved from his seat to Ambrose's lap. The heat and weight of him filled Ambrose's throat with so much passion he thought he'd choke on it.

His heart had beat anew upon his resurrection, but this was the first he'd felt alive.

The witch king had only ever kissed a brand of control and possession into his skin. It had been devouring in a way that made Ambrose feel consumable. It did not compare to the feeling of Emery's mouth coaxing his to open, or Emery's thumb hitched under the hem of his shirt, or Emery's hard cock against his hip.

A buried voice protested and scraped like fingernails at the insides of his skull. Not the witch king's. Ambrose's own. *You aren't going to survive this.* He thought he'd understood starvation, but he'd suffered it so long that the gnawing of his insides had become background noise. Now the ache was fresh.

It awakened the unsavory thought that this kiss was only his second, but it could also be his last.

So he made it last.

Emery's body went pliant, his kissing shyly hungry. All his carefully hidden nerves couldn't be concealed because, with their chests pressed together, Ambrose could feel him shivering. All those desires surfaced in the quiet plea of a stifled moan, a tongue sweeping between Ambrose's lips.

And the ravenous, devouring hunger sheathed its claws and was briefly, blissfully quiet.

When they finally drew apart to catch their breath, Emery's mouth was reddened, and he wore a dreamy smile.

"Not bad, for someone who hasn't had much practice," he jibed.

"I could use more."

Emery leaned in again. Between the press of their lips, he said, "The food will go cold."

A HEX FOR HUNGER 261

Ambrose remembered the purpose of all this. He looked at his hands, still spell-stained, but the magic was . . . quiet. "Should we see if the counterspell worked?"

Emery nodded and awkwardly maneuvered out of Ambrose's lap. He sat in his own chair, looking flushed and anticipatory. His slicked-back curls were mussed from the attentions of Ambrose's fingers.

In that brief snapshot, Ambrose could imagine a future in this kitchen, with this boy in his rumpled clothes stained from cooking, his undead familiar begging under the table, having a domestic evening of home-cooked dinner and reading by candlelight.

"How do you want to test it out?" Emery looked down at his chest, then looked up again with a sheepish smile. "No offense, but I'd prefer not to be a test subject."

Ambrose looked mortified.

"Joking." Emery looked around. "Try to get a mug out of the cupboard without opening it?"

It was as good a test as any. Ambrose got up and touched the panel of the cupboard door.

For a brief moment, as he studied the whorls in the wood grain, he called to his magic, and it did not answer. There was no rotten hunger, no slavering violence, and the wood remained impenetrably solid.

But it was only a brief moment, the lapse of half a second, chalked up easily to the distraction their evening had been. For the next second, his limb came poisonously alive and sank through the cupboard door until the mugs clinked within.

Their efforts weren't entirely in vain. The roast dinner had been delicious, and Ambrose was well-fed, even if the spell haunting him wasn't.

Plus, it meant that Emery now spent the evening cuddled up to Ambrose's side while searching the grimoire for answers, using it as an opportunity to let Ambrose try and read along.

After a cryptic passage about the fallacy of memory, how the stories we tell ourselves about our lives are colored too much by feelings to be truly honest, Emery said, "I don't know how to break the pact, but I just thought of a way to find out what Morcant does with us during the second half of his initiation rite."

Ambrose had never been to Bellgrave's dormitories. He didn't particularly relish going to the girls' ones, but Hellebore would not willingly relinquish the truth about the ritual behind the corpse door, so they would have to take it from her while she slept.

The spell Emery crafted could extract memories. They'd spent the better portion of the day collecting the tithes necessary, and an entire evening bent over the cauldron on Emery's stovetop brewing the potion.

Now they crossed the moor, where Ambrose remembered jousting competitions taking place, now reserved for "football." A familiar two-story cottage with a thatched roof came into view ahead.

"The dormitories are in there?" he said.

Emery still didn't look at him. "Yes. The boys are in the ones on the south side, the girls in the north, but Hellebore's a senior warden. She'll be in the central cottage."

Ambrose shouldn't have been shocked the cottage still stood. The entirety of Bellgrave had been well preserved, modernity clinging to its carcass like limpets on the side of a beached whale, but he'd never thought he'd return here.

In his time, it had been the king's summer quarters. A place he'd gone when he wanted a reprieve from duty and responsibility.

Ambrose's memories of the place sat as uneasily in his gut as curdled milk, but when he tried to identify why, he didn't know.

He kept his discomfiture to himself as they marched through the dewy grass. Emery had used the last of his gathered tithes to craft the spell for stealth, but he only had enough to last them an hour. They'd need to be swift before the invisibility wore off.

They'd considered waiting for a delivery of more materials, but they couldn't leave Morcant and the witch king enough time to gather themselves for a counterattack. Leaving the sanctuary of the wards at all felt risky, but they couldn't hide forever, and the sooner one enemy was dispatched, the easier it would be to handle the other.

Emery pointed to the first window on the left of the second floor. "That's Hellebore's room."

Ambrose looked. The window was an unlit hollow eye in the building's face. Good. Hellebore was probably asleep already.

Emery cast the stealth spell over them, his magic settling comfortably around Ambrose's shoulders.

They approached the door. In the grass next to the stoop was the iron boot scraper Ambrose often used after the witch king went riding. A strange thing to have endured there for centuries. The door's engraved

A HEX FOR HUNGER   263

handle, which once bore his seal, had been replaced with one shaped like a rose. Stickers and rainbow flags pasted in the window surrounded a sign he struggled, but succeeded, to read.

All are welcome.

He doubted that included him, but they passed through the door all the same.

Ambrose's heart rate ticked faster with every step up the turning staircase. He remembered rushing up them when he'd first arrived at the castle, barely fourteen.

He'd felt so special at the time. The witch king's youngest knight, tutored by him personally.

Why did it all make him feel sick now? The sting of his eventual betrayal, certainly, but some other memory made its sluggish way to the surface.

Emery led them to a door in the hall and listened for a moment before unlocking it with a muttered spell. He peered through the cracked door, then let it swing the rest of the way inward to reveal a dark room and empty bed.

Hellebore wasn't here.

That didn't draw Ambrose's attention quite like the window.

It looked across the moor onto the castle. Its silhouette still carved the same dark shape out of the sky. A branch from a tree outside the cottage still pointed to the castle like in a painter's composition.

Ambrose's throat closed seeing it. He remembered how the wood of the windowsill felt under his palms. Remembered that exact view. He thought he could remember the witch king's muffled voice from the garden below.

What had he been saying?

It was as if Ambrose could hear the voices again. Two.

Then he recognized them. Sneaking up to the window, he glanced outside. Crossing the green at a clip were Hellebore and Saoirse.

And with them, his memory came back in a rush.

"Shit." Emery ran to the door and locked it so it wouldn't appear broken into. "We need to hide until she goes to sleep."

On the night bandits had murdered Ambrose's family, someone else had been there. Another knight. Not Sir Aric, the one Ambrose had spoken to at the jousting competition, a younger man with a bold cant to his chin, who stared into the eyes of the witch king without a speck of obsequiousness. A man who walked the tightrope between brave and foolish.

He'd been looking at the witch king just the same way as they argued on the green outside that window.

Emery cast around the room for an appropriate spot, but while a nicely proportioned room, it was not fit to host four people, two of whom were invisible.

Ambrose was still reeling as memories came back to him. "The wardrobe," he said faintly.

He'd only just begun his training. He'd been given this very apartment, a bed so luxurious and clothes more fine than he'd ever known before.

The knight hadn't liked it.

"He isn't of noble blood. The lords won't allow it."

Ambrose had latched on to that statement. What bearing did his breeding have to do with how well he held a sword?

But as the memory began to crystallize, other facets of detail shone in a new, sharper light.

The door downstairs clicked open.

Emery pushed aside the clothes hanging in the wardrobe, but the bar was too low for them to stand inside.

Footsteps sounded on the stairs.

I know what you asked Sir Aric to do. Are you hoping you can groom this commoner to look past the gruesomeness of that wretched ritual?

"Get in," Emery hissed.

Those bandits were uncommonly well-armed. Do you expect everyone to believe what happened that night was a tragic accident?

Ambrose sat himself in the bottom of the wardrobe. His hands shook.

My family—I've told them. The world will know our liberator has become a tyrant.

Emery hesitated. Perhaps because there wasn't a lot of room, but more likely because he'd seen the stark terror in Ambrose's face and knew it had nothing to do with Hellebore coming up the stairs.

His last words had been uttered through a spout of blood as the witch king cast a spell to carve him up like a jack-o'-lantern.

Do you think your new pawn will remain naive forever?

"Oh, hell, Ambrose . . ." Emery got into the wardrobe with him.

CHAPTER 39

The silence spell muffled the sound of hangers clinking together as they tried to arrange themselves modestly, but there was frankly no *appropriate* way to maintain a respectful distance while crunched into the bottom of someone's wardrobe. As things stood, Ambrose had a stiletto poking him in the hip, Emery knelt awkwardly over his lap, the lace of one of Hellebore's dresses hanging over his head like a funeral veil.

"Never thought I'd find myself back in here," Emery muttered.

It momentarily distracted Ambrose from the flood of unwelcome memories. "In Hellebore's closet?"

"No, I mean—"

The sound of the door opening silenced them. They both held their breaths, listening.

"What sorts of colors do you like?" That was Hellebore's voice.

"Mm, I wish I was a winter, but I think I'm more of an autumn, if I'm honest."

"I didn't ask what some Alakagram star thinks your colors are, I asked which ones you *like*." The usual edge to Hellebore's voice had softened to butter, more teasing than acerbic.

Ambrose found it hard to concentrate on what they said.

Had the witch king arranged the deaths of his parents? Had he orchestrated it to make himself look like a savior?

Of course he had. Then he'd silenced the only other man who'd known.

Ambrose had just turned fourteen. He'd watched the witch king perform powerful magic to murder a healthy young man in his athletic prime.

With no surviving relatives and nowhere else to go, he'd curled up in that exquisitely comfortable bed, and when the witch king came up and put a hand on the back of his neck to tell him, with affectations of warmth and kindness, that the most difficult part about being king is that everyone had a story to tell about you, and most of them weren't true, Ambrose had nodded and smiled and pretended he hadn't seen what transpired on the green.

Why hadn't he remembered it until now, though?

He couldn't recall what the witch king had said. Had he been angry, calm? Had he explained himself? Ambrose shuddered violently as wave after wave of realization came with each chipped memory.

Emery shifted uncomfortably, probably kneeling on one of Hellebore's shoes. "Are you okay?"

"Sit down," Ambrose whispered, grateful the silencing spell allowed them to converse.

"You look upset."

"Just sit down?"

Emery lowered himself gingerly until his weight settled into Ambrose's lap. His warmth and solidity were a grounding rod, helping to dispel some of Ambrose's anxiety. In any other circumstance, it might have brought up the memory of kissing in the kitchen, it might have brought heat to his cheeks, but instead he found himself thinking about all the moments he'd defended the witch king or acted for his benefit.

He tried to focus on what he could see outside the door. Through the narrow crack, Saoirse sank, bouncing, on the end of Hellebore's bed. She wore a knee-length dress with star-spangled tights and leather boots—the kind of clothes she hadn't worn to guild meetings since Morcant's quip.

"I like jewel tones," she said. "But—"

"I think jewel tones would look lush on you. Now, sit still. I'm not used to doing this on someone else." Hellebore sat on the bed next to her with a palette open in her lap. "Let's start with your eyes."

It was a different side of Hellebore from the one Ambrose had seen standing over Emery with a dagger. Her fingers gently dabbed something clear over Saoirse's eyelids, then followed it up with shimmery emerald powder.

They weren't eavesdropping on anything nefarious related to Morcant, only a girl teaching her friend how to apply makeup.

"*In the closet* is a euphemism," Emery said quietly. "For people like us, it means the time before you told anyone you were queer. I've never been in *Hellebore's* closet before."

A HEX FOR HUNGER

"Oh," Ambrose said. "I . . . see. When did you—?"

"Come out of the closet?" Emery supplied. "I think I was eleven when I told my nonna. But she already knew."

"Your nonna?"

"My grandmother. She raised me. Mum and Dad, they couldn't really take care of me. Or didn't really want to. Mum liked parties and traveling more than me, and Dad went in and out of prison, so—" He shrugged, abruptly shifting the conversation, uncomfortable with the personal turn it had taken. "Hellebore never struck me as the nurturing queer elder sort," he added.

"You're the same age."

"Older than Saoirse, I meant."

Ambrose didn't want to let Emery distract him from the morsel of detail about his upbringing. If he had to dig up his own past tonight, they might as well share a shovel. "Where's your nonna now?"

"She died." Emery shrugged again, a compulsive gesture, as if to say *pay no attention to how wounded this made me*. "Nothing dramatic. She was old. When Katzica died, too, I thought about resurrecting my nonna instead of you."

Ambrose's throat tightened. He was grateful for the second chance Emery had given him and afraid that Emery might regret that choice now. "Why didn't you?"

A shaft of light from between the wardrobe doors cast a bolt across Emery's face. In it, his eyes shimmered too much. "And tell her that, in her absence, I'd become a murderer?"

"You didn't mean to kill Craig Kendrick."

"But I did."

"I didn't know her, but I think she'd have forgiven you," Ambrose said.

Emery said nothing to that, just looked away.

Ambrose added very quietly, "Perhaps it's selfish, but I'm grateful you brought me back."

"It's not as though I didn't benefit. And I didn't bring you into a time of happiness, sunshine, and daisies."

Ambrose thought about his life before, the knot in his belly the moment he saw the view out that window.

"In my time, I *lived* in here." The cramped interior of the closet pressed in on them, hardly room to breathe.

Emery put both hands on Ambrose's arms and squeezed. "Are you going to tell me what had you so freaked out a minute ago?"

"Here?"

"We've got no place else to go. Hellebore and Saoirse can't hear us."

If it was anyone else, Ambrose could never admit to the things he'd seen, the things he'd done, the things the *witch king* had done. It made him look like such a fool, to have followed so blindly.

Then he remembered Emery saying, *He was kind to me, in the beginning.*

The darkness made it easier to confess. Ambrose recounted the things he'd remembered. How the witch king had first found him. The death of the knight outside that window. The rituals which made him a living weapon. The moment he erred and was forced to kill his horse and submit to the arcane collar. Who had he been, by then? Who had he become?

Not the hero he'd dreamed of, that was for certain.

Emery listened without interruption. Sometimes, he rubbed his hands up and down Ambrose's arms in a gesture of comfort.

When Ambrose finished the sordid tale at last, he said, "I don't understand how I could bring myself to trust him. How could I just forget what he'd done?"

Emery said, "You were young, with no one to turn to, and you'd just found out the man who rescued you had orchestrated the deaths of your family. What else could you have done?" Emery asked.

"Fought him."

"You were a boy. You would have died."

"I would have died instead of being made into . . . *this*."

"I happen to like *this*."

"But how could I think I *loved* him?"

"Because it was the only way to survive." Emery took one of Ambrose's hands from where it was knotted around his waist and kissed a scar across his knuckles. "The mind is no different from the body. It can be wounded. Your body freezes near a cliff's edge because it knows the fall will kill you. Your mind knew that to do anything but adore and obey the witch king would result in the same thing, so it erased the memories that made following him impossible to endure."

Outside, Ambrose vaguely heard Hellebore complimenting her work then getting up to leave, telling Saoirse she needed to grab something from the bathroom. Saoirse said she'd make them tea.

Ambrose considered Emery's words. Could his mind have done that? Sutured injuries with romantic embroidery to make the pain endurable?

A HEX FOR HUNGER   269

Though it made a twisted sense, the pretty stitches had rotted through gradually, and as that rosy outlook faded, he'd felt less like a lover on the cusp of a reunion than a sword ceaselessly dulling its edge against the necks of anyone who stood in the witch king's way.

Why he'd remembered now, he couldn't be certain, but he thought it had to do with the hospitality of Emery's arms around him, in the thump of one heartbeat steadying his, providing a safety from which he could face the truth.

"Thank you," he said, just as the last motes of Emery's silence spell ran out.

The emotionally fraught conversation had distracted them from how much time had passed.

Outside, Saoirse's head snapped toward the wardrobe.

CHAPTER 40

Ambrose and Emery held their breath, but Saoirse rose from the bed and marched toward the wardrobe.

She flung it open. Ambrose could not have felt less dignified if they'd been caught naked. Emery guiltily leaned away from him.

Saoirse gasped. "What are you doing here?"

The whole cottage had one communal washroom, and Hellebore could be back any moment.

"Not spying on your makeup tutorial, that's for certain," Emery said peevishly.

"Are you and your *cousin* necking in Hellebore's wardrobe?"

"No!" they said in unison, so violently she took a step back. They'd both forgotten the fictional story of their association.

"Obviously that was a lie," Emery said, more quietly this time. "He's my . . ."

Saoirse's eyebrows rose and rose. Her smile grew and grew.

"Don't—"

"You know Hellebore is going to call you 'cousinfucker' until the day you die."

"*He's not my cousin!*" Emery threw his head back and covered his face. "Look, that doesn't matter."

"Agreed. The fact you're in there at all does. Give me one good reason I shouldn't go tell Hellebore right now."

"We came to find out what happens during the second half of Morcant's initiation rite," Emery said.

"By snooping through Hellebore's things? She wouldn't keep anything like that *here*."

"No, with this." Emery removed the vial of sleepy blue potion from his robes to show her. "I was going to extract the memory from her while she slept."

"Why is that so important you'd risk getting caught creeping around her dormitory?"

"Because we have good reason to think the ritual has something to do with Morcant's immortality."

Saoirse absorbed that impressively fast. She did not seem surprised to hear Morcant was immortal. Perhaps Hellebore had told her, which would mean they were closer friends than anticipated. If Saoirse was too loyal to help, that didn't bode well.

She said, "So you're trying to kill him, then? Morcant?"

Emery grimaced, "If I saw another way—"

"I'm in."

Emery blinked twice. "What?"

"On the condition nothing happens to Hellebore," Saoirse finished. "I'll help you if you swear on your life that potion won't hurt her."

"No. Not at all. It just extracts a memory."

"Swear it!"

Emery held up his hands, "On my honor, I swear."

Ambrose hadn't seen whether Saoirse used a tithe, but she must have. Magic coursed through the air smelling strongly of hyacinths—her magical signature.

"Then give it to me." She held out her hand for the potion, waiting.

Emery didn't hand it over right away, staring at her suspiciously. "Why are you so eager to help?"

"Because Morcant is an evil cunt, and I hate him, and she'd never admit it, but Hellebore does, too."

"You know, she tried to kill me," Emery said.

"On whose orders?" Saoirse shot back, then winced. "Look, obviously that was a bit not good, but she failed. And how do you think Morcant took that? She beat herself up terribly, but you don't see that side of her. She gets it in the neck every time you step a toe out of line. Not blaming you, just saying. She's his daughter." A fiercely sad look drew the corners of Saoirse's mouth down in a grimace. "She's suffered him her whole life. I'd be a worse person in her place."

272 ALISTAIR REEVES

Ambrose never thought he'd find kinship in Hellebore, but the moment Saoirse said it, it struck true.

Emery placed the potion in her palm. "In that case . . . thank you."

"Don't mention it." Then she added a little sheepishly, "Really, don't. I was awful to you, when you were only trying to warn me about Morcant. I thought you believed I was too weak for the guild. My stubbornness got me into this mess." She sighed, glancing sideways at the mirror on the inner panel of the wardrobe door. She ran a finger under the paint of her lower lip to even it. "I'm not even sure if I regret it, given what a friend Hellebore's been. I guess you have to find something good while going through hell."

They heard steps down the hall.

Saoirse said, "Meet me at the hanging tree," and shut the door, nearly hitting Emery in the face.

Emery rifled through his tithe belt for bone powder and cast a portal onto the inner wall of the wardrobe. They practically fell through it, landing in the grass a furlough away from a crooked tree, partially fenced off and glimmering with protective wards. Some of Hellebore's shoes tumbled out with them, which had to be tossed back through the portal before closing it.

They waited for Saoirse to meet them. Dawn's glow haunted the horizon by the time she came through a portal of her own. She held out the same bottle Emery had given her, only now the dark navy liquid inside held an undulating spool of red light.

"That should be it," she said.

"Thank you." Emery took it from her. "I feel like I should give you something back for helping us."

"Kill Morcant," Saoirse said. "Just do it properly this time."

Emery took the potion bottle straight to the cauldron on his stovetop. He emptied the tiny vial, the crimson memory releasing the scent of fungal putrefaction into the kitchen.

Emery held his nose while he stirred in the tithes for psychic transference. "I read the potion's smell reflects whether it's a good memory or a bad one. Safe to assume this one's terrible."

Whatever they were about to discover about the ritual, it wasn't likely they'd relish it.

Emery finished throwing tithes into the brew. A gecko's mummified toe, a shard of sea glass. He ladled it into two cups, took the one with a chipped rim, and gave the other to Ambrose.

A HEX FOR HUNGER 273

It had a flag bearing a skull with heart-shaped eyes designed on the side. It looked like some of the pride flags Emery had taught him about, though this one he didn't recognize. He couldn't quite sound out the phonemes.

"Neck-roh?"

"Nec-romantic," Emery said.

Ambrose snorted.

"I made that one." Emery looked both sheepish and proud. "You're getting better at reading."

"I have a good teacher."

Emery flushed. "I'm no good with flattery. Should we drink it together?"

Ambrose nodded. Emery clinked their mugs and said, "Cheers."

It smelled like petrol—an aroma Ambrose had recently been introduced to and did not translate well to drink. It took remarkable constitution to hold his gorge.

Emery pinched his nose before quaffing his own. "That was vile."

"How long before it takes effect?"

"Not . . . lo—"

Emery tilted sideways. Ambrose caught his head before it hit the kitchen floor, then the exhaustion hit him, too. The potion did not lull him to sleep so much as hit him over the head with a sleep cudgel. The cold tile under his cheek and Emery's face snoring softly a foot from his own faded away.

Then he was not in his own memory at all.

He found himself looking down at a pair of hands, connected to him but not his own. They looked fit for playing instruments—long-fingered with short nails in chipped polish the color of steel.

Delicate. Feminine.

His stomach swooped with a familiar repulsion.

Looking down at himself, he wore Hellebore's body like an ill-fitting suit, reminding him of a time when his real body felt more like meat. Separate, detached, not fit for purpose.

He had to forcibly ignore the sensation. This wasn't his body—it lay back on Emery's kitchen floor. This body belonged to Hellebore. This was her memory, and he was experiencing it through her.

Instead of her hands, he focused on what she held. A shard of quartz glowed faintly in her palm. A spell jar.

She looked up, giving him a view of the room around them. Dimly lit by the quartz and a floating mote of witch light, he made out the tomb where they'd found the grimoire. There was the wall of weapons, including the axe that killed him. There was the open sarcophagus in the center. Morcant stood next to it, speaking softly to a figure sat cross-legged inside.

Emery.

He was younger, a sparse few strands of silver to his hair, eyes bright and heart-crushingly naive. He looked at Morcant as Ambrose had never seen him do before. Eager to learn, eager to please.

Morcant was instructing him. "You must focus inward. Forget your body. Detach from your mind. Embody only the ephemeral. It will open you to the world beyond the veil and make you more sensitive to the spirit world."

Emery nodded firmly. "I'm ready."

As he closed his eyes and fell into deep meditation, Morcant gave soft, occasional instruction. "You are neither alive nor dead. You are as the spirits are. Like music. Like light. Sensed but not sensing."

As he continued, the words became more like a chant. Rhythmic. Unsettling.

"Empty your mind, empty your heart until you feel nothing. Are nothing. You feel lighter and lighter because of how much nothing you contain. You are empty."

His hypnotic murmurs caught in the cavernous space, echoing like a susurration of dry leaves caressing a stone path. The tiny hairs on Hellebore's arms stood up, and her heart hammered faster. Ambrose couldn't hear her thoughts, but he felt her fear.

Had she already undergone the same ritual? Had she been the first?

Finally, Morcant took lavender and eggshells from his pocket, his whisper adopting magical intent. The tithes evaporated into smoke, which Emery inhaled on his next breath. He swayed. Morcant caught him as he slumped back, laying him inside the sarcophagus.

Seeing Morcant touch him, conveying him into the coffin like a corpse for burial, drove Ambrose mad. He felt as he had when Emery commanded him to hide, helplessly forced to watch and incapable of intervening.

Morcant turned to face his daughter. "Hellebore."

Her heart plunged. Quickly, eager to get it over with, she approached the sarcophagus. She clutched the spell jar in her hands so tightly it cut into her fingers.

"Everything's prepared." Morcant dropped the soft, soothing tones of hypnosis he'd employed with Emery, now cold and direct. "You know what to do."

A HEX FOR HUNGER

275

"What if I get it wrong?" Hellebore said.

"You'd best not."

The shivering anxiety felt like a trapped bird in her chest, but she nodded. Emery's robes and shirt had been opened to mid-chest, where a charcoal rune mark had been drawn, just as it was with the initiates Ambrose had witnessed. Hellebore placed the spell jar over the rune, alongside a black rose. Emery did not twitch or seem to feel it.

"I'm ready," Hellebore said.

"Good."

Morcant took out a dagger. It had a petal-shaped blade, still rusty with stains—the dagger used to kill Craig Kendrick.

Ambrose's heart lurched. Instinct drove him to try and move, to shout, to wake Emery, but he could no more affect what happened years ago than he could control the changing seasons. Although he felt the pounding of Hellebore's heart and her shaking hands, he could not force her to stop.

All of this was only an echo of her mind. Something which happened and could not be undone.

She took the dagger. Morcant opened the front of his robes, revealing a sigil of runes over his heart, intricate as lace.

He said, "Stop shaking."

Hellebore swallowed the lump in her throat and tightened her grip on the dagger. She held it up, but faltered.

"You can't hurt me," Morcant said. "Strike true."

Hellebore tried again. She held the dagger aloft, overhand, staring at the sigil of runes on her father's chest like a target.

She let out a noise of effort as she brought her arm down but pulled her strike at the last moment. A prick of blood dripped from Morcant's skin.

He seized her wrist in an iron grip, nearly making her drop the dagger. Her wrist bones ground together in his fist, making her whimper. Ambrose felt it, too.

Morcant didn't snarl when he spoke. The quiet tone was almost worse. "Coward. Do it properly this time."

The words wounded more readily than the dagger could. They hurt, but she seemed to use his insults as a whetstone on which to steel herself.

This time, she raised the dagger and plunged it into his chest with enough force it sank to the hilt.

She let out a stifled cry. Blood seeped from between her fingers, encrusting them with red rings. She held the blade there for a beat, Morcant staring down at it and murmuring an incantation, which seemed to heat his blood until it boiled. Hellebore wrenched the dagger free in a spray. Droplets rose in shivering globules as light poured out of his wound. It seemed to bleach the blood, draining it of color, until it condensed into a single mass. A gray orb of both liquid and light.

Ambrose had felt disconnected from the body he inhabited when first he'd opened his eyes in Hellebore's mind, but this horror they experienced in tandem.

Morcant held his hands around the orb. The wound in his chest stitched shut, the blood spent in the spell, leaving him looking as though he'd never been harmed. The dagger, too, was clean besides what remained of Craig.

Morcant approached Emery.

Hellebore took several steps back, while Ambrose wanted to rush forward. He couldn't. He had to watch as Morcant poured the gray bile of his soul into the spell jar perched on Emery's chest. The quartz abruptly turned from cloudy white to arterial scarlet. The black rose wilted, its petals turning brown. Then Morcant pressed on the spell jar, and it began to sink through Emery's skin. Through the rune. Through flesh and bone. Carving out a space for itself in the open, empty vessel he'd made of Emery's body.

CHAPTER 41

Ambrose slammed back into his own body, coming awake on the kitchen floor at the same time Emery did.

"No." Already, Emery was moving as if possessed.

Indeed, possession was perhaps the best descriptor, his body an unwilling host to a portion of Morcant's soul in a dark twinning of Ambrose's experience with the witch king.

"No." He wrestled out of his shirt and clutched the rune over his chest. "No, no." His nails left red welts as he scratched.

Ambrose seized his hands. "Stop."

"Get it out."

"You're hurting yourself."

"I can't have that twisted bastard's soul inside me. You need to get it out." He took Ambrose's hand and placed it, palm flat, against the rune. Ambrose cringed when he understood what Emery meant.

"It's made him immortal." Emery had one hand over Ambrose's, the other holding his wrist, keeping his palm over the place where his heart thundered and, presumably, a fragment of Morcant's spirit resided in its spell jar. "All this time I've been trying to kill him, but I've been keeping him alive. I can't. I *hate* him. He's wrecked my life, and—Please. I need it out."

"I can't."

"You can pull out hearts, you can pull this out of me."

Emery's chest already had red hatches from his fingernails. Ambrose didn't want to envision it with his heart carved out. To make matters worse, the witch king's magic, which had felt like a hollow, aching starvation for weeks, renewed with the prospect of feeding.

"I'm afraid of hurting you."

"When you took that book out of a locked chest for me, the chest was unharmed, wasn't it?" Emery pressed Ambrose's hand tighter against him. "Why not my chest? Is it any different?"

Ambrose shuddered, but Emery's tone made him pause. He sounded terrified, panicked, but also . . . revolted. Sick. Violated.

Ambrose would feel the same in his stead. The magic imbuing him with his abilities often felt like pollution in his blood. Not for the first time, it struck him how similar their situations were: two powerful immortals had infested their lives. Deep down, he believed it was too late to excise the witch king from his heart without cutting into something vital. How did you heal from a corruption that rotted through whole parts of who you were? The idealistic youth who'd dreamed of being a hero had long since been devoured by the Grim Wolf of Bellgrave.

But it might not be too late for Emery.

In theory, Ambrose could do this. He'd used his abilities before without causing lasting harm. If he kept his hand non-corporeal, he could feasibly transmute the spell jar and extract it. It had been inserted without pain or a scar beyond the rune used as an anchor point, so why should removing it be any different?

Still, the idea of using his abilities on Emery frightened him more than anything they'd done thus far. What if the hunger tried to gorge itself? What if Ambrose couldn't stop it from feasting? What if a scrap of the witch king hid inside him and used this as an opportunity to kill Emery?

He'd been staring down at the floor, but Emery lifted his chin with a gentle touch. His fingers spread to cup the edge of Ambrose's jaw.

"Please, Ambrose."

Emery had such wide, deep brown eyes—the color of black coffee, dark chocolate, comforting things Ambrose had only come to taste in this era. He looked completely trusting. Ambrose had yearned for that trust, but now he had it, he wasn't sure he trusted himself.

Emery's face was steely. Determined. He squeezed Ambrose's hand tightly.

"*Please.*"

"You'd trust me to do this?" Ambrose asked.

"Yes," Emery said. "I trust you."

A HEX FOR HUNGER   279

If there was anything he could have said to convince Ambrose, that was it.

"All right."

Emery looked relieved. "Thank you. Where should we—?"

"Perhaps you should make yourself comfortable."

"Bed, then."

Emery led the way through the twisting stacks of books making a labyrinth of his bedroom. He lit a cedar-scented candle and turned on the lamp with the stained-glass shade. He swept a hand over the coverlet until it was flat, then laid himself on top of it.

Ambrose's pulse thumped seeing him like that. It looked too medical. Too much like he was attending to someone who'd taken fatally ill. Too much like the pose in which the spell jar had been inserted in the first place.

"Hey," Emery said.

He turned onto his side and patted the bed. Ambrose sat on its edge, taking a ragged breath. Emery took his hand. Just the ends of his fingers, so Ambrose didn't feel chained, could break away, but could let Emery tether him to solid ground if he so wished.

"You'll tell me if I hurt you?" Ambrose asked.

"Right away," Emery promised.

"You'll stop me if anything feels wrong?"

"Of course."

Ambrose believed him, but somehow it did little to comfort him. The thing about reaching into someone's heart was that it going *wrong* often meant *fatally*, and he'd come to care for Emery a great deal. Enough to defy a king.

His memory strayed to their kiss—the soft way Emery had opened his mouth and let Ambrose in. If only they could make this as easy and gentle.

"Okay," Ambrose said to signal he was ready.

Emery lay back with his head against the pillow. A stray lock of hair tumbled over his forehead, and if Ambrose couldn't do this now, then when?

He twisted the lock loosely around a finger before tucking it behind Emery's ear, his cheeks flushing as their eyes met. Ambrose stroked the same hand down Emery's throat, his magic singing hungrily for the pulse fluttering under his fingertips. He trailed his hand lower, over the curve of Emery's clavicle, the central line of his chest. He traced the rune with his index finger, letting his magic seep and attune to Emery's body, his skin, his blood, his percussive heartbeat.

He'd dreamed of touching Emery, but under circumstances much different from these.

"Ready?" he asked.

Emery's chest rose and fell shallowly under Ambrose's hand, but he hardly looked afraid. He sounded breathless when he said, "Yes."

Ambrose focused his magic, letting it coalesce in the place where they touched. When his fingers sank through an inch, Emery's chest inflated on a sharp intake of breath.

Ambrose froze. "Does it hurt?"

Emery shook his head fervently. "No, keep going."

Ambrose waited a second to confirm nothing had gone wrong. Emery's body was tense with anticipation, but he didn't shake or flinch when Ambrose pushed farther inside.

He had to keep a tight rein on his magic, which snapped its teeth and begged to unleash every ounce of its insatiable hunger, but Ambrose had spent his life starving for something altogether different, and he knew how to suppress hunger when needed. He clenched his teeth, concentrated, and as he did, the magic subtly shifted. It did not necessarily become docile, but when used for violent means, it felt viscous and congealing. While muzzled like this, he found it silky. Almost amenable.

His hand glided past the vital protection of Emery's flesh, into the cage of his ribs, where he could cup Emery's fluttering heart in his hand. Emery, staring down at the place where Ambrose's wrist protruded from his chest, let out a soft noise.

Ambrose tensed. "Is it too much?"

Emery let his head fall back against the pillow and shook it. "Can you feel it?"

"Not yet. Can you handle more?"

Emery let out a gusty breath that was half a laugh. "Ambrose, trust me, this *doesn't* hurt." The knot in his throat bobbed. "I'm—just hurry up? I'm trying not to be indecent, but—" He let out a little gasp as Ambrose shifted to angle his fingers differently, searching. "Oh, *hell.*"

Realization made scorching heat rise to Ambrose's cheeks.

Oh. *Oh.*

Emery wasn't gasping because it hurt, he was . . .

He was enjoying this.

All Ambrose's worry fled him. Conviction that he could do this without causing harm transformed into curiosity at the prospect he could make it feel *good*.

He adjusted his position on the bed, devoted now to finding that spell jar, but also keenly interested in Emery's reactions. The magic still teethed, frustrated, but something felt different about that, too. Like a feral animal shocked silent by the stroke of a kind hand.

Ambrose leaned forward, bracing against the mattress over Emery's shoulder. Emery's eyes flew open, an attractive color high in his cheeks all the way to his ears. Ambrose kept a tight hold of his magic as he trailed his fingers searchingly through the harpsichord keys of Emery's ribs. Deeper, feeling his lungs inflate when Emery's breath caught, counting the vertebrae when his spine arched.

Then his fingers brushed something sharp and foreign, like a razor stuffed in a soft toy. It was lodged just behind Emery's heart.

"I think I found it."

Emery nodded quickly. "Can you remove it?"

"I think so."

Ambrose tried to be delicate and precise as he judged the length of the spell jar. It was small, about the size of his first two knuckles, and the magic within prickled like a sea urchin's spines. Gently, careful to keep the spell jar and his own hand non-corporeal, he curled two fingers around the loose end and tried to wiggle it free.

Emery's hand flew up to clutch Ambrose's arm. His mouth fell open on a stifled whimper.

The spell jar teetered, caught between ventricles. If it had been a corporeal object, it could cause damage, but in Ambrose's grip it was harmless. "I almost have it."

"Okay."

"I think I can pull it out now."

Emery blew out a breath between pursed lips. "Do it."

Ambrose focused all his energy on drawing the spell jar to the surface. It felt a bit like cupping water in his hand and trying not to let it spill between his fingers, but he slowly pulled it through. Emery's back arched, his fingers tightening around Ambrose's arm. His knees cocked apart as his heels dug into the mattress. The magic, the spell jar, and his body adhered to one another, and Ambrose was slowly loosening the threads binding them. He could feel the tension reach a cresting point, a brief slip of it loosening, and then the release as it all unraveled.

Ambrose's hand burst free, clutching the spell jar in his fist. His magic unspooled, freed from his tight control, but instead of jerking at its leash to be loosed like a hound scenting blood, it seemed only to . . . to *sleep*.

Emery was unharmed. The only marks on his chest were the fading scratches he'd left himself.

Ambrose held the spell jar out in his open palm. "It's out. It's done."

He could hardly breathe, but Emery was breathing hard, still holding on to Ambrose and looking from the spell jar in his hand to Ambrose's eyes. He had the flushed, sweaty look of a man debauched and—

And Ambrose could defy the magic's hunger, but not his own.

He tossed the spell jar aside, took Emery's face in his hands, and kissed him.

CHAPTER 42

Where the first kiss had felt like a drizzle after a long drought, this one was a downpour.

The moment their lips met, Emery opened his mouth, and like the spell jar dredged from the depths of his heart, a noise was dredged from depths of his throat, greedy and wanton.

Ambrose's senses overloaded. He was drenched in the smell of Emery—spiced cider and wood smoke. He soaked in Emery's arms around him, hands exploring him.

"Wait, wait." Emery pushed him back with two hands fisted in his shirt. "If we do this, I just—I need to know. Your loyalty to the witch king. You . . . Are you still—?"

Ambrose thought the phrase that came immediately to mind was most ironic, since the witch king was now—after several centuries—truly alive. But Ambrose said it anyway. "He's dead to me."

Emery's smile, and the kiss that came after, tasted of relief.

All hesitation burned up in the rising heat of it. One of his hands wound powerfully around Ambrose's neck, the other roaming in an unfettered exploration of his body, raking down his ribs, then—finding the hem of his shirt—underneath clothes, mapping a scorching path up the curve of his spine and along the landmarks of each scar. Emery touched the tributaries of burns on his shoulder, the slim crescent where a dagger had slid between his ribs, then the lightning bolts under the line of his chest.

Ambrose shivered so violently it broke the kiss.

Emery smiled against his mouth. "Sensitive?"

"Mm." Nobody had touched him like this. Like his body was a story and they were dying to know what happened next.

If he hadn't been so fixated on kissing, he might have told Emery about those particular scars. How they were the only ones he'd chosen. The only ones with a happy ending.

They could do that in the morning.

He'd snatched stolen looks at Emery's body before, but now he had permission to touch and explore. Still braced against the mattress, it was unfair he only had one hand to thumb over a perked nipple before stroking down his ribs. Years of Morcant's abuse had left him thinner than he'd been in Hellebore's memory, the bumps of each rib countable by touch.

Emery didn't stop kissing, but self-consciousness bowed his body inward. Ambrose paused.

"Sorry. Sometimes Morcant's curses left me unable to eat much for days," Emery said.

Ambrose wasn't ignorant to his own insecurities, which would doubtless surface if he acted on his desire to be as close to Emery as two people could be. He was no Prince Charming, but he recalled the lessons from the books he'd read thus far.

"I find you criminally attractive," he said. And winked.

Or tried to.

It was not particularly seductive.

Emery's face turned an incandescent shade, then he burst out laughing.

Not the response Ambrose had been aiming for, but at least he'd put Emery at ease. "I've still not mastered winking."

"I don't care. I want you so fucking bad right now."

Ambrose couldn't contain his grin.

Morcant was still out there. The witch king, too. They really ought focus on the danger, but within Emery's wards, in his arms, Ambrose thought, *I could die tomorrow, and my sole regret would be never having spent this night laughing and touching and loving him.*

So he did.

Emery arched, encouraging him to touch farther south of his belt. Ambrose still braced against the mattress. Now, he couldn't resist pressing Emery back until he had to choose between falling into the bed or holding on. He chose the latter, an arm flung around Ambrose's neck, the other hand seizing a handful of Ambrose's arse.

Ambrose's eyes widened.

"Sorry. Shit, am I moving too fast?" Emery said. Ambrose had spent so long desperate for this sort of affection, he was not keen to wait a second later. He didn't want to be treated delicately. He took Emery's hand and put it back where it had been.

Emery looked relieved and said, "Okay?"

Ambrose pinned him flush against the mattress to demonstrate just how "okay" this was. He hooked Emery's legs apart with a strategically placed knee and groaned when Emery responded by trying to grind against his thigh. For a moment, Ambrose let him, before grasping Emery's hips and holding him still.

"Ambrose. Are you teasing me?"

"You seem to like it."

Emery let out a long, tortured groan. "I *do*. Should have known you'd be that kind of top."

"Top?"

"Another of our gay little words. Means, like, the one who, uh, *gives* while the bottom receives." At Ambrose's disconcerted look, he added. "Unless you prefer to—?"

Ambrose wasn't, well—He didn't have certain equipment to hand. He'd never gotten to take full advantage of his current anatomy, either.

He kissed the spot on Emery's neck beneath his ear. "How else can it be?"

Emery's breath hitched. "Well, there are, like, tops and bottoms, or you could be vers, or a side—Fuck, keep doing that." Ambrose had lowered his mouth to one of Emery's nipples after noticing how sensitive he'd been to the ministrations of his hands. "Fuck. Okay—uh. There's doms and subs, too. You can be a dominant bottom, like a power bottom, so you take it, but you're in charge. Or a service top. You're the giver, but you're really, uh, handing all the control to—to—" Ambrose had tongued a line down to Emery's navel, marveling at how violently he shivered. "God, what was I saying?"

"Control?" His tongue ventured lower.

"*Fuck*, Ambrose. Fuck it. I'll teach you the queer sex lexicon—sexicon? *Later*. I'll teach you later. They're just words, and they don't matter, because right now I'd let you do whatever you wanted to me."

A tug of satisfaction nearly made Ambrose smirk. "So, you're a bottom."

Emery's mouth fell open. "I'm a switch," he said weakly.

"You never covered that one."

Emery made a frustrated noise. "It means I don't care who's in charge or where my dick goes, but right now I'd like you to touch it."

Ambrose didn't need telling twice. His mind had explored many possibilities, some he wasn't sure how to discuss, but he could start with the obvious.

He tried not to look too eager as he tugged Emery's trousers down, freeing his cock. It had a slightly upward curve, a perfect circle of pink peeking out from the ring of his foreskin.

Ambrose's mouth filled with too much spit. He ran a curious hand along the length, marveling at the different textures of skin over the head and shaft. He had no clue what he was doing, but lust crushed any anxiety over his inexperience.

Emery had propped himself up on his elbows, but at the first stroke, his eyes fluttered shut on a muttered curse. "Spit. Spit on your hand."

Ambrose did, wetting his palm, firming his grip, and at the second stroke Emery fell back against the pillows.

After a few shivering groans, he said, "No, okay, stop, or this will be over too soon."

"Am I doing it wrong?"

"No. There are other things I'd like to try."

"Tell me."

"Well"—a soft gasp as Ambrose thumbed the sensitive spot below the head—"I want to please you, too."

Ambrose's nerves fluttered. He'd reached a point of uncertainty. He didn't know what he liked, let alone how Emery's preferences coordinated with his own, and he didn't want this first time to disappoint for fear it could be the last.

He'd been caught up in the kissing, in how natural it was, but this part—giving and receiving, tops and bottoms, doms and subs. It swirled in his mind as he tried and failed to place himself within categories built by people whose bodies weren't like his own.

Seeing him floundering, Emery reached down to still his hand. "Would it help if I asked questions?"

Ambrose nodded.

"All right. Where do you want it?" Emery squeezed Ambrose's hand around his cock to leave no ambiguity about what he meant.

Ambrose's mouth watered. "Anywhere."

Emery tilted Ambrose's chin up, his gaze hot and intent, reading Ambrose closely. "Be specific."

He could think of two places he'd particularly like, but one made him more nervous than the other.

"My mouth."

"And do you want me to take charge?"

Ambrose nodded.

"All right. Get up."

The deep vibrato of Emery's voice was more compelling than any arcane charm. Ambrose rose and stood at the edge of the bed. Emery kicked his trousers off the rest of the way and swung his legs over, standing.

He was only a few inches shorter, but didn't seem that way when he gripped the back of Ambrose's neck and said, "Get on your knees."

Ambrose very nearly buckled to them. He kneeled, holding Emery's hips, now face-to-face with what he wanted.

"Listen to me," Emery said, gently demanding. "If you want to stop for any reason at any time, say *petrichor*." He smirked. "Or tap my leg thrice if your mouth is full."

"Is that a spell?"

He let out a breathy, endeared laugh. "No. It just means 'stop,' no matter what. It's important. While we're both, well . . . not new to this, but new to each other, and given this—" He ran his thumb along the rune line of the arcane collar. "It's important."

Ambrose could not conceive of wanting this to stop. All his nerves centered around being good enough so that it never would. But something about the way Emery said it all, like he'd thought about it before, rehearsed it—

He'd fantasized about being together like this before.

It made Ambrose weak. He wanted to ask what else they did in the theater of Emery's dreams and fantasies, but not now, when one was about to play out.

"What was the word?" Emery asked.

"Petrichor."

"Good." Emery put a tender thumb to Ambrose's lower lip, parting it from the top. "Now open your mouth."

Ambrose's stomach swooped pleasantly. He did as instructed, and Emery placed the salty head of his cock against his tongue. He closed his lips around it, tasting. The sucking noise didn't sound half so lewd as Emery letting out all his breath in a hissing groan. He tangled his hand in Ambrose's hair, the grip firmly guiding him to take more. To bob his head.

288   ALISTAIR REEVES

Emery's voice was a purr. "Good."

The praise made a molten wet tension reel tightly in Ambrose's belly. This—being commanded—was familiar. It might have picked at old scars, but he didn't mind wearing a collar when it was Emery holding the leash.

His confidence grew. Emery's instructions petered off into muffled moans as Ambrose used his hands, slickly stroking up and down with his mouth. Then over Emery's balls and behind them.

Until the fingers in his hair tightened and pulled him off. A glimmering string of spit still connected his lips to the tip of Emery's cock.

He gazed up. Emery looked down at him with a wrecked expression. The hand in his hair settled at the nape of his neck again, guiding him.

"Come here."

Ambrose got to his feet, met with a sloppy kiss because of how wet his mouth was, though Emery didn't seem to mind. Ambrose took him in hand.

"Stop," Emery said.

"You don't want to finish?"

"Not before finding out what you like."

"I liked that. Very much." Though his body ached.

Emery pulled him closer. "Where do you want me to touch you?"

"Anywhere." Ambrose felt keenly aware of Emery's erection against his thigh. His words came out shivering. "Everywhere."

Emery yanked on his belt and deftly popped open the button on his trousers, eyebrows raised in question as he pressed his palm flat to the trail of hair leading beneath the hem.

"Lie back on the bed," Emery instructed.

Ambrose obeyed, but he'd begun to worry whether the things he wanted Emery to do to him were wrong for men, or if Emery had somehow forgotten that he wouldn't find the same thing in Ambrose's pants as other men kept in theirs.

Emery said, "What are you fretting about?"

"How do you know I'm fretting?"

Emery touched a finger between his brows. "You get this worry line right here." He smoothed it out, and Ambrose did find himself relaxing. "What's wrong?"

If anyone else had asked Ambrose to bare his vulnerabilities this way, he'd have denied he had any. Not with Emery.

"I've never been touched . . . *there*."

A HEX FOR HUNGER

289

"Do you want me to?"

"Yes." *Desperately*. Ambrose closed his eyes. "But . . . does that make me less a man?"

Emery searched his face for a moment, then dropped a hand to Ambrose's stomach. He raised an eyebrow as if to ask, *May I?*

Ambrose gave a shaky nod, letting Emery's touch undo some of his tightly wound tension. Then his hand slipped lower, trailing beneath clothes and between Ambrose's thighs, parting him with his fingers, and if his thoughts had been blurry before, they were oblivion now.

All his life, he'd only known the hunger of the magic in his blood. It drowned out all else so he could never address the things he truly wanted. Now he couldn't think for how much he wanted.

He wanted and wanted and wanted.

"Good?" Emery's lips quirked in a self-effacing smile. "I'm new to this myself. So let me hear you."

Ambrose pushed his face into Emery's shoulder and *moaned*.

"You sound like a man to me." Emery's voice brushed, husky and laughing, against his ear. "Most of us sound the same with our faces down and our arses in the air." His fingers slipped deeper and curled. "I don't care what other people think makes a man. I'm only interested in making you cum."

Ambrose reached for Emery, finding his cock still slick, but it was awkward to stroke him while lying on his back, and besides—

He wanted more than Emery's fingers inside him.

Twisting, he rolled Emery onto his back. It took a frantic moment to wrestle out of his trousers. Finally naked, he crawled over Emery's body, straddling and kissing him. The rasp of stubble against Ambrose's lips grounded him enough to make unambiguous his aims.

Experimentally, he lowered himself to rub Emery's cock between his lips.

"F-fuck, Ambrose, holy shi—Hold on." Emery abandoned the garbled attempt at speech to lean over, wrest open his bedside cabinet, and fumble out something in a square packet. "If we're going to—which I *very much* would like to, by the way, but if we are, we should—" He paused to rip the packet open with his teeth, producing a rubbery, slimy disc of some sort, which he rolled over his cock. "There. Carry on."

Ambrose looked confused.

"I'm not sure what the medieval equivalent of a condom was, but I don't think either of us are ready to be dads," Emery elaborated.

Comprehension dawned, and Ambrose's eyebrows shot to his hairline. "*Oh.* No."

"Good. Now, come back here."

Ambrose went to him. The interruption had disrupted some of his courage, so his kiss was almost shy, but Emery's hands on his hips and his clever tongue quickly emboldened him anew. He sank into it, testing his weight. He liked the sense of power it brought to feel Emery go soft and pliant under him. To take Emery's hands, lace their fingers, then pin them above his head.

Emery liked it, too. His cock twitched.

Ambrose rose onto his elbows and knees, repositioning himself. He watched Emery's face for any sign he was doing this all wrong, but he only looked hot and eager.

Ambrose held his breath. They both did. He lowered himself, slowly, slowly down.

He'd heard this could hurt the first time, but he was so wet that it only took a careful, prolonged stretch before he glided down. Pleasure sang a verse through his body, plucking at sensitive chords, hinting at the melody of the chorus to come.

Once Ambrose settled into his lap, Emery's breath let out all at once, caught between their lips as he leaned in for a kiss. Ambrose tested raising his hips and bringing them down again. It drew a huffed breath from both of them, then another as he did it again.

"Am I—?" he asked.

"Yes. Fuck yes, that's good. Keep going."

Pleasure spiked as he took Emery into himself. Again and again. Pinning him down harder, slamming his hips harder. Taking up a rhythm that made the mattress creak.

Something rusted in Ambrose's mind creaked, too. A bent nail in the ramshackle construction of his sense of self.

In the world he'd come from, love had been a complicated array of conditions and contradictions. He was a man, so his affinity for other men had to stay secret. Yet there were parts of him connected to womanhood, which other queer men rejected. He felt as if he'd had to carve himself up to match a diagram like the ones butchers used to carve a cow, only his body had parts labeled "male" and "female."

The witch king had never touched him like this, and he'd said it was because the risk of discovery was too dangerous, but Ambrose had understood that in the ramshackle scaffolding of his body's construction, he was both lovable and loathsome, desirable and disgusting.

He didn't know it could be like this: Emery, under him, moaning and begging him not to stop when minutes earlier he'd stood over Ambrose with a hand on his neck and ordered him to kneel. That he could want Emery inside him tonight, and ask tomorrow if any modern magic would let him into Emery the same way. He could desire someone without being unmade by them. He could rip out all the rusted nails and haphazard pieces and call himself a man and his body a home, regardless of what went into its making, or how he lived there.

Emery took Ambrose just as he was—grinding up into him, grasping at his hips, whispering his name. The normally quiet sanctuary of his bedroom was loud with their panting, the creaky mattress, and the supple percussion of Ambrose riding Emery's cock.

The pleasure felt urgent now. Where before, it had been a steadily growing burn, getting hotter, now it spiked and blazed and made him clench. Ambrose's thighs started quaking the nearer he got, as if he'd been riding horseback for days. Emery's teeth scraped his shoulder.

"Ambrose."

Fingers dug into his hips. Ambrose's thighs gave out. He shivered as ecstasy crested through him, spiraling from the place Emery was buried snugly inside. Emery's hips gave grinding, abortive thrusts as he let out a strained, growling sound of satisfaction.

They tensed, holding on to each other as the wave ripped through them, before the tide of it finally let them go.

Lethargy made his limbs heavy, made Ambrose hyper aware of his pulse ticking under his overheated skin.

Finally, he rolled onto his back. Emery stared up at the ceiling, his chest still inflating rapidly as he caught his breath. Flushed and shiny with sweat, he looked like a sunbather luxuriating on the beach in summer. One of his knees he'd cocked outward, revealing the tender skin of his inner thigh, paler than the rest.

Ambrose thought about kissing that spot.

Emery caught his look. "Have mercy."

But he said it with an indolent moan that implied he'd only like the mercy to be temporary.

Ambrose chewed his lip. He didn't know what came after. He'd never shared a bed.

Emery's head flopped sideways to look at him. "Do you want to cuddle?"

Ambrose turned scarlet. It was ridiculous. Why should he find this part mortifying? He'd just ridden Emery like a prized stallion.

Being treated softly was new in a different way.

Emery looked a little coy, rolled closer and tucked himself under Ambrose's arm. Flushing, Ambrose dropped a kiss into his hair.

"The Grim Wolf of Bellgrave turned out to be just a sweet puppy," Emery said.

"With you."

Emery looked pleased by that.

"We still have to deal with the spell jar." *Jars.* Every initiate likely had one.

"It can wait until morning," Emery said.

He drifted off first, his breaths softly tickling Ambrose's skin. His lashes made dark fans across his cheeks. The candlelight and deep shadows caught on all the pretty architecture of his face—the hollow between his collar bones, the deep groove of his upper lip, still red from being kissed. He looked so calm and at peace.

Vulnerable.

They had to find a way to destroy Morcant's spell jar and extract all the others from the initiates, including Hellebore. Now that Ambrose had a taste of this, the thought of losing Emery was intolerable.

But what if the worst threat came from him?

He waited, listening for a voice while tracing a lazy pattern over Emery's skin. If any crumb of the witch king remained, surely he could not resist castigating Ambrose now.

His mind was silent. Calm. The witch king was not there.

He was *out there.* Somewhere.

But not entirely. Ambrose rubbed the bump of his spine, where the witch king's vertebra had temporarily replaced his own his own. How to extract someone who'd scarred him so indelibly?

Perhaps he would have to die . . .

Yet, as he drifted off to the sensation of tingling skin and Emery's breath on his shoulder, he couldn't help but think, *I'm alive, I'm alive, I'm alive . . .*

CHAPTER 43

Ambrose woke to a kiss.

He'd never been roused from sleep this way. Of the many new experiences this world had given him, he cherished this one in particular.

His eyes fluttered open. Emery hovered over him, tucking hair out of his face.

"Good morning," Ambrose mumbled sleepily.

"You talk in your sleep, you know."

Well, that was mortifying. "What did I say?"

"Oh, that I was the best lay of your life and you can't wait to ravish me again, and also that I'm the sexiest weasel you ever laid eyes on."

Ambrose covered his face with his arm and groaned, "True."

"Wait," Emery choked. "I was joking. Well, not about the sexy weasel part, you did mumble that."

"But you're not a weasel."

"You said, *Your sexy wiles weasel-y me*. Which I think was sleep-talk for 'You weaseled your way into my heart,' but I can't be sure."

If that was true, Ambrose's heart felt lighter with a weasel in it than without. Regretfully, he looked over the edge of the bed toward the stack of books where he'd idly tossed the spell jar last night. "We should deal with that."

"Mm." Emery leaned in, tracing a finger along the scar tissue knotted up Ambrose's chest. "I was thinking. If that thing is linked to Morcant's immortality, he's probably put one in all of the initiates."

Ambrose had considered that, too. Rolling over, he got out of bed to retrieve the foul thing.

It had fallen inside one of Emery's shoes by the wardrobe. Given the chaos of Emery's room, it should have taken hours to find it, but the spell jar had an aura to it, malignant and unsettling. The moment Ambrose got close, he sensed it as if he'd stepped in an icy puddle.

Holding it, he couldn't imagine how Emery had felt with it inside of him for so long.

He sat on the edge of the bed, and Emery shifted closer to lean his chin on Ambrose's shoulder to look at the spell jar in his palm.

"I think it's safe to assume that, in order to kill Morcant permanently, we have to destroy all of them," he said. "But will he . . . I don't know, feel it?"

"It's impossible to know until we do."

Turning it over, Ambrose examined the quartz. Its coloration had the rust and crimson shades of blood both new and old, but he could tell nothing else about it.

Morcant's aim was to make these as unobtrusive and difficult to retrieve as possible. The more of them he had, the more secure he could feel in his immortality. It had been placed with magic, and barring invasive and potentially dangerous surgery, only magic could retrieve it, but you had to know what you were searching for.

"He spoke of moving away from Bellgrave and taking up their business elsewhere." Emery paled. "What if we weren't the first guild he started? If we aren't the only ones he's implanted with these things, searching for the others—"

Ambrose put a calming hand over his. "No. In Hellebore's memory, it was the first time she'd performed the ritual with him. If there were others, I doubt he wouldn't keep them close at hand. You're the source of his strength, but also his vulnerability." He thought about the power he wielded for the witch king, and how that could so easily have been turned against its creator if not for the collar. "Most power is a kind of cage. We'll trap Morcant in his."

Emery relaxed a fraction. "The most obvious place to start is with the other initiates, but getting them to hear me out might be a . . . unique challenge. They all avoid me, mistrust me, or believe I'm off the deep end, thanks to Morcant."

"They must hate him, too."

A HEX FOR HUNGER   295

"They fear him more. They'll expect retribution. I have to convince them to let some bloke they've never met go bobbing for apples in their chest cavity using arcane magic cast by a dead king. To do that, they have to believe I can beat him."

"Or their fear of retribution will be stronger than their desire to be free of him," Ambrose concluded.

A heart-aching look of fractured hope shone in Emery's eyes. "In all my years at Bellgrave, they've only seen me lose."

They required a show of force. A demonstration that Morcant was not as powerful as he seemed, to prove they could beat him.

"We have one spell jar. If we could keep Morcant restrained, we could destroy it for all the other initiates to see him weakened."

"What about Hellebore?" Emery said.

True. Convincing the initiates would be challenging. Convincing Hellebore to help kill her own father seemed impossible.

"That's if we can even find a way *to* destroy the spell jars," Emery added.

Experimentally, Ambrose let a few grasping snakes of magic form a fist around the spell jar in his hand. The hunger took longer than usual to answer his call. That it was still there at all disconcerted him, but if it could be useful for not only retrieving the spell jars, but destroying them . . .

The spell jar shivered at the touch of destructive magic, but as Ambrose closed his fingers around it to test for any weakness, he found none.

"We need an enchantment strong enough to break its protections," Emery said.

All their problems: how to convince the initiates to help, how to corner Morcant, and how to destroy the spell jars—felt monumental and impossible, but as Ambrose considered them all, solutions began to fit into each like missing segments of a puzzle.

"We should speak to Saoirse."

She agreed to meet them within the safety of Emery's wards. Wearing a coat the color of daffodils, she stuck out through the thick fog as she came to their door.

She said, "Bitch, you *live* here?"

"I happen to like it here," Emery said.

"Whatever you say, swamp witch."

"It's a lot cozier inside than it seems," Ambrose assured her.

She came inside, looking up at the hole in the ceiling, enchanted to keep out the rain but not the sight of a starry sky. After a pause, she looked at the disaster of the living room—tithes gathered, scribbled notes, and the grimoire open on the coffee table.

"What did you find?"

They told her about the contents of Hellebore's memory—the spell jar filled with a scrap of Morcant's soul, and where he'd placed them. They explained how it made him immortal, and they'd need to destroy *all* the spell jars in order to finish him.

She listened intently. "You're not having me on, are you?"

In the end, it was simpler to show her.

Though touching it didn't seem to hold any danger, they'd wrapped the quartz in a dish towel to dampen the stomach-turning aura it exuded. Ambrose peeled it open.

"They weren't that color before." Saoirse's reaction, though less visceral than Emery's, was no less repulsed. She sounded very far away and touched the spot on her chest where the rune mark would be. "How'd you get it out?"

"Ambrose has a unique talent for it," Emery said.

Ambrose rolled up his sleeves to show her the spell stains of his magic. "It allows me to phase through objects. And people."

Saoirse winced. "Sounds painful."

Emery's cheeks turned color. "No. Not really."

He had asked jealously if Ambrose would have that *particular* effect on everyone while removing the spell jar. Ambrose had, in as kind a way as possible, informed Emery that he was possibly the only little freak who'd *enjoy* the process.

"And you want me to do the same thing," she guessed.

"Do you want his dirty, scummy soul in there until the day you die?" Emery asked.

"Obviously not, but a fat lot of good mine will do you if he has five more in the other initiates. And Hellebore." The name was said with a milieu of emotion. "She knew about all of this."

"That's why we came to you first." Emery cleared his throat. "We hoped you might convince everyone else to help. Including Hellebore."

"Help kill her own father."

"You said yourself, she has more reason to hate him than any of us."

"Of course, but hating him doesn't negate, well, the whole load of everything else she feels. He's had his claws in her for years. She isn't a bad person, but a bad person controls her every move. How much she eats, where she went to school, who her friends are, who she dates. How much of that do you suffer before he controls who you are?"

Her words were an arrow through Ambrose's heart. She said aloud all the things he'd thought himself.

He hoped he could convey as much conviction from the depths of his own experience in what he said. "Perhaps, if she could not choose any of those things, that means she will appreciate it all the more when you give her another option."

Saoirse looked at him as if he'd said something very revealing, narrowing her eyes.

"Just to confirm, you two *definitely* aren't cousins?"

"No!" Ambrose said.

"He was born *several centuries ago*," Emery added.

Which only meant they had to explain a step further who Ambrose was. It led to describing the rest of their plan: how they might trap Morcant, convince the initiates, and destroy the spell jars in one fell swoop. Saoirse absorbed it all gamely. After falling in with an immortal necromancer's cult, perhaps not much surprised her.

They laid it all out. The rest of their plan had come together piece by piece, but it all hinged on Saoirse's cooperation. They couldn't do it without her.

"Will you help?" Emery asked.

Saoirse waited, clearly relishing the chance to badger him a little. It was a hint of the friendship they might have fostered under better circumstances, where Morcant's poison didn't turn good-natured banter into cutthroat repartee.

"Of course," she said. "You can start with me."

CHAPTER 44

It took a challenging quarter of an hour to dredge the spell jar from Saoirse's body.

She found the process uncomfortable and harrowing, a far cry from Emery's experience. He did his best to reassure her until, finally, Ambrose's hand emerged with the quartz grasped tightly in his fist, magic dripping gorily from his arm.

Now they just had to convince the other initiates . . .

Saoirse wanted to speak to Hellebore alone. It seemed the safest way to approach her, but the others posed a problem. Emery didn't like the idea of opening his home to anyone but Saoirse. He didn't trust them not to reveal everything to Morcant rather than cooperate, and they'd never enter another secrecy pact after the last.

What's more, what did it matter if they had all the spell jars, if not the means to destroy them?

It was from the seed of this last problem that a plan was sown.

The tomb where it all began seemed the best place for it all to end.

They met Saoirse outside, on the dewy green of the necropolis, surrounded by gravestones. She rubbed her fingers together and whispered to them through chattering teeth, a mix of cold and fear making her shiver. "Hellebore isn't here," she said.

Of course, not everything could go right.

"Where is she?" Emery said.

"I don't know. I've called and called, but she hasn't answered." She rubbed her arms to ward away the chill. "I'm scared he's done something to her."

Ambrose exchanged a look with Emery. If Morcant suspected they knew about the spell jars, he might have hidden Hellebore away in order to protect her own.

To finish this tonight, they needed her.

"Should we delay to search for her?" Ambrose asked.

Emery shook his head. "It will give Morcant more time to mount a defense against us. We have the chance to weaken him now. We should take it."

Saoirse said, "What if she's hurt?"

"He needs her alive and well to protect the spell jar she carries. If we destroy all but one, he's that closer to dead. It will weaken him," Emery insisted. "Which makes all of us safer, including Hellebore."

Saoirse sucked her lips between her teeth and nodded. "I just hope she's all right."

"You remember how to cast the spell I taught you?" Emery said.

Saoirse opened her glove to show them the bloody handful of nettles she carried. "*I'm* not the senile one between us."

Emery smiled. "That's the spirit."

Entering the tomb, Ambrose thought he might have felt anxious. Instead, a meditative calm kept his breaths even, his senses alert. It was the same state of mind he'd entered before battles with the witch king, as natural as donning armor.

Of all the battles he'd fought, this one was most important he win.

They descended the steps halfway. From there, Saoirse went alone.

Distantly, the murmurs of the guild hushed at her arrival. Morcant's resonant welcome echoed eerily up the stairs, but even whispers carried in the cavernous tomb.

So the meaty thunk of a body hitting stone carried just as well.

"Where's Hellebore?" Saoirse shouted, her words a cacophonous din through the catacombs.

Morcant might have hidden Hellebore to protect her, but he hadn't foreseen how protective Saoirse would be of her friend. She wasted no time in enacting their plan.

Ambrose and Emery took their cue, running the rest of the way down the stairs.

Morcant's voice came wet and muffled, speaking through a bloody nose. "Ah, Saoirse. Your decorum today is so very ladyli—*Ungh!*"

"*Where is she?*"

They arrived in time to see Saoirse's fist catch Morcant in the jaw, followed by gasps and a scream from the initiates. She'd used the spell they'd learned from the witch king to bind Morcant to the floor, shadowy magic encircling his neck, wrists, and ankles. His water deer was similarly held down by the neck, its hooves scraping against the stone.

Morcant could not cast spells. He could not move.

"Why you—" Morcant whipped his head up to glare at Saoirse, his nose bleeding freely. At the sight of Emery and Ambrose rushing in, his gaze narrowed. "Ah, I see. They've recruited you, have they?"

Emery swiped a tithe of salt water and spit before crossing the threshold to dispel any waiting sigils or traps. Saoirse stood over Morcant, her knuckles bloodied to match his nose. The initiates backed against the far wall, shocked speechless.

One of the new apprentices, Iris, shouted, "What is happening?"

"What is he doing back here?" another said, pointing at Emery.

"Yes, why don't you enlighten them?" Morcant said. "I'm sure they're eager to hear of your many attempts to murder me in cold bl—"

His voice cut short, slapped silent by Saoirse's open palm. "Explanations can come later. First, tell me where Hellebore is. I won't ask again."

There was a glint of mockery in Morcant's smirk. "If you insist. Hellebore, **come say hello to your friend**."

His whistle in the echoing tomb split the air painfully. Ambrose's skin prickled with goose flesh. Some world-weary soldier's instinct told him they should have gagged Morcant and executed the plan without Hellebore.

But the corpse door already rumbled aside.

The tomb beyond was dark as ever. The initiates had gone still and silent as scared rabbits.

Saoirse approached the door, calling, "Hellebore?"

"Hello, Saoirse," said a voice from within, tremulous and angry. *"Run."*

"Hellebore," Morcant said, "**restrain these upstarts**."

Saoirse didn't move quickly enough. A figure burst from the tomb. The candlelight stripped the darkness from her. Hellebore, her makeup smeared, her hair stuck to her forehead under a hooded cloak, moved with supernatural speed. She rushed to her friend and seized her by the wrists.

"I said, *run*."

"Hellebore, what are you *doing*? *Stop!*" Saoirse screamed hoarsely.

Ambrose's heart dropped. He thought he understood, though he wanted badly to be wrong.

Saoirse wrenched her arms away. Hellebore cast a spell like the one she'd used to bind Emery the night she nearly killed him. Ropes coiled like snakes around Saoirse's wrists and torso. In the ensuing struggle, the hood of Hellebore's cloak fell back.

There was a circle of runes around her neck, glowing sickly green.

Saoirse, bound and uncomprehending, did not react in time. The enchanted ropes tied her so tightly she collapsed to her knees, skinning them on the stone floor.

She may not have had time to react, but Ambrose did.

"**Deal with the others**," Morcant ordered, just before Emery cast a spell to gag him.

Ambrose caught Hellebore's arm and twisted. He didn't see what she drew from her cloak in her free hand—only the glint of steel right before she lashed out blindly, burying a blade in his shoulder.

Emery turned just in time to see. "Ambrose!"

Pain registered through the adrenaline, but Ambrose had weathered worse, and a shoulder wound was mercifully easier to fight with than if she'd struck anywhere vital. He hooked an arm around her neck and squeezed. She fought, scoring his flesh with her nails because the collar compelled her to. But he sensed her desire to succumb. To let him squeeze and squeeze until unconsciousness took her.

Her energy drained like blood from a poisoned wound, she went limp, and Ambrose lowered her to the floor.

Saoirse, still on grazed knees, looked at her fallen friend with tears in her eyes. "Is she—?"

"Alive, but unconscious," Ambrose grunted.

"Why did she—What is that around her neck?"

"It's a compulsion collar," Ambrose said gravely. "Like mine. It forces her to follow Morcant's commands. He couldn't manage it on Emery, so he put it on her instead."

This news rippled through the initiates, horror tinging their hushed whispers. Emery rushed to Ambrose's side at once, hands hovering over the dagger's hilt.

"Tell me what to do." He started rifling through his belt for healing tithes.

"I'm fine. Restrain Hellebore before she wakes up."

"You've been *stabbed*."

"I've come back from worse."

Emery made a noise of frustration, but he did as requested, binding Hellebore with spell chains to match Morcant's.

Ambrose tested his grip around the dagger's hilt, estimating just how much pain he'd be in. Emery pulled crushed petals and dried snake skins from his tithe belt, the latter turning his palm cool white. He pressed it around the wound, the numbing anesthetic seeping through.

It helped, but it still didn't feel good to wrench the dagger free. Emery quickly applied the petals to the gout of blood, magic turning them to sutures, knitting flesh until the flow staunched.

"Are you—?"

"I'm fine now," Ambrose assured him.

Though they exchanged no affectionate gesture—now wasn't the time—there was something tender enough in the way Emery tended his wounds that it made the initiates whisper more intensely.

Who is he? What have they done to Professor Van Moor? What did he do to Hellebore?

Emery took Hellebore's dagger from where it had clattered to the floor and used it to cut Saoirse free. She kneeled to check on Hellebore, Morcant watching the exchange with a silently murderous stare. He could neither speak, move, nor cast magic, but they'd be fools to consider him harmless. If beheading him right away were an option, Ambrose would opt for it, but they needed the initiates to cooperate, and they weren't liable to after witnessing his murder with nary an explanation.

Ambrose had expected a fight when they confronted him. Ambrose knew how to fight. He knew how to weather an injury. Familiarity and experience went a long way to making a knife wound feel like the easy part.

Now, the time had come for explanations, and he found he was more afraid of the initiate's responses than of any hidden dagger.

He had to recall, they were as he had been—convinced of their abuser's good intentions. Convinced they deserved whatever punishment he wrought.

"Can any of you tell us what the hell is going on?" Windsor demanded.

"If you'll listen, that's exactly what we came here to do," Saoirse said.

"You and him?" Windsor jutted his chin to point at Emery.

"Why should we trust what he says?" Dalton agreed.

Saoirse said, "Because you trust me, and I know he isn't who Morcant made him out to be."

The initiates looked discomfited but unconvinced. Their gazes strayed to Morcant, bound but still alive and dangerous. Each wore hardened, weary expressions. Ambrose recognized them from battlefronts where spirited soldiers went to war and returned with wounds both bleeding and invisible.

They'd seen how Morcant punished Emery for slights and failed rebellions. How might he respond to this affront?

Looking at them now, Ambrose understood why anyone who had not suffered as they had might not understand why they didn't fight. They couldn't see how things had begun, how slowly Morcant had built their tolerance to his cruelty, how twisted the mental arithmetic leading them to believe if they were good enough, perfect enough, sensitive enough, they could avoid his foul moods and earn a drop of praise, which felt like a wealth of approval and generosity when compared to the dearth they normally subsisted on.

He remembered craving the witch king's crumbs of affection, never knowing there would be a man centuries later who didn't ask him to degrade himself for it.

Emery, faced with their doubt and apprehension, didn't falter. "Morcant is not the encouraging mentor he styles himself to be." He had spent years subject to lies and derision. Morcant had woven a new identity for him, and none of his peers, save for Saoirse, had seen beyond the costume. Given the opportunity to purge himself of the slander, his voice carried weight in the cavernous space, so that it seemed even the ghosts rose from their graves to listen.

"I've known him longer than all of you, barring Hellebore, and look what he's done to her." He gestured to the rune collar. "Subjugated her with a compulsion charm that forces her to do his bidding against her will. He isn't a teacher or a mentor. He has no interest in cultivating your talents or helping you reach your true potential. He's a greedy lich who tricked us into committing harrowing acts of arcane magic in order to make himself immortal. And I can prove it."

He slammed the spell jar onto the lid of the central sarcophagus. The magic within made it sound like a rhapsody of shattered glass rather than quartz striking stone.

"My—Ambrose, here . . ." Emery paused, looking at Ambrose. The word *friend* felt tentative and wrong. The word *lover* too personal. But the way it had come out—*My Ambrose*—that felt right.

Emery gestured to the spell jar. "He pulled this out of me. The rats we sacrificed were people, used to hollow out a spell jar powerful enough to contain a part of Morcant's soul. Then he placed them in us during the second initiation rite so we might never find and destroy the thing which makes him so powerful. We helped make him immortal."

The initiates' wan faces looked from the spell jar to Morcant, shock turned to revulsion. Windsor clutched his chest, where a rune marked the spot a shard of Morcant's soul had been shoved into his heart.

"It doesn't have to be this way," Emery said with finality.

He turned to the open corpse door, giving Ambrose a look that asked plainly, *Are you ready?*

Ambrose answered by walking into the dark, following the dull glimmer of light at the other side of the tomb.

This had been the best and most compelling reason they had to do this here, now. The axe was the only weapon they knew with the power to shatter enchantments.

Its haft made his fingers tingle with the pins and needles of magic. *Still there, even after all this time. Even though the witch king should, by all rights, be dead.*

He was met with a sharp intake of breath when he emerged holding the weapon.

"Wait, you're not going to kill him in front of us, are you?" an initiate asked. It was the boy with the burn scar who'd cowered from the torch at Morcant's fundraiser. Dalton.

Ambrose, rather than correct them, swung the axe down hard on the spell jar. It burst asunder, and at the moment of its destruction, Morcant let out a harrowed scream that even the spell gagging him could not muffle.

His pallid cheeks had a green tinge, his eyes bloodshot and sunken. Inexplicably, he looked to the stairway, as if searching for an escape.

Or a rescue.

Ambrose positioned himself nearer the door in case, but they had to focus on the current task—convincing the initiates to relinquish the phylacteries they carried so each could be destroyed.

"You've all been the victim of his ire at one point or another," Emery said. "You all know what he's really like, and he won't stop. He has us under his thumb. The secrecy pact keeps us from speaking of this to anyone but each other. When I tried to get around it, he told me what we'd *really* sacrificed during our initiation rite and threatened to have me put away for murder. He has every single dagger we used lined up in there."

Emery gestured to the tomb behind him. "This is our best chance to be free of him once and for all."

"By killing him and getting put away regardless?" Dalton asked. "I'd rather just take my dagger and run."

"You think he won't find you?" Saoirse snorted. "There's a part of him inside you. You want it to stay there?"

She took her own spell jar from her pocket, holding it up for them to see. She set it on the sarcophagus and looked Morcant dead in the eyes.

"This is for all those things you said to me when no one else was listening."

She took the axe from Ambrose. He helped position her hands apart. She swung it down, missing on the first attempt and striking true on the second. Her phylactery exploded into dust, and Morcant once again howled like an animal.

When he looked up at her, fury made dark shadows beneath his eyes, his shoulders rising and falling with ragged breaths, but he could not speak to defend himself.

The initiates still looked uncertain. They shifted back and forth, regarding Morcant like a rabid dog close to slipping his leash. They knew what had transpired tonight would not go unpunished. Rather than finish him, they were most eager to find some way they could avoid that punishment. Dalton said, "Aren't we more valuable to him alive, if we have that thing inside us?" He pointed to the remains of the spell jar. "If we take it out, and your plan fails, what's to stop him from killing us?" Ambrose was no great diplomat. He didn't know if he could say anything that would add value to their argument. But he had experience with men like Morcant.

"If you believe you can make yourself indispensable enough that he'll never turn his wrath upon you, I think you misunderstand what you are to him. He does not care for you. He does not need an excuse to harm you. He already has. All you do by changing yourselves to suit him is surrender to the idea that you brought that harm on yourselves."

The boy bristled. "What do you know about it? Who are you, anyway?"

"He's Emery's friend, and he's helping us," Saoirse interjected. "Look, I understand. You're afraid Morcant will kill you, but isn't he doing that already?" She looked down at her feet. "Sometimes, I say things so mean I don't even recognize myself anymore. I never used to. I don't want to die, but I don't want to become some loathsome, spiteful monster either." She looked around at them all, gathered in the candlelit tomb as if buried there themselves. "He can't kill all of us without attracting attention."

The initiates said nothing, silently fearful and contemplative. Iris finally stepped forward. "I don't trust you," she said to Emery.

"Thanks," Emery muttered sardonically.

"But I trust Saoirse."

Ambrose felt himself unwind, a sigh of relief nearly to his lips.

It stoppered at a sound from the stairs.

Footsteps.

What did it mean, when you knew someone so well you could identify his mood by the sound of his approach?

How cursed was this tomb, that twice now a man who should have been dead appeared in that precise place?

Ambrose didn't know, and didn't wish to wait and discover he was right.

Before the source of the steps appeared, he made a desperate bid for the axe. He got three paces before a voice—paralyzing in its familiarity despite an age since hearing it aloud—cracked like a whip.

"Stop."

Ambrose had thrown his tether onto the pyre. He'd watched the bone become a lantern of fire before sundering in the heat.

Yet the collar cinched around his throat. His free will fled him. And he stopped.

Ambrose could not find it in himself to be surprised.

Of course, of course the witch king had returned.

"Hello again, my sweet wolf."

CHAPTER 45

He looked just as he had when Ambrose had loved him.

Half the witch king's golden hair was tied up by a pin, the rest falling loosely around his shoulders. His eyes were too blue for comparison to sea or sky. The soft, smooth angles of his cheeks, the curves of his mouth, were plush as silk and idyllic as sculpture. The crown left streaks of red through his hair where it wove beneath skin and bone, an enchanted illusion of rubies replacing the lost jewels.

He bared his teeth in a smile to wage war for, yet his appearance inspired none of Ambrose's old passion or yearning. It only made him sick.

The moment he appeared, several things happened in rapid succession.

Emery lunged for the axe Ambrose hadn't gotten to in time.

The witch king was faster, lashing out with the same spell binding Morcant. Snaking coils of magic throttled Emery and the other initiates, slamming them into the walls, where they remained pinned like insects. The percussive thump of their bodies hitting stone and their screams echoed cavernously throughout the tomb.

The witch king draped a hand around the back of Ambrose's neck and whispered in his ear, "My obedient dog would **never speak out against his master**, would he?"

The collar twisted a notch tighter, and Ambrose understood the worst was yet to come.

Emery, who had not heard the witch king's order, twisted against his bonds and growled, "Get your hands *off him.*"

"He deserves to determine for himself whose touch he yearns for." The witch king trailed a hand along Ambrose's shoulder as he spoke, raising the skin in goose flesh, but the collar kept Ambrose from refuting it. "Has one night spent in his company fooled you so thoroughly? Why don't you tell him, sweet wolf? Or better yet . . . let's show him."

Emery's face drained of color. "Show me what?"

The witch king's fingers swept from Ambrose's shoulders to paint fractals into the air, a tithe of lavender leaving a sleepily fragrant scent in the spell's wake.

It hung like an aurora, playing out recent memories that, for all their familiarity, didn't seem real.

In them, the witch king lurked visibly over Ambrose's shoulder, guiding him with a hand on the small of his back, an intimate whisper in his ear.

They showed Ambrose hunting for hints of the grimoire through books he'd secreted into his room.

Ambrose killing Morcant, as much at the witch king's behest as Emery's.

Ambrose seeking out the skeleton in the cellar and taking with him a single, solitary piece of his master's spine.

Ambrose slipping it onto his finger in the tomb and the witch king's spirit pouring into him, piloting him through the motions of killing Emery, only for Valenti to get in the way.

Ambrose taking the grimoire through the portal as they escaped.

Gathering the witch king's animated remains for the pyre.

Why, in these haunted visions of the past, did it look like Ambrose embraced the witch king before twisting his head until his neck cracked?

Lighting the pyre, eyes shining with tears, only now they seemed in mourning for the king he'd burned.

Then he and Emery walked away, hand in hand, and from the blaze, smoldering parts melted together. A figure wreathed in flame rose from the ashes, and before his skin became the alabaster it was now, before the soot was cleansed from his flaxen hair, the smoke clothed his body in stains just like the ones on Ambrose's arms.

They hadn't killed him that night. They'd brought him back to his own body.

And now it looked as though Ambrose had planned it all along.

The initiates, Saoirse, even Morcant, all watched the play. Most looked confused, scared. Only Morcant looked . . . interested.

A HEX FOR HUNGER 309

The vision concluded. Magic rained down from the air, removing the screen between Ambrose and Emery. They looked at one another. Ambrose didn't know what sort of story his face told, but Emery's was a tragedy. He hung from his bonds against the wall, tension leaving him limp with excruciating revelation.

"You did this?"

No. But Ambrose had been ordered not to speak out against the witch king. The curse glued his tongue to the roof of his mouth, rendering his denial nothing but a desperate thought. His urge to lash out, to strike the witch king down with the very magic he'd bestowed upon him, was strangled out of him. He couldn't even take a threatening step toward him.

He'd watched his tether destroyed in the fire, but evidently it was something more powerful still which kept the spell alive. Which kept the *witch king* alive.

Emery was shaking his head, a few wild strands of hair falling into his face. "No. No, he wouldn't do that." He met Ambrose's gaze, pleading with him. "You wouldn't do that."

Never.

"No? He's loyal to his last breath." The witch king walked around Ambrose and tilted his chin in a parody of a lover's caress. The scrape of his nail was the point of a dagger. "He's delivered you to me as a gift for our reunion, but still you don't believe it? He must have affected you deeply . . ."

Now, it looked as though Emery were the one whose heart had been cloven in twain by an axe. He kept shaking his head, denial warring with what he'd been shown.

In response, Ambrose's magic, which had been so blissfully, peacefully quiet, growled and bared its teeth. The hunger awakened.

Repulsed by the witch king's touch, Ambrose managed to wrench his head away. The collar punished him like a garrote, but he managed it. Something had changed. The collar didn't glow like it used to. The compulsion was strong. It still worked, but the magical stake driven into the meat of Ambrose's heart had come a little loose.

There had to be some way to tear it out entirely.

"Ambrose?" Emery pleaded. "Tell me he's lying."

Ambrose opened his mouth, but it was a step too far. The collar kept him silent.

You know me, he thought. *Please don't believe him.*

But as far as Emery knew, the compulsion charm had been broken when they'd destroyed the tether.

"I think you have your answer," the witch king said. "I wouldn't humiliate yourself any further by belaboring it." He paced away, turning instead to the bound initiates. And Morcant.

Morcant knew the secret behind the witch king's magic. He'd recreated it with Hellebore. Something Emery and Ambrose had said to each other in that tomb gave him the missing piece of the puzzle.

Perhaps Ambrose could trick him into revealing it to them in turn.

He hated to follow the charade. He hated the heartbroken uncertainty in Emery's face. He hated the witch king. But if he was to discover the true key to the witch king's immortality, he had to play along and find some way to alert Emery.

"What is to be done with Morcant?"

The witch king cast Ambrose a curious look. He did not trust the redirection, but nor did he fear Ambrose enough to disregard it. "Let's speak with him."

The witch king swiped two fingers through the blood still soaking Ambrose's shoulder and slashed them through the air. The blood wicked into a spell, breaking Morcant's gag. He sputtered, and while the witch king's attention was elsewhere, Ambrose cast Emery a wink.

It was as clumsy and awkward as the first time he'd tried, but Emery's expression slackened with recognition.

Hopefully it was enough.

The witch king addressed Morcant tonelessly. "Who are you?"

"Morcant Van Moor." The professor inclined his head. "A teacher at this school and great admirer of your work."

The witch king's gaze drifted to Hellebore. Specifically, the rune collar on her neck. "I can see that."

They regarded each other like two vipers.

Could it be possible for one to drag information out of the other concerning the exact peculiarities of their immortality?

Better yet, could they be goaded into ending one another and save Ambrose the trouble?

"Perhaps, if you freed me from these bonds, I'd be amenable to sharing the specifics of my own immortality," Morcant hedged. "Though different from yours, it has, thus far, proved quite robust."

"So robust you find yourself at the mercy of a few students?"

A HEX FOR HUNGER 311

Morcant's expression darkened. "I have returned from the dead twice now, while you were successfully locked away for centuries."

The witch king gave that reluctant consideration before turning to Ambrose. "You've already deduced his methods. Tell me."

He didn't compel Ambrose. He didn't have to. If they wanted a battle of immortal bastards, they could have one.

Ambrose pointed to the initiates still tied to the wall, silent as field mice avoiding the notice of a prowling farm cat. Without mincing words, he explained what Morcant had done with the rats, the spell jars, and his students.

"Phylacteries," the witch king corrected. "An old, crude method of achieving immortality."

Morcant's simper looked more like gnashing teeth.

The witch king said, "I see. Retrieve the phylacteries for me, Ambrose."

Morcant said, "I wouldn't do that."

"Why not?" the witch king sounded genuinely interested.

"Now I've used your methods, destroying the phylacteries alone won't kill me. I make a better ally than an enemy."

The witch king had never shared power, and he did not intend to start. "Ambrose."

Ambrose inclined his head to hide his expression. As he crossed the tomb, he chanced a look at Emery, who watched with a mix of uncertainty and brittle hope.

"No!" Morcant snarled. "This is a grave mistake. When I'm free, I will—*Mmf.*"

The witch king gagged him once more. "You are a pretender, your power a meagre fraction of my own. Your hold on your daughter cannot compare to what Ambrose and I have."

Ambrose's ears pricked to that. What did their relationship have to do with power?

While he turned it over in his mind, he started toward Windsor, who'd been the most cooperative of the initiates. At Ambrose's approach, he yanked at his enchanted chains, which crackled and snapped, making him yelp.

Lowly, Ambrose told him, "Hold still and this won't harm you."

Windsor froze, trembling in fear as he regarded Ambrose's spell-stained hands. The knot in his throat bobbed, but he didn't struggle.

Ambrose's magic came to him stickily, like dried spit in a parched mouth. Rather than slavering for blood, it sniffed weakly, so weakly that when Ambrose first placed his hand against Windsor's chest, it felt as solid and impermeable as stone.

He gritted his teeth.

The witch king's laconic tone held a hidden edge. "Shall we do this the old-fashioned way?"

A bolt of fear made Ambrose's heart trip. No, he could do this bloodlessly. He had to. He didn't wish to contemplate Emery bound behind him, or what could happen tonight if he failed, but the image came to him unbidden anyway.

Morcant inscribing a new collar around Emery's neck, subjugating him to an eternity as his loyal lackey.

The witch king cutting Emery open to wear his body like an expensive coat.

It struck him, then. Why Emery?

There were other witches he could have bid Ambrose to sacrifice in his quest for true resurrection. Valenti had, inadvertently, served just as well. Yet the witch king still wanted Emery. Still looked at him with venomous intent.

Your hold on your daughter cannot compare to what Ambrose and I have.

But that was no longer true. Not since Ambrose had discovered all the ways he'd been betrayed.

He recalled something else. When Morcant had tried to ensorcel Emery with the collar, he'd put a *third* rune on Ambrose. Somehow, Ambrose had been an additional, necessary ingredient.

It was starting to come together, but not quickly enough. If he didn't figure this out, if he couldn't even retrieve this phylactery, they were doomed. He and Emery would never share more dinners, more nights spent reading, more lazy mornings tangled in bedsheets.

The magic's quiet appetite seemed to catch the scent of his fear. It snarled awake, growing hungrier, until finally Ambrose's fist sank through Windsor's chest.

He let out a whimper, but otherwise held still. Ambrose searched past the thundering beat of the boy's heart to the phylactery lodged within.

It took less time than with Saoirse's. He extracted the sliver of crimson, and when it was finally out, Windsor went so green he fainted.

Ambrose showed the witch king, then placed the quartz on the sarcophagus. He took up the enchanted axe.

A HEX FOR HUNGER

"Stop," Morcant said hoarsely. "There is more power I can barter with. There is more to this world than the one you came from. I can teach you."

"You know nothing of true power," said the witch king.

Ambrose tightened his grip on the axe's haft. In the depths of his heart, he yearned to swing it toward the neck of the witch king, but he could feel the collar forbidding it.

The pact had to be destroyed first.

What had kept his magic alive all this time?

Hunger.

That's what the grimoire claimed, that's how the magic *felt*.

But what fed it?

He swung the axe down on the phylactery. Morcant's scream echoed into the tomb, over and over, finding its own immortality in the cavernous chambers and adjoining tunnels.

Ambrose said, "All of them need to be destroyed to kill him."

The witch king tipped his head. "Then you best move quickly."

There were hidden depths to his words. Ambrose knew that, once he'd successfully removed all of the witch king's obstacles, the only obstacle left would be himself. He'd betrayed him. He'd fallen in love with someone else. That meant he'd ceased to be useful.

Or had he? He still bore the collar. He still caved to the compulsion.

But it felt weaker.

One by one, he extracted the phylacteries from each terrified initiate. One by one, he lay them on the sarcophagus and sundered Morcant's power one glittering shard at a time. Morcant waned with each loss of his soul, his screams becoming nought more than anguished mewls, the once powerful necromancer brought low by his ancient idol.

All the while, Ambrose tried to put his finger on the true source of the witch king's power. Not phylacteries, not grimoires, not runes carved into bones—there was a deeper, older magic.

Somehow, he'd turned hunger into a tithe.

There isn't much a man won't do when he is hungry.

Only Hellebore's phylactery remained.

Ambrose knelt in front of her. She looked exhausted, barely returned from consciousness, but her gaze was intense. She wet her lips and tried to speak, but her voice had gone hoarse from fighting Morcant's orders.

"Hunger," she whispered.

Yes. Hunger. That was the tithe. He knew that. But—

"What feeds it?" he whispered.

But the witch king did not suffer their conversation. His clawed grip dug into the meat of Ambrose's injured shoulder.

"Is there a problem with hers?"

"No," Ambrose said, and prepared to dig it out.

Her breath came in ragged huffs as he hunted for the phylactery. Hers was so enmeshed, it felt like it had grown its own veins, embedded itself into the blood and muscle of her. She coughed, and the spit that landed on Ambrose's wrist was pink.

"Stop it, you're hurting her!" Saoirse screamed.

"Don't—you almost—have it," Hellebore said.

The phylactery tore from her, laced with blood. Saoirse begged for either of them to heal her friend. Hellebore told her it was fine, but it wasn't. She needed urgent medical attention. She wouldn't receive any until the witch king was slain.

Ambrose held the bloody shard in his palm and tried to think what to do with the things he now knew, with the time they had left.

Emery could heal her. Emery could fix all of this.

Ambrose got up and roughly slapped the last phylactery onto the sarcophagus. He took up the axe. He was so close to understanding. He could taste the iron of the final key to his salvation.

He raised the axe above his head.

He looked at the witch king, and the magic simmered but did not come to boil.

Then he looked at Emery, watching him with guarded, fragile hope, and the hunger flared so monstrously it left Ambrose hollow.

He understood. He knew with sudden, immaculate clarity what the hex on his soul truly hungered for, and what would feed it.

He would perhaps have the hair of a second once the phylactery shattered and the witch king was distracted. He had to get to Emery. Would Emery know what to do? What was needed?

The witch king said, "Is he distracting you, sweet wolf?"

Ambrose's heart stuttered mid-beat.

"Perhaps we should have dealt with him first, then."

No.

"Ambrose, **kill Emery.**"

A HEX FOR HUNGER   315

The collar jerked. Ambrose's strike went askew. The axe's edge sparked off the stone face of the sarcophagus. The compulsion righted him like a puppet, dragging him toward Emery, the magic so ravenous Ambrose thought he'd succumb to famine before he reached the other side of the tomb.

"Ambrose!"

Emery slammed his hand against the wall behind him, leaving a bloody print. His bindings evaporated. He fell to the ground. On the stone behind him were runes, drawn in blood from his cut palm. He must have broken the skin against the shale and prepared the spell for the right moment.

He righted himself in time to cast something else, but the witch king still had blood on his hands from Ambrose's injury, and in a spray of magic he eviscerated Emery's hex before it landed.

Ambrose tried to fight the collar, but it made him raise the axe.

"Not with a weapon, **with your bare hands**," the witch king ordered.

The axe clattered to the floor.

Ambrose understood now. Why it had to be Emery. Why he had to use the magic to kill him.

Emery had the power to break the curse, or to keep it alive.

Ambrose struggled with all his strength. The collar choked the air out of his lungs, but he managed to strike the stone behind Emery rather than Emery himself. Shaking with the effort, Ambrose raised his head to look at him.

Emery's wide eyes drank him in, searching for the man Ambrose had been the night before. Not the monster the witch king made of him.

"Are you going to rip my heart out now, Ambrose?" he said.

Ambrose shuddered. A little of his will was restored. Something in the depths of Emery's words weakened the magic. Fed the hunger.

Compassion. Trust. Intimacy.

Love.

Not a feast for the belly, but food for the heart.

This was the reason the witch king sought to inhabit Emery's body, the reason he insisted on using his hands, his magic rather than a weapon that could irreparably mangle Emery as a vessel.

All his life, Ambrose had hungered for the witch king's approval, his high regard, his heart. He'd adored him. He'd worked hard to earn every scrap of reciprocation.

It was a yearning hunger. One the witch king never rewarded with more than scraps.

And so long as Ambrose had hungered for it, the witch king's magic, his immortality, sustained itself from that hunger. Ambrose's spirit had yearned long into the afterlife, keeping the spell alive, perpetual and renewed unlike any common tithe.

Then Emery had come along, and Ambrose had started to yearn for another.

The threats of this evening had starved Ambrose anew, forcing him to reckon with the fact one night might be all they'd ever have. But it didn't have to be.

With every ounce of power left to him, Ambrose said through the collar's choke, "I would never take your heart from you, but you can have mine. And if you gave me yours, I would protect it for all my living days."

Emery gazed into his eyes, scared and hopeful and trusting. "You know I already have."

The witch king advanced upon them. **"Kill him now!"**

The last winking remains of the compulsion charm slammed Ambrose's hand against Emery's chest.

And no further.

Emery gasped around the impact. Winded, he collapsed to the ground.

"No! No, you wretch, you spoiled wretch. Kill him!"

The collar gave barely a tug. The hunger, sated, drained out of Ambrose like a retreating tide. His fingers paled to the color of skin as he wrapped them around the haft of the axe on the floor beside Emery.

He spun on his heel and swung the blade in a horizontal arc. It split the witch king's head from his shoulders before he could utter another word.

Hot blood sprayed Ambrose's face, then evaporated. The air tasted of thunder in the collapse of the witch king's magic. His body hit the floor like ink hitting water, consumed in curls of smoke, leaving behind only empty clothes.

Ambrose stared at his hands. They were flesh-colored, drained of the magic which had sustained the witch king all this time, but the scars of countless tithes remained.

It had not been a rune on his bones, it had not been his own mortality tethering the king to this life. It had been hunger. Yearning. Ambrose had never tasted love that wasn't fed to him in tiny, poisoned doses, and so he'd gone hungry. Always hungry.

And so long as he was hungry, the witch king lived.

A HEX FOR HUNGER

317

Emery had fed him.

Now the witch king was dead.

A razor of peculiar grief cut through Ambrose at the thought. Not for the witch king, whose demise brought nothing but relief. The grief was for himself. The lost time, the life he'd lived, the person he'd been. All sacrificed on the altar of the witch king's pride.

Now he had to find out who he was when no one held his leash.

It was something to reckon with later.

The spell binding the initiates died with the witch king. They dropped to the floor, wobbly on their feet but taking to them quickly. Without a backward glance, Dalton ran. The others followed. Save for one.

Saoirse rushed to Hellebore's side, pouring petals out from the pouch at her waist, pushing magic into her until color returned to her cheeks.

Ambrose held out a hand to Emery, still slumped against the wall, chest rising and falling in staggered breaths. He took it, allowing himself to be helped to his feet.

Ambrose silently offered him the axe. It was just an axe now. Its enchantment had died with the witch who cast it, the blade still slicked with his blood.

Emery curiously took Ambrose by the hand. He held Ambrose's index finger and drew it gently across the axe's crimson edge, muttering an incantation. Light poured from the steel, following the path of his touch, igniting the enchantment anew.

"How do you know this spell?" Ambrose asked, awed.

"I didn't. But if the blood of a beheaded, immortal necromancer and the touch of a man who broke a centuries-long spell weren't powerful enough tithes, I'm not sure what would be."

Saoirse helped Hellebore to her feet. Emery turned to face her. "It's your phylactery."

"It won't work."

Morcant's voice was hardly recognizable, its rich tenor reduced to a wheezing rasp.

"Not just . . . protected by the phylacteries . . . anymore. The hex for hunger—"

"Is broken," Hellebore spat. "Go on. Command me."

He stared at her, comprehension dawning. He still said, "**Kill them.**"

The collar's light was a dull thing. It pulsed faintly, and only a vein throbbing in Hellebore's temple belied any effort on her part.

Morcant's expression twisted, pale eyes flicking from her to the other witnesses of his fall from power. **"Kill them!"**

"Don't you understand?" Hellebore said through gritted teeth. "It's over. I'm done."

Saoirse silently took her hand and squeezed.

The last phylactery still glimmered like a bloodstain on the sarcophagus. Ambrose offered Hellebore the axe.

Morcant went pale as the grave. "You can't do this. I'm your father!"

Hellebore paused. "I wish you were. But if today taught me anything, it's that you'll never be. That's why the hex didn't last. But—" She turned to Emery, voice strained around a pit of emotion. "I don't want to be the one to do it."

"Stop!" Morcant pleaded, but Hellebore's heart was cold to it. She'd suffered too much. Forgiveness was a distant impossibility.

Emery took the axe. "If you're sure."

She nodded.

He looked at Morcant, who'd begun to beg in earnest, all pride forgotten in the seconds before execution. He found no mercy from those he'd sought to subjugate completely.

Emery brought the axe down like a guillotine. The last shard of Morcant's soul burst apart like a collapsing star. His head wrenched back with an earsplitting, unearthly scream as icy light crept like cracks up the veins in his neck and through his face. His body burned up, consumed in a wisp of pale smoke, leaving nothing behind to bury or resurrect.

EPILOGUE

THREE MONTHS LATER

W hat does fell-ah-tee-oh mean?"

Emery poked his head out from the kitchen. "That isn't a word."

Ambrose held up the book he'd been reading. "Yes, it is."

"Spell it for me."

Ambrose did and Emery made a noise halfway between a snort and a guffaw. He laughed a lot more lately.

"Fellatio," Emery said. "Fuh-lay-shee-oh."

"That sounds nothing like how it's spelled. What does it mean?"

Emery raised his eyebrows. "Would have thought the context might give that away."

Ambrose read the sentence to him aloud. "*Afternoon tea with Bigglesby was about as tempting a scenario as fellatio from a shark.*"

Emery frowned. "All right, I understand your confusion." He wiggled his eyebrows. "Fellatio is what you were doing with my dick last night."

Ambrose's mouth formed an "oh" of comprehension. "I see. Bigglesby sounds like torturous company."

At that moment, his stomach growled.

Emery said, "Come torture my company instead. I'm making pumpkin-spiced cinnamon buns this time, and I'm about to gut the pumpkin." Emery hadn't forgotten his promise to let Ambrose try those cinnamon buns from the charity bake sale, and had endeavored—since their new-found freedom—to introduce Ambrose to as many new books and baked goods as he could find. It was, in the wake of what had happened, therapeutic to indulge themselves in simple pleasures.

To cover up the death of her father, Hellebore had insisted upon burning his remains along with the witch king's and sealing the tomb permanently. She'd then set fire to her family home.

It was quite simple, given the tithes and taboo spell tomes of Morcant's laboratory, to make the whole thing look like an accident. Morcant's remains were never recovered, but others were. People who'd gone missing over the course of his three years at Bellgrave. His mother's trapped spirit. School faculty were eager to deny all knowledge, and his death was ruled an accident or misadventure, but the pall of what he'd done still lingered.

Most of all in the hearts of those he'd hurt.

Three months had passed since then.

They still heard from Saoirse every now and again, but aside from her and Hellebore, the other initiates had carried on with their lives alone. It was better that way. They reminded each other too much of a time they'd rather forget.

Ambrose only felt the collar's choke in his nightmares. Emery would wake him and stroke fingers through his hair until he fell asleep again. For his part, Emery didn't suffer in his sleep, but little things would put him ill at ease. A particular gait of footsteps in the school halls, the vibration of his mobile phone, or the receipt of a spontaneous gift.

But one evening while reading by the fire, he'd tipped his head back against Ambrose's shoulder and said that he'd never felt so safe before.

Ambrose, in spite of all his newly acquired vocabulary, still had no words to convey how it felt knowing his presence provided security and comfort rather than intimidation or danger.

He had not heard the witch king's voice in months, and some days could not remember what it sounded like.

"This is the best bit," Emery said, rolling the pumpkin toward Ambrose on the table. He'd carved a hole in the top and, tugging the stem, revealed the long strings of pumpkin innards with seeds tangled throughout. "Some people use a spoon, but I prefer to get my hands dirty."

He reached in and pulled out a squelching fistful of pumpkin guts, dumping them into a bowl. "I'll need to separate the seeds out from the pulp. Do you want to have a go, or would you prefer seed picking?"

A HEX FOR HUNGER

Wrinkling his nose, Ambrose reached into the pumpkin's innards and dug his fingers into the pulpy mass. He pulled out a slimy, stringy lump that smelled very uniquely of *vegetable*.

"Hopefully not too much like ripping hearts out," Emery said.

Ambrose flicked a pumpkin seed at Emery. "No. It's far too cold."

"I never did thank you," Emery said. "For taking care of my heart, rather than ripping it out."

Ambrose drew him close, getting orange smears of pumpkin on his apron. "I don't need your gratitude for that."

"Well, I appreciate it anyway," Emery said, allowing himself to be drawn in for a soft kiss, familiar as coming home. "It would be harder to love you without it."

Ambrose kissed him harder.

Months ago, Emery had planned an elaborate evening where he'd cooked a roast, opened a bottle of wine, and then—quite awkwardly and abruptly—told Ambrose he was falling in love with him. What followed afterward was an anxious, rambling monologue about how if Ambrose didn't feel the same, he understood, and that he'd tried to rein in his feelings for fear he was moving too fast. In the end, Ambrose had kissed him quiet and explained rather bluntly that he thought it could already be taken for granted—after he'd forsaken his oath, his lover, his king and helped Emery kill his enemy—that he loved Emery, too.

Though he hadn't felt the stomach-gnawing hunger of the witch king's magic in months, he did feel a different sort when Emery rose up on his toes to deepen their kiss.

He broke away when Ambrose's hands wandered, saying, "Later! We have buns to bake."

Ambrose raised his eyebrows. He'd recently been made aware that "buns" could be used as a euphemism for buttocks.

"Teaching you modern slang was a mistake," Emery said.

They managed to mix and knead the dough, slather the batter in pumpkin-spiced sugar, and roll them into perfect spirals with only minimal sex jokes and interludes for kissing. While the buns proofed, they read together, had dinner, and headed to bed with the taunt of the buns they couldn't bake until tomorrow following them.

Since they couldn't give in to the temptation of eating them, they gave into the temptation of each other instead.

As the night grew heated, and clothing more scarce, Emery said, "Wait. I have something for you."

Ambrose nudged Emery's cock with his thigh. "I noticed."

Emery slapped him playfully. "Pervert. Actually, never mind, that's quite . . . astute of you. Hold on."

Emery opened the bedside cabinet, removing a gift bag tied shut with a purple ribbon and decorated with—

"Is that pattern floral or phallic?"

"Yes."

Ambrose stared.

"Open it!"

Ambrose adjusted his position leaning back against the pillows to untie the ribbon. From inside, he pulled a crystal potion bottle shaped like a cut jewel and filled with an iridescent fuchsia liquid.

Ambrose raised his eyebrows and popped the cork to drink it, but Emery slapped a hand over the opening. "You're not even going to read the label or ask me what it does?"

Ambrose shrugged. In the passionate context of their bedroom, he'd forgotten he could read. "I trust you."

Emery flushed. "That's—lovely, actually. But before you drink it, read the label."

The label on one face of the potion had been written in Emery's familiar curving letters. As Ambrose's eyes crept along each line, they widened with comprehension.

He and Emery had discussed this before—if there was magic that could change his body a step further.

Emery affirmed that there was, but it was the sort of spellcraft he'd like to be very careful about, and the ones he knew of only effected temporary change. Ambrose once feared he'd like the results too much to go back to the way he'd been, but after months of sex with the body he had, he felt quite sure he'd be satisfied either way.

"This will only last a day," Emery said. "But I've been working on it, and I thought—I don't know if it's possible yet, and you can tell me if you hate the idea, but I wondered if we could adapt the old magic that affected you before and use it for something better. Instead of a tithe of hunger, maybe it could be one of . . . fulfilment. Wholeness. The kind you find by being yourself."

Ambrose ran a finger over the edges of the potion bottle, emotion welling inside of him.

"Sorry if that's too cheesy," Emery said.

Ambrose swept Emery's hair back from his face and kissed him. Then he tipped the potion bottle to his lips, drained the sweet brew, and went back to kissing Emery again as the magic took effect.

His skin was still marked by runes and scars, but every kiss turned his dark memories into the faded marks of a letter gone illegible with age.

Emery had said the type of spell he'd suggested might not work. They might have to work years to perfect it. He marveled that something as awful as that old, hungry hex could be turned toward a kinder purpose.

Emery was under him, hard and waiting after being prepared by Ambrose's fingers and tongue. And then Ambrose was inside him, seeing stars, and he had to reflect, as they kissed, tasted and devoured one another, that not all hunger was awful.

Come morning, they rose early to check on the buns, which had risen enormously in the baking tray. After pouring cream between the crevices, they put it in the oven and drank tea on the sofa. The aroma filled their home. The scent would forever be associated with Emery warming his cold feet by shoving them under Ambrose's arse.

The oven dinged, and Ambrose's newfound affinity for sex jokes continued as Emery basted the buns with dollops of icing, which looked—well. Ambrose made a rude gesture to imply they could home brew that sort of thing.

The smell was mouthwatering but didn't compare to the taste of that first bite. Ambrose had to close his eyes, the soft, doughy pastry oozing icing sugar down his lip. The peculiar blend of pumpkin and spices reminded him of a warm hug.

Emery had taken a bite, too, and looked pleased with the result, but he seemed to derive more delight from watching Ambrose discover a new thing to crave.

For all their cravings, Ambrose didn't think they'd ever go hungry again.

ACKNOWLEDGMENTS

They call your second published book your "sophomore novel." There's a special term for the feeling that's evoked when writing one: the sophomore slump. So coined because, after publishing one book, it's intimidating trying to follow it up with another. I'd love to say I had perfect confidence in myself to write something as good, if not better, than *A Spell for Heartsickness*, but I'm as neurotic as an Italian greyhound. *A Hex for Hunger*, like the dwarves of Moria, mined a little too deep. It was a difficult book to write (understatement), but it would have felt impossible without the support and encouragement of many friends, family, fellow writers and my publishing team.

I'll try and keep rationalisations to a minimum so this doesn't end up as long as the book itself, but know that you're all the bee's knees.

I want to start by thanking my agent, Ellen Goff, who kept me accountable under my first big deadline and gave me feedback on the messiest first draft I've ever written. In addition, I want to thank my editing team, Melissa Frain, Crystal Wang, and Felix Chau Bradley for helping me take this from a hot mess to one of the most rewarding books I've ever written. Likewise, to my entire team at Podium, Cass Dolan, Nicole Antos, Stephanie Beard and Taylor Bryon, thank you for all your hard work behind the scenes and championing this book when it turned out way spookier than originally intended.

Thank you to my writer friends, who are quickest to remind me that, yes, *every* first draft has you feeling like Jeff Goldblum standing over that steaming pile of you-know-what in *Jurassic Park*. In particular, thanks to Avrah, August, Cee, Monica, Sio, Mary Ann, Niamh, Erin, and Steve.

ACKNOWLEDGMENTS

Thank you to my many other friends and found family, without whom I might never leave my house. Many of you also write books, but were "friends" before you were "writer friends" so consider yourselves beloved, special snowflakes who defy categorisation. All of you inspire me to keep going. In particular, thanks to Cait, Manuela, Natalie, Sam, Becca, Aidan, Fen, Kat, Steph, Elliot, Alexis, Helen, Jonny, Helenx2, and Will.

To the family I miss every day from across the sea: Mom, Dad, Marney, Shannon, Duncan, Jenna, Ben, and of course the littles, Burke and Maeve. Thank you for supporting me and my weird little gay books.

Thank you to all of the booksellers, booktokers, bookstagrammers, and reviewers for telling more people about *Heartsickness* and making my first book launch feel far less terrifying.

Lastly, thank you to all my readers in general, especially you reading this. Just as books don't get created in a vacuum, they don't truly exist until they play out in the theatre of a reader's mind. I hope you found this one worthy of your imagination.

Much love to you all.

ABOUT THE AUTHOR

Alistair Reeves is a romantasy author whose stories feature messy queers and morally gray characters. His influences range from video games to Chinese danmei, and when he's not writing, he can be found playing *Dungeons & Dragons* or tending to his frankly absurd collection of succulents. Born in Canada, Reeves now lives in England, indulging his addictions to hot beverages and rainy weather.

Podium

FOR A GOOD TIME
follow us on our socials

 podiumentertainment.com

 @podiumentertainment

 /podiumentertainment

 @podium_ent

 @podiumentertainment